'Does David know what sort of a woman you are?' She knew that Gary was joking, but the laughter died inside her.

'No.' She looked straight at him.

David had returned from Penzance only hours ago, looking happy, bursting with news of Fern's successes at the craft fair. As if he had imagined Claire would want to hear about it . . . He hardly seemed like the same man who had kissed her with such intensity before she left for London. It was as if that conversation, that desperate touch, had been wiped already from his mind. It haunted her, the force of it seemed to press inside her still, but perhaps to David it had held little significance.

'Sometimes,' she said, 'I think that David doesn't know what sort of woman I am at all.'

About the author

Jan Henley began writing successful feature articles and short stories for women's magazines when her children were small. Since then, she has combined family life and her writing career with her studies for a B.A. with the Open University and has now achieved a first class honours degree. She lives in West Sussex with her husband and three children.

Family Ties

Jan Henley

CORONET BOOKS

Hodder & Stoughton

Copyright © 1998 by Jan Henley

The right of Jan Henley to be identified as the Author of
the Work has been asserted by her in accordance with the
Copyright, Designs and Patents Act 1988.

First published in Great Britain in 1998 by Hodder and Stoughton
A division of Hodder Headline PLC
First published in paperback in 1999 by Hodder and Stoughton
A Coronet Paperback

10 9 8 7 6 5 4 3 2 1

A CIP catalogue record for this title
is available from the British Library.

ISBN 0 340 69554 4

Printed and bound in Great Britain by
Clays Ltd, St Ives plc

Hodder and Stoughton
A division of Hodder Headline PLC
338 Euston Road
London NW1 3BH

For Luke

My thanks go as always to my husband, Keith, and to my parents, Daphne and Bert Squires, for their tireless support and encouragement. And thanks to Wendy Tomlins, Elizabeth Roy and Carolyn Caughey at Hodder for their helpful advice.

Special thanks go to Leisa Tomaszewski, David Edwards, Kim Kausse, Lindy Stannard, Juliet Weissberg, Terry and Joss, and to Keith for taking up fishing.

And last – but never least – my thanks go to my children Luke, Alexa and Anna, without whom this story would never have been told.

There's a certain slant of light,
Winter afternoons,
That oppresses like the heft
Of cathedral tunes ...

Emily Dickinson
From number 36

Chapter 1

———◆———

Check the staff rota . . . send a reminder for milk money . . .

Claire Harrison ticked the items off her list. Oh, and buy some new teaspoons for the staff room.

'Dinner smells good.' Ben watched his mother hopefully. 'I'm starving.'

'Won't be long.' Claire shoved the paperwork for school back in a folder, retied the apron she was wearing over sweatshirt and jeans and went to rescue the lamb casserole from the oven. 'Tell your dad it's ready, will you?' If she hadn't been so distracted, Claire would certainly have registered the guilty nervousness of her son's expression as he watched her giving the vegetables a final stir.

But, as it was, she only frowned at what was in front of her. So, she was no Delia Smith, but what the hell, it was food, wasn't it? She replaced the lid, slung the tea-towel she was using as an oven-glove over one shoulder and grabbed forks from a drawer as her husband entered the kitchen and Ben chose his moment.

'Hey, Mum, Dad. You know that money Gran and Grandpa gave me on my eighteenth?' His voice was impressively casual. So casual that Claire, who had taken a firm hold of the casserole pot with her tea-towel, didn't falter on the way to the kitchen table.

'Mmm?' She became half aware that something was up. Not all of it on CDs and sports clothes, she was thinking. Claire liked to think of herself as easy-going, which wasn't hard since Ben had never caused her the kind of worries that most parents gnawed and nagged over. But he was eighteen now. Wasn't it about time he thought of something else to do with his money? A small investment, perhaps? A car? Wasn't it about time he came to a

1

decision between university, business studies at college or getting a job?

'Well, I thought I'd use it to . . .' He hesitated. 'Get out of this dump for a while.'

Claire did not usually go to the trouble of cooking lamb casserole for the two men in her life. Neither was she clumsy. The odd item might slip through her fingers and out of her mouth – particularly at certain times of the month – but she had never before dropped the dinner.

'Shit,' she said.

David and Ben leapt up to give assistance, both staring in horrified disbelief at the thick puddles of gravy and lumps of meat and sodden vegetables. Unappetising was hardly the word.

'Shit,' Claire repeated. She stamped her foot. It was a childish reaction, but all of a sudden she felt childish. She should be used to Ben's lack of tact by now – teenagers were supposed to be tactless, weren't they? But this *dump* was their home. And Ben . . . She simply couldn't think of him leaving.

'Shall we scoop it up and pretend it never happened, or do you want me to get a pizza out of the freezer?' David, unflappable David, could be relied on not to shout about the loss of his dinner. But today his very calm made Claire want to scream. She ignored him and reached for the kitchen towels.

'So . . .?' Ben must have known this was only the beginning. There he stood, hands on hips, watching his parents on their hands and knees on a gravy-laden floor.

'Get out *where*?' she demanded, gingerly removing a soggy parsnip and almost throwing it at her son. As for David – he was staring at her in a pretty strange sort of way. Did he think she was overreacting? Probably, but she didn't care.

'Oh, you know . . .' Ben shrugged in his careless teenage manner.

'I certainly don't.' Claire found herself grinding her teeth as she fought to control the rising panic. She knew David was right, even though he hadn't said anything. Ben was eighteen, for heaven's sake. Why shouldn't he want to leave home? It was natural, wasn't it? David thought so: that was why he was still staring at her as if she'd gone stark raving mad.

2

Ben stooped down until their faces were level, put a hand on her arm and smiled the smile that had always been able to move her. It was the smile that had got him his own way when he was a toddler, the smile that had made her believe, long ago, when Ben was just a baby and she had wanted so desperately to leave Cornwall, that she should stay, that it could work. That this family unit – David, Claire, Ben – could be a happy one despite everything, that Ben could eradicate her sadness in a way that David didn't seem able to.

Somewhere along the endless maternal line of cuddles and hurt, of anger and understanding, Ben had become everything to Claire. When David let her down, when David refused to leave the village that he'd grown up in for her sake, when she and David stopped talking, stopped laughing, stopped . . . Stopped loving, perhaps. When that happened, this child had made everything worthwhile. Perhaps she had loved him too much, in the way mothers often do, but now . . . Now, he wasn't so easy to love. Because now he was no longer a child. And yet she was supposed simply to smile back at him as he waved goodbye.

'Mum,' he said, the smile not quite reaching the blue-grey eyes that she knew to be so like her own, 'I want to go and do some travelling.'

'Travelling,' she echoed. Like Freddie. But her brother had never come back.

'I don't want to stay around here for the rest of my life, Mum. I want to see a bit of the world.'

He was asking for her understanding, that was all. One word from Claire and everything might seem to slide back to normal. She could give her blessing very easily, she knew that. One word . . . And if she didn't? She and Ben had reached a turning point, and Claire knew that straight ahead arm in arm wasn't an option any longer. 'I haven't cleaned the kitchen floor this week,' she muttered.

The pressure of Ben's hand on her arm lightened. His smile faded as he took his hand away. Claire knew that for once in her life she hadn't told him what he wanted to hear.

David was still staring at them. 'Pizza, then,' he said, with a slight catch in his voice. And then, in irritation, 'He only

3

wants to live a little, Claire. He only wants to –'

'See a bit of the world, I know.' She ladled the rest of the casserole back into the pot. 'He said.'

They were in accord for once, her husband and son. For years it had been she and Ben against the world, she realised with a start. It had never been intentional. David had always been obsessed with his work – except, perhaps, when they had first met. Work and fishing, they were his passions. The village of Trevarne that was their home, his two aunts in the house up on the hill. And Fern who lived with them.

Claire blinked. These were the things, the people, that meant so much to David. There had never seemed enough time left for . . . For what? For the family life that had once meant outings to the park and celebrations at the sight of Ben's first adult tooth. For time, a time that was Claire and David's time. It seemed that family life had now become a competition where she and David were on opposing sides.

'I wouldn't be going away for ever,' Ben said.

'Mmm.' But still, he was going.

She remembered the Ben at seven or eight who regularly went out fishing with his father. She remembered how she had cherished the rare peace and quiet. Now Ben was leaving her again, but this time it was different. This time there was distance between them and she wasn't talking about mere miles. 'Don't go too far away, Ben,' she heard herself whisper. But his smile didn't return and she knew she hadn't spoken out loud.

'Lots of people go travelling,' Ben said.

'Lots of people go to college.' Claire got to her feet and grabbed the mop.

Ben sighed. 'I told you, I'm not sure about college. Take your time, you said. Have a think about it.'

'I never said you had to travel thousands of miles away to think about it,' Claire snapped. 'It's time you grew up, thought about the future.'

He glanced at her in surprise.

She had never, she realised belatedly, said that to Ben before. She had never put on the pressure, told him to get himself organised, urged him on to the next step before he was ready. She'd done none of that – and been proud that she hadn't.

Ben scraped back his chair. Cue for a stormy departure, Claire thought, cross with herself. She had spent all afternoon cooking that casserole. And she had spent the last eighteen years developing a good relationship with her son. Of course she'd always known that one day he would leave. And she knew moments of leaving were gradual – they began with first school-days, it was all part of the same process; the first time he didn't kiss her goodnight, the first bed-time he wanted privacy in the bath, the day his voice broke. Each was a step in her mind's eye.

And even going to college would mean him leaving. It was silly, really. But a son at college meant there was still a thread between them. A son in another country – for heaven knows how long – was a son displaced.

'And how do you imagine you're going to do all this travelling?' He hadn't left the room – a pity, because Claire could feel herself bent on self-destruction.

Ben gazed back at her, a strange expression in his eyes that she was unwilling to unravel. 'I'm going to use some of the money to buy a bike,' he said softly.

'A bike.' She hardly noticed as David shoved a plateful of pizza on the table.

'A motor-bike.' Ben's voice was gentle.

He knew that she hated motor-bikes, he knew because he had asked her once as a child why they no longer walked past the bike shop when they went to Bodmin. Claire remembered him tugging at her hand, slowing to a crawl to stare at the gleaming machines just sitting outside, just waiting . . . But all that shiny chrome had begun to get to Claire too; that was why she had started walking a different way.

The story of my life, she thought now. When the going gets tough I walk a different way. 'I hate motor-bikes,' she had told him then. Not true. Once, she had loved them.

'Ben . . .' She disliked the pleading she heard in her voice.

'I know you never wanted me to get a bike, Mum.' He looked sad.

'You promised me you never would.'

David shot her a sharp glance. Yes, she knew it was emotional blackmail, but David could have his say later.

'But, you see, I'm into bikes, Mum,' Ben said. 'In a big way.' He poked with little enthusiasm at the pizza, which looked flaccid in the middle and burnt around the edges, with slices of pink pepperami perching meekly on top. 'I always have been.'

'Oh.' And had she always known that?

'That's why I want to get one. I'm sorry I can't keep my promise but it's dead important to me.' He touched her shoulder.

She didn't trust herself to speak.

'I've discussed it with Dad.'

'I see.' Claire pulled away, hurt. She still couldn't meet David's eye. And she knew, without having to look, that Ben's mouth would be clamped shut, the eyes so like her own giving even less away. She was aware of this because she knew her son very well – but she couldn't look at him now either. She was far too angry. It seemed like a conspiracy. Had Ben imagined that he needed moral support, or a referee?

'You can't stop me.' Ben's eyes weren't calm any more. She wasn't sure she recognised what he was thinking, but he wasn't calm at all.

He grabbed his leather jacket and left the room, lean, lanky, and awkward, as if he had more elbows and knees than were strictly required. His shoulders were pulled back in defiance, the pony-tail that most people disapproved of, and Claire loved, giving him an unreasonably jaunty air.

'Oh, Ben . . .' Claire put her head in her hands. Ben's pony-tail reminded her of the boys she used to fancy but never date, back in London in the early seventies before she met David, boys with long hair, brown skins and checked shirts they wore with faded jeans.

They were never part of her world. She always chose instead young men in suits with wide lapels, kipper ties and button-down shirts. Smooth types, her friend Laura called them. The kind whose trousers were perfectly creased, the kind who were going places – already on the first steps of management and only in their early twenties. The kind that took you out to wine bars for long liquid lunches and still managed to impress their bosses when they got back to work. They had the gift of the gab, they were sharp, they were making money and they could show a girl a good time. But Ben . . . Ben was of a different kind. Ben was very like David used to be . . .

'You can't bloody stop me,' she heard Ben shout as he slammed out of the house.

'He's eighteen, Claire,' David said.

'Yes.' How could she explain to David? David's life was work, fishing, and the village of Trevarne. Her life had become Ben.

'Why do you mind so much? Is it because if he goes away –'

'It's because of the bike.' She couldn't let him finish, because that would mean she would have to face it, the cold fact that she and David as a partnership might have become dependent on their son.

'The bike?'

'Everyone knows bikes are dangerous.' She cut into her pizza, but the tantalising scent of the lamb casserole still hung – along with lemon floor cleaner – in the air. Claire gave up. She wasn't hungry now anyway. 'I'd be worried sick every time he went out.' Needing to move, she went over to the sink, rinsed out the floor mop, tried not to cry.

'He'll be careful. You don't need to worry.' David came over, stood beside her, within touching distance – a big man, his hair dark, streaked with white, grey, even ginger, curly and pushed away from his face. There were specks of dried grey clay in it that showed her how often he had done that today. His brown eyes were kind, but although he was so close, he didn't touch her.

He never touches me now, she found herself thinking, unable to remember exactly when he had stopped. 'I will worry.'

Still, he watched her. 'You had a bike yourself,' he reminded her. As if she needed to be reminded . . . 'I don't see what's so terrible about it.'

'No, you don't see.' She swung away from him, losing the moment, knowing she was being unfair but unable to help it because now she really felt like crying, and she didn't want David to be around to see.

'Claire . . .' The Cornish lilt of his voice was soft, so appealing that she almost crumpled there and then and flung herself into those big arms. But she didn't do that any more, did she? All that was in the past. So she only shook her head.

'Why don't you admit it, Claire?' When she looked up at him his eyes were cold, his mouth twisted with a bitterness she didn't understand. 'You just can't let him go.'

'I have to let him go.'

'But you can't bear the thought of him leaving, can you, Claire?' His voice cut into her.

'Stop it.'

'Why, Claire? Why can't you?'

'He's my son. I love him.' But she knew what David was trying to make her say.

He grabbed her arm. 'You can't bear the thought of him leaving home because then it'll just be the two of us, won't it? You and me. And you can't stand the idea of that, can you, Claire?' He was shouting.

'Don't be ridiculous, David.' But her voice was shaking.

For a moment he held on to her arm. His grip was hurting, but she hardly flinched as she looked up at him. Had it come to this, then? What would he do? Did he want to hurt her – this man she had loved? Did he want to pay her back for not being the woman he'd thought her to be, for not fitting in with his life, his family, with Trevarne?

She couldn't tell what he was thinking, what he wanted. She didn't even know why he was so angry. What did he expect? Claire had always taken second place. He hadn't loved her enough to leave Cornwall. And perhaps she had never forgiven him for that . . .

David seemed to find it all so easy – to live for his work, to throw himself into the things that she had no time for. Who could blame her for finding solace in motherhood? For turning to her son for companionship when she and David no longer had a word to say to each other – a word that meant anything at least, a word of love.

'We'll find out now, won't we?' Abruptly he let go of her arm. 'Ben was right. You can't stop him getting a bike, you can't stop him leaving.'

Claire remained silent. Had she tried?

'We'll find out what we've got left,' he said.

She closed her eyes, but she heard him leaving the room. Leaving just as Ben had left. She heard his footsteps, the click of the door as he went out the back. She heard the fabric rustle and imagined the navy boiler-suit being pulled over his jeans and T-shirt, on to his bulky figure. It sounded very final, that slam of the door as he entered the workshop, entered his world – that of artist and craftsman.

Oh, David . . .

People come from miles away to see his designs, she reminded herself. He was more than just a potter. They come and they buy, not just the odd jug or planter, but whole dinner services sometimes. They commission so much, he can't keep up with demand, he has more work than he can handle. He . . .

The tears came.

Claire had told David when they first met that she had once owned a motor-bike. She had dropped it into the conversation as if it weren't important, as if it had never been important, as if it were a small piece of her past that no longer mattered. Perhaps it had all been too close at that time. She was still hurting, still damaged, and she had never told a soul, simply kept it wrapped up in her own mind, her own nightmares, as if that way it could be extinguished, almost as if it had never been.

And once not confided, it then became impossible to confide; it seemed too late. Perhaps it even created the first barrier between the two of them. But Claire would never forget it, or the way it had made her feel. A Triumph Bonneville 650cc, her own bike; she'd bought it second-hand and it had still taken her ages to save up. Everyone had said it would be too heavy for a girl like her to handle, an English bike, a proper bike. But she'd shown them.

Claire sat down at the table, platefuls of half-eaten pizza beside her, took another forkful, and remembered. *Why do you mind so much?* David had asked her. He might well ask.

Sometimes, round about midnight, on a Sunday afternoon, or at other odd times when a flash of chrome, or the sound of an engine revving reminded her, Claire thought about the days when she too had been passionate about motor-bikes. Although passionate wasn't strong enough – it had been more like an obsession. God knows where it had come from, but as a teenager it had been all she wanted – a bike, and not just any old bike either.

There was a second-hand motor-cycle shop down the road from where she lived with her family, a run-down place, where a thin, dark and scruffy bloke called Jerry did up bikes that he'd bought cheap, spending weeks lovingly fixing and sprucing, getting them roadworthy or just plain good-looking again. *Up to scratch*, as he used to say, grinning at her, adjusting his oil-stained working gear, rubbing his hands across his face to deposit a smear of oil in much the same way as David now deposited clay . . .

He fascinated the eighteen-year-old Claire, or at least the bikes fascinated her. Jerry was in his twenties, he had dark eyes and a beak of a nose, and he didn't talk much – at least not to her. He was okay, but the thrill she experienced watching his skinny body crawl around under bikes had nothing to do with him and everything to do with what he did for a living.

It excited her to see some old heap coming into the shop, to be there when Jerry was working on it, day by day, shaking his head, frowning, fiddling, fitting new parts, then finally polishing and testing it out. That was the biggest thrill – watching him turn the throttle, hearing the engine rev into life, seeing him sit astride the machine in his dirty blue jeans and black boots, before disappearing down the road in a rush of pure speed and power that left her breathless. It was a perfect feeling, that breathlessness.

She waited for his return with a thudding heart. Perhaps Jerry the mechanic thought the girl who liked watching him working on the bikes had a crush on him. Maybe that was why he was so nice to her, never minding her questions or the way she just stared and stared. Or perhaps he recognised that she had a bit of that passion – the feeling for bikes that some had. Nothing between wind and face . . . Being able to feel the engine throbbing beneath you.

'Which bike d'you like the best?' she asked him once.

He frowned. 'What d'you wanna know that for?'

She shrugged. 'I just do.'

'Dunno why a girl would give a shit about that.' He shook his dark head.

She was used to it, used to certain men who came to the shop and laughed at the way she hung around just watching. They even made crude suggestions sometimes, but it was easy enough to ignore them. It didn't put her off coming to the shop to see Jerry. Nothing put her off that.

'Which one?' she persevered.

'English bikes are the best,' he told her. 'These Japanese machines are crap.' He threw a dirty rag in the direction of a yellow Kawasaki. 'They whine at you – even in a big bike you ain't got no power there. No real power.' She heard the contempt in his voice. 'It's a bit like riding a bloody vacuum cleaner.'

Claire giggled. 'You see a lot of people riding Japanese bikes.'

'Oh, them things are light and fast off the mark.' He snorted. 'They're reliable enough. Japanese bloody mass production. Taking over the bloody world.'

'But . . .' Claire smiled encouragingly.

'They're pieces of plastic. No character.' He scratched his forehead. 'There ain't no getting away from it. Them classic British bikes are the best if you want something solid underneath you. No bloody contest, girl.'

Claire liked to hear him talk. Sometimes she went into the back of the shop and made him a mug of hot sweet tea just so that he would down tools and talk to her. 'You like the Triumphs,' she remarked. She'd seen the look in his eyes when he got one in the shop.

'Course I do.' He got up and stretched, for he'd been bent double the best part of the morning. 'Wouldn't have one of me own otherwise.'

Claire eyed him speculatively. 'Would you take me out on it?' She saw his expression change. Until now she knew she'd just been some crazy female who liked hanging round the bike shop. 'So I could see what it feels like, I mean,' she added, to make it clear to him that it was the bike she was interested in.

He laughed. 'I s'pose.'

'You don't mind?'

'Nope.' His expression changed once more, as if he were weighing her up. 'Lots of girls like riding pillion. I had this girl once said it was like sex.'

'Okay, then. When?' If he was expecting her to be shocked then he'd be disappointed. Claire was confident she could deal with Jerry. And she was about to find out how good it was to ride on one of those bikes, to discover if the reality could possibly match her expectations.

It did. Right from the moment she climbed on to the machine, felt that solidity he'd talked of underneath her, the power of it as the engine throbbed into life, she knew this was where she wanted to be. She was hooked. From the first moment it took her – bodily sensations, emotions and all – into a roller-coaster of speed, power and total exhilaration.

Jerry took her out towards Dorking somewhere, about twenty minutes out of London, to a dual carriageway more like a racetrack. *Deceptive Bends*, she read on a road sign, and she wanted to giggle. It hadn't taken her long to get the hang of leaning at the right angle and at the right moment – banking it round a corner, Jerry called it. She sensed that Jerry could deal with all the bends, deceptive or otherwise, and she knew without being told that this road was a biker's paradise.

'Hold on tight,' he shouted.

She did. She clung to his waist, burying her face in the sweet scent of black leather, conscious of the wind funnelling through her hair, tugging it from under the crash helmet. No visor, the wind stung her eyes too, scored into the soft skin of her face. She had no idea what speed they were doing. She wanted to whoop with excitement, only the breath was torn out of her body before she could make the sound.

They swept down to the next roundabout, round and back again, she didn't know how often. But by the time they got to the biker's café, and Jerry motioned for her to jump off, her mouth was dry, her legs were weak, her face was numb with cold and she was shaking uncontrollably.

'What did you think?' He grinned.

12

'Bloody marvellous.'

'You're OK. You can ride pillion with me one Sunday. We all come down here. Load of bikers. It's the business.'

Claire kissed him on the cheek. He was a terrible show-off – she knew how much he'd wanted to impress her – but he was kind and she knew he was paying her a great compliment. 'Thanks, Jerry,' she said. 'But I won't be riding pillion for long.'

His grin faded. 'Didn't go for it, then? Too scary for you?'

She shook her head. Was he mad? 'I'm gonna be riding my own bike. That's what I want. To get my own bike.'

She could see why Jerry's girl had compared it to sex: there was a sense of arousal, of being all stirred up, body and mind. But the eighteen-year-old Claire had only tried sex once and it had been an unmitigated disaster. This was better on all counts. There was no end to it – it could go on and on and, better still, it could be done alone.

A week later Claire landed a secretarial job – she'd finished at college just over a month ago and had been waiting for something like this to come up.

'Things'll change now,' Jerry prophesied gloomily. 'You'll probably start driving a Mini.'

She put her hands on her hips and pushed her carefully made-up face closer to his. 'Who do you think you're kidding? I'm gonna start saving for my bike.'

'What kind? A Honda? Like this joke over here?' He pointed to a 70cc bike that he was working on.

'A British bike.' She'd quickly learned to hear the difference the second the engine started up. British bikes let out a throaty rumble that was unmistakable. But it was more than that. The difference was the sense of unleashed power, and that was what she wanted.

He laughed. 'You wouldn't be able to even kick-start a heavy bike. Look at the size of you.'

Her eyes narrowed. 'I bet I bloody could.' She'd been watching him. She knew there was a knack to it – it wasn't just brute strength. 'I bet I could kick-start a bike as well as you do.'

'No chance.'

'Let me try.'

He seemed to be sizing her up, not wanting to back down – she could tell. Then he chucked her a key and gestured to a bike he'd got in that day.

'That thing?' She let her contempt show. It was only a 250cc.

'It's big enough.' He waited, hands on hips.

Claire sauntered over with a confidence she was far from feeling. She took a deep breath, swung herself into position, turned the key and kicked – a slight jump and then down hard, feeling the resistance, giving it force and confidence in the way she'd seen Jerry do it hundreds of times. Jerry never doubted that he'd start a bike: there was nothing half-hearted about it.

The engine growled into life. Claire grinned in victory.

'Not bad.' He was impressed, she realised. 'I suppose I could look out for something . . .'

'I want a Triumph Bonneville.'

He laughed once more. 'A Bonnie! Who the bloody hell do you think you're kidding?'

'That's what I want.' She felt the stubbornness of her own mouth. She'd made up her mind. She loved the shape of them, the feel of them, the sound of them.

'You'll never be able to handle a Bonnie.'

'I'll learn.' Claire switched off the engine and threw the keys back at him. 'I'll get myself a decent pair of boots, and I'll learn. Just watch me.'

It had taken a while, two and a half years to be precise, during which time Claire learned to ride on a smaller bike, passed her test, and saved up for her very own Triumph Bonneville 650cc. Jerry found it for her, and as soon as she stroked the silver lettering of the Triumph emblem down the red and white fuel tank, she knew that this was the one. A beautiful beast of a bike, it was. They did it up together. Claire was patient. She trusted Jerry, knew he'd do his best for her.

She began to lead a bit of a double life – it seemed to be the only way. Monday to Friday she was Claire Trent, personal secretary to the junior manager, cool and organised at all times. She wore short skirts and make-up, and went out to wine bars with those young men in kipper ties who thought having a good time was knocking back the lager at weekends and having the money to take a girl to a club after.

But at weekends she was a biker, a part-timer, riding down to Dorking, wearing leathers, taking the deceptive bends as fast as any of them, relishing the same risks, living for the thrill.

'I don't understand you,' her friend Laura complained. 'What's the appeal?'

'It's the freedom of the open road,' Claire told her. But it was more than that. It was like a drug. There was nothing to match it. It was fantasy and excitement, an instant whip-up of the emotions, an utter arousal, a thrill unlike any other.

Or it had been until the summer before she met David. Until the hot Sunday at the end of August 1976, that dry and dusty summer when everything had changed. Claire hadn't so much as sat on a bike since then.

'I'm sorry, Mum.'

Claire looked up. She didn't know how long she'd been sitting there, but it was growing dark and Ben had obviously come back in without her hearing him.

'It was bad timing, I can see that now.'

Slowly, she smiled. 'Any time would have been a bad time, darling. But I'm sorry too.'

He came closer to the table. She could smell the sweet scent of his leather jacket and it brought back the memories again so vividly that she had to close her eyes, just for a moment. 'If you're really against it,' he put a hand on her shoulder, 'I won't get the bike.'

She glanced up at him in surprise, knowing how much that would have cost him because she remembered what it was like to want something so much. 'Don't be silly.' She wanted him back, that was all. 'It's your life.'

His face lit up. 'Then you don't mind?'

She reached out, stroked his cheek. The pony-tail was nothing. On her son's jaw there was always a thick line of stubble these days; he wasn't just growing up and away he was already there. 'Oh, I mind.' Her smile was lop-sided this time. 'But you're damn right that I can't stop you. And I won't even try.'

He hugged her. 'I'll be careful, Mum.'

'And not just of the road.' She drew away from him. 'Bikers are a different breed.'

'I'm not a biker.' He grinned. 'What do you think? That I'm in some kind of gang?'

She knew he was laughing at her. And she deserved it: this was the 1990s, for goodness sake, they weren't in the seventies any longer. Once upon a time she had understood only too well the difference between the biker who was simply out to impress, to whom image was everything, who hung around in a gang and liked to cause trouble, and what Jerry had called the genuine motor-cycle enthusiast, the guy who just loved bikes. But over the years the boundaries had become blurred in her mind – she'd become guilty of tarring them all with the same brush, she supposed. And, after what had happened, who could blame her?

'Oh, all right. Be what you want, do what you want.' She laughed with him, trying to forget that on this bike he would be going away.

His expression became more serious. 'Will you help me choose?'

'Choose?'

'A bike, I mean.'

God, it was almost as if he knew. But she didn't think she was ready for that. 'No, you make up your own mind.' She put the kettle on for some tea. 'It's you that's going to ride round the world on the thing.'

He nudged her gently. 'Will you miss me?'

'I won't miss doing your washing, that's for sure.' Oh, yes. Claire wiped a tear from her eye. Everything had slid back to normal even though her whole world had changed.

Five days later a gleaming Japanese motor-bike – a bright red Suzuki 100 GSX, for nowadays there were strict rules about the kind of bike learners could ride until passing their test – was parked in the garage beside the cottage. Ben tended it with love and care. Claire had to smile. Jerry would have thrown down his tools in disgust.

Chapter 2

'Have you got a moment, Claire?' The headmaster of Trevarne primary school stuck his bald head around her office door.

Wistfully, Claire gazed at the pile of correspondence and registration details sitting in front of her word-processor. It was the beginning of the academic year, the school possessed only one receptionist, secretary, telephonist, first-aider and occasional dinner-lady – and that was Claire. 'Of course, Richard.' She sighed.

She waited patiently while Richard Stickler went through the usual pantomime of rubbing his hands together, peering among the contents of her desk and then sitting none too carefully on top of it. He was her boss, in a manner of speaking, but as David often reminded her, 'You don't have to like him.' And she didn't.

'It's about the summer fête.'

Richard was clearly waiting for her response, so she smiled encouragingly. Anything to be left to get on with her work. 'I thought it went rather well,' she said. 'Didn't you?' The day in June – highlight of the village calendar – was still being discussed up at David's aunts' house, where any village event provided material for at least three months' gossip and complaint.

Richard's wife – the most famous golf widow in Trevarne – had organised the fête, just as she had since the beginning of time, or so it seemed to Claire. But this summer Iris Stickler had also been responsible for two fatal flaws, which Claire was far too sensible to mention now. All the programmes given out on the day had referred to the famous soap actress Georgie Hamilton as *the fine actor George Hamilton* and, as if that weren't enough, Iris had omitted to buy the first prize for the

17

raffle, traditionally the greatest money-spinner of all.

Iris is losing her touch ... The rumour had swept around the village, and in no time at all it was decided by the powers that presided in Trevarne – a committee calling themselves the Friends of Trevarne, or Friends for short – that something must change.

Claire happened to know all this because David, in his status as village craftsman with more roots in Trevarne than the old yew in the churchyard, was a Friend. He and Richard Stickler had never seen eye to eye, but Claire supposed that the donation of a Harrison pot or vase worth a hundred quid to the raffle prizes allowed Richard to overlook David's more bohemian qualities.

'Not this year's fête, my dear.' Richard leant closer and Claire caught a whiff of BO. 'I'm talking about next year's bash.'

'Next year?' Claire squeaked, feeling threatened. 'But it's only September.'

'Hah!' Richard Stickler eyed her with compassion. 'It's never too early to begin preparations, you know, Claire.' As he spoke his eyes seemed to glance lightly over her crossed legs, his right knee twitched, and he placed one hand firmly on top of it. 'I can tell you haven't done this kind of thing before.'

'What kind of thing?' She pulled ineffectually at her skirt. It wasn't short, but Richard Stickler would make a woman in a wimple feel sexually harassed.

He chuckled. 'Didn't David tell you?'

'Tell me what?' Silently, she cursed David for leaving her open to this, whatever it was.

Richard leant closer still. 'That we want you to become a Friend.'

She stared at him.

'So, what do you say?'

Was she supposed to thank him? Claire frowned. She was so taken aback she didn't quite know *what* to say. Everyone who wasn't one laughed at the Friends of Trevarne, but the fact remained that the committee was powerful. It was absolute cliché and reeked of snobbery; a bit like the masons, only more public and members didn't have to roll up their trouser leg. Oh, yes, and women were allowed. But, God, they remained a select bunch. The members were predictable and home grown – the local headmaster and his wealthy but still obsessively picking-her-own-for-jam wife, the vicar who hardly ever made the meetings and when he did couldn't hear half of what was going on, the owner of the local post office cum bakery cum village store, who represented the nearest Trevarne came to free local enterprise, and the local craftsman, her own dear husband. But with Claire they were veering dangerously from the home grown. So what in heaven's name had made them choose her?

'Why me?' she asked the headmaster.

'I could tell you we need some fresh blood.' Richard smiled a gruesome smile. 'Or I could be honest and tell you that the Friends have decided to come into the nineties.'

'The nineties?' Claire was beginning to feel decidedly unwell.

'Even the most fuddy-duddy Friend knows we have to keep in step with modern times and technology,' he told her, thus excluding himself neatly from this category. 'It's nineteen ninety-six. Time to turn to a younger brain.' His gaze drifted back to her desk.

'And to a word-processor?' It seemed a fair guess. Claire wasn't exactly in her first flush – forty had passed her by with a mere whimper two years ago – and the school's word-processor was light years away from the forefront of technology. But Iris had steadfastly refused to let anything with a face like a computer lend a hand with arrangements. Claire on the other hand, already a member of staff of a school that often profited from the proceeds of the fête, already the wife of a Friend, was also computer literate. She could save Iris Stickler's dignity, give the committee their fresh blood, and presumably do all the work required in her spare time.

'It would give you a say in village affairs, my dear.' Richard's eyes narrowed. 'You would belong.'

But did she want to belong? Claire wasn't so sure. Did she want to play a leading part in the committee of a village that she had spent most of her married life hating?

'It's the first time that anyone from London has been asked to join our little band,' Richard said, as if the city were a den of iniquity, and this small village in Cornwall a corner of paradise. 'Some people would feel honoured.'

'What would I have to do?' Claire's first instinct was to refuse.

She was more than busy enough already. And then there was her family to consider . . .

What family? The thought struck her. Her parents still lived in London and she rarely saw them. Ben was about to go off travelling around Europe and she had no idea when he would be back. And David . . . A thought occurred to her. Maybe, just maybe, this might bring them closer together again. She had always scorned the small-village mentality of Trevarne. But if David saw her making a contribution to his beloved village . . . if he knew she was trying to belong . . . And Richard had a point; being a part of this particular committee would at least give her a say. She might really be able to drag Trevarne into the 1990s at last.

'We want you to be the main administrator,' Richard told her. 'Organise the rotas, programmes, find a celebrity to open the proceedings, that sort of thing.'

Claire realised that if she refused her life wouldn't be worth living – at school and probably at home too. 'Oh, all right,' she agreed ungracefully.

'Wonderful. I knew you wouldn't let me down.' Richard, BO and all, smirked, bent forwards and had the nerve to kiss her cheek before she had a chance to get out of range. If that was what being a Friend entailed, Claire thought, she might very well resign. 'So, if you come round to the house tonight, Iris will give you all the info you need.'

Claire thought of the book and early bed-time she'd promised herself. 'Does it have to be tonight?'

Richard rubbed his hands together again and eased his backside from her desk. 'As I said, Claire, it's never too early to begin. The first item on the agenda is to get some leaflets printed, *Can you help with our summer fête?*, you know, that sort of thing. The offers will come flooding in and then you can sort it all out, delegate, start getting the show on the road.'

'Oh, God.' What had she done? Was she mad?

'I know you can do it.' Richard smoothed back imaginary hair. 'The resources of the school are at your disposal, my dear,' he reminded her. 'And there's always overtime.' He winked.

She glanced at him in surprise. But if Richard were really

suggesting that Claire should take advantage of the school facilities *and* be paid overtime – which she wouldn't put past him – he should know better. Claire wasn't the type, and besides, unpaid overtime came with the territory. To work in a school like this one meant being committed, and those who were committed didn't need the incentive of mere money. More likely they needed to be committed to a loony bin, she thought.

'I'm sure you'll be able to get the leaflets ready to be delivered on Saturday,' Richard trilled as he left the office. 'After all, Sunday is a day of rest.'

'Not on a bloody golf course it isn't,' Claire muttered.

If Claire had imagined David would offer to help deliver the leaflets she'd spent half the week preparing, then she was mistaken. She awoke on Saturday to find only a conspicuous gap in the bed they shared, telling her that David had been drawn into a fishing trip by the excitement of a pink-grey dawn or possibly the anticipation of several hours away from the marital home and bed. And Ben was nowhere to be found.

TREVARNE SUMMER FÊTE the bold black letters printed on sunflower yellow paper shrieked at her as she left the cottage. *CAN YOU HELP?*

'Preferably not,' she muttered.

We need willing helpers to make jam, sell raffle tickets, man the stalls . . . She began to tackle the other cottages in the small row that led to the bridge. Shouldn't that be 'people the stalls'? she wondered, sticking a leaflet into Marion Chaney's letter-box four doors along. 'Person' the stalls? 'Woman' the stalls?

'Do you want a hand, Claire?' Marion called, from an upstairs window. The permanently harassed expression of Trevarne Primary's new and unofficial deputy head appeared.

Claire was tempted. She liked Marion, but she also knew that Marion was even busier than she was. She'd just switched year groups and she always took on a lot of the work that was the Stickler's by right. Marion was already overloaded. 'I'm fine,' she called back. She could always ask David's aunts, she thought, as she reached the final cottage of the row – now occupied by the new year six teacher and art co-ordinator, Gary Stockwell. But she'd rather eat a wedge of Aunt Veronica's lemon curd cake – wickedly referred to as lemon turd cake by Ben – than trail around the village with the aunts and a pug dog or two in tow.

She paused when she reached the bridge, over which scores of children played Poohsticks every day of the summer holidays. A pretty river of the same name ran through Trevarne, just one of the reasons, Claire supposed, why tourists flocked here in the summer. There were the bridge, the clematis and rose-trellised cottages made of granite with blue-grey slate roofs, a shop so old and tiny you had to shuffle into and out of it with arms glued to your sides, the sixteenth-century church up on the hill and slabs of granite perfectly placed for picnicking by the river.

Oh, it was pretty all right. Trevarne had made all the guidebooks, and many of its inhabitants had hungrily grasped the mixed blessings of providing B-and-B. The result was hell in the summer and peace with relative prosperity the rest of the year. Some, at any rate, would say that it was worth it.

Claire leaned over the dusty granite. Down there, somewhere, for the anglers liked to keep their favourite swims secret, was David. It was odd to think of him, so close to her, so hidden . . . And he was hidden, David was the quiet and secretive type by nature. His air of gentle calm had always made her feel safe, just when she'd needed it the most. 'We don't need words, Claire,' he had told her once. But now she wasn't so sure. Now she wondered if words were exactly what they did need. How else could they understand the other's world, the other's feelings? How else could they know how far they had drifted apart?

She sighed. A grey film hung over the day, reflecting her mood. Typical September, Claire thought, neither one thing nor another, unable to make up its mind or accept summer's end, leaving every-one not knowing what to wear. The leaves of the birch trees looked dull enough to drop, and the dampness of autumn had swollen the river, leaving rock surfaces smooth and wet as sealskin. But behind the grey film she traced the beginnings of a thin pencil-line of sunlight. David would be staying by the river a while yet, for sure.

As she made her way up the hill, Claire glimpsed Iris Stickler heaving what looked like an orchard-load of English Coxes from the boot of her Golf hatchback into the house. But she didn't speak. Was she resentful or relieved that Claire had taken over her job as organiser of the village fête? Claire wasn't sure.

At the aunts' house she tried to sneak past Fern's workshop and up to the front door without being seen, but a yapping pug caught her on the way.

'Ssh,' she urged the small insistent animal. But the aunts' pugs knew she disliked them. Claire could become fond of almost any animal, given the chance, but the sight of a pug in full yap, its tiny tail flicking from side to side, globular eyes watering, spittle dribbling from some gap in the black folded face that she supposed was its mouth . . . No matter how she tried, she could find in her heart no affection whatever. She hated pugs. She suspected that they weren't really dogs at all.

'Claire!' This was Aunt Veronica of lemon curd cake fame, waving from her usual place on the other side of the kitchen window and making it impossible for Claire to pretend she hadn't seen her.

She waved back and Veronica trotted out, small and squat as a barrel. For years Claire had been fascinated by the thick tufts of white down unevenly spaced across her chin, but David had told her that Veronica had once been beautiful.

'And very sought after,' he said.

'Poor Veronica.' For some reason this saddened Claire. 'But she never married?'

'No.' David's brow creased. 'No, she never married.'

Now, Veronica fixed her short-sighted blue-eyed gaze on Claire. 'Have you come round for tea, dear? How nice.'

Tea. That meant warm milk and water and a tea-bag dunked in it for five seconds, long enough to leave only a drop of oil and a promise to the taste-buds of what might have been. 'Not exactly, Aunt.' Why did she find it so hard to be firm with David's aunts? 'Actually, I'm–'

'What've you got there, girl? Let's see.' As was her habit, Aunt Emily lunged into the foreground from nowhere, the volume of her voice making Claire jump guiltily for absolutely no reason at all.

Some reflex action made her clutch tightly on to the leaflets and

Aunt Emily – as stubborn as she was strong – had practically to tear them from her grasp.

Ever since her marriage to David – for the clever man had hidden both aunts from her until that date – Claire had been half terrified of Aunt Emily. David said she shouted because she was deaf, but Claire suspected she simply preferred the sound of her own voice to anyone else's. Besides, she was a bully. And Claire, who under normal circumstances preferred to avoid confrontation, gave the impression of being a bully's dream. So did Aunt Veronica.

Claire smiled in what she hoped was a friendly but firm manner at Aunt Emily. She was of indeterminate age, tall and bulky with wiry grey hair, steel-rimmed spectacles and eyes and skin to match. Big Emily and little Veronica – it didn't seem quite right and Claire could never quite escape the conviction that their names belonged to each other, that somehow their parents had got them mixed up all those years ago.

'I want some help,' Claire told her. That was true enough – help to escape wouldn't come amiss.

'Help for the fête?' Emily yelled, reading the black print. 'Already?'

Claire was going to repeat what Richard had told her but there was no need, for Veronica had already taken up the refrain. Perhaps she had heard it before. 'It's never too early to start, Em.' She spoke with the usual apology in her voice. 'There'll be jam to make, and raffle tickets to buy and . . .' Here her imagination failed her. 'And all sorts of other things.'

'I know that,' Emily shouted crossly. 'I'm not stupid.'

'Well, now that you've got a leaflet, I really must be –' Claire tried to nudge with her toe the yapping pug currently attempting illicit sex with her ankle while making good her exit from the garden. The dog, however, seemed to consider this one of the games of love and chased more frantically than ever. Veronica and Emily were oblivious to the animal's behaviour – probably, they were used to it, Claire thought.

'Put the kettle on, then.' Emily, perhaps still smarting at her sister's effrontery in voicing an opinion, glared at Veronica and Claire with equal distaste. 'And isn't there some of your . . .?'

'I really haven't time –' Claire began, watching hopelessly as Veronica trotted off to do her sister's bidding.

'No trouble, no trouble. Yes, some tea and cake,' she whispered to herself as she went.

Claire's shoulders sagged.

'And I'll do you a list.' Emily took a leaflet and folded it in two.

'A list?'

'Of everything that we're prepared to do.' Emily's eyes glinted behind their spectacles. David said that under the bluster was a heart of gold, but Claire suspected more sadistic tendencies.

'You're very kind.' In desperation, Claire bent down to shoo the bristling little dog away. Her legs were bare and both ankle and leather-thonged sandal were disgustingly wet – with his saliva, she hoped – by now. 'Go on. Shoo!' She kept her voice gentle although she was unable to suppress a distinct quaver of irritation. Once and only once Emily had accused Claire of shouting at her dogs, with the venom of a mother protecting her young. From that day Claire had understood. Effectively, they *were* her young.

They had Fern, but she was only a lodger, although her mother had once worked as Emily and Veronica's housekeeper. Housekeeper? It was pretty obvious that she was no longer around. Despite Veronica's domestic interests, the furniture and carpets in the best front room smelt musty and were matted with dog hair. Claire couldn't imagine Emily tolerating a housekeeper and she certainly couldn't see how anyone could tolerate Veronica and Emily without going crazy. Poor Fern. Both of the aunts were difficult. Together they were indescribable.

True to form, Veronica produced tea of the milky variety that turned Claire's stomach, and a plate bearing a doily and the unmistakable lemon curd cake. She was just wondering how she could decently refuse and make good her escape when two more pugs entered the room, a look of supreme confidence on the folds of their faces. They either considered Claire's ankles to be asking for it – she must remember to wear jeans next time – or they were assuming their right to share the cake. That is, Claire thought with horror, if they hadn't taken a few dribbling mouthfuls already.

'I'm surprised David didn't bring it round earlier,' Veronica twittered as she tried to refill Claire's already full cup.

'Earlier?' Claire got to her feet. 'I really can't stay. I've got so many to deliver.'

Veronica clicked her tongue. 'He could have saved you the journey, dear.'

'Oh, he's gone fishing.' But privately Claire agreed with her. After all, he was on the committee too. The only leg work he did was walking down to the village hall for the monthly meetings.

'Yes, dear, I know.' Veronica smiled. 'It's in the kitchen.'

'In the kitchen?' Claire edged towards the door. She often felt sorry for Veronica – especially for having to live with Emily – but sometimes she couldn't make sense of her at all.

But Veronica was nodding frantically. 'Oh, yes. Fern likes it lightly grilled with butter.'

'Lightly grilled, does she?' Comprehension dawned. So David had returned from his fishing expedition. But not only had he still deprived Claire of any help to deliver these damned leaflets, he had also apparently deprived her of the fish he'd caught. And where the hell was he now?

She made her way back down the garden towards Fern's workshop – just a shed, really, but David had fixed it up quite nicely for her over the years. He kept an eye on this house and his aunts because they had no one else. And he helped Fern because . . . well, because she was almost part of the family, Claire supposed. And because he believed she had artistic talent that should be encouraged.

He was a good man, everyone said so, but still Claire was cross with him. Joining the committee, agreeing to all this work, had been partly for David's sake, to bring them closer together. But here she was delivering leaflets alone. Wasn't it becoming a little one-sided?

She had assumed Fern to be in the house, but as she passed the workshop, she saw her sitting at her easel, facing the light with a rapt, intent expression on her face as she worked. She was painting one of her intricate nature studies, although Claire couldn't make out the subject. She couldn't make Fern out either – the woman was a complete mystery. Today her small frame was swamped by an outsize blue paint-daubed shirt, and her long brown hair was wound loosely around her shoulders, tied at the back with some sort of ribbon.

She considered knocking on the door. Fern was only a few years younger than Claire, but despite her close relationship with David – maybe because of her close relationship with David, Claire admitted to herself with a twinge of jealousy – they had never become friends. Perhaps it was that something which Fern and David shared that made Claire feel excluded, outside some special circle. Certainly she could have done with a friend in Trevarne, especially in those early days. But now Claire recognised the absorbed look of the artist who would hate to be disturbed, the same look she sometimes saw on her husband's face.

Hadn't she, once upon a time, always been running into his workshop – a lot more up-market than this one, for sure, but with certain similarities nonetheless – whenever she wanted to see him, thrilled that her husband was always around, always available since he worked from home?

She soon found that wasn't the case. When David was working he was working. He didn't want to be disturbed – even by his new wife – and before she was aware of doing it, Claire had designated his workshop a no-go area. She didn't want her pride to be dented any further. She never went in there now.

The same rules applied to Fern's workshop, but just as she was about to turn to go, Claire saw Fern's mouth curve into a smile, realised she was speaking to someone, knew there was someone sitting back in the shadows in the far corner of the shed with her, watching her in these intimate moments.

She froze as Fern laughed, she saw his familiar bulky figure as he got to his feet and moved into the light, and somehow she managed to stumble away.

Imagine if they'd seen her . . . That was all Claire could think at first as she half ran back down the hill, and started on the high street. What would they have thought? That she was spying, perhaps?

And then as she made for the small housing estate and council places behind the school, she began to get angry with David once again. It was one thing helping Fern out, one thing nurturing an artistic talent, as he liked to put it. But what the hell was he doing in Fern's workshop with her today? There didn't seem to be much nurturing going on.

So what *was* going on? Claire was speeding through the estate now, high on self-righteous indignation. Surely they weren't . . . Surely they couldn't be having an affair?

She realised, as she finished the estate and headed for the farm and the old barn, that she had never spelt this out to herself before, never considered it as a possibility. David was the loyal type – wasn't he? David would never be unfaithful. And yet . . . And yet, the thought plagued her. How long since she and David had laughed together? How long since they'd kissed? How long since they'd made love?

She didn't understand Fern Browne, that was for sure. How could a woman like that bear to lodge with Veronica and Emily, even if she did have her own bed-sitting room, and a shed that had been converted into an artist's workshop? Didn't the aunts drive her bananas? Weren't there other places she could have lived after her mother died? What could she need them for? She seemed to exist self-sufficiently. If she needed anyone it was always David she turned to . . . And perhaps that was why she stayed.

But Claire couldn't dwell on that, not now. Instead, she made her way back through the tiny park that led to the copse and the scenic route to their cottage, her footsteps crunching on the gravel path that provided a route up to the main road as well as a detour through the trees. Fern, she told herself firmly, was just a friend. So why did she keep remembering how David's voice could always bring a smile to Fern's small and serious face? And how Fern could always bring a whisper of tenderness into David's tired eyes?

'What the – ?' Her thoughts were abruptly broken by the man jogging along the path. He narrowly avoided cannoning into her.

'Sorry.' He was winded, bending over to get his breath back, and Claire recognised Gary Stockwell, the school's new teacher.

'You gave me one hell of a shock,' Claire snapped, not knowing if she was glad or sorry for the diversion.

'Sorry,' he muttered again. 'Claire, isn't it?'

'People don't run in Trevarne,' she told him. The curve of the beech trees had hidden him from sight, but the truth was she'd been too preoccupied.

'Then people must be very unfit.' He sounded friendly enough, but she registered caution in the dark blue eyes and for a moment wondered why.

She was going to tell him that fitness wasn't an issue in Trevarne, but that wasn't quite true since horse-riding had its followers, and the village hall provided a venue for an activity she'd heard referred to as tums 'n' bums by women in the playground. 'Maybe they are.' She smiled back, to reinforce her own status as a Trevarne outsider, before remembering the leaflets in her hand. She was a Friend now, wasn't she? She belonged to the damn place now, for better, for worse.

He looked around them. 'But it seems a nice enough village.'

'It can be.' She surveyed him with undisguised curiosity. The clean-shaven beginning-of-term look had already degenerated into what would have been called designer stubble some years ago, but at least his jeans were clean and he had a nice smile. Also a silver stud in one ear, she noted, which wouldn't have gone down well with Richard if he'd noticed it at school. He was, she supposed, in his mid-thirties.

'We're in the other end cottage,' she told him. 'Tumbledown.'

'And is it?' His eyes gleamed.

'Not so as you'd notice.' She smiled once more. 'But if you want anything . . .' she brandished a leaflet ' . . . or any gen about the school you know where we are.'

'I appreciate that.' He stared at the leaflet, a question in his eyes.

Claire held it closer to her chest. 'It's just, um . . .' She found herself embarrassed to tell him. That showed, she supposed, that she didn't belong after all, and on balance she couldn't help feeling relieved about that. 'We're beginning to plan next year's village fête.' Reluctantly, she flashed the leaflet in front of his face.

He blinked. 'Christmas?'

'Next summer.' Their eyes met and both grinned. Claire sensed an ally, and in a school with Richard Stickler as the head you could never have too many of those.

'Well, I'll certainly try to do something to help out.'

She eyed him quizzically. 'Really?'

'If you join a small community, and all that, you have to, don't you?'

'Mmm, I suppose.' But Claire was wondering why a man like this had joined the small community in the first place. He clearly had no ties here – well, he wasn't married anyway, no ring, no woman in evidence. The school wasn't exactly an ace draw in the way of career moves. And . . . he didn't seem the type.

'You're not from Cornwall?' he asked her.

They always knew, didn't they? And he *was*, of course – she recognised the accent although it differed slightly from David's. 'London,' she told him. 'I moved here when I got married.' David . . . She pushed the thought away.

He eyed her with renewed interest. 'Of course. You're David Harrison's wife, aren't you?'

Claire's heart sank. He appeared casual, standing there scuffing one trainer along the gravel. So why did she feel the entire conversation had been leading up to this point? 'You know him?'

'I've seen his work.' He smiled. 'It's good.'

'Yes, it is.' Claire tried to dredge up some enthusiasm, but this morning's events had left her sounding even less convincing than usual. And over the years she had grown tired of people only talking to her because they were interested in David's work. She supposed praise for her husband should make her proud, but it didn't any longer. It made her feel as if she were simply living in his shadow. Sometimes it was hard to believe she had a life of her own; these days she seemed positively swallowed up by David's achievements. And that artistic success, that look in the eye that he shared with Fern and maybe with this chap too, for he was the art co-ordinator and so probably another failed artist like the rest of them. Well, it all had a price, didn't it? And Claire suspected that she – or, rather, her relationship with David – had become that price.

But Gary Stockwell was looking at her as if he understood some of what she was feeling. 'I'm glad we bumped into each other. I wanted to test the water . . .' he began.

'Yes?' She moved one step away, knowing what was coming. Of course he could meet David any time he wanted to. They were neighbours and, anyway, David never minded meeting people who appreciated his work, although if they expected to be inspired by words of wisdom then they would be disappointed because David wasn't in the habit of doling out advice. He was a listener. There was an air of tranquillity about him that she had always half-envied. Perhaps it was all that fishing, she thought resentfully.

' . . . about organising a school visit,' Gary went on. 'To the new Tate Gallery in St Ives, perhaps. It's really exciting. Have you been there?'

Claire stared at him in surprise and shook her head.

'I think it makes art come alive for the kids to see it *in situ* so to speak. Don't you?' He was getting into full flow now, moving his arms around, enthusiasm streaming from every pore.

'Oh, yes.' Claire was impressed. But would Richard be? His idea of a school outing was a visit to Bodmin jail five miles away.

'And the younger they are when they get into it, the better.' Gary paused for breath. 'Year six will be doing a lot of contemporary stuff later on,' he confided.

'Really?' Although Claire was perfectly accustomed to the imitation Monets and Van Goghs that lined the corridor from playground to school hall every summer.

'They usually get some good post-Impressionist stuff from the London Tate,' Gary said thoughtfully. 'I'll get a brochure of their contemporary exhibitions while I'm at it. I saw this wonderful installation there last summer – the kids would have loved it.'

'I'm sure they would.' Claire laughed. His enthusiasm was contagious, and it was an enthusiasm that was long overdue as far as the school was concerned, she felt.

'So what do you reckon? Do you think it's a good idea?' He looked hopeful. 'Or just plain daft?'

'I think . . .' I think it's a brilliant idea, she was about to say, for she had long been campaigning for more visits for Trevarne's school-children. They might be too far away for visits to London, but there was so much to see in Cornwall alone. This could be just the start.

But she didn't say any of this, because she was distracted by the sound of an engine. A motor-bike engine – she knew that immediately. Her son's motor-bike engine, she realised almost as quickly.

Ben? She glanced up the path to the other end of the track where

31

gravel met main road, and saw him in the distance, saw the pillion passenger jump off the bike, take off a helmet and shake out a lot of very long blonde hair.

Claire's mind went into fury mode: Ben had not passed his test, he shouldn't have anyone riding pillion. But fury changed into disbelief as Ben took the blonde pillion passenger into his arms with a passion that Claire had never associated with her son somehow. And then came panic, for she suddenly knew the girl's identity only too well. It was Tiffany – Richard and Iris Stickler's precious teenage daughter.

'Are you all right?' Gary looked in the direction on to which Claire's eyes were totally locked.

'Not really.' She frowned. 'This is getting to be a bit of a day for surprises, that's all.'

Gary Stockwell seemed as if he would ask her more, so she touched his arm lightly. 'Look, I've got to go.' She wasn't ready to confront Tiffany Stickler, who would, no doubt, be sneaking back home this way while Ben, presumably, would be returning innocently alone and by road. First, she needed to think.

'Bloody hell,' she muttered, screwing the few remaining leaflets into a ball as she strode off.

Once, Ben had told her everything and she would have known there was a girl. She didn't even mind a girl, for heaven's sake – there had been girls before, casual affairs, only almost too casual to be called affairs for Ben never seemed that bothered. He had amused his mother no end by regaling her with every detail of their infatuation. But – as far as she knew and she had thought she knew it all – there had never been a girl on his bike. God, when she recalled how she'd drummed into him the importance of that when he didn't have his full licence yet . . . And there had certainly never been a girl like Tiffany Stickler.

'Bloody, bloody hell,' she repeated. And it had all started with that motor-bike. The one she had never wanted him to have. The one he was supposed to be travelling around Europe on, not impressing girls like Tiffany Stickler with. That damned motor-bike. The one that *would* keep reminding her of the past. The one that made her so bloody angry.

Chapter 3

Claire arrived home to a silent house and a letter on the door-mat. She picked it up, barely registering her mother's small neat handwriting, went into the kitchen, put the kettle on and tried to work out how she could handle this.

David . . . Well, David had been sitting in Fern's workshop while she was painting, nothing wrong in that. It could be – surely it was – totally innocent. She trusted him. Claire watched the kettle slowly steaming, coming to an angry boil. Well, didn't she?

But Ben . . . Ben was seeing Tiffany Stickler and, worse, they were keeping it quiet. Knowing Richard and Iris as she did, she could hardly blame the youngsters for that. It wasn't a crime. Why should they tell the world their business? The narrow mentality of *some* in this village would have the pair walking down the aisle with her in the family way before anyone could so much as click a finger. No wonder they didn't want to go public.

Oh, God . . . Claire hesitated, kettle in hand. Pregnant? Surely Ben wouldn't have . . .? Surely he and Tiffany hadn't . . .?

No. Resolutely she poured boiling water into the pot. They were keeping it quiet because the headmaster's daughter was normally kept under lock and key, that was all. The girl was chauffeured to horse-riding, tennis club, badminton practice and what-have-you. Claire never saw her around the village in the way she saw most people. Tiffany Stickler was slightly apart, slightly superior in Richard's opinion, no doubt, to be protected from mere heathens. So how on earth had Ben . . .?

Claire reached for a mug. How they had met wasn't her concern.

Neither was their decision to keep it secret. They were having a bit of a fling. A laugh, as Ben always called it. End of story. Next week there would be another girl. Next week Tiffany would still be playing badminton.

But there again . . . As she poured the tea, Claire attempted to drive away the image of teenage passion that she'd just witnessed, but it was now apparently indelibly imprinted on her mind. Ben was no innocent, she knew that. Still, it had come as a bit of a shock actually to see him . . . see them . . . But that was the young for you – even a five-minute wonder had more unresolved sexual tension than *Brief Encounter*. And, in her son's case, she wasn't sure that it was unresolved at all. Belatedly she stopped pouring and grabbed a cloth to soak up the surplus tea.

To hell with it, she *was* concerned. She wouldn't brood on Ben's potential status as village Don Juan, but when it came to Richard's daughter . . . that was *her* business too. After all, she worked for the man. And now, she reflected gloomily, she was even one of his Friends.

'I'll talk to Ben,' she told the unopened letter on the kitchen table. 'It's the only way.' She heard the front door open.

'Hi, Mum,' called out Trevarne's answer to Casanova.

'But not right now,' Claire whispered to the letter. 'Hi,' she called back. 'Did you have a good morning?' God, she sounded so natural, she was wasted as a school secretary and Jill-of-all-trades. She should be on some West End stage at least.

Ben breezed in. 'Any breakfast around? I'm starving.'

But that was going too far. 'You know where the eggs are.' In defiance, Claire slit open her mother's letter. 'But *I* would call it late lunch.'

'I'll just have some cake, then.'

This, she recognised as Ben's way of getting her to cook for him. He had learned it by some sort of male, I'm-good-at-disguising-my-chauvinistic-impulses instinct. He was also good at ironing his shirts badly and at redecorating the bathroom with smears of cleaning fluid after he'd subjected it to death by steam.

But today she wouldn't let him get away with it. If he needed to seduce someone, why the hell had he chosen her boss's daughter?

What was he trying to do to her? Her village status – not to mention the blasted committee – would never stand the strain of being his mother and therefore probably to blame. And worse, he hadn't even *told* her. 'Right you are.'

A moment's baffled silence was followed by Ben loping round the kitchen, seeming too tall for the cupboards and worktops, his legs too long for the chairs, his hands too big for the cutlery and plates. She suppressed a minor ooze of affection. He clattered the cake tin around, sighing, because an egg was what he really wanted. Needed the energy, probably, she thought, after whatever he'd been up to this morning.

'And don't make too much mess,' she snapped.

'Do I ever?' He stooped to kiss the top of her head.

Claire realised that instead of reading her mother's letter she was squeezing it into a ball of repressed emotion inside her fist. She forced herself to open her palm. 'So . . . Made any plans yet?' she asked casually.

'Plans?' For a split second the blue-grey eyes widened, and she thought she could detect a shade of guilt.

'Plans to go away.' Claire spread out the letter on her lap. How would he get out of that one?

'Right. Yeah.' Ben's mouth was full of cake.

Claire waited patiently.

'I reckon I might wait till the summer.'

'Why's that?' Probably, she'd spoken too quickly. His eyes registered surprise.

'Weather.'

'Hmm.'

'And money.' Ben licked his fingers and began collecting crumbs from the plate. Warily he glanced at her. 'I might look for a job. Try and get some dosh together first.'

Claire swallowed her first reaction. 'I see,' was about all she could manage. It wasn't looking good, but she wouldn't confront him now. She might drop a few hints . . . give him the opportunity to tell all. And then she would pounce.

'So you'll have to put up with me for a bit longer.' Ben chucked his plate in the washing-up bowl. 'Will you manage, d'you reckon?'

Once again Claire withheld the tenderness. She had to admit she was relieved that the time of leaving had been postponed – more relieved than she could say. But she would have preferred the reason not to be Tiffany Stickler. 'I'm sure I'll cope.' She kept her voice brisk and her gaze pinned to her letter. Was this how it had been with Freddie? Sometimes, just sometimes, she felt a good deal of sympathy for her mother.

Ben left the room at last, whistling, and Claire began to wade through rambling descriptions of a neighbour's irritable bowel syndrome, the height of her mother's late hollyhocks, and the intricacies and intimacies of the new wallpaper in the dining room. *I hope you'll come to see it before it fades*, her mother had added in her acid prose. And then, worst of all, and as always left to the end of the letter, was the stuff Claire was dreading, the stuff about her father.

David's bulky figure appeared at the back door at the same moment she finished reading the letter. 'Anything interesting?' He came in, smelling of river, reeds and fish – but not, she noted, of Fern Browne – took off his hat and put his big hand lightly on her shoulder. He left it there for a moment. She waited, but she didn't feel a thing.

'From Mum.'

David grunted.

No *and how are they*? Claire suppressed a sigh. David and her mother were not friends. They never had been. Patricia Trent had never forgiven David for uprooting Claire and carting her off to what she called the back of beyond. And David couldn't cope with people who never said what they really thought and yet still expected everyone to know.

'What difference does it make which bloody tea-cups we use?' he had been known to growl at her.

They lived in such different worlds that Claire, whose sympathies were stretched both ways, had long ago given up on bringing them closer. 'And you?' she asked him.

'What?' David seemed distracted, although his face was glowing as it always was after a fishing expedition. Although he hadn't *just* been fishing, Claire reminded herself.

'Did you have an interesting morning?' This was his chance to tell her. She waited.

'Not specially.' David pulled off his coat.

'Catch anything?'

'A few trout.'

'Where are they?' Claire was cross with herself for doing this. Why couldn't she just *tell* him, for heaven's sake? He might even have seen her there, heard Emily's booming greeting, the pugs yapping. But she didn't think so, and something perverse inside her stopped Claire from speaking out.

She watched as he opened his bag. Most of the fish he caught went straight back in the river, but the angling association agreed to a small catch being retained – for a fee, of course. And she knew only too well where today's catch was sitting right now.

David had the grace to look shame-faced at least. 'I took them round to the aunts' house on the way home.'

Claire turned away. On the way home, indeed. He must have been there for hours.

'Well, they said they hadn't had fresh fish for ages, they love trout.'

Fern loves trout, she thought.

'And last time you moaned about having to gut them.'

Claire saw red. '*You* could always gut them.' Hardly fair for her to do the nasty bits when he'd had the pleasure of them, so to speak. But it was always the same. He put his family – his old childhood family, that is – first. Claire and Ben came a poor second. In everything.

'Next time –' he began.

'Bugger next time.' She saw the confusion on his face. Poor David, he wasn't to know that it wasn't just the fish. And neither was it just because she'd seen him with Fern. She was concerned about Ben and Tiffany Stickler. And worried to death about . . .

'Is it your dad?' Surprising her, he came closer, smoothed her hair from her face in a gesture of comfort. She tried to relax, longed to fall back against him, allow his solid figure to take her weight, her burdens. But she couldn't quite let go. It felt strange, that gesture of comfort: they no longer had easy contact with each other's bodies,

37

she realised. Once they had touched continually. And now . . .

She nodded. 'Mum reckons he's not safe to go out on his own. She says . . .' Claire pointed to the letter ' . . . she has to get a neighbour to watch him, even when she just goes out shopping for half an hour.' She stared up at David, willing him to say it wasn't true.

It couldn't be true, because Josh Trent had always been, like David himself, a big and powerful man. A wise man, a man who liked to give out advice and was damned good at it too. He had always been Claire's anchor; she sometimes wondered if that was why she had married David, because his size and something about his gentle, measured way of speaking reminded her of her father. She had been hurt when she met David. She had needed the kind of security he seemed to represent.

Claire shook the thought as far away as she dared. No. Her father couldn't possibly be ill – especially not mentally ill as her mother seemed to be implying.

But David didn't reassure her. 'Has she taken him to their GP? Have they done tests?'

Claire pulled away from him, screwing the sheet of paper into a ball once again. 'It hasn't come to that. It won't come to that.' She couldn't look at him. 'Dad might get a bit confused from time to time, but that's all. You don't know what Mum can be like, not really. She just wants someone to mother. Ever since Freddie and I left home she's been the same. She can't bear not to be needed by someone. She's treating Dad like a child. Somebody should stop her.'

He took her gently by the shoulders, and Claire found herself looking up into his eyes. She read the concern, but she didn't want concern, she wanted . . .

'I'll have to go and see them,' she said, waiting for him to say that he'd take her. 'Next weekend.' It had to be as soon as possible, she'd left it too long already, scared to see what she might see, scared to acknowledge her mother's fears.

She watched the lines of his brow curl into a frown. 'Next weekend I've already promised to –'

'I can go on my own.' She turned away, not wanting to know

what he'd promised to do, something that couldn't be cancelled or postponed, quite clearly. Something so vital that she'd have to face this alone. Ben, her father, David and Fern . . . These days it seemed she must face everything alone.

'The week after.' David sounded uncertain. 'Why don't you let me take you then?'

'Next weekend.' Claire remained firm. 'I need to find out how bad he really is. I need to see him as soon as I can. It's important, David.'

'You've waited this long –' He seemed about to say something more so she broke in to save him the embarrassment of further explanations.

'I'm perfectly capable of going on my own.' She was an independent woman. She didn't need David. 'I can probably find out more that way.' And it was true that with David there, Patricia would be hostile; she'd never open up. But, still, if things were as bad as her mother hinted they were, then Claire might need some moral support. Badly. 'Or . . .' A thought occurred to her.

'Or?' David looked sad.

'I could take Ben.' That long train journey to London, for she didn't relish driving all that way, was a perfect opportunity for a cosy heart-to-heart. And it was perfectly clear that David didn't want to come. When she needed him, he wasn't there. Second place again, as ever.

'Are you absolutely sure?' Once more David seemed to be asking her something else. And still she didn't know what it was.

Claire hesitated for the last time. 'I'm sure,' she told him.

She walked into the staff room on Monday morning to find Gary Stockwell being lectured by Richard.

'So you see, Gary, old chap . . .' The clap on the shoulder, was the – never to be trusted – Stickler sign of mateyness. '. . . I don't think a gallery visit is quite the thing. Anyway, these kids are too young to appreciate it.' He turned. 'Morning, Claire.'

'Morning.' Claire smiled sympathetically at Gary behind the Stickler's back. She might have known Richard would find an objection. Money spent on art was money wasted, in Richard's book.

'Kids on coaches.' The headmaster ticked a list off on his fingers. 'Singing, shouting, being sick.'

'It's not far to St Ives.' Gary was stubborn, she'd give him that. 'And you won't discount the idea? I mean, if the parents were to approve?'

Fat chance of that if they knew Richard was against it, Claire thought.

'Yes, yes, of course. No one could accuse me of being narrow-minded.'

Claire's eyebrows rose.

'I'm always open to new ideas. Claire will tell you that.' Boredom flitted across Richard's features and Claire had to smile. He'd had his say, made his decision known and he was accustomed to his staff lying down and playing dead at this juncture, not arguing the point. The truth was that Richard was about as open to new ideas as the Pope.

'Well . . .' He glanced pointedly at the Rolex on his wrist. 'This won't do. Assembly to organise. I must run.' But Claire noted that his parting grimace of a smile did not embrace Gary Stockwell.

'You've upset him now.' She chuckled.

'But will he ask the parents?' Gary frowned. 'I've told him what's on at the Tate. It could be a brilliant day. Don't you reckon the parents would fork out to let their kids see a bit of the real thing?'

'They might.' But she doubted it.

'A chance for some hands-on, if you know what I mean.' Gary seemed wistful.

'I certainly do.' Claire began to clear away coffee cups. Another of her duties was to keep the staff room manageable, and this too was a lot more hands-on than she had envisaged when she first took the job. 'But if he does ask them it'll be a bloody miracle,' she muttered disloyally. 'He's made his mind up, couldn't you tell?'

Gary stared at her. 'And that's it?'

'Very probably.' She grabbed the dustpan and brush for someone had left crumbs all over the red chintz of the armchair.

'So everyone has to accept it's no go? No debate? No questions asked? No one else's opinion counts?'

'Not exactly.' Claire couldn't help laughing at his mixture of enthusiasm and naïvety. 'Richard isn't the end of the line. But . . . Is this the first time you've worked in a village school, Gary?'

'What if it is?' He stuck his hands in his pockets, looking for all the world like that son of hers might look in ten years' time.

Claire softened. 'Come for a drink at lunch-time and I'll explain,' she offered. She didn't know why she felt compelled to offer the hand of friendship to this man, but there was something about that enthusiasm of his that appealed to her. Trevarne could do with a few more like him to shake it up, to ask a few questions for a change.

'All right.' He grinned.

'And if I get the chance,' she grabbed her bag and made for the connecting door and her own small office, 'I'll have a word with the Stick – I mean Richard – about the gallery visit. Maybe I can clarify the benefits, so to speak.'

His face brightened. 'Would you? But . . .?'

She could see him trying to work out why the school secretary might succeed where he had failed, but Claire didn't have the time right now to explain the complications of village politics and marital status, let alone Richard's penchant for a good pair of legs – even if the woman who owned them was over forty. 'Half twelve? In the Lionheart?'

'Well, yes, but why don't we meet here first, in the staff room?'

My God, but he had a lot to learn indeed. 'Oh, no. I'll see you in the main bar. And mine's a tomato juice.'

'We had to meet in here,' she told him when they were settled with their drinks. 'If we'd been seen leaving the school building together, then that would be it.'

'It?'

She put on a serious expression. 'Full-blown affair at the very least.'

He choked on his coke with ice and lemon. 'What?' he spluttered.

Claire wasn't sure it had been that awful a proposition, but still . . . 'Village mentality,' she told him with despair. 'But don't worry, you're quite safe. I'm not making a pass at you.'

'I never imagined you were. It's just –' He broke off, taking a sip of his drink.

'You don't indulge at lunch-time either,' she observed. 'Very wise. Richard has been known to smell people's breath when they get back from lunch.' Claire giggled. 'And it's not a pleasant experience to have him getting that close.'

'I bet.' They exchanged a conspiratorial glance.

'And, by the way, I'm sorry about rushing off like that in the copse the other day.'

'I thought you'd seen a ghost.' Gary's remark coincided with the arrival of their prawn sandwiches.

'Worse than that.'

'Anyone I know?' He had the most amazing dark blue eyes, she registered. Also a very nice smile, and . . . well, she could do with a confidant. He obviously felt the same way about the Stickler as she did – or he would do, once he'd been here a while.

'It was my son,' she informed him.

'Oh?'

'And . . .' she rolled her eyes '. . . Richard Stickler's daughter.'

He paused, sandwich half-way to mouth. 'And not just talking, as far as I remember?'

Claire recalled the scene. 'Definitely not just talking. Their mouths were,' she sighed, 'otherwise engaged.'

Gary chomped thoughtfully on his prawn sandwich. He'd demolished two of them already, she noted.

'Okay, so run this past me again. Your son is having a –'

'Relationship,' she provided smoothly.

'A relationship with Richard Stickler's daughter. Aged?'

'Hell . . .' That was something that hadn't even crossed her mind. 'Sixteen. Or . . .' She caught his eye. 'I'm not sure. She *may* be sixteen.'

Gary finished the sandwich and went back to his coke. How could he eat at a time like this? 'Or she might be only fifteen?'

'I don't know,' Claire croaked.

'And Ben is . . .?'

'Eighteen.' She was on sure ground there at any rate.

'An adult.' It took Claire a moment to catch his meaning.

'An . . .? Oh, hell! You mean he'll be responsible if . . .' She couldn't go on, couldn't voice her fears, even to this kind man who was frankly making her feel worse than ever.

'What did Ben say when you asked him about it?' Gary leant forward, his expression sympathetic. 'Have they . . . well, you know, gone the whole hog?'

'I didn't ask him.' Claire pushed her plate away.

'You didn't?'

'I didn't want a confrontation.' She thought of Fern and David, of her father . . .

'You were scared?' He was so understanding, a bit of a Claire Rayner in trousers.

'I'm good at running away,' she admitted. 'I didn't want to hear about it. I've never pushed Ben into telling me anything.'

He raised dark eyebrows in an unspoken question.

'I never needed to,' she told him. 'I've always hoped I was a liberal parent . . .' Her voice tailed off. It sounded so corny. Why was she telling him all this?

'And what did David say?' Gary spoke as if he already knew David well, not just that he'd picked up a few of his earthenware pots in a gallery somewhere to admire the glaze. For some reason this annoyed her.

'Not a lot. I didn't actually tell him about it.' Cautiously, she met his look of undeniable amusement. 'Like I told you, I'm good at running.' And she was beginning to wish she hadn't told Gary Stockwell either.

'I suppose you were hoping it would all go away?'

That was rather close to the mark. Although it struck her that she often chose not to confide in David, these days, whereas once upon a time it had been basic instinct. But Ben had always seemed her responsibility, hers to worry over. And now? 'It might go away.' She shrugged. 'Ben has a new girl every week. It's never serious. They're young . . .' She tried not to remember that kiss.

'If you really want my advice . . .' Gary glanced at his watch and got to his feet, preparing to go.

She followed his lead. It was time to get back for afternoon lessons. 'Of course I do.' Depending on what it was.

He held the door open for her. 'I'd just ask Ben the score.'

'Ask him?' She stared at him, it seemed much too simple. 'You mean ask him if he and Tiffany are . . .?'

'Well, why not? Surely people practise safe sex, even in Trevarne?' His grin, when it came, was once again pure conspiracy.

'Safe sex?' Claire shrieked, looking up to see Iris Stickler on the other side of the road getting an eyeful. Claire might have warned Gary that they mustn't be seen entering the pub together, but talking of Ben had made her forget entirely that they shouldn't be seen leaving it together either. And they certainly shouldn't be talking about sex, safe or otherwise.

'Hell,' she said again.

Gary too had seen Iris, but his grin merely widened. 'What does it matter what people think? We can have lunch together, can't we? We're both consenting adults.'

'I wish I could say the same for Ben and Tiffany,' Claire grumbled. In theory, surely, Ben could even go to prison. Having sex with a minor . . . If they had. 'Oh, hell,' she said again.

'And by the way . . .'

'More words of wisdom?'

'For a school secretary your vocabulary is a tad limited, if you don't mind me saying.'

And Claire laughed – causing Iris to stare even harder – because she was beginning to get the feeling this man would become more than a mere ally. She might get lucky. He might become a friend.

'You don't think he's a troublemaker, do you, Claire?' Richard had the look of a nervous rabbit, she thought, with his thin, brown face, the carefully cut brown suit, and spasmodic twitch of the knee in tricky situations.

'Gary?' She wondered if Richard had spotted the silver stud in Gary's left ear-lobe that he'd clearly forgotten to remove before coming to school this morning. 'Oh, no.'

'Not the kind to stir things up at all?'

Privately Claire rather hoped so. 'Not a chance,' she lied. 'He respects what you've done here, Richard. He was telling me. At lunch.'

'Really?'

'Oh, yes.' She sat down in the chair opposite him, ignoring the fact that he was staring at her legs as her skirt rose a good, oh, four inches above the knee. Perfectly respectable, but the Stickler was a desperate man. She leant forward with absolutely no shame. 'And let's face it. A man like you could teach him so much.'

'I could? Well . . . yes, of course I *could*.'

'This Tate Gallery visit, for example.' Claire smiled her most bewitching smile. 'Wouldn't it be great? I know it's not *the* Tate, but still, it's so *contemporary*. It would give the school such . . .' she groped for the right word '. . . such status. To be at the cutting edge, so to speak. At the artistic forefront. If you get my drift.' Had she gone too far?

But if she had, Richard didn't seem to notice. He had got a good look at her legs if nothing else, and the glint in his eye told her that he was mentally working on the top button of her blouse. She ploughed on. Richard was a lech, and she liked to get her own back on leches – but he only *looked*. He wouldn't hurt a fly. 'The governors love these educational visits, don't they? Just because we're so far away from London, we're not living in a backwater. The children of Cornwall are never too young to experience the culture we have on our own door-step.'

'Quite.' Richard had his hand firmly placed on his knee. 'But would it be educational, Claire? I mean, at the end of the day it's just, well, just art.'

Claire suppressed the sharp comment that came to mind. 'Even at this early stage of their education we need to focus on the marginalised subjects,' she told him reprovingly. 'Hands-on. Discovery learning. Enrichment. Broadening their minds.' Oh, yes, she knew all the buzz words, all the right buttons to press.

'Perhaps you're right.' He was weakening. 'But who would take them? Who could we spare?'

She pretended to give this some thought. 'I could go, I suppose. If Gary were to come too. And a few of the year six parents.' She smiled confidingly. 'They'll jump at it. The coffers will be rattling with donations, they'll boast to their friends about the school . . .'

'All right.' Richard got to his feet and adjusted his jacket. 'We'll put it to them.'

'Good idea, Richard.' Claire got up too. 'I'm with you on that. I'm all for democracy. That's why you managed to persuade me to join the Friends of Trevarne.'

'Hmm.' She could see that her point had gone home.

'And I'm sure you're right to follow your instincts.'

'I am? Er . . . I am.' Richard moved to open the door for her but Claire had one other little matter on her mind.

'And how's Tiffany?' she murmured. 'It's a long time since I've seen her. She must be . . . oh, how old by now?'

If the Stickler was surprised by her interest then he didn't show it. 'Fifteen.'

Claire suppressed a groan. 'And I suppose she's still doing all her horse-riding and things on a Saturday morning?'

Now he did look surprised. 'Gym club,' he told her. 'In Bodmin.'

'Yes, of course.' Claire decided to make a hasty exit. Mustn't push her luck. 'Gym club in Bodmin. That's what I was thinking of.' He was looking so self-satisfied that she was ever so slightly tempted to tell him the real definition of gym club in Bodmin. But she resisted. Self-control, that was the thing. And Gary was right. Before she did anything else, she must speak to Ben. To find out, as he so succinctly put it, the score.

Chapter 4

———◆———

'What are you doing, David?' It was late afternoon the following Friday, and for the last half-hour Claire had been watching David armed with the cartons in which he stored his pottery, going back and forth between garage, workshop and van.

'Packing pots.' He stooped to kiss her, but she dodged it.

'I gathered that much.'

David was clearly taken aback. 'I thought you were just off.' He glanced at his watch. 'You'll miss your train.'

'Probably.' She glared at him. 'You're going to a craft fair?' Was that why he couldn't take her to London? Because he was going to another blasted craft fair? She could hardly believe it.

'Didn't I tell you?'

'No, you did not. I thought you'd finished until mid-October.' She struggled for a sense of proportion. Mid-October was when the round of craft fairs started again, indoor this time, ready for the Christmas rush. But what did all that matter when her father was ill? She had needed David's support, damn it.

He rubbed his eyes, depositing plaster-of-Paris dust across one cheek. 'This is the one I'm doing with Fern. It's a bit special.'

It would be. 'With Fern?' Claire took a step further away from him.

'I told you.' David sighed, as if he knew there'd be trouble. 'She needs more outlets for her watercolours. There's some chap who'll be at Penzance. That's why it had to be this weekend. So he could see her work.'

'I see.' It was all perfectly reasonable. Why shouldn't David, who had already made his reputation as a designer and craftsman, help Fern establish hers?

He caught her tone. 'You could have come with us, love.'

'Maybe I would have done – if I'd known about it,' she snapped.

His brown eyes grew troubled. 'I did tell you.'

'I don't remember.' Although, to be fair, there was a faint glimmer.

'It was on the calendar, Claire.'

'I never saw it.' She didn't even know what they were arguing about by this time. Or, rather, she was arguing, David was calmly defending. He was good at holding his emotions in check. So good she sometimes wondered if he had any in the first place.

He took her arm, tried to look into her face. 'You've always said you hated those things.'

'I do.' Oh, she'd enjoyed them at first. David was often the centre of attention, and during the day he would have more than his fair share of people watching, admiring, buying pieces and ordering more. But after a while she'd grown tired of being in the shadows, watching people fawning up to him – although to David's credit he took little notice of all that. Still, she resented running to the refreshment tent and back all day long, hour after hour being told how lucky she was to be married to David, how proud she must be. 'I do hate them,' she repeated. 'It's just . . .'

She wanted to tell him that she needed him, Claire realised with a slight shock. She needed him to know about Ben and Tiffany, and yet she had told a colleague at work whom she hardly knew rather than her own husband. She needed him to be with her when she saw her father – she wanted *him* to see her father, so he could at least give his opinion. She valued David's opinion. She was worried sick.

But a craft fair with Fern Browne was apparently more important to David. So be it.

'What, Claire?' As always his voice was gentle. 'What is it?'

'Nothing.'

'Don't lie to me.'

At last she allowed herself to look into his face. It struck her that he wasn't calm at all. He was holding his emotions tightly in check. 'I have to go. We'll miss the train.' Her voice was dull.

'But we need to talk.' He shook her, not roughly, but as if she were an obstinate child.

'What about?' Not now, she thought.

'You know what about. How long do you think we can go on like this, Claire?'

She remained silent. What was he trying to tell her?

'I don't know how we came to live separate lives.' A small crease appeared on his brow. 'But I do know that it's been going on for too long.'

It sounded as if he were blaming Claire for the wrong turnings. But what about Fern? What about Trevarne? Had David forgotten how much she had wanted to leave? 'What do you want, David?' Even now, part of her wanted to reach out to touch his face, his dark hair streaked with white and ginger.

He bent his head closer towards her, his face almost touching hers. 'I'll show you.' And then his lips were on her lips – not tender, but hot and insistent as he pressed himself against her.

For a second she felt the full force of his weight, the threat of him. Fear and longing twisted together, briefly in her mind, before indignation took over, and she was pushing him away. 'Stop it, David.' Not like that . . .

'You see?' His brown eyes were blazing now. 'You won't let me come near you.'

'It's not that. It's not *me*.' Furiously, she spun on her heels. Talk, he had said. But it wasn't talking he wanted. And for the rest he had Fern. Where was he when she needed him?

'I would have come with you any other time,' he shouted after her, 'but I couldn't let Fern down.'

And that, Claire thought, as she grabbed her bag and yelled up to Ben to hurry, just about summed it up, God help her.

'I envy you sometimes, love.' Josh Trent was looking tired, Claire thought. Tired, but thank God, not *ill*.

After lunch the four of them had gone for a short walk, and although Claire had been surprised at how quickly he tired, there didn't seem to be much wrong with his mind.

'Why's that?' she asked.

'Peace and quiet.' Josh smiled. 'Living away from the city.'

'It doesn't seem much like the city right now.' They were sitting side by side on a wooden garden bench, placed by Claire's mother under the apple tree. Fine in spring, Claire thought, but a bit dodgy in September. Still, it was pleasant, and Claire stretched out like a cat in the late-afternoon sunshine. She loved these warm days: they were like unexpected birthday presents, coming just when you thought summer was over.

'But do you think you'll stay in Cornwall for the rest of your life now, love?'

Claire glanced at him sharply. 'Who knows?'

It was true that once upon a time she hadn't been able to accept that Trevarne would be her home for ever. It was so small and, frankly, so boring. And now? Well, she had learnt to live there, hadn't she? She had made the best of a village life that had so stultified her at the start of her marriage that for two pins she would have upped and left it.

She really would have, if David hadn't told her he couldn't leave Trevarne . . . if she hadn't loved him with every fibre of her being . . . if she hadn't found herself pregnant with Ben. She would have left, because in the early days Trevarne had driven her half crazy. And the arrival of a small baby had made things worse, not better.

She couldn't help loving David, she certainly couldn't help her pregnancy. But David could have agreed to leave with her, couldn't he? When he saw how unhappy she was . . .? There was nothing to stop him. He could work anywhere.

Oh, he said it was his family home, that he was part of the community, his roots were in Trevarne, he had family ties like his aunts. But . . . second place. That's what it was all about. He could have left back then. And perhaps Claire had never forgiven him for that.

'Then again, I suppose one place is much the same as another,' Josh remarked.

'Is it?' She wasn't sure she could agree with that. Places seemed very different to Claire.

He glanced at her from under his ragged brows, such a perceptive glance that she was left in no doubt. His mental powers weren't damaged in the slightest – at least not at this moment in time. 'It's the people you're with that make the difference,' he told her.

Was this her father's way of enquiring after the health of her marriage? It wouldn't be the first time, but Claire had no intention of burdening him with her problems – especially when he happened to be one of them. 'David loves Trevarne,' she told him. 'He'd never leave.'

'And what you want is by the by, eh?'

Claire smiled back at him. 'Oh, it's not so bad. My job could be a lot worse. The air's clean. It's a pretty place, you know that.' She laughed. 'And then there's all that peace and quiet you were talking about.'

He sniffed. 'You were never one for quiet. That motor-bike . . .'

Claire remained silent. She didn't need reminding. Her mother had hit the roof, but her father hadn't seemed surprised by any of it – when she first became addicted to bikes, when she saved up to buy her own, when she abruptly put it up for sale and never touched it again.

Even now he was watching her but not pressing the point. *Leave her be . . .* That was what she remembered him saying most in her teenage years.

'I'm older now,' she said obliquely. 'People change.'

Josh shifted on the bench. 'Remember those holidays?'

'Hmm?'

'In Cornwall, when you were a nipper. Land's End. When was it now?' He slapped his knee. 'Nineteen sixty-one, you fell over on the cobblestones and gashed your leg open.'

Claire laughed. 'I was only about seven.'

'And Bude. At that holiday camp. 'Sixty-three that was. Your nan and grandad were there. We entered the fancy-dress competition as Snow White and the Seven Dwarfs.'

Claire pulled her cardigan around her shoulders. The evening was drawing in. 'Who was Snow White?'

'Your nan.'

She counted on her fingers. 'Nan, Grandad, you, Mum, me and Freddie. That makes six.'

He laughed. 'The couple in the chalet next door joined the party. He was Sneezy – had hay fever something rotten. And his wife was Dopey.'

Claire giggled. 'And Mum?'

'Was Grumpy.' They roared, and Patricia, on her way out to tell them dinner was ready, frowned her tense little frown.

'What's so funny?'

'Old times.' Claire got up and put an arm around her mother's shoulders, but the tightness she found there forced her arm back to her side. 'We were talking about old holidays in Cornwall. You remember, Mum.' She marvelled at how much her mother found to disapprove of sometimes – even Claire and her dad having a laugh together.

'Of course I remember.' Patricia fussed over Josh, pulling his thin jacket closer around him, taking his arm as if he were a cripple.

Claire caught his eye and suppressed another grin. Dad had always let Mum assume she was getting her own way. Not like David, she found herself thinking. That wasn't even in the equation of marriage for him.

'So which young lady are you honouring with your attentions this week, son?' Josh asked Ben as they sat down to dinner.

Claire almost choked on her wine. Ben and his steady stream of girlfriends had become a family joke, although Claire wondered if she had always remained so light-hearted about it simply *because* it was a steady stream, rather than a one and only. She wasn't sure how she would feel about *that*.

'Oh, you know . . . no one special.' This was the stock response, but Ben didn't look up as he toyed with his broccoli.

Guilt, she thought.

'That's the best way, if you ask me.' Josh patted his shoulder.

Claire half agreed. The other half was irritated by this all-boys-together stuff.

Patricia sniffed. 'No one *is* asking you.'

'Us lads should stay fancy free for as long as we can. Give 'em an inch . . .'

Patricia clicked her tongue. 'Talk about giving . . . Don't *you* go giving him ideas.'

'He's already got them.' Claire was tempted to enlarge on this, but told herself it would wait. Going home on the train was plenty soon enough.

'Mum . . .'

'I bet he has an' all.' Josh chuckled. 'A boy after me own heart.'

'And, besides, he can't afford to get too involved,' Claire eyed her son thoughtfully, 'when he's planning to go off travelling for heaven knows how long.'

Patricia Trent dropped her knife and fork. They fell on to her plate with a clatter that hardly dented the strained silence. Claire wouldn't look at her mother, but she knew what she was thinking. *Like Freddie . . .*

'They all get itchy feet some time or another,' Josh murmured. 'It's nothing so unusual.'

'You're right.' Once more, her father had smoothed things over, and Claire found herself smiling at her son. 'They do, don't they?' She had too, in her own way.

'And when you lot have finally stopped talking about me as if I wasn't here . . .' Ben pulled a complaining face that somehow restored their relationship to its old footing.

They laughed, but as Patricia got to her feet to clear the table her expression was still troubled, Claire noted. And it was a weary face these days, the grey perm a loose frame for tired lines and shadows, although the cornflower-blue eyes remained alert, and Patricia still kept herself looking smart. Today she was wearing a flared skirt in navy, a white blouse and a pretty silk scarf at her neck. Claire fingered her own scarf. She never used to wear them but they seemed to have become an essential part of her wardrobe in the last few years. She looked, she realised dismally, rather like a younger version of her mother.

Claire followed Patricia into the kitchen.

'Dad seems absolutely fine.' There was no point pussyfooting around the subject. She squirted washing-up liquid into the bowl.

Her mother's expression told her she'd used too much. 'You haven't been here five minutes.'

'I've been talking to him most of the day.' Claire was aware of her own slow anger. She might avoid confrontation where David's aunts were concerned, but she had no such reservations with her own mother.

In reply, Patricia merely pressed her lips into the thinnest of lines.

'We've covered every subject under the sun. I'm sure there's nothing seriously wrong with him.' Claire hesitated, her mother's hurt look forcing her to be scrupulously fair. 'He's getting a bit scatty, I won't deny that. But everyone gets forgetful as they get older, Mum. Look at me. I'd forget my own head. I put a pint of milk away in the oven only last week.'

'Don't be flippant, Claire,' Patricia snapped.

'You wanted my opinion.'

'He's having one of his lucid days.'

'I see.' But Claire didn't, not really. All she saw was that her mother was determined for Josh to be ill.

Patricia picked up a tea-towel. 'I need help,' she said.

The guilt passed over Claire in waves as she sank her hands into the hot soapy liquid. 'I'll do what I can, Mum. But I'm miles away. I've got a full-time job. I've got –'

'I mean professional help.'

Claire turned to stare at her. 'Surely it hasn't come to that?' She remembered David's words about seeing a GP. If he were here he'd probably be agreeing with Patricia right now, urging her onwards to the surgery. 'Everyone forgets things,' she said again.

Patricia picked up a plate and dried it carefully, base first as she had once taught her daughter, although it wasn't a skill Claire used that often. Left in the drainer, plates tended to dry naturally.

'One day last week he decided to heat up some soup. I was in the bathroom.' Her voice drifted into monotone. 'He switched the gas on.'

Claire looked over at the cooker. 'So?'

'He turned round to get the matches to light it. They weren't where he thought they'd be. He sat down to read the paper.'

'I don't get the point.' Claire scrubbed ferociously at some gravy that had hardened into glue.

'The point, dear,' Patricia picked up another plate, 'is that he left the gas switched on without lighting it. The point,' her eyes darkened, 'is that he forgot he'd switched it on in the first place.'

Claire's hands stopped moving in the bowl. She waited. The steam from the hot water seemed to be making her dizzy, making her head swim. Or had she just drunk too much wine?

'When I came down from the bathroom he was coughing. The kitchen smelt disgusting. He hadn't even noticed.'

'What did you do?' She tried to control the feeling of faintness but now the blood was pounding in her head, making her nauseous. It wasn't the heat of the water, nor the wine. It was what her mother was telling her.

'I realised it was the gas, switched off the cooker, got him out of the room, told him he shouldn't have touched it in the first place.' She paused, out of breath. 'He knew I was just coming down to do the soup. I'd told him. So why . . .?'

'And what did he say?' Claire murmured.

'He said, "*Shouldn't have touched what, love?*" ' Patricia's shoulders began to shake. 'He didn't even know what I was talking about.'

'Mum . . .' Claire took her hands out of the water, moved to her mother's side and held her close. Patricia wasn't crying, she was simply shaking.

'He hadn't even smelt the gas,' she whispered. 'He could have gassed himself and not even known.'

She wouldn't think about that. 'Perhaps it was a one-off,' Claire heard her own voice saying. 'I'm sure it won't happen again.'

'Claire.' Her mother's voice hardened. She drew away and Claire saw again the authority of her childhood. 'This is not the sort of forgetting you can shrug off.'

Claire knew she was right. They couldn't ignore it. *She* couldn't ignore it. 'Have you told Freddie?' she asked. As the baby of the family, born when Claire was already at school and virtually independent, Freddie had always been adored and always been spoiled. Perhaps that was why he had moved away from home at the earliest opportunity – in true hippie style, taking little more than a rucksack and his guitar – and settled in Amsterdam, where he stayed, mostly unemployed, usually stoned, and rarely even at the other end of a phone. But Claire didn't see why he should be spared *this*.

'I don't want to bother Freddie.' Patricia frowned.

She had bothered Claire . . . 'He's Freddie's father too.' Claire stared her out. 'Don't you think he has a right to know?'

Patricia's vague shrug of the shoulders disguised whatever feelings she had on the matter. 'He's so far away. What could he possibly do?'

'He might come over,' Claire said gently.

Patricia turned away. 'You take care the same thing doesn't happen to you.'

Claire knew how much it hurt her mother that Freddie didn't visit more often. She'd poured herself into her only son, and yet she hadn't seen him for years. Claire knew she even sent him money, hoping he'd spend it on the fare – though she was probably too proud to ask him to – but doubtless Freddie, being Freddie, found more interesting things to do with it. A few drinks, a meal out with one of his girls perhaps. Ben, she was sure, would never behave like Freddie. He would be back. 'It's different with Ben,' she said.

'Perhaps. Perhaps not.' Patricia seemed unconvinced. 'But it's not that I'm protecting Freddie from knowing about his father. It's just that if I told him he would say I was exaggerating, you know he would.'

Claire waited for what she knew was coming.

'But *you* believe me, Claire. Don't you?' The cornflower-blue eyes gazed into hers. 'I'm relying on you to see how it is.'

Against her will, Claire was transported back into childhood. She had always been the grown-up one. Everyone told her so; they had for as long as she could remember. She could be relied on, they all said it. Even at an early age she had a strongly developed sense of responsibilities being thrust upon her, a trust she wasn't always ready for, didn't always want. And those family responsibilities made her want to escape whenever she could; at first into a world of her own imagination, and later . . . Later, into a world of speed and excitement, where the pure thrill was the only thing to worry about. And any risk was a responsibility she had only to herself.

'Of course I believe you.' Claire spoke automatically. Her mother was totally strung out, she realised. She might be a touch sniffy and more than a little repressed, but she did need help – and at least she'd had the sense to ask her daughter for it. No, Claire could not dismiss her mother's worries any longer, no matter how lucid her father had seemed today.

Patricia appeared to be satisfied. 'I knew you'd understand. That was why I needed you to come.'

'You should see the doctor,' Claire said at last, admitting it. 'Tell him what you've told me. And the rest.' Lines of worry like this hadn't appeared on her mother's face after just one incident. This must have been going on for a while. And was it her imagination or had the atmosphere between them now lightened?

'What will he do?' There was a touch of fear in Patricia's eyes.

Claire didn't have the faintest idea. 'Maybe there are tests they can carry out. They can at least offer advice. And –'

'Yes?' Patricia looked almost eager, like a child herself.

'You need a holiday, Mum. Both of you do.'

She turned away, her expression proud. 'We can't afford it, you know that. Not on our pension.'

'Come and stay with us. For as long as you like.' Claire heard herself saying this with a kind of horror. She didn't want to think about what David would say. But she had to offer. It was partly the guilt, oh, yes. But it was Dad too, the way he'd talked of those old Cornish holidays when she was a kid, the barely disguised nostalgia in his eyes.

'That's kind of you, dear.' For the first time since they'd arrived, Claire saw her mother smile. And that made her sure she'd done the right thing.

'So you'll come?'

'I'll ask your father.' Claire saw she had already decided. 'But I expect he'd love to.'

By Sunday lunch-time, Claire felt justified in sneaking away for a quick drink with Laura. She'd done her bit, and besides, she didn't get to see Laura nearly often enough.

'So what brings you to London?' Laura asked, as they ordered their drinks. 'Parental duty or desperation for a bit of culture?'

Claire smiled. She and Laura had been close once upon a time, but now she made a snap decision not to tell her why she was here. And, after all, she had never fully confided in Laura. She had never told her why she had packed in motor-cycle riding, or what had happened at the back of that café on the Dorking road. But, then,

57

she hadn't told a living soul about that. 'I thought it was about time Ben saw his grandparents.' She sipped her tomato juice. 'And that it was about time,' tentatively, she touched Laura's arm, 'that I saw *you.*'

'Mmm.' Laura's half-smile told her that she, too, wasn't exactly on top of the world. Would she say what was troubling her, or didn't their friendship include confidences at all?

They found a table, and Laura lit a cigarette. 'So, sweetie, how's life treating you? What have you been up to?' She tapped Claire's glass of tomato juice. 'I see you've stopped lunch-time drinking – that's a bad sign.'

'A sign of age, more like.' Claire knew Laura wasn't referring to village high spots like the summer fête. She meant, What do you do that's bad – or at least remotely interesting to a girl from the city? 'Not a lot by your standards. Same job, same house, same husband. I don't get here, there and everywhere like you.'

Laura smiled in response. 'Me? I just bum around.'

'But I bet you went to the Cézanne exhibition.'

'Oh, yeah, well, everyone went to that.' Laura eyed Claire cautiously as if she'd just nose-dived from another planet.

'Not everyone in Cornwall.' Claire laughed. 'And the William Morris at the V and A? Degas?'

'Mmm. The Degas was wonderful.' Laura's expression became dreamy. 'I would have posed for him any day.'

'You would not. He was a slave-driver. I heard it on good authority that he forced his women to stay in back-breaking poses for hours.' Claire watched her thoughtfully. 'And concerts? Earls Court maybe?'

'Wembley. The big reunion.'

Claire looked blank.

'You know, the Eagles. You must have heard about it?'

'Not in our backwater we didn't.'

It was supposed to be a joke, but Laura shrugged. 'You didn't have to move away, Claire.'

'I know.' She was aware of the tightness in her own voice. But she'd had to move away to marry David. And what did she expect? Laura was still doing the same kinds of things that they had once done together. Why shouldn't she be? As for Claire, at least she looked likely to be heading for the Tate in St Ives with Gary. That was something. 'How's work?' she asked, to change the subject.

'The same. I still run the place.' They laughed, back on an easier footing since this was something they had always shared – a conviction that it was the PA who organised the company, kept it going, even made it successful, the boss being just a front. And working for Richard Stickler at Trevarne village school wasn't so very different.

'And men?'

'Well . . .' Laura became about as coy as she ever got. 'There is someone.'

'I knew it. You're wearing extra blusher and you've got a distinctly predatory gleam in your eye.'

'Cow.' Laura grinned.

'Who is it?' Claire had never understood why a woman like Laura had not grabbed herself a happy and lasting relationship. She was one of those women – suffering from serious delusion, in Claire's view – who determinedly avoid the good guys, only to lie down and die for some out-and-out bastard. In all other respects Laura was an independent, bright and attractive woman. Watching her being trampled on had always been soul-destroying, to say the least.

Laura hummed and hawed like a teenager. 'Graham,' she said at last.

'Graham?' Claire's jaw dropped. 'You mean Graham as in Graham your boss and Graham married to Frances?'

Laura became defensive. 'What's wrong with Graham?'

'You mean apart from the fact that he's married?' Claire got to her feet. She wouldn't mention the halitosis or the dubious line in office calendars. 'I need a drink.'

'I thought you didn't –'

'This is an exception.'

Claire returned from the bar to find Laura buffing her nails and looking cool.

'Really, Claire. You're becoming a terrible prude, stuck in that tiny village in Cornwall,' she said. 'It can't be good for you.'

Claire put the glasses down smartly on the table top. She was conscious of a strange desire to defend Trevarne, which was extremely irritating to say the least. 'It's not because he's married . . .'

'Really?'

She re-considered. 'Well, okay, it is that too. But we used to laugh at him, Laura, we used to think he was a right –' A sharp look from her friend silenced her. She struggled for their old footing. 'Has he changed much?'

'He's richer.' They both laughed, but Laura's laughter seemed brittle, and Claire's ended in the faintest of frowns.

She wondered if Laura still chose the expensive jewellery he used to buy for his wife on birthdays and anniversaries.

'And older,' Laura said, and once more Claire detected a sadness on her face.

'Aren't we all?' Claire took her hand and attempted to change the mood once more. 'But you're happy? That's what counts.'

Laura seemed unsure. 'I sometimes think of what I'm missing.'

Like me, Claire thought. Often she thought back to her life before David, and wondered . . .

'Marriage, kids . . .'

Claire did a rapid calculation. Laura was a couple of years younger than her, surely. 'You could still have kids.'

'I'm thirty-nine.' Laura sighed. 'I think I've sort of missed the boat.'

'I don't think you ever really wanted to board it,' Claire reminded her.

'Maybe.' They exchanged a look. 'And now I can't imagine it somehow.'

Claire felt a pang of sympathy but, knowing it wouldn't be appreciated, she didn't give way to it. In a moment Laura would pull herself out of this mood and then she'd probably regret being so honest. She watched her as she lit another cigarette.

'How about you and Dave?'

As always, Claire struggled with the thought of her husband as a Dave. But he was Laura's cousin, and she supposed that he had been a Dave once, in childhood perhaps. 'Oh, well, you know . . .'

Laura leant forward. 'No, I don't.'

'We've been married a long time.' She thought back to when she had first told Laura of their impending partnership. In some ways things hadn't changed so very much . . .

'Getting married? To Dave?' Laura had squawked. 'You can't!'

Claire bristled. 'Why on earth not?'

Laura seemed momentarily lost for words. 'You're so different,' she said at last.

Claire knew what she meant. Laura thought of David as her country-bumpkin cousin, and she supposed in a way that's what he was. He wasn't at all like the men she'd dated before. But that was part of the attraction. She *wanted* someone who was as different as possible. And, after what had happened, she wanted a different life. She agreed to marry David because he didn't belong to the city, he had never been near a motor-bike. He was gentle, he respected her, he didn't try to push her into sex. She agreed to marry David because he would always look after her, and because she loved him, of course because she loved him.

'You knew we were seeing each other,' she reminded her friend.

Laura might have laughed when she introduced Claire to David at that party of hers. 'He's only staying for a few days,' she had whispered. 'Be nice to him.' But she'd done more than laugh when he took to coming to London almost every weekend.

'I thought it was a bit of a joke,' Laura said. 'I knew he fancied you, but . . .' Words failed her. Her expression said that anything she added would be downright rude. 'You and Dave?' she muttered.

Claire had been irritated back then. No, she hadn't confided in Laura about what had happened out on the Dorking road that Sunday. No one knew. Claire had locked it away. But David had never been merely an escape route. Oh, she had loved him . . .

And didn't she love him still?

Claire looked at Laura, facing her across the table in the smoky pub, only half aware that Laura had spoken. 'What did you say?'

'I said,' Laura leant further over the table towards her, eyes gleaming, 'has there ever been anyone else?'

'Anyone else?' For a moment Claire's mind went blank. 'Oh, no.'

She recognised the disappointment in Laura's eyes. Would she be any happier if she thought there might be someone else for David? If she knew about Fern? Claire hoped not, but she wasn't taking any chances. Her doubts about her marriage were for herself alone – at least for now.

As they rose to leave, Claire found herself thinking about Laura's life. Would she return to her flat for a lonely Sunday lunch, or had she planned an assignation with Graham? Would she go to visit some gallery this afternoon, while Claire was sorting out her family and their problems, or would she wander alone in the park, wishing she had a kid to throw bread to the ducks, a man whose hand she could hold in broad daylight?

Outside the pub they kissed. 'If I had someone else, it would be all round the village in an afternoon,' Claire told her. 'So we don't do that sort of thing in Trevarne.'

'I bet.'

They both smiled, but Claire imagined there was a certain sincerity lacking. Each time they saw one another there seemed to be less shared.

'Next time,' Laura said, 'call me on a Saturday, and we'll go to one of our old haunts. We'll do a gallery. Or maybe I'll take you to one of the new clubs.'

'Clubs?' Claire echoed. She wasn't sure about that.

'In Chelsea. Webster's is cool these days. And there's a new bar opposite. It used to be called the George and Dragon.'

'I remember it.' She and David had gone there a few times. It was an old-fashioned place with oak beams, a log fire in winter, and the kind of real ale that David enjoyed. 'Yes, all right, let's. What's it called now?'

Laura laughed. 'It's a bit more up-market now, sweetie. It's called the Shattered Soldier.'

'The Shattered . . .?' Claire blinked. But Laura was moving off with a smile, a wave and an air of blithe unawareness. Ah, well. Claire turned to go. She had to admit that she was more of a George and Dragon person herself, these days. Perhaps she and Laura were drawing apart. Perhaps London was, after all, moving into her past.

* * *

'It's not me, you know,' her mother told her as they finally said their goodbyes. 'I'm not making any of it up.'

'Yes, I do know, and that's why you have to go and see the doctor.' Now that she had accepted it, the words were becoming easier to say. And, hopefully, the GP would put all their minds at rest. 'Let me know what he says. But . . .' Claire wasn't entirely convinced '. . . go easy, Mum. I still think you might be worrying over nothing.'

'You think I just like to fuss. You think your father would be better off without me, no doubt.'

Claire looked across at her father and suppressed a grin. 'Of course not, Mum.' She hugged her.

'We will come,' Patricia promised. 'We'll come to Cornwall and stay with you for a few days. And then . . .'

'And then?' Claire smiled.

'And then perhaps you'll see.'

Chapter 5

'Ben . . .' Claire gazed across the deserted carriage at her son, not sure what to say or how to say it. The train hadn't obliged her by filling up, and she couldn't run away for ever. Gary was right – *Just ask him*, he had said. And why not? Ben might be eighteen – an adult in most senses of the word – but . . . She took in the perfect curve of his bent head, the wide-apart, even eyebrows that gave him a permanent slightly startled look, the long legs clad in scruffy denims. He was still her son.

'Yeah?' He barely glanced up from his magazine, the blue-grey eyes hardly flickered.

Oh, well, in at the deep end. Claire braced her shoulders. 'All that stuff you fed Grandad about no one special . . .'

He looked up, his attention caught. 'So?'

'So I know you've been seeing Tiffany Stickler.'

Ben remained silent for what seemed like minutes, and in that time she could almost see the barriers rising. 'How?'

No attempt at denial, she noted. And that pleased her, because whatever else he did she wanted him honest. 'I saw you.'

'Saw us?' Ben shifted uncomfortably on the seat of the railway carriage. 'Where?' He seemed confused rather than resentful.

'On the other side of the wood, by the main road. Last Saturday when I was out delivering leaflets in the village.'

'Oh.'

'You were pretty wrapped up in each other. Literally.' Claire hadn't meant to say this. But Ben seemed so cool about the entire thing, she wanted to spur him into some sort of reaction.

She got one. 'Spying, were you?'

'No.' Perhaps she deserved that. 'Of course not.'

'Then why the Spanish Inquisition?'

'Why the secrecy?' she retorted.

'I don't have to tell you everything.' They glared at each other.

'No, you certainly don't.' Claire felt the anger surge. Didn't he realise she had his best interests at heart? Didn't he know how much she cared? But all that care and protection, once essential, had now become intrusive apparently. 'I'm only thinking of you.'

'Doesn't look like it,' he grumbled.

'Well, she *was* riding pillion.' Claire let this sink in. 'Wasn't she?'

He nodded.

'But you haven't passed your test yet. And I told you –'

'Everyone does it,' he blurted. 'For God's sake, I was only giving her a lift back to the village. Half a mile. You know I can ride the damn thing, don't you?'

'Maybe I know it, and maybe you can, but you still need a full licence to prove it.' Their eyes locked in combat. He knows it's not only that, Claire thought. She looked away, out of the window to where the world was getting dark, not wanting to see the expression on Ben's face. Wary, resentful . . . She had seen it before, on the face of her brother Freddie, but she'd never imagined she'd see it on Ben's.

'I've always thought you could talk to me,' she said. 'About anything.'

He remained silent as Claire looked back at him.

'So . . .?'

'I haven't got anything I want to say.'

She took in the stubbornness of his mouth. It was hard to see him as separate, but she knew she had to try. He was growing away from her, and the leaving would be on his terms – it had to be if there was going to be anything left for Claire. And she must have *something* left. Their partnership had always worked so well. Perhaps too well. It had become too important to lose.

She thought of Gary. Yes, she should be asking questions about Tiffany's age and questions about safe sex, but she couldn't just plunge in. 'Am I allowed to ask how you met her?' God, here she was, another whining mother. No wonder he didn't want to confide in her any longer.

'I've known her for ever.'

For a moment Claire couldn't take in the significance of this. It was, however, a very un-Ben-like thing to say. 'I mean, how was it that you started seeing her? That girl's always been wrapped in cotton wool, we both know that.'

Ben seemed to soften slightly although she didn't much care for his soppy expression. 'I met her in Bodmin. One Tuesday night about seven o'clock, a month ago. She was supposed to be doing piano practice but she'd bunked off. She was down by the river. Just walking.'

First gym club and now piano. What else was there? Despite the trouble she seemed to have caused, Claire felt a sympathy for the girl so hot-housed by her parents that they didn't even know all she wanted was to walk down by the river sometimes. 'So she was doing a bunk from lessons even before you met her?' That was one black mark removed from Ben. At least he hadn't been responsible for corrupting her – not entirely, anyway. And girls were so mature at fifteen these days. Maybe she'd misjudged him. Maybe Tiffany Stickler wasn't at all what she seemed.

'She's tried to stop it.' Ben's eyes hardened. 'She doesn't want all that crap forced down her throat. She's sick of it. Piano lessons, horse-riding, ballet, gym club. She's had the lot since she started school. But her parents won't let her give any of it up.'

'Every advantage,' Claire murmured. Richard might be only headmaster of a village school, but he had married money, all right, and he was going to make good use of it in the status stakes.

'Advantage? I'm surprised she hasn't had a bloody nervous breakdown.' Ben glared out of the window.

'And they – her parents – don't have any idea she's missing all those lessons?' Claire was incredulous. 'They must pay the fees. They must talk to the people who are supposed to be teaching her.'

He eyed her warily as if not quite sure of her loyalty. Well, she was a parent, wasn't she? One of them. A potential enemy.

'She goes sometimes. She makes up decent excuses. And she's got quite good at giving them the slip.'

'I'm sure she has.' Privately Claire had to admit to some admiration. It wasn't every girl who'd have the guts. Richard and Iris had ensured their daughter would be a good liar, even if she did grow up to hate ballet and piano. 'And what happened that day in Bodmin?'

He blushed, and tactfully Claire looked away. What was happening here? Ben blushing over a girl? It didn't seem quite right somehow, it made Claire feel uncomfortable, as if part of her day wasn't slotting into its accustomed position.

'When she first spotted me she avoided me – reckoned I'd give the game away, I suppose. But there was something about her . . .' His expression altered once more. 'I followed her down by the river. We talked, went for a coffee . . .' A broad grin stretched over his face. 'It went on from there.'

'And when you say *went on* . . .' Claire braced herself. This was it, then. She'd never shied away from any facts of life as far as Ben was concerned. It had all been out in the open and up front. But this, she knew, in some indefinable way, was different. 'Exactly how far has it gone?'

He seemed shocked. 'What the bloody hell has that got to do with anything?'

'Ben.' She leant forward, closer to him. 'You've always told me about your girls and I've always told you to be careful.' She took hold of his arm and her voice dropped to a whisper. 'I've even bought you condoms, for heaven's sake.'

'Mum . . .' He tried to pull away.

'But this girl is different.' She had to make him see.

'Yeah, but . . .'

'This girl is the headmaster's daughter and I am the school secretary. This girl is only fifteen.'

But Ben hardly blinked. 'Maybe you'll have to trust me, Mum,' he said.

She let go of his arm. 'How can I trust you when you never told me about her?' Perhaps she wasn't being fair. Perhaps she was changing the perimeters. Claire wasn't sure any longer.

'I swore to Tif I wouldn't tell a soul,' Ben muttered.

Tiffany Stickler was deceitful, he'd said as much. And now Ben had become deceitful too. Claire's anger against the girl resurfaced. 'But why?'

'Her dad would kill her if he found out.'

'Don't be ridiculous.'

'He'd give her grief. Large portions of it too.' He shot her a telling look. 'And listen to you. You're not doing so bad yourself. Can you blame us for keeping it quiet?'

'Oh, Ben, that's not fair.' But he had a point. Confrontation was all very well, but Ben was a big boy now. He was an adult with adult problems and she had to let him solve them himself, she had to let go.

'I promised Tif,' he repeated, for a moment looking very young again. 'On my life.'

Claire felt a lump in her throat. Her son . . . She covered it up with a quick laugh. 'That's terribly romantic and King Arthurish of you, darling, but –'

'You don't understand.' He said this less as complaint than as statement of fact.

Oh, I do, she wanted to shout. I really do. She understood about parents and about space. She knew about love and loyalty and that sharp pain that could disappear with a look, a kiss.

And she wondered how many of them had been like this in her youth, those boys with big dreamy eyes and long curly hair who spent their evenings playing guitar in folk clubs, going to poetry readings, sitting around and rebuilding the world – in theory. Ben reminded her so strongly of those hippie types, with his thick dark blond hair tied back in the pony-tail, his gentle ways, eyes translucent as the sea, his long legs draped in blue jeans that never looked entirely clean.

She had wanted something that those boys seemed to represent, but instead she had opted for the smoother types, those with money in their suit pockets, those who laughed loudly and drank lager in the pub at lunch-time. They couldn't get close to her, and that was good. She didn't need the excitement of romance because she already knew how to get her kicks – on her Triumph Bonneville with the sensation of speed in her belly and the wind flying through her hair.

Had she been secretly searching for something else? For a man a tiny bit like her Ben, perhaps, with romance burning strong in his eyes? If she had understood what she wanted, if she'd even half-way understood herself, she would have gone for it. And perhaps that was what she'd hoped for from David, all those years ago. He'd been different all right, perhaps too different.

Claire reached out for her son's hand, but he resisted. She thought of how easy it had once been, and was saddened. 'Maybe if Tiffany were a little more honest with her parents?' she said. 'You never know. They might understand.'

He snorted disbelief. 'D'you think they'd understand? They'd get stark raving stressed, more like.'

Claire sighed. 'But how long does it have to be a secret? How long do you think you can keep it quiet when the two of you are practically eating each other in broad daylight?'

'You won't tell them?' Another step away.

'No.' For better, for worse, she thought.

He relaxed slightly. 'When she's eighteen she can do what the hell she likes.'

'That's three years away.'

'Just over two.'

'And in the meantime you'll help her deceive her parents, even if I ask you not to?' Even as she spoke, Claire sensed she was wasting her time.

'I haven't got a choice. She needs my help. She needs me.'

Claire looked away. Men were such fools sometimes, especially young ones like Ben. Did Tiffany Stickler know she could twist Ben round her little finger? Probably. Did she enjoy doing it? Quite possibly. Claire was irritated. Why did her son have to be so damned easy to walk over? *She needs me*, indeed. What next?

'And besides, I'd *never* get to see Tif if anyone told them.' Ben's eyes became bleak at the prospect. 'They'd probably try and ground her for ever.'

'So you'll carry on seeing her . . .' Claire hesitated. 'Until you get bored,' she added hopefully. That had always been the pattern. It wouldn't be long, would it, before another girl came into his life?

They always did. All she could do was pray that this happened, or that Ben became tired of subterfuge and snatched moments, before the Sticklers discovered what their darling daughter was really doing after school and on Saturday mornings.

'I won't get bored,' he told her.

So certain. Claire's eyebrows rose. 'I know you and your girls, Ben,' she reminded him.

'Tif isn't just one of my girls.' This was what she had been dreading. Ben looked her squarely in the eyes. 'I love her, Mum.'

'I see.' And now she knew exactly what was different. It wasn't because of who Tiffany was, it wasn't because Ben hadn't confided in her. It was that dreadful four-letter word, the one with which her son had transferred himself neatly and in one cruel swoop from her to another woman or, in this case, girl. That was the killer blow, the reason why Claire wasn't involved as she had always been before. It was pretty hard to take, but it had had to come sooner or later, she'd always known that. But why, oh, why, did it have to come now – and with Tiffany Stickler of all people?

An hour later Claire opened the front door with her latch-key to find the house in darkness.

'David?' she called. But it was plain he wasn't home.

There was, however, a message on the answer-phone.

Claire listened to it, groaned, went into the kitchen to make some coffee. It had been a long day.

'Where's Dad?' Ben's head appeared round the kitchen door.

'The craft fair ended much later than they expected. They had a meal and decided to stay the night in Penzance.' Claire heard her own voice, weary and emotionless.

'It'll be all right, Mum.' To her surprise Ben was suddenly beside her, pulling her into his arms. 'Don't worry.'

'About what?' Her voice was muffled by his shoulder, and relief that they could still have these moments of closeness was vying with grief over David. Ben didn't know, did he, of her irrational fears about Fern? He couldn't.

'Don't worry about anything.' Awkwardly, he patted her hair and she took the comfort he offered, absorbing every last drop in the precious few seconds before he drew away. He didn't linger. 'Better now?'

She looked up at him. 'I'll survive.'

The phone rang. It might be David, Claire thought, but Ben was the first one to move.

'That'll be Tif. She said she'd phone.'

From the hall, Claire could hear the soft murmur of his voice. No wonder he'd taken so many calls upstairs lately. It was Tiffany all right – Ben was positively oozing tenderness. He wouldn't let Tiffany go, he would linger for her.

And that was how it should be, she reminded herself. She must let him go. She wouldn't cling to him, as her mother had clung to Freddie, only forcing him further away.

In the hall she could still hear Ben's voice, and for a moment she felt close to her mother, for she, too, had invested too much emotion in what would soon be lost. They had never got on, mother and daughter. But perhaps she was closer to Patricia Trent than she'd ever imagined . . . Claire shivered.

Her mother had loved Freddie, but she had also loved Josh. What about David? Claire wouldn't think about him in Penzance with Fern, sharing a drink, sharing supper, holding one of their intimate conversations that seemed to exclude the rest of the world. What about David? What of their marriage? Those were the questions she had to face. Once Ben left, would there, after all, be too little left behind?

Claire didn't manage to catch Gary Stockwell at school on Monday – he had a full timetable all day, and later was occupied on detention duty, supervising Nigel Jones and his cronies from year six, so she nipped round to his cottage after dinner. It was a bit of a liberty, perhaps, since she hadn't been invited, but she felt their friendship had progressed at least this far.

'Claire.' There was little doubt that he was surprised to see her. And *she* was surprised at the transformation. He had changed from schoolmaster's jacket and trousers to loose black cords and a black polo-neck sweater, he had a silver star-shaped stud in one ear, and he was smoking a thin roll-up cigarette.

'Am I barging in?'

He opened the door wider. 'Go ahead and barge.'

Inside the cottage were more surprises. The living room, into which he led her, was decorated in shades of aubergine and grey, and was cluttered with furniture, including an antique pine dresser stacked with a motley collection of art-deco plates, tea-pots and candlesticks, a couple of delicate asparagus ferns and lots of books – of modern art and poetry. She recognized the sound of Mozart drifting from the hi-fi, and the scent of incense hanging in the air.

'What a lovely room.' Claire was intrigued. It was hardly the kind of setting she would have imagined for a village school-teacher. 'Is this one of David's?' She picked up an earthenware urn full of dried flowers.

He nodded. 'Coffee?'

'Why not?' She watched him straighten an Egyptian-style throw draped over one chair, move a couple of cushions and shift a pile of school exercise books from the coffee table, before disappearing into the kitchen. There was something that didn't quite fit . . .

'So how did it go with Ben?' Gary reappeared, put the tray of steaming coffee where the exercise books had been, and motioned her to sit down. 'You've had a chance to talk to him by now, haven't you?

'Mmm. Not good,' she told him.

'Not bad,' he corrected, when she'd related the gist of her conversation with Ben. 'At least he didn't pack a suitcase and leave home.'

'Only because darling Tif lives in our village. And, anyway, he's got no money. God knows how he can afford to take her out.'

'She probably pays.'

'Maybe she does.' Getting to her feet, Claire wandered over to the dresser, picked up a photo in a walnut frame – of a good-looking man of about Gary's age. He was grinning back at the camera, very sure of himself. 'Your brother?' she asked him, without turning round. Surely there was some likeness between them?

'A friend.' Gary didn't move from his position on the sofa, but something inside Claire's brain clicked into place. She had been a bit slow on the uptake, she felt.

She turned round. 'Did your parents let *you* go your own way, Gary?'

He shook his head. 'Hardly. They had everything mapped out for me and Max.'

'Max?'

'He *is* my brother.'

'So did they want you to go to college?'

'I'd always wanted to teach. It seemed . . .' He gave a self-conscious laugh 'Worthwhile.'

Claire examined the photo once more. 'Did you meet him at college? Is he a teacher too?'

The smile faded. 'He was a tutor at the college I went to. Look, Claire. I –'

'I'm sorry, Gary,' she cut in. 'Ben as good as told me I was a nosy cow yesterday evening and he's right. I didn't mean to pry.'

'You weren't.' Thoughtfully Gary sipped his coffee. 'You were just asking normal kinds of questions. But this . . .'

She remained silent, waiting for him to continue.

'This was supposed to be a fresh start.'

'Without your past?' She hazarded a guess.

Abruptly he got to his feet. 'I didn't want to let people in.' He glanced back at her. 'But it's obvious, isn't it? I'm a bloody fool to think no one's got a clue.'

'Absolutely not.' Claire pulled a face. 'It was just the picture. Your reaction.'

'I should have got rid of it.' He smiled ruefully. 'Only thing of his I kept.'

'Still . . .'

'It's not a pleasant story, Claire. I won't bore you with the details. I was a naïve kid, he turned out to be a right bastard.'

'It happens.'

'Only too often, unfortunately. If you're gay and keeping it quiet you tend to be taken advantage of by people like that. I was pretty cautious, and he liked to taunt me. It amused him, he said.'

'Did your parents know?' she asked.

'About my being gay, you mean?' His eyes met hers.

'Not at first. I tried bloody hard to be one of the lads, even when it felt all wrong. Dad was a bit of a lad himself – still went surfing in the bay at Trebarwith Strand every Friday night with the rest of them, even when he was forty. You know the type?'

Claire knew exactly the type. 'And Max?'

'Max is all right.' Gary shrugged. 'He's a bit of a rebel in his own way, but it never bothered him, not fitting in. In fact I reckon he prefers not to. He just gets on with his own life. He doesn't see a lot of the parents either but, then, he doesn't see a lot of me.'

'So when did you decide you couldn't carry on pretending to be one of the lads?' Claire felt so sorry for him, she could see how different he must have felt. It was hard for any child not to fit in.

'At college. This guy, Simon his name was, he really screwed me up. I loved him, you see. So I decided to come out.'

'You told your parents? That must have been hard.'

'It wasn't easy.' He looked away. 'The funniest thing about it was my dad didn't believe me. He thought I was having him on. He kept saying, "Yeah, sure, and I'm queer too," until suddenly he looked at me, stopped laughing and . . .'

'How did he take it?'

'He flipped.' Gary grinned, but his voice held some bitterness. 'It's supposed to be a parent's worst nightmare, isn't it? Well, it was certainly my father's.' He glanced at her. 'And you're worried about Ben . . .'

'Do you still see your parents?' Claire had the distinct impression that Gary had become a loner, and that he preferred it that way.

'They washed their hands of me, as the saying goes. At least, Dad did and Mum went along with it. He couldn't stand the humiliation, Mum said. He certainly didn't want people to know about it.' Claire sensed his anger. 'As if it's in the genes, as if people would blame *him*, you know?'

'Mmm. I know.' Her heart went out to him.

'That's when I started moving around. It's not so easy to come out and stay out. When people know you're gay things can get a bit on the sticky side.'

'In this day and age?' Claire was amazed. 'We're more tolerant than that, surely.' She thought of his dad. 'Well, most of us are.'

'Not as much has changed as you might think,' Gary told her.

'Superficially maybe. There are bars gays can go to, we're more up front . . . when we're allowed to be.'

'And when aren't you allowed to be?' she asked him.

'People pretend that your sexuality isn't an issue – but they still look at you a certain way. They don't always know how to handle it.' He shot her a significant little glance. 'And schools certainly don't like it.'

Claire thought of Richard. 'I suppose they don't.' And it wasn't just men like Richard, was it? For certain parents, teacher homosexuality could well be a thorny issue. She went over to look at the photo once more. 'Have you met anyone since?'

'No one I cared about.' Gary started making another roll-up, carefully scattering tobacco on to the cigarette paper. 'I have my needs, like anyone else. I travel. I have . . .' he licked the paper and looked up at her '. . . interludes.'

'Interludes?' She chuckled.

'But they're meaningless. There's no . . . emotional investment, if you know what I mean.' He rolled up the cigarette and stuck it between his lips. 'It's not what I want, so I don't indulge very often. These days I spend a lot of time on my own. It's a hell of a lot easier. And I reckon I'm happier that way.'

'You never left Cornwall, though?' Claire was surprised at that. She would have thought a small village in Cornwall was the last place you'd want to be if you were part of any minority, ostracised or not.

A spark of passion flamed in his eyes. 'I love Cornwall. No one's going to drive me out of Cornwall.'

Claire was reminded forcefully of David. Was that how he felt too?

'It's the only place I seem to belong.'

Claire laughed as she sat down beside him. 'We're a couple of misfits, you and I. Outsiders.'

He raised one eyebrow. 'You're no misfit. You're respectable. You organise village fêtes and God knows what else.'

'I'm not really respectable in the slightest.' Claire shook her head in mock despair. 'I never was. But I'm pretty good at pretending.'

He leant forward. 'This is beginning to get interesting. Come on, then. You've dragged my unsavoury past out into the open, let's hear a bit of yours.'

Claire thought of her bike-riding days. She thought of Dorking, and of Jerry at the second-hand bike store. 'Maybe I'll tell you about it one day,' she hedged. Would she? She had kept it to herself all these years.

'Dirty cheat,' he remarked. 'One confidence deserves another.'

'I've told you about Ben and Tiffany Stickler.' A thought occurred to her and she giggled. 'No wonder you almost had a fit when I told you everyone would think we were having an affair.'

He smiled. 'I'm glad you know, Claire.'

'Me too.' She got to her feet again, wandered over to the dresser, this time picking up a book on post-Impressionism. Cézanne's magnificent blue bathers met her eye.

'And I'm very glad we're going to the Tate in three weeks' time.'

'It's all fixed up?' Claire felt more pleased for Gary than she was for herself. 'For definite?'

'For definite.' His eyes narrowed. 'So are you going to tell me how you did it?'

'Did what?' She was all innocence.

'Persuaded Richard to change his mind.' He looked her up and down. 'Didn't offer him your body, did you? Is that what you mean by being non-respectable?'

'You must be bloody joking.' Claire sat down with the book and kicked off her shoes. She was beginning to feel very much at home here in this cosy and cluttered room. 'I just steered him towards thinking that (a) it was a good idea, and (b) it was his idea. I may have blinded his intellect with a flash of female thigh, but that's irrelevant since he doesn't have much intellect to start with.'

'Does David know what sort of a woman you are?' She knew that Gary was joking, but the laughter died inside her.

'No.' She looked straight at him.

David had returned from Penzance only hours ago, looking happy, bursting with news of Fern's successes at the craft fair. As if he had imagined Claire would want to hear about it . . . He hardly seemed like the same man who had kissed her with such intensity before she left for London. It was as if that conversation, that desperate touch, had been wiped already from his mind. It haunted her, the force of it seemed to press inside her still, but perhaps to David it had held little significance.

'Sometimes,' she said, 'I think that David doesn't know what sort of woman I am at all.'

Chapter 6

————•◦•————

During the next two weeks, preparations for the November jumble sale and firework display moved into fourth gear. Fifth was possible in Trevarne, but only hours before the event in question.

'Jumble sale and fireworks?'

Claire could see Gary's mind struggling with the concept and she smiled, for she too had struggled with it almost twenty years ago. These days, it seemed a fairly conventional combination.

She told him what David had once told her. 'It's traditional.'

'And what's so special about tradition?' Gary grumbled.

'Trevarne thrives on it.' As if he didn't know. 'Without tradition, the entire village would fold up and die.'

'Heaven forbid.' They exchanged a telling look and a grin.

'Here's the list of the little darlings we're taking to the Tate.' Claire handed it to him. 'Only half of them on voluntary contributions, I might add, so let's hope the school gets some of the profits from all that jumble.'

Gary scanned the names, groaning at the point which coincided, alphabetically speaking, with the name of Nigel Jones.

She peered over his shoulder. 'His mother once told me art was Nigel's favourite subject,' she observed.

'Nigel doing as little as possible is Nigel's favourite subject.' Gary seemed annoyed.

'Is that boy causing more problems?' Claire had been wondering the same thing, but it was Marion Chaney, entering the staff room even as Gary spoke, who asked the question. 'Because if he is I'll have a word with Richard. It wouldn't be the first time.'

Gary's brow creased. 'There's no need for that, thanks anyway, Marion.'

Claire guessed that he didn't want to give Richard any ammunition – as a new member of staff, Gary had not been exactly docile so far. Richard didn't like that. He was also full of new ideas. And Richard liked those even less.

The kettle boiled and Marion went over to make tea. 'Anyway,' she said, 'I'm sure Claire will keep Nigel Jones – and the rest of them – under control on the school trip.'

'You make me sound like a sergeant major,' Claire complained.

'Well, you are a born organiser.' Gary grinned, joining in the game. 'And that's only one step away.'

'I'll say.' Marion laughed. 'Look how early you got those summer-fête leaflets out. I was very impressed.'

Claire scowled. 'I was under pressure.' In actual fact she had done very little for the fête so far. School days were full with work, and any spare time was more than occupied with brooding – about Ben's liaison with Tiffany, about David and Fern, and not least about her father.

Marion passed mugs of tea to them both. 'I'm surprised you haven't bullied me into running the plant stall. I could judge a dahlia competition or something.'

'Should I be bullying people?' Claire sipped her tea. A dahlia competition sounded ghastly. Perhaps she wasn't cut out for this job at all.

'Oh, yes.' Marion winked at Gary. 'I'd say a bit of bullying is vital for someone in your position.'

'Well, if you're offering, Marion,' Claire teased, 'then I won't say no. And while you're in the mood, just think of all the cuttings you could propagate in that greenhouse of yours.'

'Only if you promise to come round for tea on Sunday, my dear. And you can bring that husband of yours if you like.'

'I *would* love to.' Although Claire doubted if David would have gone. Sundays meant fishing – rain or shine – help with the roast dinner if she was lucky, and a retreat into the workshop as soon as possible. David might have made it clear that they should talk, but since his return from Penzance he had avoided every opportunity. She sighed. None of this would happen this Sunday, though. This Sunday they had an engagement that would *never* be postponed.

Marion's eyes twinkled. 'Would you, indeed? Even if it meant a couple of hours' hard work?' She sat down in one of the staff room's sagging armchairs. 'My greenhouse may be perfect for propagating, but it's also in dire need of a winter clear-out.'

'Even that.' And Claire was being perfectly sincere. She enjoyed Marion's company – the school's deputy head had become if not a close friend then at least one of the few people she could talk to in Trevarne. 'But,' she clutched her stomach and rolled her eyes, 'unfortunately you're not the first to ask us.'

'David's aunts?'

'David's aunts.'

'I see what you mean.' Marion looked sympathetic. 'Never mind, my dear. The greenhouse can wait.'

As they left their cottage the following Sunday, Claire asked herself once again why she felt compelled to accompany David on these awful visits. Ben had learnt very early on how to get out of them, but she never had. And today Ben had scarpered straight after lunch and not been seen since. Which out-of-school activity was Tiffany Stickler not attending today? Claire wondered.

At the top of the hill they were treated to the sight of Iris opening the rear door of her Golf hatchback to reveal mountains of plums.

'Victorias,' she yelled to David.

'What?'

'Iris has been to "pick your own",' Claire whispered. 'Hello, Iris. Plenty of jam on the way, then.' She visualised a thick and sticky torrent of the stuff rolling down the hill and shook her head sharply to chase away the disturbing image.

'I'll be making a few pounds.' Iris's voice was so curt that for one mad moment Claire imagined she'd found out about Ben's involvement with her precious daughter. But then she remembered the Lionheart and Gary.

'Lovely,' David said, in the same tone he used to congratulate Aunt Veronica on her lemon curd cake. 'I can't wait to try some.'

'Dear David, I'll bring some round.' Iris gazed at him with neighbourly concern.

'But you won't give it all away, will you, Iris?' Claire asked her. Chance would be a fine thing. 'I can put you in charge of jams and marmalades for the summer fête, can't I?'

She watched Iris struggle between her desire to be high-handed with a supposedly adulterous wife and the dread that charge of jams and marmalades might go elsewhere. Power won over morals. 'Of course you can, Claire,' she said. 'It's all going to a good cause.'

'Oh, the very best.' Claire laughed, as they turned in at the aunts' gate. 'The school fund needs every penny it can get.'

'She seemed a bit off, today.' David was thoughtful.

Claire wanted to share the joke – as they used to share things. 'That's because she thinks I'm having an affair with Gary Stockwell.'

But he gripped her hand so tightly that she wondered if she should have kept quiet. 'And are you?'

'David!' He had some nerve. Didn't *she* have more reason to jump to those sort of conclusions? 'No. No, of course not.' She was about to add that Gary was gay, but stopped herself. Rightly or wrongly, Gary wanted to keep it quiet. She should not tell anyone – even David. And, besides, why the hell should she tell him? Perversely, his behaviour made up her mind. David should trust her.

'Why does Iris think it, then?' His voice was carefully controlled, and to an outsider, David's question might seem quite normal, but Claire sensed an undercurrent of anger that was most unlike him.

'Oh, you know Iris and small-village mentality. She saw us coming out of the pub one lunch-time, that's all.' She didn't add that she and Gary had been giggling at the time, nor that they'd been discussing safe sex. Since then, Iris had literally jumped out of the bushes once or twice when she and Gary had simply been standing around chatting. Gary found it hilarious and Claire had to agree. They couldn't be just *friends*, could they? They weren't the same sex.

David grunted, and it wasn't until they were installed in the aunts' living room that a glimmer of good humour returned.

Pretty soon the same old routine resurfaced; Fern and David in one corner huddled over pencil and paper and discussing framing techniques, and Claire left to fend off Aunt Emily, and in this case her suggestions for the summer fête.

'A dog show,' she boomed. 'That's what has always been missing from the fête.' She preened herself. 'Best trainer, best-groomed dog, rosettes . . .'

'I'm not sure there would be enough people interested.' The last thing Claire was intending was a miniature Crufts. It was worse than dahlias.

'Pretty Pooch,' Emily declared.

'Pardon?'

'The name of the competition, dear. Such a ring to it, don't you think?'

'It's certainly alliterative.' Claire glared at a particularly ugly pug that was apparently poised to attack her ham sandwich. She moved the plate out of range and thanked God that although pugs had ugly faces they also had extremely short legs.

'Do what?' Aunt Veronica had re-entered the room. 'Do what, Claire dear?'

'She said,' Emily yelled, as if Veronica were the deaf one, 'that she thought it was a wonderful idea.'

Claire struggled to her feet. 'No, I did not!' She was in no mood to allow Emily to put words in her mouth.

'I'll do a cake stall, of course,' Veronica sang out. 'My lemon curd . . .'

Inwardly, Claire groaned.

'A lucky dip,' Emily screeched. 'I love a good lucky dip.'

Claire searched for control. Who would know what they were putting their hands into?

'Bric-à-brac, of course.'

'Of course.' There would always, in the history of the universe, be bric-à-brac pouring from people's attics. Bric-à-brac, clutter, junk, it was all the same to Claire.

'But who will the celebrity be?' Veronica was becoming quite excited. She began to clutch at the grey wool stuff of her dress with thin, nervous fingers. 'Who will you choose, Claire? Will you be asking someone terribly famous?'

'Oh, probably.'

'Barbara Woodhouse?' Emily put in. 'Or has she passed on?'

'She certainly has.' Although even if she hadn't, the woman who had made dog training famous would not have been high on Claire's list.

'I thought maybe an author, someone well known, they could autograph books while they're here, even sell some.' An author might not be so expensive, she thought. After all, the purpose was to raise money, not spend it.

'Pooh!' Emily pulled one of her faces. 'Authors aren't celebrities. What do they do that's so wonderful? Anyone could tell their life story. *I*'ve lived.'

Veronica nodded to confirm this.

'Now if I were to get down on paper some of the things that have happened to me . . .'

Claire decided that she'd had enough. How could Fern live with these women – albeit in a separate bed-sitting room for much of the time? She looked across at her, but Fern, her eyes dreamy, was totally absorbed by David, to the exclusion of all else. Claire couldn't bear it. 'I must be going,' she said. She couldn't watch them any longer.

David got to his feet.

'You don't have to leave just because I am,' Claire snapped, but he'd already shrugged himself into his old brown jacket. Well, he wouldn't want to hold the fort alone, would he? He might actually have to speak to an aunt or deal with a stray pug or two.

They walked in an uneasy silence, and Claire could sense him watching her. Was he wondering why she had behaved badly? Did he regret ever marrying her and bringing her to Trevarne?

'Claire . . .' As they crossed the bridge he turned to face her, put his hands on her shoulders.

She flinched.

'Oh, don't worry.' His expression changed. 'I'm not going to try to kiss you again.'

'You're not?' She stared back at him, aware of disappointment. And something else . . . Something missing.

'I can see you're unhappy,' he said softly. 'If I could make it right . . .'

What was he telling her? Hadn't he just been huddled in a corner with Fern all afternoon? What did he think that was doing to her?

'It's not just you, David,' she began.

But he put his fingers to her lips, barely brushing the skin. 'Ssh. Don't say anything. Not yet.'

'All right.' For a moment there was understanding between them.

He took her hand, and they walked the rest of the way home in silence. Silence and sadness, Claire thought. His hand was warm, but they remained miles apart. I loved this man, she reminded herself. So where had they gone wrong?'

That night Claire went to bed early, before David. Lying there, she found herself thinking, How long since we made love? And, wasn't it odd that she couldn't even remember?

The more she considered this, the more it shocked her. He was her husband. How could she not remember the last time?

David had treated her with care and caution in the early days. If he wanted to make love with the city girl he met at his cousin Laura's party, he had never made it obvious. He was a gentleman in all senses of the word, and for Claire that was a revelation.

They kissed, yes, clinging together for warmth and reassurance, they touched all the time as if needing to confirm the other was there, that all the flesh-and-blood tenderness was real. And when he returned to Cornwall, Claire missed him, longed for his return, made a promise to herself that with this man she would overcome her fears, she would be complete.

But he never pushed for more. Until one day he asked her to marry him – a simple question, David's way, as she was to discover.

She knew she wasn't quite ready, but suddenly she was scared she might lose him – this caring man. And she dreaded losing him. She had seen enough of the dark side of life, she wanted to get away from London, she wanted to be safe. David offered her all that and more. How could she refuse him?

She had seen Trevarne once before – in the spring – but when they returned there after a non-eventful and rather dismal three-day honeymoon, it was raining, awfully grey and pallid rain. David's cottage looked very different in the rain, and the damp seemed to seep right through her.

While she shivered in her thin coat, David lit a fire in the grate, his hands expert at forming quills of newspaper, at arranging the kindling, at fanning the first hesitant flames.

Claire watched him. On their honeymoon, she and David had not come together in the way that she had hoped for. It had been hard to relax in the formality of the hotel, especially hard since this was the first time for her, since her world had been turned upside down. But now she couldn't tear her eyes from those hands, couldn't separate the vitality of them from the vitality of her feeling for David. His hands seemed almost part of her.

He rubbed her cold fingers between his warm palms. 'You're freezing.'

'Warm me, then.' She flung her arms around his neck, buried her face in his shoulder.

'I'll do that all right.'

They were both kneeling beside the fireplace. He drew away momentarily, chucked a couple more logs on the fire.

She stared into the blue-orange glow, sniffing the spicy damp smell of the wood, listening to the crackling of the crisp embers of kindling, startled by the spurt of flame as more newspaper caught alight.

'Claire . . .' His hands were on her shoulders now, he was pulling her gently round to face him, his lips moving towards hers, his eyes glazing with passion.

He tasted of the wood himself, she thought, as she responded to his kiss. And he smelt of the woods outside – of pine and beech, the dampness of the river Trevarne, of bark and fresh wet grass.

'I love you, David.' She slipped her hands inside his coat, eased it away from his big shoulders and helped him pull it free, throw it to one side. Her fingers played with the buttons of his fleece shirt; she undid the first three and tangled her fingertips through the dark matted hair of his chest, leaning forward to plant a kiss on the warm skin, amazed at her own temerity.

'Still cold, are you?' He was teasing, but his voice was hoarse, his breath becoming shallow. He caught her exploratory fingers, brought them to his mouth and kissed them.

'Not a bit.'

His hands were on her body now, where she wanted them to be, easing her coat from her shoulders. He slipped his hands inside her sweater, unclasped her bra, cupped her breasts in his palms.

Claire stood up, pulled off her sweater, stripped off her jeans and knickers, and stood, in front of the fire, stark naked, as the flames scorched her thighs.

'Beautiful,' he said, watching her. 'I have never seen a sight more beautiful.'

She laughed. 'I look good by firelight, do I? Does it hide a multitude of sins?'

'No sins.' Not taking his eyes from her, he too stripped off the rest of his clothes and pulled her down on to the patchwork rug in front of the fire.

They made love, and this time she felt it – the beginning of an unknown passion surging through her, lifting her way past the tenderness. She felt his surprise, his delight in the hands exploring her body in a way they hadn't explored it before. She felt his urgency and matched it with her own. She groaned as he came inside her. Yes . . . She had been right to marry David. He could cure her of what had gone before.

At last it was over. Exhausted, they lay together on the patchwork rug, and Claire was conscious of a deep satisfaction – physical, and emotional too. She felt more joined to this man than she had when they'd made their marriage vows. She was content.

'I shall always remember this day, love,' he said, as his fingers traced a path from breast to belly to thigh. 'I shall always remember the day I brought you home.'

By morning, though, the dampness had taken hold once again. And the more Claire saw of both cottage and village, the more she realised how much they left to be desired.

'Give it time,' David said. He said that quite a lot in those early weeks. 'Give it time, love.'

David's warm arms and the passion that had taken her almost by surprise could always make her forget the coldness that she found in Trevarne, but each night of lovemaking held an undertow of something left unsaid – something she should have told him. And each morning the village was always still there, always just the same.

'I don't belong,' she told him. She was a city girl, a different animal entirely. She shouldn't be living here.

'You belong to *me*,' he said. 'Give it time.'

Claire gave it time, and she hated it. She didn't mind that the neighbours all knew who she was, but she hated the fact that they seemed also to know her business. She didn't mind having a local post office cum grocery store, but she minded that you couldn't just go in there to buy bread and walk straight out again if you didn't feel like talking. If you did such a thing, it would be round the village in minutes – that Claire Harrison thought herself superior, too good to talk to the likes of folk in Trevarne.

And it wasn't just the close-knit community that made her feel hemmed in, it was the very smallness of the village as well as the minds. There was nothing to do outside the cottage, nowhere interesting to go, the place was a cultural backwater.

She said as much to David.

His face darkened. 'What are you saying, then?' The Cornish lilt to his voice no longer sounded gentle.

She thought it was clear enough. 'Can't we move? You can make your pots anywhere, can't you? Do we have to live here?'

His mouth moved into a stubborn line. 'This is my home, Claire.'

'But you could –'

'It's always been my home.'

'I know, but –'

'My family is here, my roots are here.'

Claire sighed. 'So you wouldn't consider it?'

He shook his head, and in that second she hated him.

'Not even for me?'

'You knew what you were marrying.'

He turned away, but she grabbed him, pulled him back, almost crying with frustration. 'I married you, not your blasted village nor your blasted family.'

'I'm sorry, Claire. But you'll get used to it. Give it time.'

'I've given it enough bloody time.'

Claire dropped the subject – for a while. But it was as if she'd erected a barrier between them and with it they lost that easy closeness. He couldn't understand, she couldn't understand. Making love became less passionate, more mechanical. Claire became unhappy, and then she became pregnant.

For a time it seemed that her pregnancy might restore their balance. David was thrilled, the village rallied round, Claire was the centre of attention. She and David made love with gentle tenderness, and it seemed a natural progression from the passion of before. Hadn't they started with tenderness? Passion would always return.

But when her child was born, something in Claire rebelled once again. It was possible to be surrounded by people and yet be lonely. She was lonely, sad and lonely. More than ever she longed to be out of Trevarne. To be in a place, any place, where she could take her baby for a walk in a park and meet other women with other babies. Young people she could chat to, those she had something in common with. She longed to be somewhere where a crèche could give her a break from the baby, somewhere with big city shops, with an art gallery she could wander into on a rainy afternoon.

'Why can't we move?' she asked David once again. 'I hate this place. I don't want my baby to grow up here.'

'I grew up here.' His expression told her she'd said the wrong thing. 'It was good enough for me.'

Claire felt wild with irritation. He wasn't understanding her *on purpose*. 'I'm not saying it's not *good* enough . . .'

She wouldn't win, she realised that. She was stuck in Trevarne because David wouldn't move away and because she loved David . . . But she blamed him, oh, yes, she blamed him, even as she decided that this child would change her life, this child would *be* her life. David might have let her down, but this child would have it all.

And he did. Claire gave Ben so much love that there didn't seem a lot left for anyone else. Even David. With the baby came their slow, slow drifting apart – physical, and emotional too. Weeks slipped into months; before long, making love had become a rarity

– and when it did happen it was a brief burning, purely from need, she supposed, a brief burning, a mockery of what they had once shared. No passion, no tenderness, and afterwards only embarrassment. Even being naked with him, Claire felt that embarrassment.

No, she never really forgave David for not letting them leave Trevarne. Perhaps she hadn't forgiven him still . . .

She heard David coming up the stairs.

They still slept together in the big bed, but Ben would move out soon, she knew it, and then she could take over the other bedroom . . . if she wanted to. People did. It wasn't so very unusual. It wasn't the same as saying, *Our marriage is over* . . .

She thought of David and Fern huddled together this afternoon, sharing so much, more than she herself shared with David, a lot more. David loved Ben, he had taken him fishing, taught him pottery in his workshop. But Ben had not brought them together. Ben had remained exclusively hers.

Claire felt his weight beside her as David got into the bed. Seconds later, she felt his touch, very gentle on her thigh. It didn't happen very often and these days it meant only one thing.

I've never denied him, she thought. Not once.

'Claire . . .'

A visual image flickered into her mind, of Fern, of David packing up his pots to go to Penzance instead of coming with Claire to London. Second place, that's how it had always been, how it would be in the future – if they had one.

Claire turned from him in one fluid and certain movement. She felt his disbelief, and then the slow exhalation of his breath. What else could she do? She'd had enough. He was her husband, but he was right: they had come to live in separate worlds.

In the building that housed the new Tate, on Porthmeor Beach, St Ives, Claire was perched on a chair beside a group of children sitting on the floor. They were watching Gary make post-Impressionism come alive. Already he had attracted the attention of a large number of gallery visitors, who were standing back, smiling, as Gary explained what he felt Van Gogh was trying to get away from, what he was reaching out for.

He should be on the stage, Claire thought.

'But why has he done all those wavy lines?' Camilla Smith asked. 'I mean, it doesn't look much like a cornfield, does it, sir?'

Claire smiled to herself.

'Movement, Camilla.' Gary waggled his fingers. 'A cornfield doesn't stay static in the wind. It makes waves. And why does it have to look like a cornfield anyway?'

Clearly this confused the children. 'Because it *is* a cornfield?' Steven Allbright said tentatively.

'No, Steven.' Gary made the shape of a frame with his hands. 'It's a picture *representing* a cornfield.'

The children frowned, looked baffled, some of them began to whisper among themselves.

Gary made a motion for quiet. 'Representing as in *re-presenting*,' he said. 'Think about it. Why does a re-presentation of a cornfield have to look exactly like the field does in real life? Or even like a photograph would show it? Why can't it be different? Why can't it be –'

'An interpretation, sir?' Camilla jumped up in excitement. 'Van Gogh's interpretation of a cornfield?'

Gary clapped his hands. 'Excellent, Camilla. Perhaps,' he looked around at the children, 'he saw different things in the cornfield than we would.'

'Perhaps he was pissed.' Nigel Jones's whisper was perfectly audible. A few children tittered.

'Ssh,' Claire hissed. This was fascinating. She wished someone like Gary had taught her about art when she was at school.

'Perhaps,' Gary went on, 'he wanted us to open our eyes a bit wider. So that we might see that cornfield in a different way, other than the way we'd always seen it before.'

As the children struggled to grasp this concept, the noise increased. Claire glanced across at Gary, expecting him to call them to order, but to her surprise his face had turned sheet white. She followed the direction of his gaze. He was staring not at her but just behind her. She twisted round to see a man of about her own age, immaculately dressed with short dark hair, striding through the gallery, apparently looking for someone or something, his eyes swivelling from left to right. It took her a moment before she realised where she'd seen that face before – framed in Gary's cottage. His old art tutor . . . Simon something or other.

As she watched, the man approached a tall, blond, delicate-featured man, and kissed him energetically on both cheeks. Of course men sometimes kissed each other . . . but the manner of the kiss would leave the casual spectator in no doubt of his sexual persuasion.

She glanced back at Gary. He hadn't yet recovered.

'Come on, kids.' Claire tried to quieten them down. 'Do you want to start on your worksheets?'

A general dissatisfaction greeted this remark. The children had been enjoying Gary's performance, but Claire could see he needed a break.

She glanced at her watch. 'Half an hour and then lunch. Okay, Gary?' She looked across at him. Come on, Gary, get control.

'Sure.' But he still looked far from composed.

'Good.' As the children slowly began to disperse, dropping pencils and muttering to themselves, she saw this Simon coming closer towards them, saw the moment when he spotted Gary.

He paused – as if he'd like to speak to him – took in the sight of the children, some of them still clustered around Claire and Gary, and walked on.

Thank God the man had some sensitivity, at least. 'Find the first painting, then, kids.' She began to usher them away, but stopped in her tracks as she spotted Nigel Jones, not moving, not speaking, his small eyes riveted on Gary's face.

Shit, she thought. Surely he hadn't twigged.

But, even as she watched, a horrid little smirk appeared on his face. Claire's heart sank. Nigel Jones was like a weasel who traded on other people's weaknesses. Like Marion, Claire knew him only too well. If there was trouble at school, Nigel was generally behind it. But he wasn't a rebel in the normal sense of the word. He was a sneak, and Claire didn't like sneaks.

So how much had the little horror seen? And, more to the point, how much did he understand?

Chapter 7

The scandal of Gary Stockwell's homosexuality hit village headlines on the day of the jumble sale and firework display in early November.

Since the Tate Gallery visit Claire had witnessed some sniggering in the playground, seemingly instigated by Nigel Jones, definitely directed at Gary. She said little, but it worried her. Surely it was only a matter of time before Richard sniffed it out.

And she sensed that Gary, too, was half expecting trouble. He was quieter than usual, he lacked his characteristic bounce. Perhaps he had seen the way Nigel was looking at him, cocky, poised, as if waiting for his moment.

On the Friday, Claire went into Richard's study to collect some paperwork, left the door open behind her, and heard – as she was sure Richard was intended to hear – Nigel complaining loudly about his latest detention and the man who'd given it to him.

'He's got it in for me,' he screeched, 'that bastard, Stockwell.'

Dreadful child . . . Claire glanced at Richard. He would have to do something, he couldn't ignore it.

With a sigh, Richard got to his feet. 'Jones!' he rapped. 'Here!'

Nigel sauntered in, grinning at Claire. Only ten, but well on the way to gruesome adolescence.

'Yessir?'

'I heard that. And I won't have you insulting a member of staff.'

'Sir?'

'You know very well what I'm talking about, boy.'

'Stockwell, sir?'

'Mr Stockwell to you,' Richard growled.

'He don't like me,' Nigel whined, abruptly changing tack. 'He's got favourites, he has.'

Richard clicked his tongue in irritation. 'Staff at this school do not have favourites.'

'He's always giving me detention, sir.'

'Perhaps you're always giving him cause.' Richard sat down at his desk. He picked up his pen and twirled it between his fingers. 'We'll say no more about it this time,' he concluded magnanimously. 'But I'm warning you, Nigel, I don't want to hear another –'

'I reckon it's 'cos I *know*, sir.' The boy spoke the word with relish.

Claire suppressed a groan and pretended to be absorbed in some papers on Richard's desk. Better to be around to hear the worst and then, at least, she could brief Gary more fully.

'Know?' Richard stared at him.

'That he's different, sir.'

Claire could quite happily have strangled him. Obviously he had manufactured this entire interview in order to cause trouble for Gary.

'Different?' The expression in Richard's liquid brown eyes moved from bored to red alert.

'Yeah, you know.' Nigel shuffled his feet and discovered a fascination with the floor of the study. If he was pretending to be self-conscious then it wouldn't wash; he just looked shifty to Claire. But she knew what he was going to say next, and there wasn't a damn thing she could do about it.

'I assure you that I do not know.' Richard looked enquiring. 'Would you care to elaborate?'

Nigel required no further encouragement. 'Well, he's a poof, in't he, sir?'

'I beg your pardon?' Claire watched the colour drain from the Stickler's face. Whatever he had been expecting, it clearly wasn't this. She fixed her eyes on Nigel and wished that looks could kill.

But he appeared oblivious. 'A pooftah. You know. Likes blokes not –'

'That'll do.' Richard got to his feet. 'And, if that's all you have to say, you can go about your business now, Jones.' His voice was low, but Claire had to admire the Stickler's self-control.

'And as you go about your business,' Claire pushed Nigel none too gently towards the door, 'perhaps you should think carefully about what happens when you open that big mouth of yours.' It might not be politically correct, but it was the only kind of language boys like Nigel understood, Claire told herself.

But he only grinned once more. 'Sorry, Mrs Harrison.' He might as well have laughed in her face.

She shut the door behind him. What now? Richard was deep in thought. She waited.

'Did you know about this?' Richard still seemed dazed.

Claire took a deep breath and wondered how she should play it. 'I'm not sure I understand you.'

The Stickler's eyes gleamed. 'Oh, I think you do.'

She stared back at him. 'You believed him, then?' Might as well give it a try.

'Didn't you?' Richard was watching her carefully.

'Nigel Jones is a malicious little toe-rag,' she said. 'You know that.'

'Ye – es.'

'I expect he's just trying to get back at Gary for giving him that detention.'

Richard tapped his pen on the desk top. 'I'm not so sure.'

'If it *were* true,' she sat down in the chair opposite him, 'how would Nigel Jones know?'

'If it were true,' Richard stared at Claire's legs, '*you* would know.'

'I would?' Claire's heart sank.

He nodded. 'I was under the distinct impression that you and Gary Stockwell . . .'

'Yes?' There was no way she would make this easy for him.

He smiled. 'The two of you get on very well. Everyone's noticed that.'

Claire didn't doubt it. 'I like him, yes.'

'Good friends, were you?'

'We still are.'

'Just good friends?'

Claire didn't like the direction this conversation was heading. She got to her feet. 'Very good friends. But surely my friendships are my own business, Richard? They don't come under the jurisdiction of the school.'

He laughed softly. 'I'm only asking. Because if you and he were an item, shall we say, then it rather puts paid to Nigel's little theory.'

Her eyes narrowed. 'And if we're not?'

Richard shrugged. 'Then perhaps he's right. Little weasels like him have a way of getting at the truth.'

The truth. So, did she have to pretend she was having an affair with Gary in order to protect him from being thought a homosexual? Claire banged her hand down hard on Richard's desk, suddenly incensed with the unfairness of it all. What the hell did it *matter*? 'I'm married, Richard,' she reminded him.

'Oh, yes.' He nodded. 'And that makes it all the more interesting that you didn't bother to put us in the picture.'

'I'm not quite with you.' She didn't trust him an inch.

'But you two had us all going, didn't you? Was that the idea? Trying to pull the wool over our eyes, were you?'

'It's hardly our fault that half the village decided we were having an affair.' She glared at him. And not half the village. His bloody wife, more like.

'You could have denied it.'

'I can assure you that I'm not trying to deceive anyone,' she snapped. 'But my business is mine alone. Not yours, not Trevarne's.'

'Claire . . . Claire . . .' Richard smiled, inviting confidence. 'I admire your loyalty, I really do. But I can be loyal too, you know. I wouldn't hold it against you.'

Not bloody much, she thought. But at this moment in time she was more concerned for Gary.

'And you're one of us now, Claire, my dear. Don't forget that.'

The blasted village committee. Why had she ever agreed? Just to please David? Because it had been too hard to say no? Claire turned away from Richard Stickler. No. She would never belong in a place like this. She wouldn't want to. She didn't want to be one of them. She wanted to be answerable to no one.

'So . . . is it true?' He rubbed his hands together. 'About Gary Stockwell? If you're such good friends then surely you know if he's gay or not.'

'Why don't you ask *him*?' Claire paused. 'If you think it's necessary for you to know.'

'Necessary for me to know?' Richard laughed. 'You little innocent. Of course it's necessary for me to know. This is a school we're running here. We take children at an impressionable age. You must be aware of that. When children come to this school, their parents expect them to be protected, nurtured, morally and spiritually guided.'

Claire blinked back at him. That was going a bit far.

He leant forward. 'And what do you imagine those parents would say if they knew they were being taught by a man like that? Who do you think they'd blame?'

'It isn't their business –' she began.

'Their children are their business.'

'Yes, but –'

'This is the real world we're living in, Claire.' His expression changed. 'But you don't have to say another word. I know a woman like you wouldn't be interested in a man like Gary Stockwell, married or not.'

'Oh?' She stared at him. What pearls of wisdom would he come out with now?

'He's far too immature.'

Nothing about fidelity, Claire noted. Richard's values were a little warped, to say the least.

'And I don't have the faintest idea how that little rat found out. But he's right about Stockwell.' He held up his hand as she started to interrupt. 'Not because you and he are just good friends, as you put it. But,' he smiled, 'because it's written all over your face, Claire, my dear.'

She moved closer to his desk. She had known him for a long time, but Claire had the distinct impression that she was only just finding out what a bastard Richard could be. He was pleased. It gave him a proper excuse to dislike Gary, didn't it? 'I must say, Richard,' she remarked, keeping her temper with some difficulty and noting with distaste the small beads of sweat that had collected on his brow. 'I'm surprised at you – believing a boy like Nigel Jones before you give a member of your teaching staff the right of reply.'

Briefly, Richard consulted his timetable. 'Call him in, then.'

'Now?' She stared at him helplessly.

'There's no time like the present.' Richard picked up his pen and twirled it in victory. 'I can hardly wait.'

Gary came out of Richard's study with a face like thunder.

'Hang on a minute, will you?' Claire followed him down the corridor at a run. 'Where are you going?' She couldn't let him teach in this state.

'Staff room. Free period.' Gary opened the door of the empty staff room, waited for Claire to follow him in and slammed it behind her.

Claire watched him. 'What did he say?'

'What didn't he say?' Gary grabbed a pile of sketches that he'd left on the coffee table, opened his briefcase and chucked the whole lot in. 'I'm finished here, Claire.' He subsided into an armchair.

'Did he say that?'

'He didn't have to say it.' Gary's fist made contact with the arm of the chair, and a cloud of dust rose into the air. 'Not in so many words.'

'But he can't. Get rid of you, I mean. Not just like that. There are no grounds, are there?'

Gary wagged his finger. 'Ah, but I wasn't honest with the man, was I? I should have ignored the experience of my life so far and come clean.'

'But then Richard wouldn't have given you the job.'

'Exactly.' Dismally they surveyed each other.

'But still . . .' Claire struggled to get it clear in her mind. 'The Stickler isn't in a position to fire you. He doesn't have the power for a start. It's up to the governors . . .' She stopped as she saw the expression on Gary's face. 'What's it got to do with the way you teach?' she asked them both.

'You tell me.' Gary put his head in his hands. Hands stained with paint, she observed. 'Richard might not have the power to fire his staff in theory . . .'

She waited. 'But in practice?'

'In practice he's pretty good at letting everyone know what he wants.'

'And what does he want from you, Gary?' she asked him.

His mouth twisted. 'He wants me to do what he calls the decent thing.'

'Resign?' She stared at him.

'Resign.' His voice was muffled. The fist came down on the arm of the chair again. 'But I'm bloody sick of running away, Claire. Sick to death of it.'

'Then don't.' She knelt beside him, pulled his hands from his face.

His expression was bleak. 'You don't understand, Claire. What other choice do I have?'

'You could force him to show his hand.' Claire guessed that Richard did not intend to come out in the open. Oh, he'd be aware that Nigel Jones would never be able to keep his mouth shut, and therefore that word would get round to the parents of Trevarne. But Richard wouldn't make any of it official. He would get Gary to go quietly so that he could sweep the affair under the carpet, pretend it had never happened, be seen as a man who could deal with such problems before they even became an issue. No doubt Richard would swing this whole thing round so that he himself would be seen in a more favourable light than ever.

'What good would it do?' All the fight seemed to have left Gary. 'Obviously the parents will be out for my blood as soon as they get to know.'

'What makes you so sure?'

Gary frowned. 'You'll see, Claire. Soon they'll start saying I'm not safe to be left alone with young boys. That I'm too much of a risk.'

'That's crap and you know it.' How could she make Gary fight this? 'You have no idea how much support you have from the parents, even from the governors. You haven't bothered to find out.'

'This isn't the first time, Claire,' Gary reminded her. 'I've got a pretty good idea what will happen.'

'But –'

He put up his hand to stop her. 'I know I have your support, Claire, and I appreciate that, I really do. It means a lot to me.'

'But it's not enough?' Claire felt very angry. For the first time she was beginning to appreciate the kind of problems Gary must always have had to deal with.

He took her hands. 'It's not pleasant, but we have to face it. If the Stickler really wants to get rid of me – and believe me, he does – then he'll make it his business to find a way.'

At the fireworks she told David, in the hope that he might have a suggestion to make, but he was just furious that she hadn't told him before.

'I don't understand what difference it makes.' Claire was more than a little fed up. She couldn't believe the small-minded mentality of this place. Why was everyone so interested in what sort of a person Gary Stockwell might prefer to go to bed with? He was being persecuted, and it wasn't as if he had even *done* anything.

David hunched his shoulders, stuck his hands into the pockets of the old brown jacket. 'Of course it makes a difference, Claire.' He stared morosely into the dark sky, apparently unmoved by a rocket exploding into hundreds of tiny but spectacular red shards.

'Ooooh!' chorused the crowd outside the village hall and the Old Barn. It was a fine night and there had been a good turn-out. Marion – for she had organised this event – would be pleased, Claire thought.

David bent slightly, to make himself heard to Claire alone. 'I've been torturing myself, don't you realise that?'

She stared at him. 'What about?'

'You were the one who told me half the village thought you were having an affair with Gary Stockwell.' He gripped her arm, hissed the words into her ear above the fizz and spark of the fireworks, the buzzing chatter of the crowd watching. 'Surely you don't blame me for having doubts?' He sighed. 'You spend enough time with him.'

'But I also told you it wasn't true.' Claire was confused. What on earth could be the matter with David? David wasn't like this, he was calm and collected. He wasn't a gossip like all the rest of them. And he was never jealous. 'I spend time with him, yes. I like Gary.'

'And you said . . .' His voice tailed off, he let go of her arm and it fell by her side. 'You said you were unhappy.'

'I was.' Claire felt cold. She wrapped her arms around herself but she didn't get any warmer. She still felt cold and alone in this darkness, even with the people and the fireworks surrounding her. 'I am,' she said softly. 'But what does that have to do with Gary? He's a friend, that's all.'

'You should have told me he was gay.' David pushed his hair from his forehead in irritation. 'Why am I always the last to know everything? Why didn't you tell me, Claire?'

'Because Gary didn't want anyone to know.' She didn't add that she had also felt perverse, annoyed that David could doubt her.

'What's going on?' He wouldn't leave it. 'Don't we speak to each other any more, Claire?' He sounded so sad, it cut into her. But they didn't, did they? At least, not often.

She shivered, and pushed her hands further down into the pockets of her duffel coat. 'You know now,' she said. She looked from David to a Roman candle spurting pink effervescence into the night. What difference had it made? He surely couldn't be implying that everything would be fine between them if only he'd known the facts of Gary Stockwell's homosexuality?

And what about Gary? Where was he tonight? Already driven out of the village circle, apparently. And she couldn't blame him for not putting in an appearance, she'd heard enough whispers tonight on the subject of Gary's sexual preferences to convince her that the entire village had little else on its mind. It made her sick, the pettiness of it.

'And then that night . . .' David fell silent, but he glanced at her, a searching look.

Claire didn't want to think about that night, or his touch on her thigh. And how was she to know he would interpret her rejection of his love-making as confirmation of village gossip? She stared up at a firework as silver rain exploded into the sky. 'I just wasn't in the mood,' she whispered.

But his gaze lingered on her face for so long that she knew he didn't believe her. And perhaps it was faintly ridiculous to say she hadn't been in the mood when they hadn't made love for so many months. She didn't even know why, except that physical intimacy was bound up with emotional intimacy, with the easy touching that had become so alien to them both. Intimacy seemed to be a word of their past.

Behind them a firework version of Postman Pat exploded into light. Someone had seen fit to accompany it with a tape of the song itself, a rendition by hundreds of school-kids. Various children screamed with delight. Various adults winced and smiled bravely.

David drew her to one side. 'Why are you unhappy? Can't you tell me?'

And all Claire could think was, What does it really matter to him? We have nothing to do with one another any more, I am not first in importance to David, I never have been.

'I'm losing my son,' she heard herself say instead.

David's breathing was heavy and very close to her. But he said nothing.

'I'm worried sick about my dad.'

Still he remained silent.

'There's Gary . . . And then there's you.'

'Me?' His hands were on her shoulders, they moved to her face, gently tilted her head until she was looking straight at him, her husband.

Claire realised that she wanted him to kiss her. How long had it been since she felt like this, since she wanted him to do that? 'You're never there for me,' she whispered.

And then, because his expression changed, because his eyes seemed to stop caring, and because she still hadn't forgiven him, for placing her second, for keeping her trapped in Trevarne, for not fulfilling his own promises, she pulled away from him and ran off into the night. She needed to escape from him. She just had to.

It was all very well for David to play the jealous husband, when some threat to his well-being or village status came along. But what about Fern? And where was he when she needed him?

Claire hardly stopped running until she got home. At first she thought David was following her, she imagined she could hear his heavy tread on the pavement behind. But she was mistaken, for of course he'd stayed at the fireworks, hadn't he? Nothing to come home for.

She let herself in at the front door, aware that she was panting, that her hair was all over the place, that she felt almost too weak to stand.

'Mum?' Ben's face appeared at the top of the stairs. And there was a look on that face she didn't much care for. 'Are you all right?'

'Yes, yes.' She flung off her scarf and coat. 'I've just had enough of fireworks, that's all.'

'I thought you'd stay to the end. I er . . .'

She'd recognise that shame-faced look anywhere, she knew him so well. 'I didn't,' she snapped, suddenly angry with Ben for being so transparent. 'And yes, I saw Iris and Richard at the fireworks, so I suppose I should be asking where their daughter is.'

She peered up the stairs until he waved towards the open doorway of his room. Tiffany emerged, a little dishevelled maybe but fully clothed at least, and with a bright blush staining her cheeks.

'Hello, Mrs Harrison,' she said.

Polite in adversity; Iris had taught her well. Claire thought of Iris's judgement of what she'd assumed to be Claire's adultery, and almost laughed. Here was Iris's daughter doing goodness knows what as soon as her mother's back was turned. And what after-school activity would this be called? Hands-on biology?

'I think you should be getting back home.' Taking pity on the girl, Claire managed a smile. She was just a girl; it wasn't her fault she was kept in chains. Ben liked her and he expected his mother at least to try to like her too. But if Tiffany Stickler ever tried to hurt him . . . 'And call me Claire, I'm not ninety.'

'I'll walk you.' Ben loped down the stairs.

'No.' Tiffany followed more slowly. 'Someone might see.'

Only fifteen, perhaps, but she looked like a young woman to Claire. Her long blonde hair was shaggy and well layered with styling mousse, and she was wearing the usual uniform of blue jeans and black bomber jacket. She had on only a little make-up, but she didn't need much. Claire could certainly see the appeal for her son. Tiffany Stickler was a very attractive girl.

'Goodbye, Tiffany.' Claire turned away to the kitchen to give them a moment's privacy, but Tiffany followed her, put a hand on her arm.

'I'm sorry it has to be like this,' she said. 'We don't want to have to hide anything from anybody.' She looked at Ben. 'We're proud of what we have.'

Oh, yes, an attractive girl. Such beautiful eyes, Claire thought. 'I'm sorry too,' she told her.

'But Dad . . .'

Claire nodded. The less said about her father the better. Richard Stickler was not one of Claire's favourite people right now.

Ben stood at the front door for ages, watching her run up the hill, until Claire yelled at him to stop letting all the cold air in. 'And I want a word with you.'

'What about?' God, he looked so defensive, she could just fold him up in a hopelessly maternal hug.

'Let me know when Tiffany's coming round in future,' she told him.

'Why?'

Claire knew that this wasn't the time for a confrontation. She tried to stop herself, but after the scene with David she felt herself hurtling towards a row. Any row would do. 'Because this is my house – mine and your father's.' Her voice rose. 'It is not a hotel, and it's not a –' she floundered '– a brothel.' Concern for him always brought out her anger. Ben had no idea. He had no thought for anyone else. Only Tiffany and his own teenage libido.

Ben barely reacted. Even as a small child, he had never taken much notice when his mother yelled at him. 'We were only listening to music,' he said.

Claire knew what listening to music meant. She, too, had been young once. 'It's not just that. You go out, God knows where, don't even bother to tell me when you'll be in for meals, treat this place like a hotel . . .' She sounded just like her mother. Was that why Freddie had left? How could she stop?

'Okay, I'll move out.' Ben's blue-grey eyes – the mirror image of Claire's own – barely flickered. 'If that's what you want.'

No, that was not what she wanted. But she couldn't tell him so, not now. Besides, she had the awful feeling that what she wanted was for him to stay here – entirely on her terms. Had motherhood made her into some sort of dictator? 'You don't work,' she said instead, unable to stop the flow. 'You're not even looking for a job. You haven't done a thing about university. You haven't even planned that famous trip you were so keen on. All you do is bum around all day and ride that bloody bike.'

'I still fancy doing some travelling.' Ben leant against the doorframe, all six feet whatever of him. His mother's tone had apparently had little impact. Oh, yes, it was all so easy for him, a matter of whim. He had no roots to hold him down, he could wander as far as he pleased. 'But I've got Tif to think of now.'

Claire felt angrier than ever. 'And you don't care about anything else,' she concluded, storming up the stairs. 'You simply don't care!'

She might as well go to bed, she thought, the mood she was in. But how could she sleep? She was far too angry.

It was only when she was in bed that she remembered she hadn't told Ben he would have to sleep on the sofa for a few days because his grandparents were coming to visit. He would not be pleased, David would not be pleased, and she wasn't sure if she could even face her parents feeling as she did right now. There was just too much to think of . . . It was hardly the time to be considering her parents' future, her father's health and her mother's sanity.

'Bloody hell!' Swearing made her feel slightly better, so she did it again, thumping the pillow this time for good measure, remembering Gary in the staff room. Poor Gary . . . There must be something she could do.

But in the meantime she needed sleep; it was definitely time for this hideous day to end. 'Bloody, bloody hell . . .'

Chapter 8

Claire's parents' visit had been planned to coincide with half-term, and Claire was determined to take them out and about as much as the weather in early November would allow. It would be their holiday. This week would be dedicated to them alone.

But when they arrived on the Sunday, she was shocked at how different they looked. She glanced across at David, saw that he thought the same; and wondered how soon this time he would make his excuses and slope back into the workshop.

'Mum.' Claire held her lightly – she'd always been the sort of woman you held lightly; she seemed to forbid the affection of a smacking great kiss or the intensity of a hug.

'Hello, dear.' Her mother looked pale and tired. She had made an effort with her appearance, but it was obvious to Claire that it *had* been an effort, that was the difference. Her turquoise silk scarf precisely matched the shade of her linen skirt, and her lipstick was the usual discreet coral. But the creased blouse, unpolished shoes and loose perm told an alternative story. Patricia Trent had been sufficiently harassed to drop her standards, and that was indication enough. She had neglected the ironing and the shoe-cleaning, and had lacked either the time or the inclination for the normally mandatory visit to the hairdresser. Even her make-up seemed different, as if she'd had one eye on the mirror and the other on an unpredictable toddler – or on her husband maybe.

Claire turned from her in some relief to hug her father. He looked tired too – the shadows around his eyes matched those around his wife's – and Patricia insisted he sat down immediately, fussed over the comfort of the chair, fetched an extra cardigan, a footstool and a glass of water in rapid succession.

'For your aspirin,' she said.

'Have you got a headache, Dad?' Claire was sympathetic.

'Don't you believe it.' He swallowed the tablet. 'She makes me take 'em every bloody day.'

'Oh.' Claire didn't know what to say. Surely her mother was worrying unnecessarily.

'Still, if it helps me get out and about . . .' He grinned at Claire. 'There's a lot of places I can't wait to see again,' he said wistfully.

'And you will. There's plenty of time, Dad,' Claire caught her mother's glance of apprehension. 'So we'll take it nice and easy, eh?'

'Oh, fuss, fuss fuss. Just like your mother.' Josh winked at David. 'You'll never let a man do what he wants, will you?'

Claire glanced at her husband. 'I can't say I've ever been accused of *that*.' She was aware of the tartness of her reply.

'Plenty of time, love. Your mother didn't start till she was sixty.'

He chuckled as he said it, but nevertheless Patricia got to her feet and slowly walked out of the room.

Should she go after her? It had been tactless of him, but surely her father hadn't meant anything by it. Claire glanced from her mother's departing back to her father's ghost of a smile, and thought she should. But she was wary of a tête-à-tête this early in the visit. Claire had the feeling that her mother was waiting to unload, and Claire wasn't sure she was ready for that, for the latest instalment of how her father had misbehaved at the hospital – already hinted at in yesterday's phone call – what the doctors had said on Friday, and where he might have told them to go.

Claire watched David take Patricia's exit as a signal that he too could vacate the room and get back to the safety of work. 'She's only trying to look after you,' she told her father. 'You should be glad she cares.'

'Women, eh, son?' Josh nudged Ben who had sat down beside him. 'What shall we do with 'em?'

Ben smiled, seemed about to make a suggestion, took one look at his mother's face and changed his mind. The soul of diplomacy, my son, she thought.

'And how's school?'

Claire had bent down to straighten some papers on the coffee table when Josh asked this, and she replied without looking up. 'Not too good actually, Dad. My boss is making waves with one of the staff.'

'Mmm?'

Claire glanced up at him, caught the confusion in his pale blue-grey eyes as he looked from Ben back to her. 'What was that, love? School, d'you say? Best years of your life.' He grinned at Ben, rather a lovable grin that tugged at Claire's heart as she realised she'd misunderstood him.

'Ben's left school, Dad.' She spoke gently. 'He left in the summer.'

Ben looked slightly embarrassed.

'Oh, yes, of course, of course.' Josh's eyes refocused. 'Working now, then? University?' There was a hint of desperation in his voice.

Claire could see him struggling and she couldn't bear it. He was fighting so hard to remember, and yet he'd lost it; he didn't have the foggiest idea what Ben was doing, what he planned to do with his future, although she'd heard them discussing it not two months ago when she and Ben were in London. And yet her father had seemed so with it, so on top of what was happening. Claire recalled her mother's words: *This is one of his lucid days*.

'I haven't decided what I'm going to do yet, Grandad.' Ben spoke with admirable composure.

Well done, Ben, she thought.

She watched her father trying to get to grips with it. He had always been an amazing figure of a man, Josh Trent, with a strength and mentality that made him a natural leader, at work, at home, down the pub of an evening with his mates. It hadn't taken Claire long to work out where her father was coming from, even as a child. Working class at roots, he had kept his principles when he rose up the ladder at the biscuit factory where he'd worked all his life. She remembered how people had always gone to him for advice: *Go and ask Josh Trent. He'll know. He'll put you right.* As a kid she used to see them coming to the house.

She remembered the time a neighbour's husband died and her

father organised a collection, took charge of the funeral when Lil couldn't cope, went round there to unblock the sink and fix her broken shelves. He had been a good neighbour . . .

And a good husband. 'I grabbed the best girl, love,' he'd told her once. But her mother had done all right. She'd got herself a man who would laugh at her sometimes and yet give her all the respect in the world. Claire felt a lump in her throat. And a great father. The best.

Knowing all this, she could hardly bear to watch him struggling to retain control, as his failing memory simultaneously tried to snatch it away. Claire knew he couldn't remember, that certain events had left him, and she sensed that he was so determined to fill in the blanks he found it perfectly possible to pretend.

She saw him turn away from her now, as if she saw too much. And maybe she did. Patricia had given Freddie, the baby of the family, most of her attention. It had been only natural, perhaps, for Claire to develop a special relationship with her father. Patricia had always had high expectations. Josh had simply always been there.

'I'm getting senile in my old age.' Josh laughed. 'What must you think of me, eh? I bet you don't blame your grandma now for fussing around me like an old hen?'

Ben laughed with him. 'Someone's got to keep you in check.'

'That's it.' He liked that, she could tell. Always he'd quite enjoyed being the lovable rogue. 'But how could I forget?' Abruptly his expression changed, his mood altering to one of agitation.

Claire realised she didn't know how to cope with him. She couldn't treat him as she always had, but she couldn't show pity – he'd flip. He was neither one thing nor another. Their relationship was changing, and would change further. It had to. She was aware of a fleeting sympathy for her mother. What did you do when the man who had always been your strength, your protector, your Sir Galahad – however crazy-mad he made you the rest of the time – how did you cope when he lost it? When he was no longer what he had always been? She touched his arm. 'We all get forgetful, Dad. Don't give it another thought.'

But he hardly seemed to hear her. 'I er, I was thinking that I should . . .' His shoulders heaved, his brow furrowed with the effort.

Smoothly Claire took control. 'I think you should have a nice rest,' she said, in a manner which she hoped was firm, kind, but please God not patronising. 'And perhaps tomorrow we can go somewhere special.' Tomorrow – another day.

The relief shone in his eyes. 'That'd be a treat,' he told her. 'Proper smashing, love.' He looked around, still disorientated, she noted.

'You're staying in Ben's room, Dad,' she reminded him. 'Up the stairs, first left, well, you know where it is.' She looked across at her son. 'Ben?'

'Yeah, I've gotta just clear a couple of things.' Instantly he was complicit, aware of her needs. 'So I'll come up with you, Grandad. If that's OK?'

Josh's brow cleared. 'Course it is, son.' He smiled at Claire. 'And your mum will be coming up soon, I expect?'

She recognised the plea. 'Very soon. You go with Ben, Dad.' Claire watched them slowly leave the room. She felt as if she were beginning to understand at last.

She found her mother in the kitchen. 'Ben's taking Dad up for a nap.'

'Does he want me?' Patricia had regained control but still seemed a touch shaky.

'He can wait for a bit.' Claire noticed that her mother had made tea. It had always been the answer, hadn't it, to any problem, large or small? Into the kitchen, put the kettle on . . .

'You don't mind, do you, dear?' Her mother indicated the tea-pot.

'Don't be daft.' Claire wondered how best to put it into words. 'Look – about Dad . . .'

'I'll go up.' Patricia made to leave the room, but Claire blocked her path.

'Leave him.'

'But . . .'

'Ben will give us a shout if he needs anything.' You're not indispensable, she wanted to say, but that sounded cruel. And in a way her mother *was* indispensable to him now. Who else was there to care for him?

Still, Patricia Trent wavered.

'Sit down, Mum.' Claire pulled out a chair. She wanted to explain to her, would like to ease away some of the shadows. 'He has to talk to you like that,' she said. 'It's not that he doesn't need you . . .'

'I know.'

'Or that he doesn't care.'

'I know that too.' Her mother fiddled with the tea-cosy. 'Claire, I have tried to tell you what it's like.'

'I'm sorry.' She watched her mother's hands, her thin, nervous fingers as she twisted the tea-cosy from side to side. 'I've been insensitive. I didn't realise how bad he was. Or the full extent of . . .' Of what? She eyed her mother helplessly. Or hadn't wanted to know, more like. 'Tell me,' she said.

'All of it?' Anxiously, Patricia looked around as if she expected Josh to materialise out of the woodwork and deny everything.

Claire took a deep breath. 'All of it.'

'Now?'

Claire poured out the tea and gave them both sugar although neither took it. She got a plate of biscuits, called up to Ben to sit with Josh for a while, shut the kitchen door, and sat down opposite her mother. 'Now.'

'We went to the GP.' Claire watched Patricia try to smile. It turned out lopsided, but at least the thought was there.

'And Dad played up?'

'He was aggressive.' Her mother sipped her tea. 'They get like that.'

'They?'

'I mean people with some kind of memory disorder.'

Claire felt her stomach dip with what she didn't want to acknowledge. 'You mean Altzheimer's? Are we talking about senile dementia, Mum?' She didn't like her own tone. It sounded awfully like she was accusing her mother of something.

'No,' Patricia replied quickly. 'We went to the hospital for tests. They think . . .'

'Yes?' Claire's hands were cradling her mug of tea, but they still felt cold. 'What do they think?'

'They think your dad has had a few minor strokes.'

There was silence as they stared at each other.

'Strokes?' Claire associated strokes with severe incapacity of some kind. A sort of nervous version of a heart attack, nerve ends getting tangled, things stopping working. Not something that could happen without people knowing it was happening. And, 'A few?'

'I know, I know. It took me by surprise as well. But . . .' Patricia reached out a hand and, without hesitation, Claire took it.

But she wasn't used to this kind of touching with her mother. Josh and Claire had always enjoyed a close physical relationship – hugs and cuddles were the order of the day. But Patricia . . . Her mother always retained her coldness and untouchability, as if she might crack, or you might spoil her make-up or something. With everyone except Freddie . . .

'It was a relief, Claire,' Patricia told her. 'Such a relief to know.'

'I suppose so.' Claire wasn't so sure. A few strokes sounded like the beginning of the end, and she couldn't face that. 'But how can someone have a stroke and not know it?'

'Minor strokes are like that.'

'But what if . . .?'

'There's no reason to think he'll have more.' Patricia spoke fast, as if knowing what her daughter was thinking.

'Although he might.'

'Yes.' Again they eyed each other over the table. 'He might.'

'And if he does?' Claire held her breath.

But Patricia wouldn't elaborate. They both knew what could happen if Josh had a major stroke; it didn't have to be put into words.

'Even with more minor strokes, they say the gradual deterioration is bound to go on – in his memory, in the way he feels disorientated. In his moods . . . He has such moods, Claire.'

Claire squeezed her mother's hand. Perhaps after all, Patricia had not been exaggerating. 'What can we do to help him?' Brisk, like a kindly nurse.

Patricia's expression grew dark with a bemused sort of anger. 'Not much. Aspirin every day.'

'Ah.' And she had imagined her mother to be fussing

unnecessarily. 'What damage can they do, these small strokes?' she asked.

'Each one may cause a small amount of brain damage.' Patricia spoke carefully and objectively, as if she'd learnt it by rote from a text-book. 'They can cause a slight weakness in the arms or legs. There can be a black-out or a fall. That's when –'

'Has he had a blackout or a fall?'

'Occasionally.' Patricia stared her out.

'And does he know all this?' Claire sipped her tea. Dear God, how did she ever tell him?

'As I said before,' Patricia looked away, over Claire's shoulder, 'he was aggressive with the doctor. He gets like that, he becomes . . . frustrated.'

'I see,' And she was beginning to.

'I've tried to tell him.' Patricia's eyes dimmed. 'He won't listen. He says I'm fussing. I thought that perhaps you . . .'

Claire gazed at her in horror. 'Me?'

'You've always been so close.' Her mother's eyes were pleading with her.

Claire shivered. It was a daunting prospect. But she was his daughter. Was it too much to ask?

Her mother took her hand once more and played with her fingers, as if going back in time, as if Claire were a tiny baby once again. 'I have tried my best, love,' she said. 'I'm getting near the end of my tether. And when I talk to him . . .'

'He doesn't want to lose his dignity.'

Claire looked up as the kitchen door opened. Ben stood there, tall, gangly and unsure. 'He's dropped off to sleep,' he told them.

Claire saw her mother's shoulders sag with the relief of tension. How much relief did she get? It must be like having a small child to cope with when you thought those days were over. Only it was different, because you knew it was a downward spiral, that things wouldn't get better, there was no growing upwards to be done. 'Thanks, Ben,' she said.

Slowly she got to her feet. 'You need a break, Mum,' she said. 'Ben and I will take Dad out tomorrow. I'll talk to him then.'

One lone tear trickled down Patricia's lined face. It met with the coral lipstick and took a detour. 'Thanks, love,' she said. 'You're a good girl. You always were.'

The next morning, Claire asked her father where he'd most like to go.

'Rough Tor.' He looked at Patricia. 'Won't you come with us, love?'

She shook her head. 'I'll stay here. I'll make the dinner, shall I Claire?'

'You will not.' Claire gave David one of her looks.

'Leave it to me.' He got to his feet. 'We want you to have a real lazy old day. That's the prescription for both of you.'

Claire smiled at him in gratitude.

'There's nothing wrong with me.' Patricia seemed somehow to have remade herself brittle again this morning. There was no sign of yesterday's warmth.

'But . . .'

'And your father can't go walking up hills,' she snapped. 'Can't you go to Bodmin? What about the prison? You could go to Bodmin. Then you could find a little tea-shop somewhere.'

'I have enough of bloody prison as it is,' Josh growled. 'And we never went to any tea-shops when Claire was a kiddie. We went walking around the tors.'

'That was then. You can't –' Patricia began.

'I can still take a look at it, can't I?' He silenced her. 'Nothing wrong with my bloody eyes.'

Claire smiled to herself. Good old Dad. 'Rough Tor it is, then,' she pronounced. She leant towards her mother. 'We'll take care of him. Don't you worry about a thing.'

Bodmin Moor was bleak in the summer, but on a chilly autumn day it was positively desolate, and certainly not a destination Claire would have chosen for a day out. But as the car hit the broad expanse of flat moorland, scattered with sheep wandering over the rocks and coarse grass, she saw her father's expression change, saw his eyes light up with the pleasure of memory.

She drew up in the deserted car park by the small stream, gazed at the bulk of Rough Tor in the distance, and waited. Her mother was right, of course: Dad couldn't possibly walk up there – she'd find it hard going herself.

'Well, Ben.' Josh grinned.

'Well, Grandad?'

Josh clapped him on the back. 'Go for me, will you, old son? Me and your mum have got a few memories to mull over.'

'Course I will.' With relief Claire watched him put a brave face on it.

'That's my boy. And tell me, son,' the pale eyes flickered, 'what it feels like, won't you?'

'Yeah.' Ben looked from one to the other of them, seeming to understand instinctively what was needed. 'Yeah, I will.'

They watched him follow the path past the stream, and slowly make his way up towards the tor, becoming a blot almost as small as the sheep themselves as he got closer to the huge piles of rocks.

Josh chuckled. 'We told you and Freddie that some friendly giant had got bored one day and decided to build a sandcastle out of granite.'

Claire smiled. 'And did we believe you?'

'Who knows what kids believe?' Josh heaved a contented sigh. 'Last day of our holidays we came up here. When we were staying near that place where the lads all go surfing.'

Claire thought of Gary. 'Trebarwith Strand.'

'That's it.' He looked pleased with himself. 'It was a windy day and it was the one place I wanted to come back to. Your mother wasn't keen. But I was set on it.'

'I bet there were more people around that day.' Claire couldn't really remember much about it. The Cornwall of past childhood memories had merged into the Cornwall of her marriage, and most of the good bits had got lost in the process.

'A few.' Josh opened the car door and eased himself out into the wind.

Claire followed. On a day like this, the wind had a way of rushing and shrieking across the moorland as if unable to believe its luck – that there were no big hills and only the odd building in its path.

'I wanted to get up high,' he shouted to her, against the force of

it. 'You kids were moaning but you loved it when you were up there
– scrambling around on those rocks, a kids' paradise, it was. It
started drizzling when we got up there. Bloody English climate, we
said. But there were all these little shelters to hide in. Slabs of rock,
you know.'

'And what was it like up high?' Claire shouted back.

Josh paused in reflection. 'You're on top of the landscape. On
top of the world, it feels like.' He pointed into the distance. 'Ben'll
tell us what it's like.'

'You don't need him to.' Claire took his arm and they moved
towards the stream. 'You remember, don't you? What it felt like.'

He nodded. 'I loved the moors.' They found a dry rock and sat
down on the flat slab of it, huddled up against the wind. 'I always
fancied it.'

Claire recalled what he had said about envying her. 'You mean
you fancied living here?'

Josh looked around them. 'I wanted the peace and quiet.'

'You'd have been bored silly.' She picked up a small stick and
poked at the stones in the stream, worn smooth and silky by the
constant trickling water.

'Are you?'

The tone of his voice changed, and Claire looked up at him in
surprise. 'Even Trevarne has its odd moments of excitement,' she
teased. She had no intention of burdening him with her problems.

'Moments? Few and far between, I bet.' Josh glanced at her
thoughtfully. 'And you were always a girl who needed a bit of life
around you. Too much energy for your own good sometimes.'

Claire smiled. 'I thought we were talking about old family
holidays.'

He patted her hand. 'You can tell me, you know, love. I'm not
past being confided in.'

'Of course you're not.' She was indignant. And reminded of
childhood in an entirely different way now. Of the time her father
just knew she hadn't given in her project on African culture – lying
barely started in her bedroom, concealed by a motor-cycling manual
– although how he knew, she never discovered. And the time when he
was equally certain of the identity of her first boyfriend, and even

when he knew she would marry David, for heaven's sake. The man was still a mind-reader, and a manipulative old rascal into the bargain.

'So?'

'So I've never liked Trevarne. It's a pretty place to live, yes, but I've never been one for admiring scenery, you know that. I don't like living in the country. I never did.' Claire looked into the distance, not sure she could still see Ben, although that black blob might be his leather bomber jacket. If so, he'd almost made it to the top. 'You're right,' she told Josh. 'Nothing ever happens in Trevarne.'

'Bar the village fête.'

'Including the village fête. And the place is run by a load of boring old farts.'

'Excluding David?' His eyes twinkled.

She paused for a moment to consider this. 'Excluding David.'

'Him too?' The shaggy eyebrows rose.

Claire giggled. 'No.' And when he obviously didn't believe her still. 'No, really. David's not one of them. They're shallow and narrow-minded, and they're living in the bloody dark ages.'

'And you can't change things?'

'No.' She looked away. 'After all these years I'm not even sure I want to try.' Although if she heard so much as a whisper that Richard might be trying to get rid of Gary, she might very well change her mind about that.

'So things are bad with David, too?' It wasn't really a question, and it seemed pointless to deny it.

'We haven't been getting along too well lately.'

'Would it help if the two of you moved out of the village?'

Claire began to laugh, although she had the feeling that if she weren't careful she wouldn't stop.

Josh seemed to understand without further explanation. 'I suppose he thinks the same of Trevarne as your mother thinks of London. It's home, and that's that. If you love 'em, you'll stay.' Josh got to his feet, Claire followed his lead and they walked slowly back to the car.

She looked at him. 'So Mum refused to consider moving to Cornwall?'

'You can say that again.' He took her arm. 'I could understand her reasons. I had a decent job, there was a family to support. She had her friends. She wanted to be safe.'

Safe . . . Claire had married David to be safe. But pretty soon that same sense of safety had seemed more like a set of iron bars.

'It's not easy, is it, love, when you want to be in different places?'

'No, it's not.' She turned to see Ben making his way back down from the tor. 'And that's why you decided to stay in London?' She thought that her father was trying to tell her something, only she wasn't sure what.

'I loved your mother.' His eyes misted over. 'Still do. Much too much to leave. She was right there.'

Claire had always been pretty sure of that. Her father might tease and her mother might grumble, but she'd always known how much they loved one another.

'And you?'

'What?' Her brow furrowed.

'You and David?' His eyes seemed to bore into her. 'When you say you haven't been getting along too well . . .'

She thought of the fishing, the lonely marital bed, the workshop that was out of bounds, and Fern's smile . . . 'Me and David?' She sighed. 'We live in separate worlds, we do.' That was what he had said. And he was right. 'I'm not sure whether love can cope.' Perhaps it was evading the question, she was good at doing that. She glanced at Josh, registered the comprehension in his eyes. On second thoughts, she seemed to have answered his question in full.

Ben returned windblown and breathing more heavily than usual, but with a big smile and a healthy glow on his face.

'Coffee?' Claire rummaged for the flask.

'Please.'

'And how was it, son?' Josh was looking at Ben expectantly.

'Bloody freezing, Grandad. Great views from the top, mind.' Ben grinned. 'Pretty exhilarating, now you come to mention it.'

Josh smiled with satisfaction. 'What could you see?'

'The quarry. The conifers round Crowdy Lake. Lots of paths across the moor . . .'

'Looking like they'd been scribbled in,' Josh murmured.

'Yeah.' Ben laughed. 'The odd farmhouse, and in the distance –'

'The land gets greener.'

'Yeah.'

'And the sea?'

'The Mouls. Just visible. It was a bit hazy.'

'Good lad.' Josh seemed pleased. 'And did you spot the war memorial?'

'Yeah.' Ben stared at his grandfather. 'How long since you were here?'

'Too long. Thirty-two years.' Josh took the coffee Claire handed to him.

'You remember it pretty well.'

Josh winked at Claire. 'Some things you don't forget, son.'

They stopped off in Camelford for pasties – Ben jumped out to get them while Claire and Josh waited in the car.

'There's something very wrong with me, love, isn't that right?' Josh gazed out of the window. After their conversation this morning he'd seemed the same as ever; now he sounded defenceless and naïve, like a child.

Claire felt herself shrink inwardly. She had been dreading this, had been at a complete loss as to how to introduce the subject. She might have guessed he'd do it himself, and while they were parked in the main road of Camelford at that. He'd never been one for sticking to conventions. 'Yes, Dad.' She spoke softly, put her hand on his arm. 'There is.'

'It's my memory. I know that.'

'Yes, you're right.'

'You see it's like a reel of film these days, love.'

Claire watched him in confusion. 'A reel of film? How's that?'

'Stills, images . . .' He let out an exhalation of breath. 'It's patchy. I can't unlock the whole thing. What I remember is in bits, it's not one continuous reel any more. Some of the links have gone. The rest is in clips, like I'd nodded off in between.'

'But you remembered Rough Tor.' On the way to Camelford he had talked again of that day – had provided them with almost every detail, right down to the picnic lunch they'd eaten by the stream.

'The longer ago it was, the easier it is to see it,' he told her. 'Bloody drives me mad.'

And that was part of the pleasure for him, she realised, in visiting these old holiday haunts. Bodmin Moor and the rest had remained intact for Josh Trent when more recent events had slipped out of reach.

'Dad . . .' She explained about the strokes, telling him what her mother had told her, all the time watching for Ben out of the corner of her vision. There was a queue in the bakery, but she didn't have long.

Her father didn't seem surprised. Maybe he hadn't even taken it in, but there was no hint of the aggression her mother had talked of. He was gentle as a lamb.

'I'm not as good to your mother as I should be,' he told Claire.

'She understands.'

'Nevertheless . . .' Slowly he shook his head. 'I get tired,' he told her sadly. 'I see things.'

'What kind of things?' Claire felt angry – not with him, but with whatever had done this to him.

'Your mother says I'm imagining it.' His voice changed into vague acceptance.

'Dad . . .' She could see Ben coming out of the shop, pasties in hand.

'I don't want you to worry about me, love. Whatever happens.' He sounded so firm.

'Dad . . .' Claire cursed the timing of this conversation for Ben was just about to cross the road. And then she realised. Of course, he'd done it on purpose. They could have talked earlier down by the stream, but he'd carefully steered the conversation on to her and David, her and Trevarne, anything to make sure she wouldn't mention his illness. He had known it was coming, probably guessed her mother would ask her to explain to him. He had avoided it. Only now – now that there was so little time – had he chosen to broach the subject.

And she thought she understood why. He wanted to know the truth, but he didn't want the time to say too much, he didn't want

Claire to be able to say too much. She could see that now. He had controlled this situation, and she must respect his right to do so.

'It's not so bad, Claire.' He was still her father, the one she had always been able to go to, her strength.

'But I don't want you to . . .' How could she say it? Claire could feel the boundaries shifting – parent and child, child and parent – and yet she wasn't ready. He wasn't ready, damn it.

He patted her hand. 'I'll stay around for as long as I possibly can, love. You can count on it.'

Claire was unable to speak, tears welled in her eyes.

'A big swallow,' he said. 'That's it. Good girl.'

She blinked them away, looked up, and then Ben was here, Ben was climbing into the car and the moment had passed. She had done what her mother wanted, done what they both wanted.

'Shall we eat them here?' Ben handed round the pasties.

'Nah.' Josh smiled. 'We're not finished yet. Let's drive down to Trebarwith Strand.'

Chapter 9

—◆—

Despite all her good intentions, however, as her parents' one-week visit stretched into two, with no end in sight, Claire felt her sympathy being tested to its limit.

Ben was doing his best, but it was time he got his own room back. And the strain was showing on David's face more than ever. While Josh went pottering off around the village, talking to all and sundry, making friends with everyone he met, Patricia had taken to standing on the threshold of David's workshop, just watching. David didn't complain about this, but Claire kept catching her at it, and she could see it must be unnerving for him. David was a private man, and Patricia was never easy. As for Claire . . . She and her mother had clashed in her childhood, fought through her adolescence and maintained a careful and safe distance in adulthood. There was no going back.

More than anything, now that she had returned to work, Claire wanted her house to become her own again; she was tired of getting home every day to find that her mother had ever so kindly cooked the dinner. She didn't want cold meat, boiled potatoes and beetroot. She wanted a burn-the-roof-of-your-mouth-off Thai curry that would justify the consumption of a large bottle of red wine shared between herself and David alone. Yes, and she wanted some time for herself, a space of her own too. She wanted to clean a kitchen that *she* had made dirty, she was tired of endless cups of tea, in the morning before the mad dash to work, in the afternoon as soon as she returned, and at very regular intervals every evening. She wanted to get drunk, or do something outrageous that her mother would find hard to forgive, and certainly never understand.

On the Thursday evening, David claimed an appointment with a client in the Lionheart, Ben was out again – the revving of his motor-bike had interrupted Patricia's commentary on the second half of *Coronation Street* – and Claire felt depressed. It seemed there was no one to turn to. And, with her parents around, communication levels with David had sunk to an all-time low.

Claire had tried to get in touch with Freddie, but there was no answer at the number in Amsterdam he'd once given her. It might be out of date by now; Freddie liked to move around, he hated to be pinned down. And that was all very well ... But Freddie had a duty, surely. And, besides, her brother should be told what was going on. It was better coming from Claire; Freddie would be more likely to take her seriously. Even if there was nothing he could do, this was a family matter, and she needed the rest of her family – even Freddie – to rally around.

By the time Josh was snoring in his armchair Claire had become a desperate woman. 'I'm going to pop out for a minute,' she told her mother. 'You'll be all right, won't you?'

'Out?' Patricia's stare transported Claire back to vitriolic 'out in the evening' stares of her teenage years. But her mother was under a great deal of stress, she must remember that.

'Only to Gary's. It's the end cottage, if you need me. The phone number's in my address book under G.' Because if she stayed here any longer, she would probably scream. She had bucket-loads of stress of her own.

It's my house, she reminded herself as she let herself out of the front door and tasted the sensation of delicious escape. Or, at least, hers and David's. And so something was very wrong ...

The air was cold, and so refreshing after the *Street* on a TV with the volume turned up too loud that Claire felt she could almost do a cartwheel from the pure delight of it. In the distance she heard the unmistakable hum of a motor-cycle engine. Or ride into the night, she thought. She could do that, she really could. With the engine throbbing beneath her, the rush of wind in her face, the whip of the speed, the cool darkness as she shot into the unknown, the smell of the exhaust and the tyres on a wet road, the throaty rumble of the engine, the vibration, the danger, the anonymity, the thrill . . . Oh, God. She hurried on to Gary's. Would she never forget?

Claire rang the door-bell and waited. She heard him padding down the stairs and across the hall, saw the dark shape of his figure approach the door.

He flung it open.

'Gary, I – Oh!' She was staring at a complete stranger.

'Hi.' The stranger grinned. It was a friendly and rather appealing grin. The man was taller than Gary, darker than Gary, with the – she had to admit rather sexy – shadow of stubble on his chin, but with a small silver hoop in his ear-lobe that was definitely reminiscent of Gary's. He was dressed in jeans and a lumberjack shirt and wore brown moccasins on his feet.

Claire absorbed all this within the first few seconds. Her next thought was that he was very attractive, and following on from this was recognition that he seemed very much at home. Not a casual friend, then, and besides, Gary had told her he didn't have friends of that variety – which meant that he must surely be a partner, and therefore gay. 'Hi,' she said. It was dreadful to think it, but what a waste.

He put his head on one side and regarded her thoughtfully. 'You must want Gary. He's upstairs.'

'Oh,' she said again. Had she disturbed them? Upstairs . . . Had they been . . .? Well, she should never have turned up like this, just assuming Gary would be free because he was always free. 'It's really not very important,' she concluded weakly.

'Who's that?' Gary's voice drifted down from the bedroom.

The bedroom. Claire took a step backwards. 'Tell him I'll see him at work tomorrow, will you?'

The stranger grinned, clearly finding her behaviour amusing. 'Why don't you come in and tell him yourself?'

'Oh no, I –'

'Is that you, Claire?' Gary ran down the stairs.

'Ye-es. Sorry to disturb you.'

The stranger opened the door wider. 'So . . . Hello, Claire.' He really was very attractive, but then, in Claire's experience, gay men often were. Or was that sexist in some way?

'Come in, Claire.' Gary pushed past him. 'What are you doing standing on the door-step?'

Given no choice, she stepped inside. 'I should have phoned first.' What an idiot. She was sure she was blushing furiously, although whether she was more embarrassed about interrupting one of Gary's interludes or whether it was the way the dark stranger was staring at her she had no idea.

'That's OK.' Gary led the way into the sitting room. 'Can I get you a drink? Some wine?'

'Well . . .'

'C'mon. Let me twist your arm.'

He obviously didn't mind her being here. And what did she have to go back home to? 'All right. Yes, that would be lovely.' She smiled warily at the other man.

Gary poured some into a glass. 'You haven't met my brother, have you? Claire, this is Max. Max, meet my one and only friend at Trevarne School, Claire Harrison.'

Brother . . . Claire took the wine. What a prize idiot she was. She'd forgotten he even had a brother. She looked up at Max, caught his grin and just knew he was aware of what she'd been thinking, had known all the time and passed by the opportunity to put her right. Oh, well . . . She'd given him a good laugh. Claire gulped the wine. Too fast – but it tasted good.

'Nice to meet you.' He held out a hand and she took it. She realised that he had thunderbolt-piercing blue eyes identical to his brother's. She should have guessed who he was. Of course he could still be gay, but she didn't think so somehow. She doubted that a gay man would hold a woman's hand for quite such a long time on first introduction.

'How long are you staying in Trevarne?' Polite and predictable perhaps, but it was all she could think of to say.

'For as long as necessary.' He grinned, leaving her to work that one out. 'I haven't made plans.'

'And he never does. Max is an itinerant,' Gary told her. 'He drifts.'

'With the tide, I presume?' But what about work? she wondered. He had to live, the same as the rest of them.

He laughed. 'Exactly right. I go wherever the mood takes me.'

'Max doesn't tie himself down,' Gary explained, with an almost envious glance at his brother. 'He's freelance by nature.'

'Freelance?'

'Writing, theatre work, barman, you name it.'

'I see.' And she did. Something in his eyes, some part of what he was saying, reminded Claire of the sensations she'd felt just now, the kiss of escape from the fresh night air as she'd closed the front door of the cottage behind her. Her memory of the freedom of riding the Bonnie along a deserted road, that part of her that seemed to be lost but not forgotten. Shoved to one side for most of her day-to-day existence but still, like now, having the power to move her. And, like Gary, she was envious. Her brother . . . Gary's brother. How was it that for some people the burdens of life – home, work, family – could be cast aside so easily?

Gary seemed to recognise her sudden sadness, for he patted the sofa invitingly and topped up her glass. 'What's up, Claire?'

Which part of it should she tell him? 'It's the parents, I suppose.' A half-truth, but they were her current millstone. 'I feel as if they're never going to leave, and then I feel guilty because I want them to.'

'But why should you feel guilty?' Gary got to his feet and began wandering around the room, switching on a lamp here, lighting a candle there, straightening the Egyptian-style throw on the chair.

'Women always feel guilty,' she informed him, not looking at Max. 'It's our heritage.'

'But it's also your house. Christ.' He sat down beside her. 'We spend long enough trying to get away from our parents in the first place, we don't want them to move in with us at the earliest opportunity.'

'Yes, but Dad . . .' Claire trailed off. She had already told Gary about her father's illness, tried to explain some of the confusion she was feeling. 'I'd like him to be able to stay here for as long as he wants. He loves Cornwall. And, God knows, Mum needs the break from the responsibility.' Why did Patricia keep standing in the doorway of David's workshop? Just watching. *What are you doing, Mum?* she'd asked her yesterday. *Just watching . . . Just watching . . .*

'But she's taken over?' This was from Max, perched on the arm of a chair. As perceptive as his brother apparently.

Claire nodded. 'She always does. It's a skill that comes entirely naturally. She doesn't even have to try.'

'It's called motherhood,' Gary put in, and all three laughed, until Claire remembered that she was one of those. Not only was she a mother but just lately she'd been a pretty bossy one at that.

'Mothers, oh, God. Look at *me*.' She put her head in her hands. And she couldn't begin to tell them about David. She *wouldn't* begin to tell them about David.

Gary put an arm around her shoulders. 'It can't be as bad as all that . . .' he began.

'It's not, it's . . .' She looked up to catch Max's dark blue gaze resting thoughtfully on her face. 'It's the wine,' she finished with a laugh.

'Then you'd better have some more.' Max got to his feet, took the bottle from the table and bent to refill their glasses.

Claire was conscious of him as he straightened. He didn't move away immediately, and she could feel the warmth from his body, very close to hers. What was wrong with her tonight? She picked up her glass. She most definitely was not the sort of woman to run round and cry on her neighbour's shoulder. And she certainly wasn't the sort of woman to be affected by some man she didn't know from Adam. So why was she drinking too much? And why was she unwilling even to look at him?

After what seemed an age, Gary went off to fetch more wine, and his brother moved away, slotted a CD into the player. As the classical music filled the room, Claire began to breathe more easily.

'There are mothers and mothers,' Gary said. He opened the wine and sank into the armchair opposite. 'I don't see you as the clinging type, Claire. You're so down to earth.'

'Hmm.' That made her sound about as exciting as a bucketful of compost. 'It's not that I mind Ben seeing Tiffany Stickler . . .' She noticed Max's questioning raise of one eyebrow. 'The headmaster's daughter,' she provided. 'It's not even because she's under age.' The eyebrow rose higher. 'And it certainly isn't the motor-bike.' She took a deep breath. How could she possibly tell them she was terrified of how little might be left when Ben had gone?

'What does David have to say about it?' Gary asked.

Claire's urge to giggle hysterically forced her into taking another large gulp of wine instead. Max Stockwell must already consider her narrow-minded, a clinging mother and an alcoholic. Why give him the impression she was hysterical too? 'Not a lot,' she mumbled. When we speak to one another . . .

She didn't say it out loud – she might have had a drink too many but that didn't mean she was about to reveal all to a total stranger, and an attractive one at that. The truth was that she could only see herself and David travelling further and further apart. What held them together? Ben was no longer a child – far from it. There was no physical intimacy, no likeness of mind. They rarely laughed together any more. They rarely saw each other any more, she realised with some shock.

'You're so tense.' Max was behind her once again. She felt the light pressure of his hands barely touching her rigid shoulders.

'Mm.' Once more she tried to relax, but she felt brittle enough to snap right in two.

'You need a massage,' Max murmured. 'To get rid of some of that tension.'

'I'm fine.' She smiled at Gary. Was his brother always this pushy?

Gary picked up a box of matches from the table beside him and leaned over to light a stick of incense. 'He's giving a professional opinion,' he said. 'You should let him get his hands on you, Claire.'

'Pardon?'

'Because he's very good at it.' Gary smiled. 'Massage, healing, that sort of thing.'

'Is there no end to your talents?' But as she listened to the music that seemed to be floating right through her, tasted the sweetness of the incense in her lungs, and felt the dim light comforting and healing her eyes, Claire knew that she needed to relax at all costs. Tentatively, she leant her head back and felt the pressure of Max's hands firmer and more confident now on her tight shoulders.

'Does that feel good?'

'Mm, sort of.' It felt like heaven. She was almost drunk from the wine and the heady perfume of the incense as it rose in small cloudy spirals into the room. She closed her eyes, slowly letting herself go, relaxing into the mood, into the movement of his hands as they worked on her shoulders, conscious only of pressure from his fingertips, light pummelling of palm and fist, skin on skin, the warmth of contact. Gradually, underneath his hands she felt soft, like a young girl again, free of the worries, of the tensions. Bliss.

'There. You're done.' He moved away, abruptly, and she felt a moment of isolation, of fear almost.

'Thanks.' She struggled to sit up. 'I should go.' Max had moved over to the far side of the room, his face was in shadow.

Gary got to his feet. 'I reckon you should give me a shoulder massage later.' He glanced towards his brother. 'I don't know about Claire, but I've just about had my fill of the Stickler this week. He's determined to force me into resigning one way or another.'

'More problems?' Claire was glad of the change of subject even if it was one that was so unsettled. Richard and Gary were tolerating one another – just – but the tension between them was palpable. Sooner or later something would give. She flexed her shoulders. The massage had left her physically eased, but at the same time saturated with a sensation she couldn't begin to define. And she felt more uncomfortably aware of Max Stockwell than ever.

'There won't be any more gallery visits,' Gary told her. 'At least not for quite a while.'

'Why not?'

' "The school budget can't run to subsidising them." ' Gary mimicked Richard. ' "We must pull in the reins, tighten our defences, count the pennies." '

'It's not as bad as all that.' Claire moved slowly towards the hall. And she should know. She'd spent two hours on the books at Richard's request only the other day.

'Of course. It's an excuse. I know he wants me to get fed up and leave.'

'But you won't?' She stared back at him.

Gary shot her a sad smile. 'I can't guarantee it, Claire. Richard *summoned* me to his study yesterday. He wanted to cross-question me about my private life, that was obvious enough. The creep kept making comments about sensitive subjects and setting an example to younger minds.'

'If he wants to play private detective and find out what you're doing in your own time, he should just employ his own wife.' Claire looked across to where Max stood staring out of the uncurtained window, but he made no acknowledgement that she was leaving.

'And he makes a lousy art critic,' Gary added.

'Oh?'

' "Some of your art work with year six is a trifle avant-garde, Gary." ' He mimicked Richard once again.

This caught Max's attention. 'What were you doing with them?'

'Cubism.'

Claire laughed with them both, relieved that Max was now following them towards the front door. She couldn't swear to it, but she sensed he was angry with her for some reason. He was an unusual man, that was for sure. 'Does he see Cubism as related to homosexuality in some incredibly devious way?' she joked. 'You know, seeing all the possibilities at the same moment?'

'Well, you know what they say about Braque and Picasso . . . All those cosy little café conversations.'

'No, what do they say?' Max asked him.

Claire giggled. 'Once Iris clocks Max you'll be accused of bringing men and corruption to Trevarne. If you don't broadcast the fact that he's your brother, then you know what everyone will think.'

'Isn't it a natural conclusion to come to?' Max caught her eye and she bit her lip, acknowledging the point. Perhaps she had no right to talk about the narrow minds of Trevarne.

'Okay, okay.' She held up her hand in defeat. 'I'm as good at jumping to conclusions as the next woman.'

'But seriously,' Max watched them as Gary helped her on with her coat, 'instead of just taking the piss, you two ought to do something about this place.'

Claire looked at him. She couldn't tell what he was thinking. 'Like what?'

'Like set up your own gallery, your own arts centre, with a village theatre maybe. Liven the place up a bit. Give it a good old shake-up.'

'That's not a shake-up, that's a revolution.' But, of course, he was right. She and Gary were all talk: they hadn't even tried to change things. And someone had to do something if Trevarne was ever going to join the 1990s.

'Would you help?' Gary turned to Claire. 'It's right up his street.'

Max looked from one to the other of them.

Claire held her breath.

He seemed to be considering carefully. 'I don't have people queuing up to employ me. I've got enough cash to keep me going for a while. We could talk about it . . .'

Claire grinned, she couldn't help herself. A stab of the old excitement hit her deep in the belly.

'So long as you two do your bit.' He was addressing them both but staring at Claire. 'Are you with me?'

'All the way.' Gary sounded exultant. 'Claire?'

She thought of the problems at home and her need to escape. She only knew that she was denying herself, denying her full potential because she was too scared to find out what the hell it was. 'Try and stop me,' she whispered.

Max's eyes gleamed. 'Then we'll set up a meeting.'

'Just like being on the village committee.' Gary nudged her. 'Claire's a great organiser, you know. She started on next year's summer fête back in September.'

'Bastard.' Claire kissed him. 'I've got to run. See you tomorrow.'

'See you soon, Claire.' Unexpectedly, Max Stockwell grabbed her and kissed her heartily on both cheeks. 'See you very soon.'

She smiled as she turned away. That sounded rather like a promise. But she wasn't about to raise any objections. Rather to her surprise, she found that she had no objections at all.

Claire felt jubilant as she walked back towards the cottage. The idea of an alternative committee appealed to her, she had to admit it. But she staunchly denied any appeal that might be more connected with a certain tall dark stranger.

She was too absorbed in her own thoughts to notice them, until she heard the laugh, unmistakably David's laugh. She looked across the road, back towards the Lionheart. David was walking with Fern and they were getting closer.

At first she assumed they'd seen her, then realised they hadn't as she saw Fern quite unselfconsciously tuck her hand under David's arm. They were even more oblivious of their surroundings than she. They had no idea she was there, and without further thought, Claire ducked behind Marion Chaney's pink lavateria, conveniently still in bloom.

She clenched her fists. Why on earth had she done that? Was she totally mad? They would certainly think so if they *had* seen her. But her worries proved groundless; they walked on, straight past her on the other side of the road. She could see them clearly in the pale moonlight, but they seemed insubstantial, not quite real.

'I'll see you up the hill,' David said in his soft voice with the Cornish lilt to it, that she'd always loved.

'Don't bother, David,' Fern replied, her voice barely audible.

'It's no bother, love.' Claire could almost feel the pressure as he squeezed the hand tucked in his arm. They were real, all right.

She waited for a full five minutes after they were gone, giving them time to be up the hill and out of sight, and not giving David time to get back down again. It was silly to mind, she knew how close Fern and David were, they had practically grown up together. And she still had nothing substantial to make her think that David would look at Fern in that light – as a woman, and a woman quite obviously in love with him to boot.

But Fern had everything in common with David that Claire lacked: she was artistic, she was a dreamer, she looked up to him, she belonged absolutely in David's world – as an artist, in Trevarne.

Claire and David hadn't been connecting for so long. They were drifting but in different directions, they no longer came close to each other, even in bed. So could she blame him for looking elsewhere? Claire had to face it: he wouldn't have far to look. And besides . . . some clammy thought stuck unpleasantly to her brain. David had said he had a business meeting tonight. With a client. He hadn't said a word about Fern.

She edged out from behind the lavateria, checked the lane for innocuous passers-by, who might think it a little odd that she'd been lurking in Marion's garden, and walked slowly towards her own cottage.

'Claire?' Her mother yanked open the door. 'There you are. At last.'

'At last?' Good God, she had thought those days were over. But as she registered her mother's expression, she realised there was more to it than the lateness of the hour. 'What is it? What's wrong?'

'It's your father.' Patricia was looking up and down the lane.

'What about him?' Claire took her none too gently by the shoulders. 'What's happened?'

'He's disappeared.'

She was about to let rip when she saw her mother's attention drawn to a point behind her. She half turned and saw a man on the other side of the road, some distance away. 'Dad?' It was an old man, walking slowly, a stumbling man who looked as if he didn't have the foggiest idea where he was going. It was her father.

'Dad!' He didn't hear her.

'He was asleep.' Patricia's voice rose. 'I only went out to make the tea. I popped upstairs for a quick wash, then I came down, and –'

'Yes, yes, never mind. He's here now.' Claire stood on the other side of the lane, about to cross, waiting for a car to pass, when abruptly he veered towards her, crossing the road without a glance to left or right. The car swerved to avoid him. The horn blared.

Josh Trent didn't seem to notice.

'Dad.' She grabbed him. 'What on earth are you doing?' He could have been killed. He didn't look before he crossed. He hadn't *remembered* to look before he crossed, she realised.

He seemed to come to. 'Hello, love. Had a nice time?'

'Dad. Where have you been? Mum was worried sick.' Weak with relief, she steered him back towards the cottage, looking up to see David striding down the hill, whistling. Not for the first time, she almost hated him.

She waited until he was closer. 'A good night, was it?' Business meeting, indeed. Who did he think he was kidding?

'Mmm?' He stared back in total bemusement. 'What's going on? What are you all doing outside?'

But Claire didn't bother to explain. She got her parents inside the cottage, made hot sweet tea, calmed down Patricia and helped

Josh into bed. It was almost an hour later by the time she sat down on the edge of her own bed.

David sat down beside her. 'Claire?'

'It's Dad. He went walkabout.'

David tried to take her hand. 'And you're blaming me for not being here to stop him, is that it?'

She shook her head. She would not say any more. Whatever David was up to, she would preserve her dignity at least.

'They can't stay here for ever, love,' David said. 'There isn't the room. And maybe your dad needs –'

'He needs me.' But she knew he was right. It wasn't fair to Ben or David to have them living here. And it wasn't fair to her either. She was losing sight of herself and losing sight of her marriage. Too much was at stake.

Wearily she put her head in her hands. But how could she do it? After tonight, how could she possibly send them away?

Chapter 10

———◆———

'You look terrible.' Claire surveyed her son critically. His long, dark blond hair hadn't come into contact with a brush this morning, and his eyes were bleary. But it was more than that – there was a deep furrow on his brow and his mouth was turned down at the corners. What is it with mothers and sons? she thought. She had no idea what was wrong with him but already she was determined to make it go away.

'Thanks a bundle.' Ben began foraging in the bread bin.

She watched him with affection. If he asked her to make him egg, bacon and waffles, she'd probably do it. More fool her. 'What's up?'

He glared back at her. 'Does something have to be up?'

'When someone looks like you do, yes.' Okay, so Ben hadn't had a bedroom to call his own for the past few weeks, but it was more than that.

Ben grunted.

'Come again?'

'I said it's Tif's birthday today. If you must know.' He chucked the bread into the toaster.

'Hmm.' Her mind raced. 'And that's bad?' She glanced out into the hall but there was no sign of her parents yet. They were having a rare lie-in and it was absolute bliss to have the kitchen to herself for a change. David had gone out fishing at some unearthly hour in the morning, muttering something before he left about the tides being right and taking the soggy bread cakes he'd made up to use as bait out of the freezer. And she'd grown accustomed to slipping easily back into sleep at five a.m. knowing she was alone, accustomed to waking up to an empty space beside her in the bed that still managed to say more than David did these days.

'It's bad, all right.'

Claire turned her attention back to her son. 'What's so awful about having a birthday? I would have thought you'd be pleased.' *She* was pleased – or relieved might be nearer the mark.

'Oh, yeah?' He made this sound like a threat.

'Oh, yeah.' She ruffled his hair as he sat down beside her, risking a sideways swipe from him with the toast and marmalade he happened to have in his hand, because these days Ben didn't appreciate being touched. 'She's sixteen now.' Did that sound as if she were condoning sex between her son and a local teenager? Probably. Claire rephrased it. 'I expect her parents will start giving her a bit more rope.'

'Huh?'

'Well, she'll be able to see more of you, won't she?'

He grunted.

A grunting teenager could be hard to take at this time in the morning, Claire reflected. 'It won't have to be so cloak and dagger between the two of you, will it?' she persevered. And Richard would find out. Richard would find out, hit the roof and probably tie the poor girl up in chains tighter than ever. She was beginning to see Ben's point.

'She's going to tell her old man she's too old for gym club.' Ben looked gloomy as he demolished almost half a slice in one bite. 'And that she hates horses.'

'Hmm.' Claire wondered how Richard would take it. Not well, she guessed.

'And she's also gonna tell him that her music teacher says she's got about as far as she ever will.'

'I see.' Claire didn't. Or at least she understood that Tiffany was planning a lot of telling, and there was nothing wrong with that. It was about time the girl came clean. But she didn't quite understand all Ben's doom and gloom. 'It might be a good thing,' she said. 'Her father might decide it's no use locking her up, after all. You,' she surveyed Ben's unwashed appearance again, 'might not be such a bad option for his little girl.'

'*She* doesn't think so.'

'What?' Claire poured herself more tea.

'She's having a birthday party,' he sneered. 'At sixteen. I ask you!'

Claire shrugged. There were parties and parties. At sixteen even Iris wouldn't expect them to play oranges and lemons. 'Are you going?'

'You must be bloody joking.'

Belatedly, Claire noticed that his shoulders were shaking, so instead of hypocritically snapping, '*Don't swear,*' as she usually did, she put a tentative hand on his arm. He didn't object. 'You don't want to, or you weren't asked?'

Ben jumped to his feet, scowling now. 'I didn't even bloody know about it. I heard down the pub last night. From Jeremy Sanderson.'

Claire was about to ask who on earth Jeremy Sanderson might be, but she realised the question was irrelevant. With a name like that, he was obviously from the right sort of family and just as obviously going to Tiffany's party. Perhaps Richard wouldn't consider Ben a valid option after all, even if his parents were Friends of Trevarne.

'It'll probably be dead boring anyway,' she said, ignoring the redness of his eyes as he turned back to face her. Claire might not be a perfect mother, but she did know that eighteen-year-old youths do not care to admit to crying. Damn Tiffany Stickler. Claire felt a burst of maternal anger. 'You won't be missing much,' she soothed.

'But why didn't she tell me she was having the party in the first place?'

Claire didn't know. 'Teenage girls . . .' she began weakly, though she'd been one herself, of course, and not a particularly nice one either.

'Why the hell did she let me find out about it in the pub? And from bloody Jeremy of all people.'

Claire knew that if she sympathised too much, if she let him know her own feelings on the subject of Tiffany Stickler – or any girl who treated her son badly, come to that – Ben would probably spring to Tiffany's defence. So she restricted herself to non-committal noises of understanding. Perhaps, even now, she was still learning how best to be a mother, she thought.

'She told me she has to spend practically all day with her *parents*.' Ben treated this word to considerable scorn. 'Visiting relatives or something. And that afterwards she'll be talking to her dad. She said she'd be busy all day. And that's why she couldn't see me.'

'Did she?' Claire didn't like the way this was sounding. She had the feeling Ben was about to be let down, and hard.

'What should I do, Mum?' His eyes entreated her to make it better just as forcefully as they had done fifteen years ago.

But now Claire was helpless. 'Confront her. Find out where you stand,' she urged. She couldn't bear the thought of Ben being walked all over.

'But how can I get hold of her?' Absentmindedly her stricken son picked up a slice of Claire's toast and bit into it.

Claire smiled. Love not running smoothly had not affected his appetite, that was some consolation.

'After all, I can hardly go round there.'

'There's a grey plastic thing in the hall called a phone.'

'Phone her at home?' He spoke with his mouth full.

'Why not?' Claire regarded him with maternal pity. 'That's where she lives.'

Two hours passed before Ben took this advice.

Patricia and Josh had wandered down to the village hall for morning coffee, cakes and crafts, and Claire was getting ready for a lunch-time drink with Gary and Max. It was going to be their first anti-committee meeting and Gary had proposed they hold it in the pub.

'Might as well start as we mean to go on,' he had told them cheerfully.

'But I thought you didn't drink at lunch-times.' Claire gazed at him curiously.

'That's when I was being a good boy.'

'And now you're being bad?' She laughed.

'Too darned right I am.'

'I want to talk to you,' she heard her assertive son tell the telephone receiver and Tiffany Stickler. Followed by, 'I don't mean on the phone. I want to see you.' Pause. 'I want to see you today.'

Attaboy. He sounded so forceful that even Claire was almost convinced. She walked past him and grabbed her coat.

'Not here, no.' Ben looked up at her.

'I'm going out,' she hissed. 'Feel free.' In her experience no one wanted a showdown with his girlfriend in public.

'All right,' he conceded. 'Come round here, then. Yes. The sooner the better. All right, that'll have to do.' He slammed down the phone.

Claire noticed that he was shaking again. Perhaps Ben wasn't destined to be the forceful type. Or perhaps he just needed a lot of practice.

'Well?' She rummaged in her bag for lipstick, ignoring Ben's faintly curious look. If it weren't for his problematic love life he would doubtless be bothering her with pointless questions such as why she was wearing eye-shadow, mascara and her tightest white jeans.

She blew a mocking kiss at the mirror. Just a touch of lip gloss would do. But she'd better make a quick getaway if Tiffany was about to descend on them.

'She can only spare me half an hour.' He spoke with heavy sarcasm, moped past her, positioned himself in front of the mirror and began fiddling with his hair, which was in its usual pony-tail by now and looked exactly the same as it always did, in Claire's opinion. 'Jeremy Sanderson's got a wedge,' he added conversationally. 'He looks a right prat.'

That was good news anyway, she supposed. 'I'll be at least an hour,' she told him, reclaiming a tiny square of mirror. 'And Gran and Grandad have only just left so they won't be back for an hour and a half at least, maybe more if Gran finds someone to talk to.'

'What about Dad?' Ben gave up on his hair and started brushing imaginary specks of dirt from his jeans. They must be imaginary, Claire reasoned, those jeans were clean on today, although they didn't look it. Just lately, Ben was providing the linen basket with so much laundry – although you'd never think it from his carefully scruff-bag appearance – it looked like she had five teenagers living in the house. And felt like it sometimes.

'He might stay down by the river all day. Who knows?' Or he could be up at the aunts' house with Fern. She might even bump into him at the Lionheart; it was possible – they both spent more time there with other people than they did at home with each other.

'It doesn't matter anyway,' Ben grumbled. 'She'll probably only be here five minutes. She sounded in a right mood.'

Claire shut her bag with a click. 'It's her birthday. She'll soon cheer up, nobody's miserable on their birthday.'

Ben emitted a grunt of disbelief.

'You have bought her a present?'

Her charming son screwed his face into a frown. 'I'm broke.'

'Oh, for heaven's sake . . .' Men had no idea. Claire spotted the flowers in the sitting room that she'd treated herself to yesterday, beautifully arranged in one of David's vases. Oh, well. She strode in and grabbed the lot. 'Give her these.'

Ben blinked. 'What, the vase as well?'

'Don't be cheap, love.' She shook her head in despair. What would she do with him? 'Yes, give the girl the vase as well, that ought to bring a smile to her face. And I'm sure you can at least manage to wrap it before she gets here.'

'Thanks, Mum.' Ben brightened visibly.

'Later on you can beg your father to make another one,' she told him.

'Okay.' Ben pulled on his trainers as if he were going out, but Claire understood about that kind of thing. He had his image to protect. She knew from bitter experience that certain trainers were sad, others cool, and – looking on the bright side – when you'd paid sixty quid for the things it was reassuring to see them getting plenty of wear.

'See you later, love,' she said, risking a quick peck on the cheek. 'And good luck.'

In the pub, Gary bought her an Irish stout. 'You look like you need building up.'

'Is that a polite way of saying I look awful?' But Claire accepted the beer, and made a mental note to avoid ivory highlighter around the eyes in future.

'You look great,' Gary assured her. 'Just tired.'

'Are your parents still staying at the cottage with you?' Max Stockwell completed the equation successfully.

'How did you guess?' Claire congratulated herself on the fact that today he was having no effect on her whatever. It had been a combination of the shock, the massage and the wine, she decided. And she was no sweet young thing – the last thing she intended to do was make a fool of herself over some man. 'I don't even know that Mum could manage him at home,' she went on. 'He's getting worse, and we're such a long way away. Although if they were to move . . .' But, from what Josh had said, Patricia was unlikely to agree to that.

'Have you thought of one of these warden-assisted places?' Gary's voice was casual.

'No.' It didn't seem at all the sort of idea that would go down well with her mother.

'They're not OAP residential homes, you know, Claire.' Max spoke softly, and Claire realised that the idea, broached by Gary, had probably originated with his brother.

She glanced across at him. 'What are they, then?' she asked. She doubted that her mother would appreciate the difference.

Max explained that they were blocks of retirement flats or bungalows where senior citizens, as he tactfully put it, could be as independent as they liked.

'They're nice places. And this is the interesting part. A warden keeps an eye on them. There are community outings, a community room. If they want it.' He looked at Claire across the table. 'If they don't want to socialise, they don't have to. But help is at hand if they need it.'

'I'm listening.'

'They offer support, that's all.'

'A kind of half-way house?'

Max shrugged. 'If you like. Do you think your parents might be interested?'

'I don't know, Max.' She smiled with rather more warmth than she'd intended. But it was kind of him to take the trouble, when he hardly knew her. 'I really don't know. But I do know I've got to do something.'

'There are quite a few of them around these days.' Max grinned at Gary. 'Our gran lived in one in St Austell up until she died. Right? And she could be a terror. There's no way the parents would have got her into a home. "*I'll stick to my own kitchen, thanks very much*," she used to say.'

'My mother prefers to stick to mine,' Claire said.

'It was a nice place,' Gary agreed. 'I'll give you the address, if you like, Claire.'

'And I'll give it some thought.' It was a good idea, she realised. That house was much too big for them these days; her mother might even be glad that Claire would be close at hand. But it wasn't up to Claire, was it? It was their choice . . . Determinedly she cleared her thoughts. 'And, in the meantime, how about this alternative committee meeting we're supposed to be having?' she asked.

Gary got out pencil and notebook. 'We wondered about the Old Barn? It's just sitting there, nobody seems to use it any more.'

'As a venue?' Claire knew it wasn't derelict. In fact, in its day, it had hosted the odd party and dance, until the more modern village hall had been built. It had once actually functioned as a barn, Claire remembered David telling her. Until the owner, a local dairy farmer, long gone from the village, had arranged its conversion, done it up a bit, put in a stage . . . Of course! 'I'm sure it's got a stage.' She tried to picture the place. 'But it would need some capital spending on it.'

'We could apply to the Arts Council,' Max contributed. 'I know several small community theatres that have done quite well out of them.'

'And then there's the lottery,' Gary put in.

'And we can do some fund-raising for ourselves.' Claire thought of the summer fête. Well, she was organising the damn thing. The money always went to the school or the church. Why not the arts for a change?

'It would all take time.' Max was thoughtful. 'What we need is a fast injection of cash, and then we can build from there.'

'A sponsor?' Claire constructed a rapid mental list of people wealthy enough to qualify. 'I can't think of anyone who'd be remotely interested. They'll probably all be dead set against the idea.'

'Who owns the Old Barn?' Gary asked. 'Not the Stickler, I hope.'

'The Church, as far as I know,' Claire told him. 'So we'd have to ask permission, pay to lease it.'

'Only for a few weeks of the year to start with. We don't have to take on anything too grand or ambitious at first.' Max rubbed his hands together in a manner totally at odds with his words. 'But a community theatre project would be really exciting. Combined with an open-air market, perhaps.'

'An environmental happening?' Claire could feel her enthusiasm growing in line with Max's. She could really see it coming off. 'A historical event?' That could be the theme of next year's summer fête, if they could organise it in time. The whole thing could coincide in a kind of mini-festival.

'Why not? Everyone in Victorian dress.'

'Support your local charities . . .'

'And craftsmen,' Claire added loyally, thinking of David.

Gary was scribbling frantically. 'And a small exhibition space in the foyer,' he said.

'Foyer?' It was, after all, only the Old Barn.

'All right, entrance hall, then. A curtained-off bit of the barn. Whatever. For local artists, of course.'

'Especially budding Cubists.' They laughed.

Max got another round in. As he handed Claire her drink, his fingers brushed against the back of her hand, probably unintentionally, but she jumped at the warmth of the contact, the pleasant headiness that would keep attacking her whenever he got too close. Who was she kidding? That night at Gary's had been no temporary blip.

'A village meeting is in order, I reckon.' Max sat back at the table. 'To elect a sub-committee to help with the legwork. To beg for a generous sponsor to keep us going until we get funding. And we will keep going, we'll see it through.'

'Of course we will.' Gary clapped him on the back.

'Absolutely.' Claire picked up her glass. 'Here's to the community arts project. To our heritage.' She smiled at Max. 'And to the future.'

Her eyes were drawn to his, she couldn't avoid it. Despite all her resolutions she recalled his touch on her shoulders, and the way it had made her feel. Sensations half forgotten . . .

'To community arts,' they said in unison.

Slowly, Max smiled. 'And to the future.'

It was a good deal longer than an hour before Claire returned to the cottage, but nevertheless she heard the raised voices as soon as she put her key in the lock. Ben and Tiffany. And discussions didn't seem to be going too well.

She paused. The voices were coming from the sitting room. She would go into the kitchen, shut the door, and if they kept going, perhaps she should consider offering half-time refreshments.

But before she had the chance, the sitting-room door was wrenched open and Tiffany Stickler stalked into the hall. She was carrying neither the vase nor the flowers, Claire noted. 'I've had it out with Dad. I told you,' she snapped at Ben, 'everything's changed. It's got to change.'

Claire tried not to glare at her. 'Shall I go out again?'

'Don't bother. I'm leaving,' Tiffany, to her credit, was close to tears. 'And I *am* going to university. After sixth-form college. I've made up my mind.'

'Cop-out,' Ben sneered, following her into the hall.

Tiffany turned to him, rather regally, Claire had to admit. 'It is not a cop-out, Ben. I'm investing in my future.' It could be her father speaking.

'You *said* it was a load of crap.' Ben kicked the skirting board. 'School, learning, books, just another piece of adult crap, you said.'

Claire's eyebrows rose. She was beginning to wonder just who was the bad influence around here.

Tiffany plucked her black bomber jacket from the banister. 'But it's necessary crap, Ben. Survival is a hell of a lot easier when you've got a few letters after your name.'

Claire gaped.

'Survival?' Ben, looking at her as if he hated the sight of her, was obviously still deeply in love.

Claire wondered if Tiffany realised that. She hoped not.

'Status, you mean. That's all you care about. You and your bloody family. Snobs, the lot of you.'

Claire sidled past him and into the kitchen. He was going a bit over the top, surely. But if she stayed too close she'd be tempted to join in the debate, and that probably wouldn't be a good idea.

'I don't *care* what you think.' Tiffany voice wasn't in the least angry, just perfectly honest. And Claire felt a twinge of secondary pain for that must have hurt Ben, even if the girl was pretending. 'I've made a deal with Dad. And I'm going to keep to it.'

'Some deal.'

He's losing, Claire thought. It was at least game and set to Tiffany Stickler. This girl had her life so well mapped out it was frightening.

'I need him, Ben.' Her voice softened.

'And what about me? Don't you need me?'

No, Ben, Claire thought. That wasn't the way. She could almost see Tiffany Stickler shaking her beautiful blonde head.

'What about love?' he asked. 'You said . . .'

Briskly, Claire walked across the room. She knew how much that would have cost him. And she shouldn't be listening. Her hand rested on the dial of the radio. But she couldn't do it, couldn't not listen to this ending that was tearing at him, her son. She was his mother. She wanted to rush out there and protect him, even if he was being a complete idiot. She wanted to do whatever was necessary to get Ben back on even keel.

'I need Dad more,' Tiffany told him. And it didn't take a lot of imagination to work out why.

There was a long pause before Claire heard them go to the front door, heard the rustle of Tiffany's jacket. Poor Ben. He'd never had the least idea how it could hurt. Love . . . But he was finding out now. Would it make him any kinder in the future, she wondered. *What about love*, indeed.

They must have said goodbye, because she heard the door being closed, and a few minutes later there it was, the familiar sound of Ben's motor-cycle engine as he started it up, revved it up, rode off, God knows where.

It was a very different sound from that of the Bonnie. *A bee in a baked-bean tin*, Jerry used to say. He always admitted that Japanese bikes were easy to look after, but they were also, he said, all the same. The idiosyncrasies of British bikes ... *Okay, they can be unreliable from time to time* ... was all part of their individual flavour. She recalled him running a loving hand along the body of his own bike. *My baby*, he called it. *You gotta appreciate a touch of class*. He had grinned at Claire and she hadn't been able to resist grinning back. According to Jerry, that was what being a motorcycle enthusiast was all about.

Ben's Suzuki was a million miles away from the deep true blue bass of the Bonnie. A long way, yes, but she understood what Ben was feeling, understood the need to take off. After all, she'd felt it so often herself. And when he returned he'd be calmer at least. Until the next time.

'Ride safely, Ben,' she whispered.

At school on Monday Richard Stickler seemed distracted, not quite his usual ebullient self, and he stayed late; he was still in his study at five thirty when Claire finished printing up the posters for their community project meeting at the village hall. Oh, yes. She worked hard enough for the school, and often in her own time. Wasn't she entitled to use their equipment occasionally?

She put her head round the door of Richard's study. 'I'm off now.'

He barely nodded, and she hesitated, sensing that something was up. 'Is everything all right, Richard?'

'Come and have a drink with me, Claire.'

For the first time, she noticed the bottle of whisky on Richard's desk. How much had he had? As far as she knew, Richard Stickler was not a drinking man, but tonight he simply looked as if he didn't want to go home. 'Well . . .'

'Kids, eh?' He groped in the desk drawer, produced another glass and poured a generous measure.

Claire felt almost sorry for him. 'The school-kids?' She perched on the chair on the other side of his desk, and accepted the glass he gave her.

Richard laughed. 'School-kids? God, no.' He took a deep slug. 'I'm talking about the other kind – the ones at home. They're even more of a worry.' He eyed her over the rim of his glass. 'How's your young lad, then?'

'Not so young, these days.' Claire shifted uncomfortably in her seat. If she'd known this subject would be on the agenda, she wouldn't have sat down in the first place.

'What is he? Seventeen, eighteen? Left school, has he? University on the cards?'

That was all it seemed to be with these people. School, university, life. No other route available. She had some sympathy with Ben. 'He can't decide,' she said.

'Which uni to choose?'

'No. What to do, where to go. He can't decide anything very much.' Especially now that he's had his heart broken by your daughter, she felt like adding.

Richard stared at her gloomily. 'My Tiffany was sixteen at the weekend, you know.'

Yes, she knew. And how. 'Really?'

'Mmm. You do your best for them, don't you, Claire?'

She sipped her drink nervously. 'You certainly do.' Well, that was a matter for debate, but now wasn't the time.

'You give them it all. And then . . .'

'And then?' She couldn't resist the bait.

'And then they throw it all back in your face.' He swirled the whisky around in the glass. 'D'you find that, Claire?'

She made a non-committal noise of assent. 'But . . . what did she er, throw in your face, Richard?'

He sighed. 'What didn't she? She more or less admitted she's been keeping bad company.'

'Did she now?' Claire felt herself bristling as maternal instincts resurfaced. She could happily strangle that little madam.

'Not in so many words. But you know these young lads.' Richard slopped more whisky into his glass. 'They're trouble, make no mistake. I'm frightened to let our Tiffany out of the house sometimes.'

'Hmm.'

Apparently struck by her tone, Richard glanced up. 'Oh, sorry, Claire, I was forgetting. Well, not your lad, of course. Goes without saying.'

Did it? She wanted to laugh, the urge to tell him was almost overwhelming.

'But some of them, you know, sex, drugs . . . Well, you worry, don't you?'

Claire nodded. Oh, yes, you worry all right.

'And our Tiffany . . .'

'She seems like a sensible girl. Very capable.' Capable of anything, more like. Certainly capable of looking after herself.

Richard brightened a little at this. 'Iris says she's got her head screwed on. I'm not so sure.' His shoulders sagged further. 'Things aren't the same as they used to be, eh, Claire? So many bad influences. Not like in our day.' He squinted at her. 'Well, in my day, anyway.'

Oh, God, he was getting maudlin. Time to go, she decided, draining her glass. 'I really must be off.' She got to her feet.

'Like your friend Gary.'

'What?' She stared at him.

'It won't do, you know, Claire.'

She stiffened. 'What won't?' She wasn't exactly sure how they'd made the leap from Tiffany and Ben to Gary, but it had been a master stroke and she was totally unprepared – as well as a touch unfocused after that whisky on an empty stomach.

'You're a Friend of Trevarne, Claire.'

She frowned. Had they made another leap? 'Yes?'

'So . . .' He paused. 'Can I be frank?'

Warily she nodded.

'The governors,' self-importantly Richard swirled the honey-coloured liquid around in his glass once more, 'are not happy. Oh, no.'

'I'm sorry to hear that.' Claire sat down again, her legs primly together. 'Why aren't they happy?'

'Simple, really.' Richard clicked his tongue in irritation. 'It was certainly made obvious enough to me at the governors' meeting. They're not happy about Gary Stockwell teaching in this school.'

Bloody creep, she thought. 'You've told them, then? You've spread the word that Gary's gay?'

Richard winced. 'One has responsibilities.'

'Does one?' Claire simmered.

'Most certainly.' Richard seemed to grow in stature as he spoke. Must be the effect that any mention of the governors had on him, she thought bitterly. 'They are not entirely sure he should be kept on.'

'I bet.'

'Pardon, Claire?'

'Aren't they happy with his work? Is that it?' She was determined to make this difficult for him.

'As you know,' Richard leant back in his chair, 'it's his out-of-school activities they object to.'

'I wasn't aware he had many.'

'Claire, you know very well what I'm saying.' Richard seemed to be losing patience.

Well, say it, then. She waited. Let him at least come out and say it.

'You don't seem to realise that it's not up to me.' His words were tinged with unconvincing regret. 'I deal with the day-to-day running of the school, yes. But, since the Educational Reform Act, it's the governors who have the real power.' Richard drummed his fingers on the desk top. 'Overall strategic management, budget, staff appointments. Dismissal . . .'

'In theory, yes.' Claire was irritated. Passing the buck again. That was all Richard seemed to do.

'Not just in theory, Claire. Believe me, they have the power to reject my recommendations out of hand.'

'But they wouldn't.' What about mutual support and respect? She knew they were pretty hot on that. She was aware that the government wanted to wean schools away from the all-encompassing control of LEAs. To foster independence and competition, or so they said. But, in practical terms, what had changed?

'Oh, they might,' Richard insisted. 'If they felt strongly enough about it.'

'But . . .'

He held up his hand. 'The governing body doesn't get paid for what it does, you know.'

'I know, but still . . .'

'These people are committed professionals. They go on courses in their spare time.'

'Very commendable.'

'And you know how involved some of them get in the running of the school.'

Only too well. 'But when it comes to dismissal?'

Richard frowned. 'Nowadays, of course, there are rules about that kind of thing,' he admitted sadly. 'There must be reasonable cause. Dismissal must be legal and fair and only the governing body can do it. The most I could do is suspend him.' He let this hang in the air. 'If I had good reason . . .'

And he obviously didn't have one. Gary's sexuality would hardly qualify – this wasn't the army. Thank God, she thought.

'People are liberated.'

'They are?' That was news to Claire.

'But not that liberated.' He eyed her disapprovingly. 'Face facts, Claire. It's the parents the governors have to satisfy. Our parents will hear about Gary – if they haven't heard already. And then . . .' He leant forwards. 'The fat really will be in the fire.'

'But why?' It may have been naïve of her – clearly it was – but coming from London Claire was used to the existence of gay school-teachers, even if their sexuality was usually left unacknowledged. Things were obviously very different in Cornwall.

'Because no parent wants their son to be educated by a homosexual teacher,' Richard said. 'It's as simple as that.'

'I don't see why not.'

'Would *you*? Honestly, Claire?'

She stared back at him. Amazingly, it was something she'd never considered, never been asked to consider. Determinedly, she dug deep, among all the old prejudices she might ever have inherited. She also recalled Gary's story about his tutor at college. It had been disastrous, certainly. But had it honestly made any difference to Gary's sexuality? 'I wouldn't mind.' She smiled, pleased with herself.

'Really?' Clearly, he didn't believe her.

'Not if he was a good teacher. If he was caring, interested in my son's education. What the hell does it matter if he likes men or women? Gary's a great teacher, not the pervert you're making him out to be.'

'Oh, Claire.' Richard looked extremely disappointed. Apparently she had irrevocably let down the Friends, and if they'd known her radical tendencies, she would probably have never been invited to join them in the first place. So much for belonging.

'I'm sorry, Richard, but I strongly disagree with you,' she said staunchly.

'Well, you're in the minority,' the Stickler informed her. 'I've talked to him. I agree he's not a *bad* teacher.'

Claire's hackles rose. 'I'm sure Gary will be relieved you think so.'

'But he doesn't seem to understand –'

'That you want him to resign?' She knew it was Richard's only way out, since Gary couldn't be accused of anything. 'I'm sure he understands only too well.'

Richard shook his head. 'It's only a matter of time. When the parents get to know, they won't be slow in coming forward, making demands. It's not easy for any of us, these days. This is a delicate matter.'

'It's not easy for Gary either.' She dug her heels in. 'Especially if he can't count on your support.' She wouldn't let this go without a fight.

But Richard seemed to relax. 'It's not a question of my support. I have other loyalties.' He unscrewed the cap of the bottle.

'Not for me.' She rested her palm lightly on top of her glass, but when she removed it he topped up her drink anyway.

'Come on, Claire.' His eyes narrowed. 'Whose side are you on?'

'I didn't know it was a war.' Liar. She picked up her glass. On second thoughts, she needed another.

But Richard continued to regard her thoughtfully. 'Anyone would think that you and he really were –'

'Were what?' Even to her own ears she sounded belligerent.

'Really were having a fling, after all.' Richard laughed thickly. 'I mean, the way you stick up for him. It's a touch over the top, wouldn't you say?'

'No, I wouldn't.' But Claire could almost hear his brain rattling into overdrive. No doubt he was reaching some sick conclusion, and she was very tempted to tell him what she really thought. About him, about Gary's situation, about the bloody governors. But she refrained. He was still the headmaster and she was still the school secretary. It wasn't, damn it, her place to say too much.

'Don't tell me Gary Stockwell fancies a bit of the other on the side?' Now the drink was beginning to tell.

'Honestly, Richard.'

But he grinned. 'I always knew you had it in you, Claire.'

She scraped back her chair and jumped to her feet. It was definitely time to go. 'I think you've said more than enough.'

'David's a lucky man.' Apparently casually, Richard also rose from his chair and walked round the desk. His eyes were undressing her, but not quite in the veiled manner in which he'd always done it before.

Belatedly, Claire took a step backwards. 'Let's leave it there, Richard.' And suddenly she was scared. Suddenly a memory returned of how she had not been quite quick enough once before, sending her brain skidding into panic. She had encouraged a bit of apparently harmless leching in order to get what she wanted – an inch or two of thigh here, a glimpse of cleavage there. She should never have done that. For she had encouraged him.

Richard strolled over to the door, not opening it as she hoped, but effectively barring her exit. 'You understand men, don't you, Claire?' he asked.

Claire tried to look firm and unattractive. What on earth could she say to get their relationship back on its usual footing? Because Richard wasn't dangerous, he couldn't be. He'd just had a few whiskies too many. 'No. No, I don't.'

'What's the matter?' His words were slurred. 'Doesn't David give you what you want?' Another step towards her.

Claire sank back against the filing cabinet. The school was deserted and no one would hear her if she screamed.

'Bloody fool.' Richard had her by the shoulders now. His voice grew thicker. 'That husband of yours is a bloody fool.'

'Let go of me, Richard.' Claire forced herself to remain calm.

Sooner or later he would come to his senses.

'Forget Gary Stockwell. I can help you, Claire. And it would be very discreet. I've got this village in the palm of my hand.' The said hands dropped from her shoulders to her breasts in one move. She was so shocked that for a second she just stared at them. This couldn't be happening to her, not again.

'Let go!' she hissed.

He let go, but only with one hand. And as he did so, he trailed his fingers experimentally along her thigh.

She'd had enough. 'I said, let go of me.' As she spoke, Claire stamped very hard on his foot, and lifted her knee into his groin. It had been a shock, yes, but Richard was, after all, an entirely different proposition from what had gone before.

He yelped as he released her. 'What did you have to do that for?' he gasped. 'It was only a bit of fun.'

'I can assure you, Richard,' she panted, as she pushed him further away, 'that it's not *my* idea of fun.'

He looked as surprised as she. 'You've got to have a go, Claire.' The ghost of a smile lingered on his mouth. 'You can't blame a man for trying.'

But Claire was not smiling as she walked out of the room. And she could blame him, oh, yes, she could blame him all right. The buck had to stop somewhere and she was damned fed up with men who shirked responsibility.

'You and me, Claire,' Richard called after her. 'Can't you see what a team we'd make –?'

Chapter 11

———◆———

Where to go? Once out of the school building Claire almost lost her bearings.

Automatically she headed home, but outside the cottage she stopped, not sure what to do next. A car went by, then another. She wasn't *upset* exactly, nothing had happened, not really, Richard hadn't hurt her. But . . .

Inside the cottage, a light snapped on. It could be one or both of her parents, David, Ben. Claire paused, turned, and made her way with brisk steps towards the cottage at the far end of the row – Gary's place. She needed a refuge, just for a short while. 'Gary, please be there,' she whispered.

She rang the bell.

Noises on the other side were reassuring. The door opened, but once again it was Max Stockwell, not his brother, who stood there.

It didn't matter. She stumbled inside.

'Claire?' He took her arm. 'What is it? What . . .?'

She shook her head, not wanting to speak, and he steered her into the familiar sitting room, propelled her into a chair. 'Delayed shock,' she muttered.

She felt a warm hand on her forehead. But she didn't need heat. Any more heat and she'd explode.

'Claire . . . For Christ's sake. What on earth . . .?' She heard the concern mounting in his voice.

A nice voice, she thought, in some distant part of her. He had a Cornish accent, like his brother's but not as pronounced. This man had travelled and returned. Yes, of course. He was an itinerant, Gary had told her that.

'Brandy.' He left her to fetch it.

'Ohhh . . .' She wasn't sure brandy was a good idea.

'Deep breaths, Claire.' And almost instantly he was back, putting the glass to her lips.

She took what was supposed to be a deep restorative gulp, but on top of the whisky, the shock and the fresh air, the heavy sweet liquid almost made her retch.

She felt a blanket being wrapped around her shoulders. He was being very kind. 'Thanks, Max,' she muttered. 'But really, I'm fine.'

'You don't seem fine to me.' Max was kneeling at her feet, a worried expression on his face. 'What the hell's happened? I thought you were going to faint on me just now.'

So had she. 'Bloody Richard,' she said.

'Richard?' He frowned. 'Richard Stickler? The head?'

'The very same.' She took another sip of the brandy and snuggled closer into the blanket. It had been a shock, that was all. Richard was so conservative. She had never imagined him likely to overstep those boundaries. More fool her. They had only ever been her boundaries.

'What did he do?'

Claire wasn't sure she wanted to tell him, but she supposed she'd have to offer some sort of explanation. 'He made a pass at me, that's all.' Putting it into words got it back into perspective. A mild grope, at worst. Of course Richard had been out of order – she couldn't deny a sense of violation – but she was pretty sure he wouldn't try it again.

'What exactly happened, Claire?' His voice was restrained, but he seemed very angry.

So he told him, as briefly as possible, already playing it down.

'The bastard.' He moved closer. His arm was around her, still warm, protective even.

Instinctively, she nestled her head into his shoulder, feeling comforted and, yes, quite glad that it was Max and not Gary who had been at home. The proximity of him was pleasant but safe. There was a delicious tingle streaking from her neck to the base of her spine, and then filtering back again. In a moment she would move away . . .

And then he stroked her hair. Something changed. The tingle intensified into desire. Something inside her seemed to leap out to meet him, something hidden and almost forgotten responded to his warmth. It was too much. She pulled away from him like a scalded cat.

Their eyes met.

'I'll go and make us some coffee,' he said.

She nodded gratefully. Coffee, that was what she needed. Not bodily warmth from an attractive man who was making her – incredibly, given the events of the past hour – feel all the wrong sensations.

'What are you going to do about this?' he asked, when he brought the tray in. 'You won't give up your job, will you?' He sat on the chair opposite, as if maintaining a careful distance between them.

'Of course not.' That hadn't even occurred to her. She sensed his approval.

'You'll make a complaint, though?' He poured the coffee. 'It's sexual harassment. Actually more like assault. Stickler really should lose the headship.'

'Hmm.' Claire took a sip. It tasted good. The brandy and coffee were making her strong again, making her realise the full implications. 'I don't think I will,' she told him. 'At least, not yet.' Richard, she knew, would regret what had happened. He should never have done it. But she wasn't at all sure that she was willing to lose him his job.

'But why the hell not?' He stared in utter confusion.

'I might give Richard another chance . . .' she murmured, doubtful that he would understand why. And, after what had gone before, she herself didn't quite understand why.

Max leant back in his chair, watching her appraisingly, a smile twitching at his lips. 'And might I ask the reason?'

She thought of the rising hem-lines she had sometimes used to her own advantage. 'I may have encouraged Richard to look . . .'

'But I presume you never said he could touch?'

'No, I didn't. Still . . .'

'He should have listened. No means no.'

He sounded like a rape counsellor. 'Yes, of course he should.'

She didn't need Max to spell it out. 'But nothing happened.'

'No thanks to Richard Stickler.' He put his mug back down on the tray with a clatter. He seemed far more indignant than she would expect of a disinterested stranger. 'You can't go on working for him after this,' he said. 'You just can't.'

'Watch me.'

He seemed about to argue further, then stopped, as if realising it was not his concern. The tone of his voice changed. 'What will your husband say?'

'I don't know.'

'I know what *I'd* say.' Max's expression was thunderous. 'I'd be down at the school before you could click your fingers. There's no way the creep should be allowed to get away with this.'

Claire was surprised, and not a little flattered. 'I didn't say I was going to let him get away with it,' she murmured. 'But as for David . . .' She should have gone to David first, Claire knew that. So why hadn't she? Was it because her parents might have been there, or because David might have been too absorbed in work to give her the attention she wanted? Or was it . . .? 'I may not even tell him about it,' she said.

The dark eyebrows rose. 'Why the hell not?'

'Let's just say I have my reasons. Personal reasons.' She wouldn't say more, wouldn't discuss her relationship with David, all the things that had never been spoken of, with Max Stockwell, no matter how unhappy she was, no matter how drawn to him she might be.

She guessed that now he was wondering even more about her. 'It's your life,' he said.

'Very true.' And, to her surprise, Claire rather felt like smiling. Because something good would come out of all this. Violence wasn't the answer. Neither were resignation or dismissal. But Richard Stickler would pay. Oh, yes, she'd make damn sure of that.

That evening, her father was in a talkative mood, David was quiet and distracted and, as Claire had half predicted to herself, she said nothing about what had happened in Richard's study that afternoon. Perhaps it was for the best – she wasn't sure how David would react, she certainly didn't want it to blow up into a village break-up, a village scandal.

After dinner, Richard phoned – a discreet call. In the background she could hear music and the unmistakable sounds of a pub, but it didn't sound like the kind of music they played in the Lionheart.

'Claire.' He sounded frantic. 'I simply must apologise, I don't know what came over me.'

'Whisky, at a guess,' she joked, amazed that she was able to.

There was a pause. She could almost hear Richard's mind racing. He cleared his throat. 'I'm overwhelmingly relieved that you've taken it so well, Claire.'

He made it sound like a bereavement. 'I'm not sure that I have . . . Taken it well, I mean.' Let him sweat, he deserved at least that much.

'I see.' Another pause. 'If there is any way I can make it up to you, Claire, for my, er, appalling behaviour.'

'I'll give it some thought.'

'You will?' She could imagining him moving the receiver from one side of his head to the other, taking a shifty look around in case anyone was watching perhaps. 'Well, anything I can do . . .'

'All right, Richard, I'll let you know.' She waited, certain there was more.

'And David?'

'Hmm?' Of course he would be wondering if she had told David, he must assume that she had. And while Richard and David had never been friends – they were far too unalike for that – they were both on the same committee, David had contacts of whom Richard was envious and David was a valuable member of the village in his capacity as master craftsman and artisan.

Keeping old village skills alive, as Richard liked to say in speeches at summer fêtes as he displayed David's latest donation for the raffle – a piece of pottery that invariably added a touch of class to the proceedings.

'Claire . . .' Richard took a deep breath. 'May I take it that the matter ends here – between ourselves? You must see how it is. I have my position to think of.'

He was so predictable, she could almost laugh. And as for keeping it quiet, the only person she had told was Max; she had even decided to keep it from Gary, on the grounds that his relationship with the Stickler was tricky enough at present. 'Richard, I'm not exactly sure that you may.'

'Then,' he was sounding desperate now, 'just what *do* you want?'

'I haven't decided on what action to take yet. But I'll let you know. And thank you for calling.' Claire replaced the receiver. At least he'd had decency enough to apologise – even if he was more concerned about possible repercussions than about Claire's feelings. Poor old Richard, she could imagine his panic, she could almost feel sorry for him. But if Trevarne were ever to progress, Richard's power must wane. It was as simple as that. The ends surely justified the means . . .

Claire had been looking forward to the meeting about the community arts project set up by herself, Gary and Max for the following Thursday night. She had pasted up posters at strategic points in the village – after the meeting they would open things up to surrounding villages and towns, but first they wanted to see what support would come from Trevarne itself. And there was certainly a good attendance at the meeting, including an assortment from the small housing estate, a few teachers from the school, the aunts, Fern, David, and all the Friends of Trevarne.

Richard Stickler was quiet at first – he'd been quiet ever since that afternoon in school the week before – but the Stickler could never stay quiet for long. Pretty soon he barked, 'I can't see why we need another committee in the first place. This could all be done by the Friends.'

Here we go, Claire thought. 'This is an *arts* committee,' she replied. 'It's very different from anything else we've done. We've introduced the concept because we need someone to lead the community arts project we're planning. Although,' she smiled sweetly at Richard, 'I don't see why the two committees can't work side by side. As a team.' Aware of Max watching her, she turned to him to exchange a knowing look.

Richard went very quiet. First round to her apparently.

'One of the Friends should have been informed,' Aunt Emily

boomed. 'There are right ways of doing things.'

And you don't know any of them, Claire thought, forcing her smile ever wider.

Gary stood up. 'One was informed.' He nodded towards Claire. 'Mrs Claire Harrison.'

'Conflict of interests,' someone muttered.

God, this lot were so damn suspicious. No one would dream this project was intended for the community.

Claire rose to her feet. 'I support Trevarne. I thought that was the idea behind both committees. I also support, specifically, the community arts project.' She thought she saw David glance at her curiously.

Someone cheered. It wouldn't be Emily, for sure.

'If you feel I can't do both,' Claire continued, 'then I shall have to resign . . .'

Mutinous rustling accompanied this statement.

'. . . from the Friends of Trevarne committee.'

A respectful and rather shocked hush filled the hall. Claire knew they had all been waiting for her to stand down from the arts project – and then perhaps a discreet cover might have been drawn over the proceedings, since without Claire it lacked staying power. Max and Gary Stockwell might have the necessary artistic expertise, but Claire was the village personality – mainly through her husband, that was true, but she belonged in the village nevertheless. As for resigning from the Friends . . . Claire suspected that no one had ever dared do that before. It was an honour to be chosen, after all. People didn't go round rejecting it. It was unheard of.

Richard got up. 'I'm sure there's no need for that, Claire,' he said heartily. 'We all applaud what you're doing.' He began to clap, turning to include the rest of the audience in his recommendation. Warily, the applause began.

Claire ignored Max's cynical wink. But if Richard thought they were now fair and square he had another think coming.

When the applause had died down, Max expertly fielded questions of a more practical and technical nature.

'We know what we need,' he said. 'A technical manager, a supervisor for set, design, costume . . .' He ticked these off with his fingers. 'Actors, of course, and we're looking into all that.' He glanced around the room, smiling with the charm of a door-to-door salesman. 'I'm rather hoping some of you might have some hidden talents. But, amateur or professional, we want you all – we need you all. This is your project, your community. A chance for you all to come together and celebrate your own heritage.' Or, on second thoughts, perhaps he should have gone into politics, Claire observed.

Gary got to his feet. 'And it's a chance for local artists, craftsmen, charity stalls . . .' He told them about the open-air market. 'All stall-holders will be local organisations, local clubs, societies and charities.'

'So what do you get out of it?' someone jeered. Looking up, Claire thought she recognised the sharp hostile features of the woman.

'Maybe we just want to do something for the community,' she said softly.

Max continued, 'As I said before, what we need most of all is you.'

'I'd say what you need most is money,' Richard drawled.

There was a sense of deflation. No one could deny the truth of that remark.

Claire got up. 'Yes, we do need money. So if Mr Stickler is offering . . .'

There was some laughter.

'But apart from money, don't forget that some of us are already giving up our free time to contribute. This is for the people of the village.'

'*He* don't come from Trevarne.' The hostile woman in the audience pointed at Max. 'And *he* en't been here five minutes.' This was directed at Gary.

There was a general murmur of approval. Aunt Emily got to her feet. 'He's an outsider,' she shouted, with impressive melodrama. Perhaps she should consider a character role herself, Claire thought.

She leant towards Max. 'They don't like suspicious strangers. You're the viper in their midst.'

'So I see.' He rose to his feet. 'I live here now,' he said. 'Most of you know Gary Stockwell. Well, I'm his brother, and I'd very much like to help.'

'Max has had a lot of experience in the theatre,' Gary said. 'He's a valuable asset.'

'But how long will he stay?' someone threw in.

Claire looked at Max. Yes, how long would he stay?

'Like I told you,' he said softly, looking back at her for one fleeting moment before addressing the audience at large, 'I live here now.'

To hide her discomfort, Claire picked up the gavel. She didn't want to think too much about Max Stockwell living here in Trevarne, and she also had the distinct feeling that the meeting might be brewing up towards more controversial matters – matters that had nothing to do with the arts project and that were best dealt with at another time. 'I call this meeting to a close. And would anyone who wants to help in any capacity whatever come and sign the list. Please!'

To her relief they were soon surrounded by volunteers.

Claire grinned at Gary and Max. So far so good. But as she spotted the hostile woman from the audience approaching, she did a rapid rethink.

'This won't be the last meeting,' the woman said, a distinct threat evident in her voice.

Claire shot her a bright smile. 'No, it certainly won't be, er, Mrs . . .'

'Mrs Jones,' Gary provided, taking a step closer to them. 'We met at parents' evening.'

Jones. Nigel's mother. She recognised her now. Claire took another look at her and remembered what Richard had said about the parents. *The fat will be in the fire . . . It's only a matter of time . . . They won't take this lightly.* The formidable Mrs Jones was glaring venom at Gary. No, not liberated at all, apparently.

Claire watched her as she drew herself up to her full five feet nothing. 'And the next meeting,' she said. 'That'll be for the *parents* of the school.' Her meaning was plain.

Gary's face turned white.

'Fine.' Claire put on the authoritative tone she often had to use in her capacity as part-time dinner-lady. 'I trust it will be well publicised. I should like to attend and make my thoughts known.'

Dismissive and cool, Mrs Jones looked her up and down. 'We'll see, won't we?' she said obtusely. 'It depends whose concern it is, don't it?' And, with a parting grimace in Gary's direction, she strode away.

'Don't worry.' Claire took Gary's arm. 'There's only one of her and she's prejudiced. Who's going to listen to a woman like that?'

But Gary didn't seem reassured. 'I received hate mail once, Claire,' he muttered in her ear. 'Once you've had shit through the letter-box, you never feel quite the same about the postman's visits.'

'Gary!' Appalled, Claire hoped for a moment that he was joking. But Gary wouldn't joke about this. 'The parents of our school wouldn't. They couldn't do anything like that.' Conscious of a tall figure standing beside her, she turned. 'Hello, David.' And, by the time she turned back, Gary had drifted away.

David put his arm somewhat tentatively around her shoulders. 'You've been keeping very quiet about all this. I had no idea you were so dedicated to Trevarne.' He grinned, to take the sting out of his words.

Claire smiled, almost shyly, back at him. 'I wanted it to be a surprise. You've always said you're the only one who wants to keep the arts alive in Trevarne.'

David seemed thoughtful. 'It was a surprise, all right.'

'But not a bad one?' She looked up at him. 'And you'll help us, won't you?'

'Of course I will.' His arm was still round her. 'But why didn't you get me in on it in the first place?'

Claire felt uncomfortable. Gary had said something similar – *Do you think David would be interested?* – but she had put him off. David was an obvious candidate, and there would have been no need of a public meeting to engender support because the entire village already adored him. 'I wanted to do something on my own.'

She hadn't wanted David to come in and take over, she realised. It wasn't his fault, but people had a way of deferring to him; it just seemed to happen. Claire had wanted this to be her project, something – another thing? – she did without him, something she could achieve alone, in her own right, not as wife of David Harrison, artisan *extraordinaire*.

'Ah.' David's expression changed. 'I suppose I would have destroyed the cosy little threesome?' He was staring straight at Max, and that was when Claire twigged the significance of the arm. He hadn't put his arm round her for ages. It wasn't a matter of affection, more a case of possession.

She moved a step away. 'Not exactly.' Although she had to admit that was part of it. There was a good chemistry between herself, Max and Gary. She hadn't wanted David to spoil it, and she hadn't wanted Max . . . Oh, blast it, she wasn't sure *what* she'd wanted. 'I thought you'd be too busy to get involved,' she said to David, who was looking more angry by the second.

'You never bothered to ask.'

'David . . .' When did they even get to talk? But before she had the chance to say this to him, Iris Stickler appeared at her side, scenting marital troubles in the air, no doubt.

David turned and walked away.

'Well, my dear,' Iris said, 'I think congratulations are in order.'

But Claire wasn't sure that they were. Because all she could see was David's dear figure in his old brown jacket storming out of the village hall. And all she could feel was an overwhelming sense of regret.

Chapter 12

———————

There was no sign of David when Claire got in from the meeting, but she could hear male voices coming from the kitchen.

One was her father's. 'Take your time, that's my advice,' he was saying. 'Everything that happens – no matter how bloody awful it seems at the time – can be seen in a positive way. You mark my words, son.'

Claire did a double take. Her father had been known in times gone by for his philosophical homilies on life according to Josh Trent, but she had thought those times were over.

Ben, for she knew it was her son in there with him, grunted disagreement.

'Oh, yes, it can,' Josh told him. 'It depends on your attitude. On whether you grin when you want to cry. I know. I've been there.'

Claire paused, her hand on the door-knob. Despite his illness, his memory losses, he was still an amazing man. Only this morning he'd had no idea what day it was, and listen to him now, dealing with Ben's problems, and making a decent job of it too.

'It's easy to *say*, Grandad,' Ben was objecting.

'Learn the lesson, son.' Josh looked up as Claire entered the room. 'She's not worth much more than that.'

'Am I interrupting?' Tactfully, Claire paused in the doorway. It was nice to see the two of them like this, although the thought crossed her mind that Ben had not confided in his father. As far as she was aware, David still knew nothing about Tiffany.

'No, love.' Josh smiled, and she moved across to them, put a hand on his shoulder.

'Sorting out the world are you?' Perhaps she should ask her father

169

to sort out her and David but she sensed it would take a lot more than one of his homilies to do that.

'Ben's been telling me about his new job.'

'Job?' She stared at her son. 'First I've heard of it.'

'I only got it today.' Ben sounded defensive.

'Well, what is it, then?' Claire went over to the sink to fill the kettle. It was high time Ben did *something*. But she wouldn't raise her hopes. He had intended to go away, she mustn't forget that. And what was there to stop him, now that Tiffany Stickler was no longer on the scene?

'Just some building work in Bodmin.'

Building work? Claire caught her father's warning glance. She contented herself with a muttered, 'I see.' But a building site was not a working environment she had ever envisaged for Ben. She couldn't see much future in that.

'Now, Claire, the lad wants a few quid in his pocket,' Josh reminded her. 'And good on him, that's what I say.'

Claire meantime was finding it hard to say anything.

'It's not permanent, Mum.' Ben grinned and she had an impulse to hug him. 'But I need some money.'

'To try and get Tiffany back?'

'To get a new bike.'

She stared at him. 'Already?'

'I'm not going to ride a Suzuki once I've passed my test, Mum.' He laughed as if she were being particularly dense.

'You're not?'

'Course not. It's a little tin-pot bike. I want something a bit more meaty.'

'Oh.' Claire suppressed the feeling of *déjà vu*. He'd be telling her he planned to get a British bike next. 'When are you taking your test?' she asked. Another thing he hadn't bothered to tell her.

'Next month.' He seemed proud. 'And then . . .'

'And then?' She quailed. She would be losing him . . .

'Well . . .' Ben glanced at his watch. 'I've gotta move.'

'You're going out?' Claire blinked at him. 'Now? It's ten thirty.'

'They're not closed yet.' He jumped to his feet.

'I'll have a cup of coffee, love, if you're making one,' Josh cut in.

He was watching his grandson thoughtfully. 'Don't bother with that Sanderson bloke, will you, eh, son?'

'I wouldn't give him the satisfaction,' Ben growled. He grabbed his leather jacket and walked out of the back door.

Claire stared at her father. What exactly was going on? And what did he know about Jeremy Sanderson?

'The new bloke,' he explained. 'Loads of dosh, apparently. Knows how to show a girl a good time. That's why our Ben got the chop.'

'Ah.'

'So you can see why he wants some money in his pocket, love.'

'And a new bike.' Claire knew that his mother wasn't exactly the first person your average teenager turned to when dumped – as they charmingly put it these days – by their latest girlfriend. But she couldn't help wishing that Ben still confided in her.

'Oh, to be young again,' Josh chuckled.

The kettle boiled, and Claire spooned coffee into two mugs. 'I don't think I could do it.'

'Me neither, but Ben's all right.' Josh patted her hand as she passed him his coffee. 'And if that mercenary little so-and-so Tiffany Stickler thinks Sanderson is half the catch that our Ben is, then she's not worth having.'

Claire couldn't help smiling. Once more her father seemed in total control. If only her mother could see him at this moment . . . 'And where's Mum?' she asked.

Josh raised his eyes towards the ceiling.

'In bed?'

'Sulking, more likely.' He sipped his coffee.

'What have you said to her now?' Perhaps they were together – her mother and David, sharing their grievances about ungrateful spouses.

Josh got a firmer hold on the mug. He was in control again, yes, but his hand was shaking, he couldn't disguise that. 'I told her I thought we should go and see this Cedars place.'

'Hawthorn House, Dad.' But she was pleased.

'Whatever.' He took another careful sip. 'Worth taking a look, I said.'

Claire put a hand on his. She hadn't even been sure that he'd taken any of it in, let alone that he would want to go and see the place. She had talked to both of them, thinking it would be her father who would object to the idea of warden-assistance in any shape or form, her mother who would object to Cornwall. But in fact Patricia had sniffed her way through the brochure and Josh had gone to sleep.

'She got the hump.' Josh seemed unconcerned.

'Perhaps she doesn't want to lose her independence.'

'Huh.' He didn't seem convinced. 'Scared of change, more like.'

'Scared of change?'

He nodded. 'I know your mum. She's plain terrified, bless her. She's always been frightened of the least thing.'

Claire was puzzled. 'I never knew that.' It might be true. With a husband like Josh, Claire supposed it would have been all too easy over the years for her mother to let him take control, make her decisions, cope with her fears.

'But I've made up my mind,' Josh seemed very determined, 'to at least see the place before we go back, so we can give it some thought.'

'You would be nearer me,' Claire pointed out. 'It would be easier for me to visit, help out if you ever need anything.'

Josh glanced at her sharply. 'I'd like to know that your mum, well, that she had someone, if I . . . when I . . .'

'No, Dad.' Claire could hear her own voice threatening to break.

But his eyes were calm. 'It's on the cards, love. Face it. I'll probably go first. And anyway, since I seem to have lost my marbles half the time . . .'

'No, Dad,' she said again. She squeezed his hand. It was an old hand, bony and paler than it had ever been before, but still her father's hand.

'We'll go and see the place tomorrow.' He had clearly made up his mind. 'And then we'll go home.' Josh leant back in his chair, his face drained now as if the effort of working it all out had finished him off for the evening.

'Stay as long as you like –' she began.

He held up his hand. 'Don't give me that, my girl. You've had enough of us. You and David need some time to yourselves. That boy of yours needs his room back.' His voice wavered. 'I might not know exactly how long we've been here, but I know it's been long enough.'

Claire was silent. It was true. She had conflicting loyalties but Ben did need his room back. It wasn't fair to expect him to camp on the sofa any longer. And David? Well, it was David's house, and yet she sensed he was feeling excluded from it, as well as from his wife's activities right now.

'We'll discuss it, I'll talk to the doctor. I'll be able to make her see.' His face contorted and Claire saw the effort he was making. Her father had such stamina: his memory might be suffering from these mini strokes, but when he was *compos mentis* he could outdo the lot of them for sure.

'You do that, Dad.' Claire smiled, but her heart was aching. 'You do whatever you think is right.'

He surveyed her with his perceptive stare that hadn't changed all that much either, although the colour of the eyes had faded. 'Are you frightened, too, girl?'

'Of what?' she hedged.

'Of letting go?'

Nothing would surprise her now. 'I don't want to let you go.' She didn't want to lose her father, and yet she felt sure that was happening. And as for Ben . . . 'I'm not sure what'll be left when Ben's gone.' Because he was going, she knew it. Every day he'd travelled a little further. Building site or no, it wouldn't be long.

'You'll find out what's left,' Josh said. 'All in good time.'

She tried to smile back at him. 'I know.'

'It might not be so bad,' he said. 'And if you take my advice . . .'

'I always did.' She looked into his face.

'You won't run away. You won't be scared of letting go.'

Claire remained silent. Tomorrow, or maybe the next day, he might forget about going to Hawthorn House, even about going home. He might forget the name of Ben's first love, get lost walking to the village shop, or pass David in the street without saying hello. That was the pattern. Film clips in his mind, sometimes out of focus, often out of sequence, rarely making sense. Everything had come together for him tonight – he had made everything come together through sheer willpower alone. But tomorrow . . .

And Claire knew he had made his feelings clear to her so that she would help him, if necessary. So that she would know what he wanted. Claire knew what she must do then. She must stay strong for that, for the man who had always been strong for her. She owed him that much at least. She had to help him see this through, no matter how long it took, no matter how little help he was able to give, no matter how difficult it proved to be. It was her responsibility. She was his daughter, and he needed her.

'Have you heard?' It was a week later when Gary strode into Claire's tiny office.

She glanced up. 'Anything in particular?'

'There was a parents' meeting in the village hall last night.' His thin face was looking weary; he was weary of peoples' prejudices, she guessed.

'What about?' But she knew from the expression on his face.

'What do you think?' He pulled a sheet of paper from his pocket. 'And this came through my letter-box this morning.'

Claire took it. It was a plain white sheet of paper with *WE WANT YOU OUT OR ELSE*, written in stark red capitals. She sighed. 'It's probably just some crank.'

Mrs Maureen Jones. They were both thinking the same, she knew it. It was Nigel's mother who had tried to upset the arts project meeting, and Nigel's mother who had threatened another meeting for the parents. She was behind the meeting, if not the nasty piece of paper, and she had kept it very quiet, considering that Claire had said she wanted to go. But the question was, how many supporters did she have?

'It could be the whole lot of them,' Gary said. He slammed his fist down on her desk in an uncharacteristically violent gesture. 'I'm bloody sick of it, Claire.'

'We don't know what happened at the meeting,' she said soothingly.

'I think I do,' Gary told her. 'I had a particularly unpleasant interview with Nigel in the playground this morning.'

'Little toad. What did he say?'

Gary pulled a face. '*They voted you out, they did*, seemed to be the gist.'

'Right.' Claire got to her feet. She grabbed the desk diary and glanced at it quickly.

'Where are you going?' Gary was staring at her.

'To see Richard.'

'Hang on, Claire.' He grabbed her arm. 'I'm about to go and see him myself.'

'To resign?' She glared back at him. 'To back off from this without a fight?'

'I never said that.'

'Maybe you didn't have to.' It seemed to be stalemate between them.

'I can fight my own battles.' He took a pace towards the door. 'I've got no intention of letting you do it for me, and I won't have you risking losing your job either.'

'And?'

'And no, I am not backing off.' He opened the door and she slipped past him. 'Claire . . .'

She turned back to smile. 'I'm sure you can fight as well as the next man, Gary. But this time . . .'

'What's so different about this time?'

'This time,' she said, 'I have a secret weapon. Trust me.'

Claire gave a curt rap on the study door and walked straight in.

Startled, the headmaster looked up.

'Richard. I need a quick word.'

She registered his expression. He knew what she wanted to talk about and he would do almost anything to avoid it.

'Ah yes, Claire . . .' She saw him preparing to bluff. 'Well, of course, any time, but I think you'll find I have an appointment.'

'Not for twenty minutes.' She stood her ground. 'I checked.'

'Hmm. Well, then . . .'

'Did you know about the parents' meeting last night?' Straight to the point, that was the way.

His eyes shifted warily. One knee twitched. 'Parents' meeting?'

'Oh, come on, Richard.' Claire felt in control. She wouldn't allow him to evade this one, no way.

'Yes.' He picked up his pen and began twirling it around

175

between his fingers. 'All right. Yes, I did know.'

'It was a bit on the secretive side,' she challenged. 'Don't you think?'

'Oh, I wouldn't say so, Claire. Not secretive. It was a public meeting . . .'

'*I* wasn't told.'

Richard smiled. 'But you are not a parent – not of a child of this school anyway. And . . .' He paused. 'I believe it was thought you might not be entirely objective.' He seemed to be doing a lot of believing.

'And you *were* objective?'

Richard got to his feet. 'You misunderstand me, Claire.' His body language confirmed what she was feeling. He was getting the better of the conversation. Bloody Richard, he was far too good at doing that. Years of going to governors' meetings had probably taught him that much. 'I didn't actually go to the meeting myself,' he told her, 'but I knew it was planned.'

'And what conclusions did they come to?' She stared at him as he paced the room. 'I presume you know that too.'

He seemed to hesitate once more. 'I was informed by telephone this morning . . .'

'Of what?'

'Apparently,' he approached his desk, 'the parents of the school do not wish Gary Stockwell to remain a member of staff here.'

'I see.'

He avoided looking at her. 'I'm sorry, Claire.'

That just wasn't good enough. And besides, he wasn't sorry, was he? He had as good as admitted that Gary's resignation was what *he* wanted too. 'And what did you say to that?'

Richard consulted his notebook. Had he written it down? Very probably. The Stickler wasn't stupid. He would make sure that everything was done by the book, that he couldn't be blamed at a later date for following the wrong procedure. Heaven forbid. 'I said that naturally the governors were concerned about certain, ah, revelations of the past few weeks concerning Mr Stockwell –'

'Oh, naturally,' Claire jeered.

'And I was sure that they would be even more concerned when

they were informed of the parents' views on the matter.' He looked over the notebook at Claire. 'But I also told them that I happen to know the governors couldn't possibly terminate someone's employment purely on the grounds of . . .' he floundered '. . . on the grounds of . . . well, you know.'

She certainly did. 'And what did the parents say to that?' She could imagine, especially if the parent in question happened to be Maureen Jones.

Richard shrugged. 'I suppose it's what they were expecting to hear. Unless Gary were to commit some sort of offence, or fail to reach certain teaching standards, something of that nature, the governors would never be able to dismiss him.' He seemed to have forgotten for a moment that Claire was in the room. 'The only thing we can do is inform him of the situation and apply a little pressure.'

'Richard!' She was shocked.

He shook his head – in despair at her naïvety, presumably. 'There's a conflict of loyalties here, Claire. We have a school to run, and a lot of people depend on me to see that it's run smoothly. We can't have bad feelings, people must get on, members of staff must be respected by the parents. And if someone doesn't fit . . .'

'I agree that the staff deserve respect.' She kept her voice icy. 'But whatever happened to the respect due to Gary?'

'Gary has lost their respect,' he reminded her.

'Then they're blind as well as stupid.' Claire thought of what Gary had told her. 'So what happens now? I suppose this is where you apply that pressure on Gary that you were talking about – *I'll give you a decent reference if you get the hell out of my school*, that sort of thing.'

'Claire!'

'Or, even worse, the parents decide to take matters into their own hands and make poor Gary's life unbearable until he's forced to resign.'

'Claire, really!'

She slapped the sheet of paper Gary had given her in front of him. 'Look at this, then.'

Richard frowned. 'I don't like this kind of thing any more than you do.' He might have been talking about the graphics for all the emotion he put into his voice. 'But I did warn you that it was just a question of time. We're old-fashioned here in Trevarne.'

'But *you* could do something.'

'I'm powerless.'

She snorted with laughter at this idea. 'Powerless, my foot. That wasn't what you told me before. Something about holding this village in the palm of your hand, I seem to recall.'

Richard had the grace to look ashamed as he sank back into his chair. 'Yes, well, in this case I am powerless. I can't *make* the parents want Gary to stay.'

Claire remained unconvinced. She glanced at her watch. But time was running out, and Richard appeared to be winning.

'However much I like Gary as a person. However much I respect him as a teacher, appreciate what he's already done for the school and in such a short time –'

Now that was going too far. 'Balls,' she said.

'Pardon?'

'You're not powerless, Richard, and you know it.' She leant over the desk, closer to him. 'Because if the parents knew you were actively supporting Gary...'

A look of horror crossed his face. 'But I told you, it's up to the governors, not me.' That's it, Richard, she thought. Pass the buck – you always do.

'And if the *governors* knew you were actively supporting Gary...'

'Oh, I don't think so, Claire.' But she sensed his discomfort. She was getting somewhere now.

'But *I* do, Richard. You underestimate yourself.' Fat chance. 'You're very influential. And with Iris's...' She let this hang in the air. Even she couldn't just come out and mention Iris's money. But she did know that Iris's family had given support to the village in all sorts of ways. Ways that were certainly appreciated by the kind of people who were now governors of the village school. Many of them owed Iris Stickler and her generosity a great deal.

He looked at her, astounded by her nerve perhaps.

'With Iris's background and status in the village,' she went on smoothly, 'I'm sure if you were to support Gary openly,' she eyed him triumphantly, 'they'd simply have to think again.'

Richard's mouth had become a thin line of anger. He glanced at his watch. 'I'd like to help, Claire, but I happen to believe that Gary Stockwell is not a suitable member of our team here. Young minds . . . they're very susceptible to influence.'

'Do you really think so?' Claire was getting angry. It had started as a fiery feeling on the back of her neck, and in the last fifteen minutes it had spread through her entire body.

'I really do,' Richard insisted. 'Call me narrow-minded, but –'

'Richard, you're *unbelievably* narrow-minded.' What about *his* influence, for God's sake? Some example he'd turned out to be.

He gazed at her in reproach. 'We believe in Christian values in this school. It really is a question of morality. I'm surprised you can't see that.'

'And I'm surprised that *you* should say it, Richard.'

He glanced at his watch once more. 'Why is that?'

She felt the surge of triumph. 'Because you're right. It is question of morality.'

'Oh?'

'Yours.'

There was a very long pause, but Richard didn't look at his watch this time.

He leant back in his chair. 'I thought we had decided to close the door on that unfortunate episode, Claire.'

Oh, very good. She put her hands on her hips. Battle stance. '*I* didn't,' she told him. 'In fact, I seem to recall telling you that I'd let you know if there was anything you could do to make it up to me.'

'Did you?' he asked weakly, refusing to look her in the eye.

'And I'm letting you know right now. You see, I feel strongly about Gary remaining at the school. Very strongly. He's an asset to the team you're so keen on. In fact, he's an asset to the community.'

'Oh, this blasted arts thing . . .' Richard brushed the idea away.

'It's important.' Claire wouldn't give in now. She had him bang to rights. She didn't care if his next appointment was standing outside the door listening, she would finish what she had come in here to say.

'I supported you at the meeting, didn't I?' Richard grumbled.

'To a degree.' She let this hang in the air between them. 'But I want more.'

'How much more?' Now she was speaking his language: she could read it in his eyes.

'Open and loyal support from you for Gary, to the parents and to the governors. Or . . .'

'Or?' He seemed almost beaten now.

'Or I have a little chat with Iris and the governors myself.' Claire could hardly believe she was doing this. It was the kind of thing you read about, intrigue in a village school. But she was quite enjoying herself; it was giving her rather a thrill. She felt as if she were living dangerously, just as she had when she'd ridden her Triumph Bonneville up and down the dual carriageways out of London, or along the dark back streets of Clapham at midnight. A bit of danger, she surmised, was a bit of a good thing. A touch of spice made life more exciting.

Richard's face went from brown – a tan recently acquired in the Caribbean – to red, to a sickly puce. Claire watched with interest.

'Well?'

'What do you want me to do?' He glared at her.

She had won. The first fight anyway, although there was work to do yet. 'I'll type up a letter for the kids to take home,' she said. 'I'll invite the parents to the school. And you can invite the governors.'

'What for?' Richard Stickler was not looking a well man.

'We'll have another meeting, of course.' She grinned. 'We'll let them all know you're on Gary's side. We'll persuade them that Trevarne isn't living in the dark ages, that it has a future. That it's time it respected people and their ability – not gossips and old-fashioned prejudice.'

'Anything else?'

'We'll tell them Gary is a brilliant teacher.' She was on a roll now. 'And let them know that you don't approve of these below-the-belt kind of tactics.'

'I don't exactly have a choice,' he muttered.

Very true. Claire felt a twinge of sympathy for the poor man. She moved to the door. 'But just think, Richard, it's all for the good of the community. And the good of the school.'

He looked doubtful.

'Gary's the best thing that's ever happened to Trevarne. So you'll be doing the *right thing*. Isn't that great?'

Richard still looked gloomy.

'It's all a question of morality, Richard. Remember?' She flounced out of the room, saw the head of the board of governors walking down the corridor. 'Richard?' She poked her head back in. He looked as if he was about to be sick. 'Your next appointment has arrived. Shall I show him in?'

Rather to Claire's surprise, David insisted on accompanying her to the meeting set up less than a fortnight later. They hadn't discussed it in detail, but Claire had explained the gist, making out that Richard had seen sense, rather than admitting to having indulged in a spot of blackmail. Gary and Max weren't there, of course, and Claire was grateful for his support. But it felt weird, walking with him down to the school, not speaking and not touching, but with the body she used to know so well still moving in tune with her own. They rarely went anywhere together, she realised. She had the school and now the arts project to take up her time, David had fishing and his work. And Fern, of course.

The hall was packed. Claire and David found seats and waited for the meeting to begin.

Richard was acting as chairman. 'We have been shocked to the core,' he said, his voice projecting to the back of the hall, 'to hear that Mr Stockwell has received what I can only describe as threats from an unknown source.'

Rebellious muttering could be heard in response to this remark.

Richard called the meeting to order. 'I would have thought the people of Trevarne to be above such things.'

The muttering this time was quieter.

'And so I have called this meeting,' he went on, 'to reiterate, should any of you be in doubt, that as head teacher of this school I wholeheartedly support Gary Stockwell – both as a member of my teaching staff and as a member of our community here in Trevarne.'

Claire had to hand it to him, he might have been reluctant to do this at first, but she couldn't complain at the way he was throwing himself into it now. No one would guess that it wasn't coming from the heart.

'And I vote that others do the same!'

'Hear hear!'

Claire turned around. Surely that had come from Iris.

'I open the meeting to comments from contributors.' Richard sat down, slightly flushed but otherwise in control.

Maureen Jones got to to her feet. Everyone stared at her, but Claire noted that there was little obvious support. The parents of Trevarne School were being cagey – despite the outcome of *their* meeting they hadn't yet decided which way to go. 'It's all right for you,' she sneered. 'But what are you going to do about it if my lad Nigel gets . . .' she took a deep breath '. . . corrupted by him?'

There were a few bursts of laughter from people who clearly knew Nigel rather well.

'He might!' Maureen Jones was most indignant. 'You read about stuff like that in the papers. It's on the telly every day, in't it?'

Very slowly, David got to his feet.

Surprised, Claire glanced up at him and noted the expression of undiluted anger on his face.

'We're living in the nineteen nineties, for God's sake.' He glared at Maureen Jones. 'Do you have any idea how many teachers are gay and simply have to hide the fact because of ignorant prejudice like yours? They want to be honest. But they also have as much right as the next man – or woman – to the job.'

No one spoke. It was like that with David, Claire thought admiringly. Sometimes he said very little, and you almost forgot. But when he felt strongly enough about something he kind of let rip, and when he did that she couldn't help being proud of him, as well as being reminded of the man she had married. Because too often that man stayed far too long away.

David looked around the school hall at the assortment of parents present. 'What on earth makes you think a gay man is more likely to cause damage to your children than anyone else is?' He pushed back his hair in a movement of exasperation. 'For God's sake, can't you see that they'd be a hundred times more on their guard? Gay men and women have to be. They live with prejudice. People are expecting them to go wrong. People want them to.'

There were a few nods and murmurs of approval. Claire continued to watch her husband in surprise. Only David could have launched such a speech on Trevarne and got away with it.

'If this is what Trevarne has come to,' David made a gesture that encompassed governors, staff, parents alike, 'an attitude little short of homophobia, then I tell you this – I want no further part in the community of Trevarne.'

There was a stunned silence. David was a craftsman, and therefore it was accepted that he might hold rather bohemian or even outrageous views. But at the same time, Trevarne loved him. His family had been here for generations, he had done a lot for the village and he commanded universal respect. He would lend a hand to anyone in need – this lot all knew that, many of them had been the recipients of David's good-humoured assistance. They wouldn't want to go against his wishes. They certainly wouldn't want to lose him.

There was a cheer from the floor. Then another. Someone shouted approval, and then the hall was resounding to a volley of applause, and in the middle of all this, David walked out of the hall.

One of the parents got to his feet. 'I vote that we show a united front. That we have confidence in Gary Stockwell until he should prove otherwise. That we apologise to him for our behaviour, and that we continue to support the school.'

Even Richard looked somewhat surprised at this. However, he stood up and counted the show of hands, gradually looking rather more pleased as he no doubt considered that he had initiated this commendable change of heart.

Iris came over and kissed Richard's cheek, Claire turned away with a smile to watch Maureen Jones leave the hall, and with that the meeting broke up with goodwill on almost all sides.

Claire could hardly believe it. In the end it had been so easy. Thanks to David . . .

He was waiting outside the building, hunched inside the old brown jacket, his expression inscrutable in the dim light.

She touched his arm. 'Thanks, David.'

But his voice was sad when he answered her. 'I didn't do it for you, Claire. I did it because it had to be done.'

'Well, anyway . . .' Of course she would have liked to think he had spoken up out of his feelings for her – at least it would have proved that he *had* feelings for her . . . But what mattered was that Gary was safe.

'I meant every word.' His brow creased. 'I don't want this place to become any more small-minded than it already is. I care about Trevarne.'

Did he imagine she didn't know that? 'Of course.'

'And as for you . . .'

Sharply, she looked up. 'Me?'

'Since you've made it clear how you feel. And since I obviously can't make things right . . .'

She moved with him as he headed back towards the cottage, but this time he kept his stride long and they were in tune no longer. Yes, she had made it clear how she felt about Trevarne. So many times in the past when she had felt trapped, stultified in this place, when she'd begged him to leave. But didn't he realise that now she was making an effort to belong? Surely her involvement in the arts project committee should have told him at least that much. Yes, she wanted to do it for herself, but she was also, like a drowning man, clutching at some straw that she thought might save their marriage perhaps.

Claire listened to their footsteps on the pavement. Definitely out of tune. But what about David? Had he given up on them completely? She glanced across at him, at the set features under the dark mop of curly hair, features she knew so well but couldn't read.

How could she tell? Since her parents' return to London, she had expected herself and David to communicate more. But it hadn't happened. He had wrapped himself inside a shell of silence and she didn't know how to force a way in.

'Ben will be gone soon. Then it'll be just you and me.' She spoke only to break the silence, to try to find something they could agree on.

They had reached the cottage. Claire scrabbled in her bag for her key, but he was there before her, fitting his in the lock.

'And what will you do then?' David spun round to face her.

'Do?'

'You're like your mother.' His eyes were cold. 'You can't bear the thought of your son leaving. You'd like to keep him with you for ever.'

'No . . . It's not like that.' But David had already turned back, he was inside the front door.

He flicked the light switch and the bulb illuminated the familiar hall and David's back, as he stomped through to the kitchen.

'It's not like that.' She sank briefly against the wall. Ben was not Freddie. She was not her mother. It was taking time, but she was coming to terms with his leaving.

To the future, they had said, she, Gary and Max. But sometimes the future was inextricably bound up with the past . . .

Chapter 13

It was some months later, when walking from the tube station to her parents' house, that Claire took a deep breath and decided to walk a different route. Perhaps it was time to confront that past.

At one time she had come this way often, the way that took her past Roper's newsagent's, and more significantly, past the building that had been Jerry's second-hand motor-cycle shop.

But since that afternoon at the café out towards Dorking, since the last time she had ridden her Triumph Bonneville, Claire had avoided Jerry's, taken a different route to get to her parents' house when she still lived there and on all her visits since, although this had meant taking some complex detours at times. But she'd made a vow then and she'd stuck to it. No more motor-bikes, no more Jerry's. No more.

It was a warm spring afternoon. The sort of day and, yes, the time of year for taking the past out of its locked drawer, giving it a dusting down and deciding what to keep and what to chuck away. Christmas in Trevarne had been and gone; Easter too. And now Claire had returned to London to help her parents pack up their belongings ready for their move to Hawthorn House.

So it was a time for the dusting down of the past in more ways than one. This was Claire's childhood home, her roots were here, and her parents had lived here all her life. It would be a big move for them all.

It hadn't taken her parents long to make up their minds in favour of Hawthorn House. Dead set against it at first, Patricia Trent had suddenly capitulated, almost physically folded, and agreed it was the best thing for all concerned. With a sigh of relief – for her father's revelations of three months before had lain pretty heavily on her shoulders – Claire made the necessary arrangements, since her mother didn't seem capable of doing very much at all. But the estate agent had done a good job. Within six weeks contracts were signed. Patricia and Josh were moving to Cornwall.

This could be, Claire thought, the very last time she walked down this road. Once her parents had moved, there would surely be no reason for her to return. Oh, she could still come back to London as a visitor – to wander the art galleries or see Laura perhaps – but she wouldn't be coming back to Highton Road, and there would be no reason at all for her to walk past Jerry's place. London was at the point of shifting firmly into her past. She might not belong in Cornwall, but she certainly wouldn't belong here any more. She would soon be rootless, weightless. Free, perhaps?

She felt a thudding of the heart as she walked past Roper's, still there, still looking much the same, and still with some red tinsel in the window left over from Christmas, or even from the Christmas before? Who could tell? The window display didn't seem to have changed since she was a teenager: there were the same old plastic dolls – Roper's hadn't discovered Barbies, although they'd been around over thirty years – notice-board complete with dog-eared postcards, and advertisements from various chocolate manufacturers.

Perhaps it was just this sense of finality in the air, which had as much to do with her parents moving as anything else, that had persuaded Claire to walk this way just one more time, to see what had happened to the place where she'd spent so many hours, hanging around looking at bikes, watching Jerry as he worked on their engines, dreaming her days away.

Her nerves built, layer upon tangled layer, until she drew level with the place. Carefully she remained on the other side of the road, not looking, not properly, until she was there, right opposite. As if she thought it would be – like Roper's – still the same, stuck in time, with an un-aged Jerry cleaning up the latest part exchange he'd acquired, muttering, '*Why don't they look after them proper?*' under his breath.

But garish lights and a red and white sign outside the shop

proclaimed the change. It was all a bit of a shock. Claire's nerves exploded into a mad burst of laughter. Jerry's motor-cycle shop had become a takeaway pizza joint. And delivery, according to the sign, was free.

She crossed over, pretending an absorbing interest in the menu taped on the door . . . Eastern Experience, featuring chicken tikka and mango chutney; the Inferno, promising lots of hot green chillies; and Burning Desire, red peppers and tuna. And, good God, even baked bean and sausage, otherwise known as Kids' Delight. What was the world of takeaway pizzas coming to?

The memory of Jerry's tatty kitchen came into her head – ripped lino splattered with oil, stained white tiles with a green and nasty something sprouting from the grout, a small makeshift cooker with only one ring operational, a rusty toaster and a scaled-up kettle. How many times had she bought some sliced white from the shop down the road and made him toast and marmalade in there? Unhygienic, perhaps, but she couldn't recall caring in the least. It was mind-boggling that the place was now a restaurant – someone must have had considerable vision to contemplate such a transformation.

Claire turned from the brightly lit shop window, her gaze moving to the brick wall outside – the same wall she'd sat on to watch Jerry tinkering with the bikes. Hour after hour. The same wall where she'd been sitting when she first decided she was going to get a bike. And not just the kind of bike Jerry said was suitable for girls – with a kind of sneer as if girls were only fit to ride pillion or at a pinch a small and tinny Honda. But a real bike.

She closed her eyes and remembered the first time she ever saw a Triumph Bonneville. *This is what I call a bike.* Jerry's pale eyes had lit up with a strange kind of glow.

She'd jumped to her feet, and when he went inside to get some tools she'd walked up to that bike, run her fingers lightly across the red and white fuel tank, over the Triumph embossed in silver lettering.

Some machine . . . Lightly, she touched the chrome. It might be stained now, but she knew Jerry would have it gleaming before he

189

sold it on. Gleaming so bright she'd be able to see her own face in it.

Jerry eyed her strangely as he emerged from the workshop. 'Like her, do yer?'

'Oh, yes,' she breathed. 'She's beautiful.'

'Triumphs are bloody unreliable these days,' Jerry moaned, getting down on his hands and knees and poking around under the fuel tank. 'But that's half the fun.' His voice was muffled. 'And they're still class all right.'

'One day . . .' Claire said. 'I'm gonna . . .'

'Do what?' He looked up at her, wiped his hands with an oily rag.

She grinned, slightly embarrassed. 'Oh, nothing.' That was when she decided what she wanted. Nothing would stop her, she wouldn't let it.

'One day you're gonna do what?'

'Oh . . .' She shrugged. 'I can dream.'

Jerry laughed. 'Oh, yeah, you can do that.' He spat on the ground. 'You're a weird one, you are.'

She held her head high and looked away from him. 'I might surprise you, one day.'

'You won't surprise me.' He poked his head back under the bike. 'Seems to me you might do anything.'

And yes, it had been a dream, and she had made it come true.

She had got her Triumph Bonneville. But they'd trampled on her dream, hadn't they? They'd trampled on her dream and made it dirty, so that she couldn't have it any more. They'd taken that dream away from her – Jerry and the others. And she'd never get it back, even now . . .

Claire sighed as she turned away. Even now it was lost to her. It had felt like a new life beginning, the day she'd got her Triumph Bonneville, the bike of her dreams, a bike of her own, a real bike. But the new life had been a joke, and a bloody rotten one at that.

And what had happened to Jerry? She ran her fingertips along the wall as she had once run them along the chrome lines of the Bonneville. What had happened to the man who had biking in his veins? A motor-cycle enthusiast, he had called himself. She must remember the distinction. But at the time it hadn't seemed to matter all that much.

Jerry must still be a mechanic – she couldn't imagine him doing anything else. And he wouldn't be retired – not yet, he'd always seemed a lot older but he'd only been about ten years her senior, she supposed.

Poor Jerry. She knew he'd felt bad. He'd had conflicting loyalties too, he'd had his membership of the biking fraternity to protect. These guys came to his shop, for pity's sake. His credibility had been on the line. And so although he seemed to have a choice – she'd thought, back then, he had a choice for sure – she supposed he hadn't, not really. To make the choice that *she*'d demanded of him would have taken more courage than poor Jerry had ever possessed. He was only a bike mechanic. He'd never pretended to be a hero.

He'd sent her a note afterwards – *Sorry, kid. They said they only wanted to get to know you. I never thought. I never wanted you to get hurt*. That was it.

She'd ripped it up but she'd never forget the words. Of course he could have prevented it, and so she could never really forgive him. But still she wondered where he was now. It must have taken something momentous to get him out of his bike shop – it was his world. It meant everything to Jerry, that place did. That and his bike.

Somewhat subdued, and strangely disappointed that she'd never see Jerry's place again, Claire walked slowly up Highton Road to number twenty two, and rang her parents' door-bell.

There was a long pause before she heard slow footsteps. Her father opened the door.

'Hi, Dad.' She moved to kiss him, saw the recognition falter in his eyes.

'Claire.' He smiled, but didn't invite her in. He stood on the doorstep jingling the money in his pocket.

His last note of independence, she thought. Gently she took his arm. How long before he didn't know her at all? 'How are you, Dad?' She steered him back inside.

He didn't reply.

'Where's Mum?'

Vaguely, Josh glanced around the room. 'I don't know.'

'I'll go and find her.'

She installed her father in his favourite chair. 'You stay here,' she told him. 'I'll be back in a minute.' She was talking to him like a child, Claire realised. She was losing sight of the boundaries just like before – child, parent, parent, child. The roles were becoming confused.

'All right.' He smiled.

She patted his hand, not knowing what to say, what else to do. She had accused Patricia of wanting to mother him, of needing to mother him, of being obsessive about it. But what other kind of love was possible now?

Still, she couldn't stay there with him; even the look of him was hurting her. He seemed more bent, his eyes were lighter, his hair more grey, his skin dry and thick like old brown paper. He had slipped a long way downhill in the last six months.

She ran up the stairs. 'Mum?'

'Claire.'

They embraced – another surprise. Her mother looked tired, but otherwise much the same, thank God. She had not regained the smart I've-just-had-a-perm-so-don't-touch-me look that she'd worn in years gone by. And it suited her – she had become approachable at last.

Claire looked around. There were clothes everywhere – on the bed, on the floor, in packing cases. 'How's it going?'

'I had three wardrobes full.' Patricia seemed apologetic, and they both laughed. 'I shan't keep them all, of course.'

'I should hope not. Oxfam would be devastated.'

'It's chaos . . .' Patricia lifted her hands in despair. 'But it helps to be doing something.'

'Let me give you a hand.' Claire found a spare box and started packing bedroom ornaments, wrapping each one carefully in newspaper. She picked up a tiny porcelain ballet dancer. Vividly, she remembered it from her childhood. Once, she had thought it the most beautiful thing.

Patricia sat back on her heels and watched her. 'Freddie phoned.' She smiled, the expression in her eyes becoming distant, and much younger.

'How is he?' In the last few months Claire had given up trying to contact him. Freddie, it seemed, could only be contacted when he wanted to be.

'He seems better.'

Claire knew what she meant. Better. More settled. Freddie was not only difficult to get hold of, but he also tended to be on another planet half the time. Better – in her mother's terms – meant able to hold a rational conversation, she supposed. Perhaps it meant he had a steady girlfriend, maybe even a job. Who was to know? Even Freddie could change.

'He said we should go over and visit.'

'Freddie said that?' Claire was surprised. They had all adored him, but Freddie had never been one for family. He had discarded those sort of ties a long time ago, and made it clear that independence came first.

Patricia nodded. 'Oh, yes, he was most insistent.'

'Maybe *he* should come over here,' Claire suggested. Wasn't it time for Freddie to lend a hand?

Patricia eyed her reprovingly. No one else had ever been allowed to criticise her son. 'He said that we'd like Amsterdam,' she told Claire. 'He has a friend who runs one of those botel things. A hotel that actually floats in the harbour. The best of both worlds, Freddie says.' She looked wistful.

'Maybe you should go, then.' Claire thought of her mother travelling with her father and his glazed baffled eyes. 'I could take both of you there,' she said. She would like to see Freddie too; it had been too long. 'After you've settled into Hawthorn House. In the summer maybe.' Perhaps David might come . . .

'I always wanted to go to Amsterdam. Your father never did.' Patricia looked Claire square in the eye.

It wasn't a complaint, she realised, simply a statement of fact. But after what her father had told her about wanting to live in Cornwall, it made her wonder. Who had been holding back whom? 'If you don't go, you'll probably regret it.'

And it would do Patricia good to have a break. Freddie's infuriating brand of irresponsibility had apparently refreshed her mother in the past. Freddie had always known instinctively how to get through that brittle veneer she wore.

'I'm worried, Claire.'

She looked up. Her mother seemed scared, and definitely not brittle at all.

What must this be like for her? Claire held out her arms. 'We'll manage, Mum. Between us, we'll manage.' For a moment they clung together, gently rocking from side to side. And this was her mother, Claire thought, whom she had never been close to at all.

On that first night, Claire blocked off the sound of the television with a novel. She accepted the weak milky coffee with a digestive biscuit at ten o'clock, and went meekly to bed.

But by the second night she couldn't contain her restlessness. Her own life, back in Trevarne, was so full with the art and theatre community project – now called *The Witches of Trevarne, the Event* – that the enforced stillness of Highton Road, accompanied by the cacophony of the TV, the clackety-clack of her mother's knitting needles in frenzied action, and her father's snores, was driving her crazy. She missed something – action, perhaps, David, or maybe even Gary and Max.

She decided to phone Laura.

'Darling! You're in London. How wonderful!' Laura certainly sounded enthusiastic enough. And was it Claire's imagination or did she sound a touch desperate too?

'So I thought we could meet up if you're free.' So what if she did sound desperate? Claire, too, was desperate, and she didn't mind admitting it.

'Good idea. We could do a club.'

'Oh, I don't know about that . . .' Claire had been thinking more along the lines of a visit to Laura's flat armed with a bottle of red plonk so they could drown their sorrows and recapture an old friendship. She must be getting old. 'I'm not sure I'd be up to it.' Her clubbing days were long gone and, besides, she'd been rooting through boxes in her parents' attic all day. Even a hot shower hadn't removed the sensation of grime and cobwebs in her hair.

'Go on.' Laura became more enthusiastic still. 'Course you're up to it. You're a woman in her prime alone in London. You can't tell me you don't fancy a night out?'

'Well . . .' Actually, I don't, Claire thought, and neither did she feel in her prime, but she *was* beginning to feel a bit of a kill-joy. Perhaps it was Laura who fancied a night out, Laura who had no one to go with. She shouldn't let her down.

'Come on, Claire, what's happened to you?' An edge crept into Laura's voice. 'You always used to be up for anything.'

Claire looked down at her cheesecloth skirt with maroon dolphins woven into it. 'I'm not exactly dressed for a night-club,' she hedged.

'Nonsense!' She could tell that Laura had scented victory. 'Dress is irrelevant.' She giggled. 'So long as you're not naked. We'll go to Webster's. That's terribly informal. And the lights are dim.'

'Oh, all right.' Claire thought of her mother's three wardrobefuls. In contrast she had nothing to change into, only jeans that were dusty and stained from the tea that Josh had spilt over them this afternoon. 'Say nine o'clock?'

'Perfect. Let's meet in the bar opposite. Remember? The Shattered Soldier.'

Claire remembered. And she felt a bit like a shattered soldier herself. She also remembered what Laura had told her about the old George and Dragon, and felt a twinge of nostalgia. She should have saved Laura for when she was feeling younger and more energetic – if that time ever came. She didn't feel up to shattered soldiers: her mother's favourite soap might even be preferable and, what was worse, she hadn't bothered to bring her mascara.

The George and Dragon was depressingly unrecognisable and, despite what she'd said, Laura was immaculately turned out in a little black dress and full make-up. She stared for a full minute at Claire's dolphin skirt as they perched on black and chrome bar stools. And to think, Claire sat up straighter, that this used to be a lounge bar. It was only a few minutes before Laura suggested they make their way into Webster's. Where the lights are dim, Claire reminded herself, with a small smile.

But Laura cheered up when they got inside, perhaps because the place was full – there were even some unaccompanied men.

'How's life?' she asked, as they sat down with their drinks. 'Has Cornwall changed? You were bored silly the last time I saw you.'

'Was I?' For the life of her, Claire couldn't remember that.

'Oh, yes.' Laura giggled and crossed her legs with a provocative swish of black-stockinged thigh – presumably for the benefit of the young blond chap at the next table. To Claire he didn't look much older than Ben.

Primly she kept her legs together but in the dolphin skirt why should she worry? The thing was practically swishing around her ankles.

'All you had on your mind was that dreadful summer fête you were organising.' Laura sounded patronising.

Had she, Claire, really been that boring? All Laura had seemed to have on her mind was her boss and married lover, Claire recalled.

'Well, it's turned into a community project now,' she told her. 'It's called *The Witches of Trevarne*.' And much amusement that had caused in the village. She, Gary and Max had spent the whole of one Saturday in the library at Bodmin to come up with that one.

'Heavens.' Laura smiled at the blond man.

'We raked up some old Cornish story,' Claire told her. 'It might only be a legend, no one's sure, but these three women were jailed at Bodmin, and then they were ducked in the river just outside Trevarne – you know, tied to a chair to see if they had special powers sufficient to save themselves with.'

'Drown or be tried as a witch?' Laura murmured, getting out a cigarette and bending forward slightly to light it, providing a flash of cleavage for the blond man.

'That's it.' She ploughed on, although clearly Laura was not enthralled. 'So we're using this story about the three witches as a kind of base for a play . . .'

'Very *Macbeth*.' Laura smirked.

'Mmm. For a play that Max is writing, which will involve the whole community. Everyone can take part, even if it's just in a crowd scene, and the play will centre around Trevarne's own history.'

Laura became more attentive. 'Max?'

'Ah.' Claire wasn't sure how to explain Max. He had remained a bit of an enigma. 'He's a founder member of our committee. There're three of us, you see.'

'But not three witches.' Laura's smile showed her teeth.

'No, not three witches. Me, Max and Gary.'

'Two men.' Laura exhaled. 'Clever old you.'

'Hardly. Gary's gay.'

'And Max?' Laura's mouth seemed to curl round the word.

And Max? She might well ask. Claire remembered the sensuality of his massage that had left her feeling confused rather than relaxed. She remembered the afternoon Richard Stickler had come on to her in his study, the shock, walking to Gary's cottage. She remembered Max's concern and the touch of his hands as he tucked the blanket over her, the brush of his fingertips on her shoulders, the feel of his arms around her. Encircled, safe, warm . . . Oh, God, and she remembered how she had responded to him. How could she forget? Unthinking, her defences down – thanks to Richard Stickler and his bloody wandering hands. But something in her had needed Max Stockwell, something had wanted Max Stockwell, longed to reach out to him. And what was more, he knew it. She had realised that back on New Year's Eve, if she hadn't realised before. He knew it all right.

'Max is just a friend,' she told Laura.

'Oh, yeah?' Laura looked unconvinced. She lit another cigarette.

Was it that obvious? Claire smiled, remembering Max's face on New Year's Eve. So pleased with himself, he'd been.

They were all in the Lionheart – half the village it seemed like. People were clustered around David in one corner of the bar, and Claire was conscious of an urge to escape, a feeling of suffocation. Gary was there too – he and David had formed a somewhat wary friendship since David's intervention on the night the governors, parents and staff had met to discuss his future in the school. Both he and Max were grateful to David, of course they were. And naturally David had got involved with the project, taking charge of the scenery, doing some papier-mâché with the kids for various props.

But while David was friendly with Gary, to Max he seemed more hostile. So much for trust . . . He had suspected Claire and *Gary* at first, she reminded herself, until finding out Gary was gay. And now he seemed to feel the same way about Max. Some people might say that was a touch paranoid, others that he had good reason . . . Perhaps he didn't believe Max Stockwell could possibly be just a friend, any more than Laura did.

And what was he exactly? That, Claire couldn't admit – even to herself.

So, in the Lionheart on New Year's Eve, Claire escaped up to the bar. Within a few moments Max was standing close beside her.

'Another?'

'Please.' She watched him signal to Louise who was serving.

He turned to her and grinned.

'You look happy.' Someone passing by jostled them closer. Claire shivered. After a couple of glasses of white wine, and with his body brushing against her own, she was already finding him a touch too close for comfort.

'I should be. We're celebrating,' he told her.

'Who is?' She looked around for the group he was with, but people had merged in a way they only seemed to manage on New Year's Eve. Having rather too much to drink and playing party games were both great levellers.

'*We* are,' he repeated. He put an arm around her shoulders and she couldn't bring herself to object. Why should she? They were friends, even if it did feel a whole lot nicer than it should do. 'We're rich.'

'Oh, sure.' He must have had more to drink than she'd thought. The truth was that the one thing holding up the theatre project at this moment in time, was – as Richard had gloomily predicted – lack of money. Funding from outside sources was hard to find and would take much too long for the money to be of any use for this summer's event. They had obtained a few local sponsors, but they were small-time – nowhere near enough for the kind of project they had in mind.

It was noisy in the pub and Max was now so close that Claire could feel his warm breath on her cheek. His arm had remained around her, he was as close as a lover . . .

'Iris Stickler has come up trumps,' he whispered in her ear.

A hot rush accompanied his whisper. It channelled speedily through to various parts of her anatomy. 'Iris?' She pulled away, caught the glow in his dark blue eyes. That was *too* close.

He patted his jacket pocket. 'She's written us a cheque.'

Claire's eyes gleamed in response. 'How much?'

'Mercenary baggage.' But he was grinning again. 'Ten grand.'

'Ten thousand?' Claire gaped at him. 'Are you serious?' Her mind went into overdrive. They might be a small concern, but they could sure use ten thousand. A sum like that could solve most of their problems.

'Kind of her, wasn't it?'

'More than kind . . .' But why on earth should Iris help them? Richard had never exactly given the project *his* wholehearted support. Did he know about this? Surely he couldn't possibly . . .

Claire looked around the pub for Iris. She was staying close to her husband's side tonight, but . . . A thought occurred to her. Could Iris possibly be supporting them simply because Richard *wasn't*? Could she have misjudged the woman?

Max looked smug. 'I suppose we'll have to commemorate her donation in some way.'

'A statue outside the Old Barn?' Claire giggled. 'Shall I ask David to start working on it?'

'Far too subtle. How about her name in neon lights by the entrance?'

'Or free advertisements for her jam in every programme?'

They laughed.

'So . . .' And suddenly he was leaning too close to her again. She caught the scent of his aftershave – sexy, Paco Rabanne, she'd seen it in Gary's bathroom when she was round there last week. It wasn't Gary's style at all. 'As I told you. We're celebrating.'

Their faces were almost touching. Without warning, without hesitation he kissed her full on the lips.

'Max!' She emerged from his embrace wide-eyed, out of breath, turned on, and feeling she should have struggled a little. Not that she'd wanted to . . . But they were in a crowded pub and she had a reputation to maintain – as well as a husband.

'Sorry.' He laughed, looked unrepentant. 'But it is New Year's Eve.'

Yes, she thought. It is New Year's Eve. She would probably have to fend off several kisses at midnight. But not kisses like that one . . .

She glanced across the lounge bar. David was staring at her, his expression unfathomable, not telling her if he had seen the kiss. She checked her watch. Yes, it was New Year's Eve, but it was still an hour and a half away from midnight.

After New Year's Eve she was more super-aware of Max than ever: the atmosphere seemed charged when he was in the room, sometimes even before he got there – the anticipation was enough. And after New Year's Eve, she waited. She supposed she was waiting for another kiss. Every day she half expected him to say something, to do something, to change their relationship in some way. But he never did. And Claire wasn't sure how she would have reacted if he had. How could she possibly know what would have happened if they had been alone that night . . . if she had been free to respond?

But Max never stepped over the line again, and instead of lovers, they became good friends. In much the same way that she and Gary were friends, she told herself. But it wasn't the same. Of course it would never be the same, because there was more. And they both knew it.

Claire realised that Laura was eyeing her strangely. 'How about you?' she asked brightly. 'Are things still on with Graham?

'God, no.' Laura took a slug of her wine.

'What happened?'

Laura closed her eyes for a second as if she were shutting out the memory. She opened them and refocused. 'His wife found out.'

'Oh.'

'So he dropped me like a ton of the proverbial.'

'I see. Poor old you.' Laura didn't *look* upset, but she seemed to have become expert at hiding her emotions. 'It must make things difficult at work,' Claire ventured.

'I had to leave.' Laura leant closer towards her as the volume of music increased. 'And that was something I hadn't accounted for.'

'Accounted for?'

'I didn't dream I'd end up losing my job. When I told her.'

'Told who what?' Claire was confused.

'I told Frances. About us. Graham and me.'

Their eyes met. Claire tried to imagine what could have induced Laura to do such a thing, and failed miserably. But, then, she had never been involved with a married man, thank God.

'How else could I get him to leave her?' Laura demanded. 'He had everything he wanted. But what about me? My only hope was to let Frances know what a shit he was. I had to tell her.'

Claire sipped her drink. 'And was it worth it?'

'Of course it bloody wasn't.' Laura stubbed her cigarette out viciously in the ashtray. 'I told you. I lost Graham and my job. She played the forgiving wife and he was eternally grateful. That was me out. Bye-bye, Laura.' She gave a mocking little wave.

'And the job?' Claire asked.

'Everyone knew about us. It was far too humiliating to stay.' Her voice rose with bitterness. 'I tell you, Claire, the other woman never wins.'

As Laura went for more drinks, Claire glanced over to where the blond young man sat drinking beer, smiling lazily. As Laura approached he looked her up and down: just another woman he might honour with his bed and body tonight, Claire guessed, noting that the top two buttons of his shirt were undone. And she was glad she was no longer part of this singles market-place, that he wasn't eyeing *her* up and down. Not much chance with the dolphin skirt – it was positively shrieking *She used to be an old hippie*, although she hadn't been, not really. Still . . . she was glad to be out of it.

Claire watched Laura sway past, take a step back, bend slightly to say something to him. She saw the man smile.

Laura and Claire left the club soon afterwards. Claire said she was tired and Laura voiced no objections. But, in truth, they seemed to have little left to say. Outside the club they kissed one another on the cheek and said goodbye. Claire knew Laura wouldn't want to share a taxi – she had seen the young blond man follow them out of the club, seen Laura's reaction too. He was standing on the steps just watching them, assessing Laura as if she were a percentage of something, not even a trophy, certainly not a woman.

'Laura . . .'

'Don't, Claire.' She touched her arm. 'I'm a big girl now. I've got my own life to live, thanks very much.'

And Claire knew that she and Laura had lost whatever they'd had in common, whatever had kept their friendship intact. She would probably never see Laura again, and worse, she wasn't at all convinced that she even wanted to.

Chapter 14

The day of the summer fête was drawing nearer, when Claire let herself out of their cottage one Sunday. She walked down the path and headed for the river. David was busy as usual, but for once, she was grateful for the solitude. Things had been so hectic lately she'd hardly had a minute to herself.

The bark of a dog in the distance alerted her, however. She spotted Aunt Emily, Aunt Veronica and three pugs approaching like a deputation down the hill.

'Help.' Claire dodged into Marion Chaney's front garden – and not for the first time either, she thought, remembering the night she'd seen David walking back from the pub with Fern. She took refuge behind Marion's beautiful flowering cherry, whose laden branches almost brushed the ground.

'I really must prune it this year.' Marion, wearing old slacks and gardening gloves, with her greying hair tied in a blue headscarf, had also been hidden by the tree, Claire realised, and was now watching her with amusement.

Claire put a finger to her lips and nodded towards the road. 'The aunts,' she whispered.

Further explanation was unnecessary. Instant understanding dawned on Marion's kind face. 'Right you are.' She bent to resume her weeding.

'Verges need doing,' Claire heard Emily boom. 'And I'll bet my bottom dollar these hedges weren't pruned last autumn. What do we have a council for? Just tell me that!'

'I don't know, dear,' Veronica replied.

Claire realised a pug was sniffing around her ankles. 'Shit.'

It sneezed on her shoe.

'Go away,' she hissed.

'Jasper!' Emily's voice could surely be heard for miles around. 'Jasper. Here, boy!'

The dog yapped but didn't budge, and behind them Marion stifled a giggle.

'Piss off,' Claire muttered. Perhaps even dogs understood the force of expletives.

'He knows he's found a friend.' Marion tried to shoo him away.

'Fine, but I'm not into doggy devotion.' Claire looked up to see Emily looming on the other side of the flowering cherry. She was wearing a pink plastic mac although the sun was shining, and clearly, there was now no escape.

'Claire? What on earth . . .?'

'Er . . .' I'm helping Marion do her weeding, sounded a little weak.

'She came round to sort out the eleven-year-olds' SATS results with me,' Marion provided smoothly, although she failed to mention why that involved crouching behind the tree in the front garden, 'but I simply had to finish forking over this bed. You know how it is . . .'

Emily's expression informed them that, no, she did not know how it was, neither did she wish to.

Claire giggled. 'You weren't looking for me, were you, Aunt Emily?'

'I most certainly am.' Emily reversed the tense and took her arm. 'David in?'

With a helpless backward glance at Marion, Claire found herself propelled out of the garden, and heading back home, the pug still snuffling at her ankles.

'Marion and I –' she began.

'This will only take a few minutes.'

'What will?' Claire shook herself out of Emily's vice-like grip, and surreptitiously aimed a threatening side kick at the pug. He hadn't stopped spitting at her once. It was perfectly revolting. Pugs weren't dogs at all; they were fat rats in hair shirts.

'I wasn't going to get involved.' Emily stood by while Claire scrabbled in her jeans' pocket for the house key. 'Were we, Veronica?'

'Oh, no, we didn't think it was our sort of thing at all,' Veronica fluttered. 'You see . . .'

'But Fern and David said it was for the good of the community,' Emily broke in.

She made them sound like one entity, Claire thought. FernanDavid. Stuck like glue.

'And as we are valued members of the community . . .'

Inwardly, Claire groaned. So much for her quiet walk by the river. Instead, she would have to make them tea. Tea would mean Veronica noting they had no cake. Maybe she'd even produce her own lemon curd speciality from under her blue plastic mac. A horrible thought. Claire shuddered.

'I decided that I would offer our services.' She nodded at Veronica.

Claire realised what Emily was on about. 'For the Event?' she asked weakly. Emily might be perfect as one of the witches, but Max would say it was type-casting and, anyway, the witches' parts were all taken.

'For the market,' Emily corrected. 'A home-made cake stall. Guess the weight of the –'

'Sounds good to me.' Claire knew better than to argue.

'So is David in?'

'I don't know. I –'

'And tea would be nice, dear.' Emily swept through to the kitchen, a ship in full sail. 'Don't you *know* when he's in? David!' she shouted.

'He might be outside,' Claire offered.

'Can't you go and see?'

There was absolutely no way that Claire would admit to the aunts that she no longer just wandered in and out of David's workshop, and they simply wouldn't understand the word sanctuary.

She stepped outside the back door. 'David!' she yelled.

She could hear the soft whirr of his potter's wheel, and music on the radio. But there was no reply. 'Dav-id!' she yelled again.

Inside the kitchen she saw Emily open one of the kitchen

cupboards and have a quick poke around, probably looking for cake or proof she used tea-bags. Why *should* she have to put up with David's horrible relations?

She marched over to the workshop door, rapped loudly. 'David!'

'What?' None of the noises inside the workshop showed any signs of ceasing.

'Your aunts are here.' And I'm going out, she was about to say, but he flung open the door and they stood, face to face, glaring at each other.

There was a very long silence.

I loved this man, Claire thought. Once, he had seemed to be everything she wanted. And now they barely spoke, or they shouted, or they held polite conversations about each other's day. Around them their marriage was gently crumbling, and they did nothing. What would she have, here in their cottage, when Ben left? Her life in Trevarne was now full, but it had nothing to do with David, nothing to do with her own husband.

She looked at David. Not hers, never hers. More Fern's than hers, more the river's or the villagers' of Trevarne. Not hers, never hers, she was second best, always had been, always would be.

David scratched the black and ginger stubble on his jaw, depositing a smudge of clay, as he invariably did. Claire wasn't sure when he had last shaved, she didn't even know that much about him. In the winter he often grew a beard, in the summer he usually shaved it off. Right now he seemed stuck in between the two.

'What do they want?' he asked her.

'Tea, I suppose.' She was just about to enlarge on this, when behind him she spotted a whole set of Fern's watercolours framed, with pride of position on the wall. There were none in the house, he obviously wanted them to himself. He probably gazed at them while he worked, she thought.

'I'm going out.' She turned on her heel.

'Claire?'

'Yes?' For a moment, as she looked back at him, she thought she saw a spark of . . . not quite anger in his brown eyes, something else, but she wasn't sure what.

'Nothing.' He glanced away. 'I'll see you later.'

She didn't bother to answer. She went back into the kitchen where Emily had dredged up a packet of fruit shortcake biscuits. 'David's coming in,' she said. 'I must fly.'

But she didn't think either of them noticed her going. David had entered the room close behind her and, as always, he commanded their full attention.

Claire paused outside the cottage, aware that Marion had spoken the truth – she was supposed to be sorting out the SATs results with her. Graphs and national averages, explanations and praise, mingled with a dash of healthy publicity for the school – all that paraphernalia. But a gardening-gloved hand waved at her as she approached the flowering cherry for the second time that afternoon.

'Later will do, my dear. This bed really does need weeding.'

Claire heaved a sigh of relief. 'Thanks, Marion. Around seven?'

'Fine.'

Claire walked on. Just past the bridge she took the path on her left that wound down to the river-bank. It was steep and slippery but she knew that, once there, the path would be passable since there had not been enough heavy rain for the river to be swollen. This narrow path walked hand in hand with the river for about four miles, and it was along this stretch that anglers, including David, often came fishing.

But some of us just like to walk, Claire thought, as she edged between the heavy birch trees to reach the first flat rocks. Fishing was peaceful, she supposed, but did man always have to hunt, even if he put most of his catch back in the river afterwards?

The river was wide at this point but the water was clear, and as she peered past the tall clumps of reeds and the plant that looked like giant rhubarb, she could make out the odd dark fish swaying and snaking along with the current, the speckled pink-grey of the granite on the river bed.

She walked along the bank for another mile or so, approaching the bend in the river where the character of the trees and the grassland changed to something altogether more marshy. There were masses of buttercups and other bog plants here and, despite her gum boots, Claire had to be careful where she put her feet. She had been caught out before – this part of the river-bank was more like a swamp – but she ploughed on for she knew that round the bend was a stack of granite just perfect for contemplating the world, life in general, and one of the prettiest riverside views in Cornwall.

She paused to catch her breath. This was a rare afternoon off for Claire and the others. Auditions had taken place under Max's jurisdiction, the main cast had been selected, and rehearsals for *The Witches of Trevarne* were now well under way. With the money donated by Iris Stickler had come a new lease of life for the project, and at least three-quarters of the population of the village had got involved in one way or another – which was pretty good going, Claire reckoned. Even Maureen Jones had hinted she might be available to stitch a costume or two so long as her husband and son were prominent among the witches-in-the-stocks crowd scene.

The necessary face-lift of the Old Barn was in the capable hands of the local painter and decorator, Claire had organised the helpers for the market that would accompany the play – in the interval and afterwards – although she would now have to fit David's aunts into the scheme of things. It was the market that they hoped would forge the separate parts – the crafts, the painting exhibition, the play – into one single event.

As for her parents, Josh and Patricia seemed to have settled into Hawthorn House. Ben was still working, had passed his motor-bike test and had come home a few weeks ago with the results of all that saving . . .

'I've got it, Mum.' His eyes were shining.

'Where?' She knew exactly what he was referring to. He had told her he was answering a for-sale ad but she didn't know any details, had been half afraid to ask.

'In the drive.' He grinned.

Tentatively, she opened the back door, closed her eyes for a second. Then she opened them.

She saw a powerful bike. But it wasn't a Triumph Bonneville as she had half hoped, half dreaded. She moved closer. Sporty . . . lightweight . . . three cylinders, this was no classic bike. In the driveway was a – rather gorgeous, she had to admit – peacock of a Japanese motor-cycle. A Kawasaki KH 750 cc.

'What do you think?' Ben was so proud, he reminded her so much of herself when she first got her Bonnie.

'Lovely,' she said.

He laughed, perhaps knowing she wasn't entirely sincere. 'I know it's not exactly what *you* would choose for me, Mum,' he said.

Little did he know . . .

Yes, things were going quite well. And Claire felt that if she didn't spoil things by breathing too deeply or speaking too fast, she'd soon be able to see the light at the end of the proverbial tunnel.

She wouldn't think about David. She felt more relaxed than she had done for ages. All that, and now this perfect solitude, a riverside walk. Peace . . .

But she paused as she rounded the bend, staring with dismay in front of her. There was a lone figure up ahead and he was destroying that solitude. Who would have believed it?

He was sitting on the very slab of flat granite she'd had in her mind's eye, shoulders hunched slightly, moodily chucking pebbles into the water, apparently careless for both the tranquillity of the river and the feelings of the fish.

And yet he, too, seemed to be lost in a world of his own, oblivious to her presence, apparently unaware that he was no longer alone. And so instead of retreating – which was her first instinct – Claire took the rare opportunity of watching Max Stockwell when he had no idea he was being observed.

He was wearing a waxy green coat and blue jeans, and his dark hair was untidy, falling over his face and the corduroy collar of his coat. But it was the expression on that face that fascinated Claire – she wished she were closer so she could tell for sure. Max looked unhappy, his mouth was turned down at the corners, his attitude was evident from the careless way he was tossing those pebbles into the clear grey-green water.

She sensed there was a part of the peace he just didn't want. Max was in the mood to make ripples, and she wouldn't disturb him.

Silently, she turned to go, but it was a second too late.

'Claire.'

Reluctantly she turned back, walked a little closer. 'Hello, Max.'

209

'This looks like an assignation,' he said. But she'd accurately gauged his mood; he didn't smile at his own joke.

'Am I disturbing you?'

'You couldn't.' By now she was close enough to register the intensity of his eyes.

She shivered. 'This is a good place to come when you want to be alone.'

'I'll bear that in mind.' His sarcastic tone affirmed that it had been a pretty dumb thing to say.

She knew that she should walk on, but she found herself unable to; she needed to know what was troubling him. 'Say if you want me to go.' She spoke softly.

He didn't reply, but she felt him watching her as she climbed on to the stack of rocks beside him, sat down and hugged her knees close to her chest. Together they stared into the water.

They remained silent for the next few minutes, but it was a companionable silence; she felt no compulsion to speak, although when they were working together on the art and theatre project they chatted incessantly, debating, advising, arguing sometimes. They often disagreed, but it never seemed to matter – they always managed to thrash it out somehow.

'Are you getting fed up with it?' she asked at last.

'With what?' His mouth twisted into a faint smile.

'With the theatre project.' He did, after all, have a life outside Trevarne and its community arts. He had family, he must have friends – a girlfriend, maybe – and he had the freelance writing work he did from time to time, *to keep the wolf from the door*, he said. But Claire realised that while she seemed to know him well, she actually knew very little about this man.

'It's keeping me busy enough, that's for sure. Busier than I expected.'

He was right. And if they'd known what they were taking on, would they have contemplated it? Would she and Max just have been ships passing in the night, instead of . . . well, whatever they had become?

'I suppose there's no going back,' he said. 'We're too far into it.'

Her stomach flipped in panic. 'It sounds as if you want to go back.' It hadn't been so much the words themselves as some quality in his voice. As if he'd had it with Trevarne, with them all. She wondered if she sounded scared. She certainly felt it.

Max turned to look at her. 'Would you care?'

'Yes, yes, of course I would. The Event –' Her voice was weak.

'Don't worry about the Event,' he cut in. 'I'll see it through.'

She was conscious of a flood of relief. Of course, he had said he would, he'd never let them down. None of it would have happened without Max. 'And then?'

'That's in the future.' He got to his feet and held out a hand to help her up. 'I don't worry about what the future holds. I just wait and let it happen.'

'I see.' She felt the warmth of his hand, and wondered if he was warning her. Reminding her not to depend on him. He was an itinerant, remember, she told herself sternly. Look at Freddie. Don't ever expect an itinerant man to stay around for long.

'Who knows what's ahead?' Once more he was staring at her until, embarrassed, she turned away.

'And the past?' she asked him. 'Are you concerned with that?' She found she was curious, very curious. And if she didn't ask him now ... The sun was warm on her back. Claire pulled off her sweater, and slung it over her shoulders.

'How do you mean?'

'I've often wondered what's in your past,' she confessed. 'You never talk about it.'

He chucked another pebble, with slightly more force this time. 'Dreams. I always had too many damned dreams.'

'Didn't we all?' Claire jumped off the granite stack and took a few steps up the path. She shouldn't intrude on his dreams.

'What were yours?' he called after her.

She thought of Jerry and her first Triumph Bonneville. That feeling of freedom and excitement, the instant whip of emotions. 'I asked first.'

He grinned, jumped off the rock to join her and together they began to walk back down the path. 'I worked in London for a while,' he told her. 'I always dreamed I could make it as an actor. Even when I was a kid that's all I ever wanted to do. I used to think about it when we went surfing at Trebarwith Strand – that was my dreaming time, you know.'

She knew.

'Yeah, I used to grab my board and ride those waves.' He laughed at himself. 'It was all a question of timing. You feel on top of everything when you're riding those waves.'

'But you never made *Baywatch*.' She giggled.

He poked her in the ribs. 'I never had the body for it.'

Claire risked a quick glance, but decided that the less she thought about his body the better. Maybe she was odd, but she'd rather have dark, thin and wiry than sun-tanned muscle any day.

She thought of the way he looked when he was organising the theatre group, the mobile features that came alive when he was reading a script. If he weren't such a good director she would have voted for Max to take the male lead in the witches project. 'So what happened to all those dreams about acting?' she asked him.

He bent to avoid a low branch. 'I got to be a really good waiter.'

She smiled. 'But you've done lots of work in the theatre. Don't pretend you haven't. It shows.'

'I did a bit of TV work.' He pulled a face. 'No speaking parts and no lucky breaks either. There was some other stuff around, but I wanted out of London.'

Claire mentally noted that at least they had this much in common.

'So I went down to the south coast,' he told her. 'I got some work there, joined a small theatre group for a while and travelled around. I went back to Sussex, helped set up a couple of theatre companies, got into the writing side, even did some directing.' He swerved to avoid a clump of nettles. 'That enough for you?'

'What did you like doing best?' She was loving this – listening to him talking about his work.

'The setting up of something from nothing,' he replied promptly. No doubt there, then.

'But you always left?'

She felt him glance sharply towards her. 'It's the building up from next to nothing that's the challenge. When other people think it's hopeless. When they all give up. It's the creating. After that . . .'

'Do you always need a challenge?' Claire wondered if she, too, was a challenge. She was married, after all.

'Perhaps I do.' He was giving her no clues. 'When the job's done there always seem to be plenty of reasons to leave, to move on to pastures new. Once the thing's up and running, it tends to lose its appeal.' He glanced at her again. 'And there's never enough reason to stay.'

Claire picked her way across a boggy section of the path. How many reasons would a man like this need? 'So you've never been married?'

He laughed.

'Is it so funny?' Her boot sank two inches deep in mud and she swore softly.

'It is to me.' He grabbed her hand and yanked her out on to the dry path. 'Marriage isn't for the likes of me.'

'What's wrong with marriage?' He hadn't let go of her hand. His fingers were interlaced with hers, and she felt her voice catch in her throat.

'What's right with it?' He stopped walking as if he were asking *her* this particular question, her and no one else. He looked at her, seemed to realise that he was still holding her hand and dropped it abruptly. 'And, anyway, I told you before. I like travelling around. It suits me. I wouldn't want to be tied down.'

'And you don't want commitment,' she teased.

He responded to the tone of her voice. 'I'd be quite capable of commitment. If that was what I wanted.'

'But it isn't?' Claire knew they were approaching a dangerous subject here. This was getting very personal. She was getting very personal.

He turned towards her, his hand lightly brushed her arm. 'Perhaps I've never met anyone worth committing to.'

'You surprise me.' Because she was so conscious of this touch, she smiled, but in response his eyes grew angry.

'And what about you, Claire? Talking of commitment, shouldn't you be having a cosy Sunday-afternoon stroll with your husband instead of asking me all these intimate questions?'

He had a point. Once, she had often walked this stretch with David. Even when Ben was small, they had taken him in a backpack, and he had always fallen asleep by the time they reached the stack of rocks where she'd just found Max, his head cuddled into David's neck. But she couldn't remember the last time. 'We're not tied to one another,' she said.

Max's voice became harsher still. 'But doesn't David know how much of a risk he's taking? Letting you wander around like this on your own?'

She knew he wanted to hurt, she'd clearly gone too far, but still her own anger flared briefly. 'I think I'm quite capable of making my own decisions about my own wandering.'

'Oh, I'm sure you are.' His laughter was harsh.

'And besides,' she sounded awfully prim, 'David and I have separate interests.'

'Very convenient.'

'Sometimes.' She walked on a little faster, but although his stride hardly lengthened he kept up with her.

'So what does David like doing?' he asked.

'Fishing.' Only yesterday she had woken up to the unmistakable whiff of melting plastic coming from the kitchen. Perhaps it seemed quite reasonable to anglers to model a plastic water-boatman with a fine scalpel, and balance it on a bread knife over the hob to soften the plastic, thus removing all those sharp edges. But to Claire it seemed little short of insane. 'And pottery.' And Fern, of course, but she wouldn't go into that.

'And what do you like, Claire?'

'You know what I like.' Abruptly, she came to a stop. They had reached the point where the path started the uphill climb back to the bridge. They would not be alone for very much longer.

The silence stretched between them, not companionable this time. He wasn't touching her but he seemed very close, not towering over her as David did, only a couple of inches taller, and that intensity had returned to his eyes.

As she watched him, wondering, he seemed to hesitate. Then he placed a hand firmly on her shoulder.

'Claire . . .' He trailed the touch down until his fingertips reached her bare forearm.

She closed her eyes. When Max was near she seemed wired up

to desire. But how much of it was frustration? How much was fantasy?

'Are you happy, Claire?' She heard the words ringing in her ears as if they were coming from some great distance away. *Are you happy, Claire?* It was one of David's questions too. Was she happy? That was the question, then. That was what it all came down to – Cornwall, David, her marriage, this man.

'I must go.' She pulled away from him, striding up the hill, not waiting for him to follow.

'Do you always run away?' He was laughing at her now, she could hear the laughter in his voice, if she looked back she'd see it on his face. He hadn't followed her, he had remained there, standing at the bottom of the hill.

Claire turned round, still walking. She remembered New Year's Eve and that kiss . . . She had wondered then how she would have responded if they had been alone, and now she had her answer apparently. She would run away. She wouldn't allow it to happen. Although she wanted him . . .

She looked at him and she knew her eyes were scared. Running away . . . Despite what her father had told her, too often it seemed the only solution.

'No, I'm not happy,' she said. There, now he knew. And much good it would do him.

She turned round again, walked on, back to the bridge, back to the cottage she shared with David. No, she wasn't happy.

That was the way things were. She wasn't happy. And still she had to run.

Chapter 15

———◆———

'God, I need you.'

Claire did not wake up. In fact, she barely heard, though in the darkness she struggled silently with the voice.

In her head, it repeated the same words. 'God, I need you.'

There was desperation, she recognised that.

Movement – in the room, in the bed, in her mind, whatever – brought her closer to the surface of waking, and she struggled against that too, fought for her right to sleep, for surely it wouldn't be a good idea to wake, to acknowledge . . .?

But the touch – coming from nowhere – clamping on her thigh so securely, as if the thigh weren't hers at all, was the end of all that.

She fought against the touch, against the darkness. 'No . . .'

But the hand moved on. Both hands were on her now, not as soft as they seemed, inhuman, cruel, holding her down, wanting what was not freely given, pulling her flimsy nightdress up over her hips, her breasts. The hands were pushing her apart, trying to find their way inside her. She was scared. A mouth fastened on her breast.

'No!' she shrieked, pure terror and gut reaction. She was back there . . .

Feeling his hot hands ripping at her clothes, sliding over her skin, bruising her flesh, bruising her mind. His wet mouth grinning.

'No!'

The Triumph Bonneville swept along the road, swallowing the miles, obeying her every touch, the engine sweet and yielding beneath her, as Claire rode out towards Dorking.

In front of her she saw Jerry – weaving in and out of traffic, cruising across the carriageway, showing off. There was nothing unusual about this Sunday afternoon for Claire often rode out this way with Jerry, and he always liked to show off. It was, maybe, two hours later than usual, that was all.

If Jerry had ever wanted to develop their friendship into something more, then he had never let her know it. And she suspected that Jerry knew their only link would ever be biking. Still, he brought her here often, and Claire didn't complain. She loved it.

But she sensed that for Jerry the Dorking trips had more significance. Each trip was part of an important ritual – cruising the carriageways between roundabouts, taking those deceptive bends too fast, hanging out in the café with the other bikers talking . . . well, talking bikes. Jerry probably spent most of his week anticipating Sunday afternoon.

But Claire wasn't interested in belonging to a pack. For her, biking was only a part of her life, the part that provided the ultimate excitement, yes, but still only one compartment. Aside from the Bonnie, she had her job, she had other friends like Laura with whom she went night-clubbing and gallery-visiting, she had her family, she even had the smooth boyfriends who regularly bought her flowers and took her to wine bars in Chelsea.

And it wasn't as if she needed a companion when she went out on the Bonnie – she could get the essential ingredients from the bike, the road and the feel of her own tight leathers. But she had to admit that it did rather add to the thrill when there were two or three bikers, sometimes more. Competing for speed, taking over the road, a group of them, wild, hungry, powerful, and maybe a little bit crazy too.

On this late Sunday afternoon they were soon joined by three other bikes. With the Bonnie, Claire managed to hold her own in the speed department, then Jerry made a signal and she followed him off the dual carriageway and along the slip road that led to the café. Today he had tired of the game rather earlier than usual.

She pulled off her crash helmet and shook out her hair. There were always bikers at this café – it had gained itself a name for that,

being perfectly placed in relation to the roundabouts and bends.
But there were fewer people around today, and it wasn't yet the
summer season when families with children and caravans stopped
here for a break on the way from London to some holiday
destination.

They stopped here but she couldn't help observing that they often
remained in their cars or made a quick dash to the loos and back.
Bikers were not, Claire noted, regarded as either respectable or
safe. It was all very well for Jerry to make distinctions between
those who were genuinely interested in all aspects of motor-cycles,
and those who were simply after Hell's Angel status. But when they
all wore black leather, how could you tell the difference? Even
Claire had some difficulty with that one.

'Pretty good, huh? It's better when the roads are quiet, ain't it?'
Jerry undid the zip of his jacket and took a look around him. He
glanced back at the main road where the other three bikers were
still racing. There was a strange expression on his thin face. In
retrospect, she might have called it fear.

'D'you want a coffee?' Claire asked him.

He seemed reluctant. 'D'you want one then?'

'Course I do.' Didn't they always have coffee before riding back?
'Yeah, all right. Just a quick one.'

She took the coffee back out to the car park, because it was
traditional not to drink it inside the café. Instead they would slouch
around outside with the bikes, admiring other machines, faintly
sneering at anything with four wheels.

Claire saw that Jerry was deep in conversation with three other
bikers, glanced at the bikes beside them and realised they were the
same three they'd been riding with earlier.

When she approached with the two coffees, the three of them
looked across, seeming surprised. But Claire was used to that. A
girl – especially one of five feet four – riding a Triumph Bonneville
650cc was very much a rarity. Usually Jerry looked quite proud to
be seen with her; today he looked uncomfortable, even embarrassed.

'No. No, she's not,' he was saying as she joined them. Not what?
Not his girlfriend?

'We didn't suss you back there.' The biggest of the three gestured

219

towards the main road and gave her an admiring look. 'Thought you was a fella.'

'Yeah?' Claire accepted this as a compliment, one that she'd also become used to.

'Introduce us, then.' The big bloke glared at Jerry, who did not look happy, not at all.

Claire was puzzled.

'Claire, this is Stan, Roger, Ade,' he muttered. He'd clearly come across them before – in Jerry's line of business that was hardly surprising. But, equally clearly, they weren't mates.

'Hi.' She kept her distance, the first flicker of unease making her feel slightly queasy. She looked down at the murky liquid in the polystyrene cup. Or maybe it was just the coffee.

'You like the old Bonnie, then.' Stan leered – although whether at her or at the bike, Claire wasn't quite sure.

'She rides well.' Claire tried eye contact with Jerry, but he avoided this. A bad sign.

'I bet she bloody does.' Stan leered once more, although this time she was pretty sure he didn't have biking on his mind.

Claire came to a decision. She wasn't entirely naïve. She'd seen enough of the world to trust certain basic instincts. She chucked the coffee, scrunched the polystyrene cup in her fist and threw it towards a nearby waste-bin. 'I think I'll be off.'

'Yeah.' Jerry sounded eager. 'All right, babe.'

Claire frowned. He never called her that. 'Are you coming?'

'Nah.' The thin scrawny one called Ade smirked. 'It's just the way he's standing, ain't it, Jerry?'

'I'm gonna stick around for a bit.' Jerry seemed apologetic.

'Okay.' Claire moved towards the Bonnie, but the big bloke, Stan, blocked her path.

'Slow down, will yer?'

'Excuse me?'

'Why, what you done?'

It was all good-humoured banter, Claire was used to that too. These guys wouldn't win *Brain of Britain*, but the truth was that most bikers – even those who were aiming for the Hell's Angel league – were harmless enough. Bikers might have gained a reputation but, in her experience, men who liked bikes were as varied as the bikes themselves. Most of them were safe – if not entirely respectable. Still . . . there was something she didn't like about this bunch, especially the one called Stan.

She pulled on her crash helmet.

'How come you're riding a big boy's bike, then?' Stan demanded, not moving out of her way.

'I can handle it.'

'She wants something big and hot between her legs,' one of the other two remarked. All three laughed – heavy male laughter.

Claire looked around. The café and car park were practically deserted. A family of four had pulled up a minute ago and departed just as quickly when they'd seen the bikers. There was another group of blokes in the café, but they were some distance from her, and when she looked towards them they turned away.

But there was always –

She heard the sound of voices, the crunch of gravel and her head spun around. 'Where's Jerry going?' It didn't sound like her voice at all.

'For a slash.' Stan moved in closer. Only he and Ade remained.

The one called Roger was walking off with Jerry, and they were already thirty yards away. She thought of shouting for Jerry to come back, but that was daft, wasn't it?

'Are you going to let me pass?' Claire heard the words rise in panic. Suddenly she was fighting for self-control.

Stan only grinned at her.

'Jerry will be back any minute.' It was supposed to be a warning. But she had an awful premonition that Jerry wouldn't be back – at least, not yet.

'He's not your man, though, is he, babe?' Stan's hair was long, dark and greasy, his eyebrows were thick and didn't stop over the bridge of his nose but ran on into each other like hairy centipedes doing battle. The smile on his face made it more threatening than a smile should.

'No. No, he's not.' What difference did that make?

'So why haven't you got some guy looking out for you, then, babe?'

Did she need one? She wondered if she could head-butt him now that she was wearing her helmet, shoot him a swift kick to the shins, or risk a knee-jerk between the legs. Would she make it to the Bonnie before he recovered? If not, she was dead meat.

But she still might have tried it, if Ade hadn't been standing there, watching, leaning casually against her bike.

Claire felt like screaming at him to get off it, to take his dirty hands away from it. But she must stay calm. Nothing had happened, she could get out of this situation, no problem.

'My boyfriend's catching up with us later,' she said.

Stan laughed again. 'That ain't what your little friend Jerry told us just now.'

God help her . . . Jerry was out of sight. Her lips were dry. She licked them nervously. 'What did Jerry tell you?'

'That you was all alone.' He leant closer as he said this, mouthing the words.

She smelt the stale alcohol on his breath. 'So?'

'I don't like people to be lonely.'

'I didn't say I was lonely.' She took a step forward.

'Hold it right there.' The tone changed. He grabbed her arm, pinching the flesh.

Claire struggled to shake him off.

'Bloody wildcat.' He tore at the crash helmet, ripped it off, hurting her neck.

She yelped. 'Hey! What the hell –?'

But he was holding her by both arms now. 'Just hold on a minute, will yer?'

She stopped struggling, but her breath was coming fast and shallow, her chest heaving. A dry fear was dipping through her, making her want to vomit.

'You're a pretty girl.'

She stared back at him. 'What do you want?'

He leaned forward, hissing in her ear, 'I just wanna talk to you. I just wanna be friendly.'

'I've got to go.'

'Not so fast.' His strength took her by surprise.

Up until that moment she had still thought he was just messing about. It was a damned nuisance, and she was scared. But it wasn't exactly dangerous. Not on a Sunday afternoon in a café car park within sight of the main road.

But in seconds he and Ade had grabbed her – one on each side – heaving her up so that her feet weren't even touching the ground. She screamed, kicked out at them as they half carried her ten yards into the bushes bordering the car park. She fought to get free, but they only gripped harder still, fingers digging into her flesh. Her throat was numb, her scream was shifting into pure panic, she twisted her shoulders, her hips, desperately flailing her legs.

But as they reached the cover of the bushes Stan slapped her face and clamped his huge hand over her mouth.

She thought she would choke. She couldn't breathe.

'Pity to spoil a pretty face.' With his other hand he stroked her cheek with cool fingers.

Ade had her arms pinioned behind her. He tried to force her down to the ground. She struggled.

The hand on her mouth tasted of oil and she tried to get her teeth free to bite it, but he wasn't having any, he pressed harder and harder, forcing her lips, her teeth, back into her gums.

She kicked hard, out in front of her, fighting for real now.

Stan swore under his breath. 'I wouldn't, babe,' he said, softly.

And it was then that she realised the cool touch on her cheek wasn't his fingers at all. It was the blade of a flick-knife, and it was caressing her skin.

'Don't scream,' Stan said. 'Or you won't be pretty no more.' He pressed the other side of the blade gently into her skin, and at the same time released the pressure on her mouth.

Claire remained silent. She had to. She stared at the knife.

'I'm warning you,' he said, sliding open the zip of her jacket. 'A little baby like this one can do a whole lot of damage.'

She looked back, from him to the knife. How could this be happening to her?

He tore open the front of her blouse, the delicate fabric ripped and a button pinged to the ground. She stared at it.

'We only want a bit of fun . . . And since you like playing big boys' games . . .' He began to breathe more heavily, he glanced at

Ade, undid the fly of his dirty blue jeans, pushed her down on the ground.

He raped her, while Ade held her shoulders and arms, kept the knife at her throat and laughed softly.

'No . . .' Claire only whispered.

She didn't struggle. She only stared at his grinning wet lips, at the thick eyebrows, at the dark tails of greasy hair stuck with sweat on his forehead. And she tried to pretend she wasn't there, she couldn't be there. But it was too real. She was there, all right.

His hands were cruel on her skin. But she didn't struggle, she didn't dare.

She half expected Ade to take his turn when Stan was finished, but he just kicked her lightly with his boot and then walked away, because she was just a crumpled-up piece of body now, she wasn't Claire Trent any longer.

She heard the sound of the engines revving, she heard them go.

And she wished she'd carried on fighting, she wished she'd fought to the death rather than this. Feeling as she felt now, afterwards, lying there in the bushes.

'No . . .' she groaned. 'Please, no.' She shuddered. 'Leave me alone!'

'I don't know how long I can go on like this, Claire.'

It didn't fit. Claire struggled towards consciousness. She switched on the light.

David was lying in the bed beside her. His eyes were squeezed tightly shut. There were tears on his cheeks.

Claire couldn't take it in for a moment. She had never seen David cry before. And slowly she began to realise about the voice and the touch.

'David . . .' Warily she put her hand on his shoulder. 'I didn't mean –' She stopped in mid-sentence. Didn't mean no?

David sat up in bed, climbed out and stumbled to the door. When he reached it, he turned. 'There's one thing you've always been good at, Claire.'

She waited.

'Making it clear what you mean.' He laughed bitterly. 'And you don't even need words to do it.'

* * *

She must have dozed off eventually, but in the morning when she woke, David was still not with her.

Wearily, Claire got up, but before she could find David, before she could try to explain or do anything, the phone rang.

She took it downstairs in the hall. Listened to the words. Spoke briefly. Put down the phone.

'Who was it?' David came in through the back way. His eyes were bleary, his hair a mess. He'd slept in the workshop, she registered.

'The warden at Hawthorn House.'

'What's happened?'

Claire couldn't speak. Instead, she crumpled into his arms.

It was the best way to go, they all told her afterwards.

Claire and David drove to Hawthorn House, collected Patricia, talked to the GP. Arrangements were already in hand – proceeding smoothly, Claire thought. Unlike weddings, no one can change their minds.

'It was the best way to go,' the warden with the sympathetic eyes told them.

And she supposed it was. To die from a stroke was to stop functioning. A massive hit to the system, a wipe-out. Claire couldn't imagine it, but she supposed they were right. So she said the same thing to her mother. 'He had no pain. It was the best way to go.'

Patricia was very calm. 'I know that, dear,' she said.

Claire supported her mother and leant on David. He took over, arranged her life, her mother's life, their days. He made tea, cooked meals that weren't eaten, filtered phone calls, fended off visitors, told everyone who must be told. And he didn't mention what had happened between them that night.

This was grief, Claire thought. Not knowing what to do next. Needing someone else to do it all. Non-functioning. Her father – the father she remembered – would deeply disapprove.

On the night before the funeral, Claire couldn't sleep. She got up, made herself some cocoa, hugged the silence to herself.

After a bit of sitting and thinking she got dressed and wandered outside. She stood in their driveway in her jeans with the kitchen door wide open behind her, and stared into the darkness.

The shape of the bike seemed to loom and mock her. Ben's motor-bike . . .

She moved towards it, found herself stroking the chrome as she had once stroked her own Bonneville, admiring the line, the curves, the sleek power. It was very different. It was a Japanese bike and proud of it; it seemed to declare its identity to the world, and loudly – one of a pack, just as the Bonneville had been a true individual.

She walked back inside the kitchen, picked up Ben's keys from the table where he always threw them, took his crash helmet from the side, his black leather jacket from the coat hook in the hall and went back out. It was two in the morning.

Walking around it, she surveyed the bike. She supposed it was all right in its own way. It wasn't a class act, it would never be what Claire – and Jerry – called a real bike. But . . . times had changed. Ben was not Claire.

She smiled. At least no one could accuse her son of being a motor-cycle snob. And at least he wasn't scared of going his own way.

She turned the key and kick-started the engine, just to get the feel of it. When the Bonnie's engine had been cold, she'd always had to tickle it – put a bit of petrol in the carburettor – to get it to start. But in contrast, this bike started smoothly and easily. And she realised that it wasn't a bad sound at all.

She pulled on the crash helmet and sat astride the bike. Just for a moment, she told herself. To relive the sensations. To remember how it had felt before she started running away.

But the throb of the engine seemed to be telling her something. It was irresistible.

With a quick glance back at the cottage, and a brief frisson of guilt for not asking her son's permission, she revved up the engine, increased the power, moved off into the darkness, into the night, feeling it almost like before – the soft velvet of the night-time hours, the bike picking up speed. The thrill . . .

Claire thought that her father might approve of this. He never wanted her to run. He didn't believe in hugging things inside. He was all for letting go.

She rode the bike up to the main road, crossed over and headed towards Camelford. It was wonderful. And on the bike, sweeping along the narrow, deserted Cornish lanes, she worked it out of her system in a way she hadn't been able to before – the rape, her marriage, her father's death.

When she eventually got back home she could hardly see for the tears that were stinging her eyes, making her throat burn. It was mad, but it was good; she had needed the release.

She cried for her father and his last months of frustrated communication, loss of memory and pain. It was unfair to imagine he'd had no pain; every day had hurt him because its events were no sooner lived than lost. Because the truth was that Claire *didn't* think it was the best way to go – unprepared and unable to understand – and she wouldn't pretend otherwise, not for any of them. She would face up to it. Because that was the way it sometimes was, and he would be better off now, she hoped. He had been released himself.

And then she cried for herself – on and on, she cried, knowing it was self-pity but unable to stop. She cried for herself – fatherless, and with a marriage that was slowly falling apart.

Chapter 16

—————◆◆◆—————

'Come on, everyone. I want to hear you putting it all into the final song.' Behind the scenes Max was addressing the cast in a low voice, for although this was an interval, people were already coming back to their seats.

Claire caught his eye and smiled.

'Everything you've got, mind.'

They tried to repress their laughter, but she could see they were bubbling with the euphoria of a project nearing completion, a project that had gone amazingly well.

The Old Barn was packed for this, the last performance of the week, and they hadn't needed to read the review in the local paper to know that the play, with its strange combination of the amateur and the professional, had been a great success.

Claire held up her hand. 'And don't forget what's happening afterwards. This is an Event, remember. In every sense of the word.'

Voices buzzed around her.

'I want everyone outside in the market. Mingling with your public, darlings. You can do it.'

They laughed once more.

'In full costume,' she warned them in a soft voice. 'I don't want to see anyone taking off the greasepaint for a while yet.'

'Honestly, Claire, where's your sense of compassion?' demanded witch number one.

'You know I don't have one, Marion.'

'I'll never be able to hold my head up in this village again.'

But Claire could see that Marion was relishing every minute. Lots of them were. For many of the actors it was the first time they had taken part in a stage play or performed to an audience – the first time they'd ever had a script to learn or felt the flutter of first-night nerves. But the professionals had helped the amateurs, and Max . . . Claire watched him with affection, Max had helped everyone. They wouldn't have been able to do any of it without Max Stockwell.

When the full cast were assembled on stage, Claire peeped through the curtains. The chairs they'd procured for performances at the Old Barn might not be the most comfortable in the world, but no one seemed to be fidgeting; they were all engrossed in the play.

Trevarne had always been besieged by tourists in the summer. But never like this. She had been astounded at the numbers they'd brought in.

The first night they'd held an open-air flower market, and the heavens had been on their side – it hadn't rained. On Tuesday night after the play and in the interval they'd had a book event, on Wednesday a poetry experience, on Thursday weaving, needlecraft and stained glass, and on Friday a local artists' evening.

It had turned into a week-long mini-festival, and some of the people roped in to help had already been heard muttering about making it a fortnight next year.

Next year, Claire thought. It seemed incredible that all this could grow from such a small beginning. From a seed of enthusiasm – Max's – Iris's generosity, and a lot of hard work.

In the village hall tonight there was an arts and crafts exhibition that had been organised by David. And when Claire had wandered in earlier on, she'd found that due to local demand he was also giving lessons on how to throw your own pot, using his own traditional foot-operated wheel, rather than the electric one he favoured for his commercial work these days. He was offering a prize of a David Harrison special one-off earthenware planter for the most imaginative and aesthetically pleasing effort.

'You've had a lot of entries.' Claire was surprised at the number.

'That's because everyone will get their pot fired and personally delivered by yours truly,' he told her. 'They can't resist it.'

She stared at the rows of strange-looking clay artefacts on the shelves beside the potters' wheel. Room in David's kiln was a precious commodity. 'That lot will take you for ever.'

He shrugged. 'All in a good cause. They're paying a fiver a time.'

Nearby, Fern was doing face-painting, selling programmes for the art exhibition, and already placing sold stickers on many of the paintings. The work of their local craftsmen seemed to be very much in demand.

And on the village green was the market itself – everything from the tombola to the cake stall, fresh flowers, trash and treasure, giant raffle, and the inevitable preserves. Most of the helpers had even got involved enough to make a stab at a costume from the Middle Ages. There were, Claire observed, before sneaking back into the Old Barn for the final scene of the play, an awful lot of ragamuffins and peasants around.

The music rose to a crescendo.

There was a movement behind her and she sensed the presence of Max.

'Almost there,' he whispered.

She smiled at the tone of suspense, at the exhilaration she heard in his voice. This meant so much to him, not for Trevarne, she suspected, but for the satisfaction of a project achieving its potential.

'Well done, Max,' she whispered back. 'You've performed a miracle.'

He put his arm around her and she could feel his lips close to her hair. 'I didn't do it alone,' he murmured.

She closed her eyes to savour the moment of intimacy. They had not been alone since the day on the river-bank. They had seen each other often, but he had not come close to her and she had resisted the temptation of going to him. But now . . . Now she found herself unable to move away.

So much had changed for Claire. After the death of her father she'd had to deal with her own grief as well as help her mother deal with hers. And in that time she had turned instinctively to David as her support. Whatever else had happened between them, he was her husband, she had needed him.

But through it all, the play and the market, the Event of Trevarne, had never gone away. Claire threw herself into it with renewed vigour and almost to her surprise it was still there, this atmosphere of tension between herself and Max. As if unfinished, as if they were both still waiting . . .

Now, she could feel his elation. It was a shared sensation, it transferred itself to her, body to body, she drummed her foot to the music and to the rhythm of Max's light breathing. She moved closer into the warmth of the physical presence beside her, she felt his hands on her hair, she smelled the male scent of him, mingling with the mustiness of the costumes, with the greasepaint, with the smell of excitement that was in the air between them.

The song moved into its climax, he held her more tightly still, and they stood, watching the actors take their bows.

'Claire . . .' His lips were on her neck, his breath warm and sweet.

She knew it was just the thrill of the moment, but she wanted to give herself up to it, wanted to feel whatever Max was offering her – even if it possessed no permanence.

She thought she heard his name being spoken, his lips moved close to hers, and then the curtain was swept aside and Gary was standing there in front of them. Gary, in the costume of the man who ran Bodmin jail.

He stared at them, clearly absorbing the situation in one glance. Shock and disapproval rapidly replaced his wide smile. 'What the . . .?'

Claire and Max moved apart.

'They're calling for you.'

'Come on.' Max tried to pull Claire on to the stage with him, but she resisted.

'It's your night,' she whispered.

There was huge applause when he appeared. The audience was fired up, she realised. So was she, and she was proud as anything as she saw him take a bow, thank the cast and everyone working behind the scenes.

'And our special thanks must go to Claire Harrison,' he said, looking towards the wings.

She smiled. He wouldn't get her on stage like that. The performance had come to an end. It was time for her to slip away . . .

* * *

Outside in daylight it seemed weird to Claire that it was still fairly early on a Saturday evening. The market had yet to get into full swing.

She wandered from stall to stall, and after a while moved over to the tombola where Iris Stickler had already emerged from the theatre and was trying her hand.

'Thanks, Iris,' she said, to the almost unrecognisable woman in the black hat. If not for her, the project might never have got beyond the thinking stage.

'Nonsense,' said witch number two. 'I had the best time.'

Claire smiled. She would never have dared cast Iris in this role, but Max had suggested it and Iris had surprised them all with her willingness to throw herself into the part.

'Haven't enjoyed myself so much for years,' she chortled. 'Can't wait till next time.'

'I haven't finished doing the accounts yet,' Claire began, 'but we've done really well, much better than we ever expected to.'

'Good, good.'

'So I hope we'll be able to pay you back the money you –' She stopped at the horrified expression on Iris's face. What had she said?

'Oh, no, no.' Iris took her by the arm. 'I wouldn't dream of it, my dear.'

'But as a sponsor . . .'

'Whatever you want to call it . . . It was a gift.' She leant closer to Claire, her voice becoming confiding. 'I've always wanted to invest in the arts a bit more, you know, my dear.' She looked across to where Richard was marching purposefully towards them. 'To tell you the honest truth, Richard wouldn't know a Renoir from a Whistler, poor lamb. And I shouldn't say this to you as he's your boss.' She paused. 'But he can be a bit of an old fuddy duddy. And . . .' she shot Claire a speculative glance '. . . a right old gossip into the bargain, as you might have noticed yourself, my dear.'

'I see.' And Claire was beginning to. She had been wrong about Iris Stickler. Iris might have thrived on little else but jam-making at one time, but her talents had been wasted. With other things on her mind she had proved a pure gem. As for Richard, it was beginning to seem as if the Stickler might be the one responsible for Gary and Claire's fictional affair all the time . . .

'And to invest in the future of the arts gives me such a thrill,' Iris breathed. 'As your lovely Max said in the beginning, bringing Trevarne into the nineteen nineties of the performing-arts world. I like that.'

'He's not my Max,' Claire protested.

But Iris wasn't listening. She was accepting praise and a kiss on the cheek from her husband.

'You were wonderful.' Richard sounded surprised.

Perhaps, Claire thought, he might begin to appreciate his wife at last.

'And you may not have noticed it, my dear,' Iris turned back to Claire, 'but our Tiffany appears to be getting on rather well with your Ben.'

Claire spun round, surprised. Sure enough, Tiffany and Ben were deep in conversation by the pottery stall. Not again. *She's not worth it* – she tried to transfer the words her father had once spoken into her son's head. He was still recovering – she didn't want him hurt all over again.

'They'll be fine.' Iris patted Claire's arm and drifted away.

Claire's eyebrows rose as she looked back at Ben and Tiffany.

'But what on earth do they have in common?' Richard was frowning. 'I've never been able to understand that. All her friends belong in the academic world. She belongs in the academic world, for God's sake.' He seemed suddenly to realise that Claire was hanging on his every word.

'You knew.'

'Knew?'

'About Ben and Tiffany.' Claire was beginning to see even more hidden depths to Richard Stickler. And not ones that she would care to explore.

Richard brushed this aside. 'I try to have a finger on the pulse. Not much escapes me.'

'I bet.' But Claire would also bet that Richard had no idea how much money his wife had donated to the arts project. If he'd known that, he would have tried to put a stop to it, for sure.

Richard's eyes narrowed. 'Especially so far as my daughter is concerned.'

A thought occurred to her. 'Was it you? Did you wangle things so that Ben got his marching orders?' Claire had always had the feeling that the financial deal Richard had offered his daughter had more to it than simply a fear that she was missing valuable piano practice.

'And what if I did?' He smiled. 'Tiffany's only sixteen. And she knows on which side her bread's buttered.'

Poor Ben. How could he compete with a man as experienced as the Stickler? All Ben had going for him was a motor-bike and a gorgeous smile. Oh, yes, she'd almost forgotten. And love . . . 'Aren't you going to go over there and break up their conversation, then?' she asked Richard. 'Ben might corrupt her.'

'She's seen sense.' Richard seemed unaware of the insult Claire felt so keenly. 'She's my daughter, all right.'

Claire watched Tiffany place a hand on Ben's arm. 'I wouldn't be too sure about the seeing sense bit,' she said.

'No offence, Claire.' Regaining some tact, Richard put his smooth smile back into operation. 'I've got nothing against your Ben –'

'It doesn't sound like it,' she snapped. Ben was wonderful. Didn't he realise? No girl would be good enough for him.

'But there are more suitable young men for Tiffany.'

'Like Jeremy Sanderson?' she jeered. He didn't have his hair in a pony-tail for a start.

Richard smiled. 'Perhaps.' She could almost see him gauging the father's annual income, contacts and Conservative tendencies.

Claire's maternal instincts rose to the surface and into full-scale battle. 'So what's wrong with Ben?'

'Potentially, nothing. He could come good.' Richard sounded as if he were assessing a deal on the stock exchange. 'But the truth is, Claire, right now the boy doesn't seem to know where the hell he's going.'

Claire looked across at her son once more. That wasn't the half of it. She and David were also part of the equation – Friends of Trevarne perhaps, but even so, not quite making the grade. Still . . . she couldn't bear the Stickler's snobbery, but he was right about

Ben. If Ben wanted to go off travelling, why didn't he just go now that he had the bike to go on? What was he hanging on to, here in Cornwall? What was he waiting for?

Aunt Veronica and Aunt Emily were arguing by the cake stall.

'Fern said some small chocolate ones would be most popular,' Veronica was insisting. 'We should have listened.'

'Oh, Fern, Fern.' Emily stamped her foot. 'Sometimes I get sick to death of that name!' She stormed off, her face florid with anger, while Veronica stayed by the cake stall, watching helplessly.

'Anything wrong?' Claire had never seen Veronica standing up to her sister's bullying before. It was rather invigorating, she found.

'Sometimes . . .' Mournfully, Veronica took some coconut pyramids from a tin and began placing them carefully on a plate and doily. 'Sometimes she just doesn't understand.'

'Oh?'

But Veronica looked over Claire's shoulder, and her face lit up as if she'd just seen an unexpected band of sunshine. 'Oh, Fern . . .'

Claire might have guessed. She'd seen a similar expression on David's face from time to time.

'Hello, hello.' The two women, young and old, contrasting and yet with some quiet bond between them, kissed one another on the cheek.

A customer approached the stall and claimed Veronica's attention.

'I thought you were doing face-painting,' Claire remarked casually to Fern, as the request for apple sponge from witch number three was dealt with by Veronica.

'There was no one left to paint.' Fern smiled and, despite herself, Claire caught a glimpse of the girl's quiet charm. 'So I thought I'd see how these two were getting on,' she whispered.

'Not too well.' Claire pulled a face. 'I think they've just had a row.'

Fern sighed. 'One of many. Emily didn't really want to do cakes. She thought you'd ask her to preside over the raffle, and when you didn't, she took it out on poor Veronica.'

Claire thought she detected some bitterness in Fern's voice. 'She did drop a lot of hints but I already had someone,' she explained.

'And I thought cakes were more their thing.'

'She didn't want to share the cake stall,' Fern told her. 'She didn't want poor Veronica to shine.'

'Ah.' Claire thought of Veronica's lemon curd cake and wondered who was the deluded one. 'Why don't you leave?' she hissed.

'Leave?' Fern looked confused.

'Leave David's aunts' house.' Claire lowered her voice still further. She had never been able to understand why a girl like Fern should stay with two old bats like Emily and Veronica, no matter how grateful she was for her makeshift workshop and for being included in the bosom of their family.

'They've done a lot for me.' Fern moved away, with a quick glance at Veronica behind her.

'Yes, but . . .'

'Veronica,' Fern's eyes were sad, 'she needs me sometimes.'

By the time Claire got back to Ben, who was manning David's pottery stall, Tiffany Stickler had gone.

'How many have you sold?' Claire ran her fingers over the green-gold glaze of a flower jug. She would not ask Ben what he and Tiffany had been talking about. Take a step back, she reminded herself. It's his business.

'Quite a few, considering the inflated prices.' Ben picked up a planter. 'Eighty quid for this. Who does Dad think he's kidding?'

'But it's perfectly lovely.' David might simply say it took up a lot of room in the kiln, but that was reducing its value. The glaze was iridescent: behind the blues and greens were flecks of silver.

She took it from Ben, moved it so it caught the light. Like all David's pieces it had incredible depth. You thought you were getting what you saw on the surface – attractive enough, strong in shape, appealing in design. But there was always more. When you looked a little closer, you could appreciate the depth of the glaze, the thought and work that David had put into each individual piece. You looked and you had to touch.

Claire ran her fingertips lightly across the planter, enjoying its rough edges, its defiant celebration of imperfection. And sometimes you could catch just a hint of yourself reflected as you got closer and closer to the core of it. The more you looked at a piece, the more you wanted it; the longer you lived with it, the more you grew to love it . . .

Her eyes misted as her thoughts wandered, and Ben's muttered 'Give it back here, then' took her completely by surprise.

He grabbed at the planter, unwilling to relinquish it, she kept firm hold, their eyes met in mutual astonishment, they both conceded, let go, and the beautiful planter fell in pieces at their feet.

'Bloody hell,' said Ben. 'That's eighty quid down the drain, then.'

Appalled, Claire knelt, picking up the pieces with loving care. 'Give me a bag.'

'He won't be able to stick them together again.' But Ben obliged, merely treating her to one of his *my mother is crazy* looks.

'I know.'

By the time Claire got to the village hall, tears were streaming down her face.

David was packing up the clay pots and ornaments. He glanced at her. 'Claire? What on earth's the matter?'

She couldn't speak.

'Come here.' Gently he took her arm, led her to the potter's wheel, sat her down on his stool. 'What's happened?' He smoothed her hair from her face, wiped ineffectually at her tears. 'Tell me.'

She thrust the carrier bag towards him. 'This.' Suddenly it was all too much for her – exhaustion, she supposed. Her shoulders were shaking and the tears wouldn't stop coming.

'What?' Carefully he opened the bag, peered inside, took out a piece of earthenware pottery glazed with blue, green and silver. His voice softened. 'You're crying about this?'

'It was so beautiful.'

'Claire –' His voice broke, his arms were around her. 'I can make another one.'

Violently she shook her head. 'You can't. Not exactly the same.'

'No.' He looked thoughtful. 'Perhaps not exactly the same.' And then his tone changed once more, as if he were remembering. 'If you're worried about the money raised for the Event . . .'

'No.' But if it wasn't that, then what was it? Sane women didn't cry over a broken pot. All she knew was that David didn't understand – he wasn't letting himself understand. And he was as far away as ever. 'I'm tired.' She looked up at the shelves of battered clay. 'Will you really fire them all?'

'Course I will.' He seemed grateful for the change of subject, only shooting her a confused glance as he grabbed somebody's effort from the shelf, holding it up for appraisal.

'A constipated penguin?' Claire was struggling to regain her composure.

David laughed. 'Could you do any better?'

'Me?' She sniffed. 'I wouldn't have the energy right now.'

'Chicken.' He opened another box. 'You're half-way there. You're already sitting in the potter's seat. And I have a luscious lump of clay reserved specially for you.'

'Really?' Her throat still felt dry, the tears damp on her cheeks, but Claire managed a smile.

Once or twice in their early days David had suggested she have a go at throwing a pot.

'I'd throw it at you,' she had joked.

And no, she'd never tried. She had known she would be useless at it, had anticipated his laughter. David Harrison . . . His talent was such, his reputation so considerable – although she hadn't been aware of that when they'd first met – that she hadn't wanted to make a fool of herself in front of him, she supposed.

'Everyone else has had a go.' He knelt at her feet. His brown eyes were smiling, there were the usual smudges of dried clay on forehead and cheek. And his voice . . . The Cornish lilt of his voice surprised her most of all, because it was tender. She realised that it mattered to him, that he wanted her to do this, although she didn't for the life of her know why.

'All right.'

'That's my girl.' He fetched her an apron, tied it around her neck.

Max kissed me there, she thought to herself, ashamed. Am I still David's girl? Was I ever?

'Now, this is the way . . .'

He crouched beside her, showing her how to throw the clay with a crisp movement into the wheel, how to spin the wheel with her foot, how to use her hands to mould the soft material, how to splash on the water.

'A bit. Not too much. Not too often.'

Her left hand didn't have the foggiest what her right was doing. She frowned in concentration.

'Make them work together,' he urged. 'Fingers, hands, feet.'

She started to use fingers which were coated in wet clay, laughing as the clay suddenly shot out to one side then the other. 'It's got a life of its own.'

'It has.' He was serious. 'Feel it, Claire. Really feel it.'

He came nearer, standing behind her now, bending so that his head was close behind hers. She was aware of the scent of him, mingling with the heavy, earthy fragrance of the clay, the scent of damp river and bark, the woody fragrance that was David.

He put his hands gently over her hands, so that the three were moulding together – his hands, her hands, the wet sensual clay.

It was incredibly erotic. Claire found herself holding her breath. She felt tense, unable to believe this was her husband whose hands were almost seamlessly joining with her own. They were moving as one – and it was the first time for so long.

'Relax, Claire. Really feel it.'

And she could feel it. It seeped through the exhaustion, the confusion, the grief. She half leant back against him, his body solid, not moving, not bending now.

'It's gone very well, Claire,' he said.

'Yes, David.'

But he wasn't talking about her pot. As she gripped it more tightly in a spasm of nerves, the fragile shape collapsed in her fingers. 'Oh, hell.'

'Seems like fun.' Gary was standing in front of them, a strange look on his face.

Claire regarded him with what she hoped was a non-committal expression. 'I didn't hear you come in.' Gary seemed to be making a habit of silent entrances today. What must he be thinking of her? Claire shifted slightly away from David. 'It looks a mess,' she said ruefully.

'It's beautiful.' She couldn't tell if David were serious.

'Everyone's packing up,' Gary said. 'There's not a lot left for us to do.'

'That suits me.' Claire heaved herself to her feet, noticing how carefully David slid her effort off the wheel with his wire, placing it tenderly on the shelf to dry. He'd done that for everyone, she reminded herself.

'Shall we go, then?' David was standing beside her. 'I'll collect the rest tomorrow.'

'All right.' She was so tired, all she wanted was to collapse in a hot bath and then bed. It was as much as she could do to walk up the road, and yet still she was conscious of the sense of something missing. 'Is there any hope, David?' she asked him. For us, she meant.

He stiffened. 'You tell me.'

'I'd like to think so.'

As they reached the cottage, David put his arm around her. She leant her head back against his shoulder. Safe, she felt safe.

As he was putting his key in the lock, Claire looked around, behind her, and she thought she saw someone's shadow, saw someone watching them from the village green.

Max, she thought. After what had happened between them in the wings he would have been waiting for her. And now? Was he waiting for her still?

Chapter 17

———◆———

Despite sleeping like a zombie from the second her head hit the pillow, Claire felt as exhausted the following morning as she had the night before. But she had certain responsibilities today. Things that she must do.

As usual David was not beside her, but it wasn't because he'd gone fishing. To her surprise, she heard him whistling in the bathroom as she climbed out of bed. Perhaps he was tired too, she thought. Too tired for the five a.m. start that a morning's fishing required.

'Are you working today?' she asked him at breakfast. She was used to that, these summer Sundays – fishing or working, that was all there was.

'I don't think so.' He yawned.

'Cooking some of those pots, then?' Claire smiled back at him, strangely shy.

'They'll wait.'

He glanced across the table at her and she wriggled inside, uncomfortably aware of him, recalling the long-forgotten physical sensations they'd once shared – sensations that she had felt spinning between the two of them last night in the unlikely setting of the village hall. An unexpected closeness, a sensual touch, the feel of his warm hands and the smooth wet clay clinging to her skin. She wondered at herself for falling asleep so quickly. If she hadn't . . . would they have made love?

'I thought we could do something together,' he said.

She gazed at him in surprise. 'What?'

'Maybe go for a walk.'

Claire wasn't exactly sure whether a walk was all he was proposing, but David seemed different this morning, very different. 'All right.' She remembered Max and the river-bank. 'But not around here.'

'Rough Tor?' He smiled, and she knew he was thinking of her last outing with her father. 'The river at Bodmin? The Camel Trail?'

'David . . .' She didn't think she could stand him being so nice. 'There's something . . .'

'Can't it wait?' Abruptly he got to his feet, avoiding her gaze, stacking plates as if his life depended on it.

Claire watched him, taken aback by his reaction. What on earth had he expected her to tell him? 'I've got to go along to Gary's,' she said, thinking of those certain responsibilities that had been on her mind from her first moment of waking. 'Just for a few minutes. We've got a couple more things to sort out.' Like her emotional life for starters.

'The play must go on?' He rubbed his forehead in the characteristic gesture that usually deposited a smudge of clay on his face. 'Will it go on for ever, Claire? Can't you take a break now that it's over?'

'Well . . .' How could she explain to him that after yesterday, after everything that had passed between them, she simply must see Max? She owed it to him. And it wasn't yet over. 'It won't take long,' she said. 'I promise.'

Gary didn't seem in the least surprised to see her.

'So . . . how do you think it went?' she asked, following him inside the cottage, her stomach churning.

'Great. You know as well as I do that it went really well.' He seemed to read her mind. 'Max isn't here, Claire.'

'Oh.' She felt a sense of deflation. She'd psyched herself up for seeing him. Then an awful thought occurred to her. 'He hasn't left?' Left the village, she meant.

'He's gone out. He didn't say where he was going.' To her dismay, there was a certain accusation in Gary's expression.

She sank down on to the sofa. 'Is he all right?'

'Not really. Claire . . .' His voice softened.

'Don't, Gary.' What she did not need was Gary's agony-uncle routine.

'You need someone to tell you.'

Claire wasn't sure that she did. 'Tell me what?'

He sat down next to her. 'You know that now it's all finished, now that the arts centre has come into being, now that someone else will take over . . .'

She thought of what Max had told her. Creating something from nothing, that was the challenge. 'He'll leave. Yes, I do know.'

'He started packing this morning.'

'I see.' She felt the bleakness, tried to test it to see what she was so sad about. Was it losing their valuable threesome, the end of what they'd worked so hard for, the anti-climax that it was over? Was it losing Max? But how could it be losing Max? She'd never had him, had she? He was an itinerant – he'd never made any secret of that. He was a wanderer, and now he had done with them, he'd be off. *Wherever I lay my hat* . . . 'He didn't waste much time.' She was conscious of her own bitterness.

Gary took her hand. 'It isn't like that. I think you know that he's hurting, Claire.'

She stared at him, the knowledge dawning that not only had Max Stockwell come between herself and David, he had also come between her friendship with his brother. Perhaps that was just the sort of personality he was – he might not intend to, but he took over. And he was good at it too.

They had needed someone like Max Stockwell in Trevarne. No one could deny that after the success of the Event. But had *she* needed someone like Max Stockwell? He did seem to have complicated her life still further, and it hadn't been exactly plain sailing before.

'Nothing happened between us, Gary.'

He dropped her hand. 'How can you say that?'

'Well, when I say nothing . . .' She supposed it wasn't exactly true. Nothing tangible perhaps. No promises.

'I saw you, Claire.'

She remembered the scene backstage and the expression on Gary's face as he'd drawn back the curtain. They hadn't been in the least discreet. Oh, she could protest that the thrill of the moment had been responsible for that brief indiscretion. She could tell Gary that it had been a few mad seconds of foolish spontaneity. But that wouldn't be true either. Because the relationship between Claire and Max had been building up to this . . . whatever it was . . . all year. She knew it, and Max had known it too. Their responsibility. But she was the one who was married.

She tried to see it from Gary's perspective.

Max . . . holding her close, cradling her in his arms, stroking her hair, kissing her neck. Yes, they must have looked like lovers.

'A kiss,' she told him now, aware of a nudge of betrayal. 'That's all it was, Gary.'

Who did she think she was kidding? Supposing it had been David who had walked in on the scene? Would *he* ever have believed it was just a kiss?

'Don't give me that. It meant much more to Max.' Gary thumped his own chest with some passion. 'He cares for you, Claire. I've never seen him like this before.'

She was confused. 'But he always said he would go.'

'Why do you think he stayed in the first place?' Gary was practically yelling at her now.

'Because of the challenge of the play and the arts centre and the committee.' Claire wouldn't shoulder all the blame; she had never made any promises, and Max had never asked her to. Neither did she believe Max was hurting as much as Gary believed. Bruised ego, more like.

'Bullshit. It was because of you.'

'And because of you,' she reminded him. He seemed to have conveniently forgotten his own part in this. After all, the entire Event had only begun because they'd all been so resentful of the parents who had wanted Gary out of Trevarne school.

Gary was silent.

Claire wanted to be honest with him, he deserved that. But the truth was that she didn't even know how she felt. Not exactly. 'I care for Max.' That was certainly true.

Gary snorted disbelief.

'I really do.' She paused. 'But the truth is that I've been lonely.

David and I haven't had much of a marriage for years. He's got his interests, I've got mine. He's got his work . . .' And Fern, she thought. 'And my life has centered around Ben.'

For too long, she knew that now. And she realised that whatever else it had achieved for Trevarne, the new arts committee and the Event itself had given *her* life new meaning. She could look at that distance between herself and her son, and she could accept it. She would always love him – it was never over between mothers and sons – but she could step back. She could give him the space he needed.

'That's all very well, Claire.' Gary didn't seem convinced. 'But it's not Max's fault.'

'No.'

'You've encouraged him.' Gary looked quite fierce. 'And you're not in a position to do that. You never were. You've got ties.'

Claire got to her feet. 'I don't even *know* what position I'm in, damn it. I don't even know if I've got a marriage left.' Her breath was coming hard and fast.

'It didn't look like that last night.' Gary stared her out.

'Last night . . .' Infuriatingly, she blushed. 'Yes, we were getting on well. For the first time in God knows how long.' Had it been more than that? David wanted to spend time with her today, he had said so. And she found herself unable to dismiss the intensity of those long-forgotten sensations.

'But he's still your husband.'

'Yes. And last night was a one-off.' She sighed. 'David and I have been strangers for too long.' Because it wouldn't all come back, would it? It couldn't. Not just like that, not after all these years of resentment and growing apart. Wasn't that mere fantasising on her part?

'And Max?' he prompted. 'Where does Max come into it?'

'I've never used Max,' she told him, knowing that this was what Gary was accusing her of. 'Right from the start Max made me feel . . .' What exactly? 'Important. Valued. He reminded me of what my life used to be like.' She struggled to express her own half-formed emotions. Those memories . . . Some of them hadn't been easy to recall. Freedom, her days of riding the Triumph Bonneville,

life in the fast lane and life before David. And the excitement . . .
'He made me feel something I didn't expect to feel any more.'

Gary's expression showed some understanding at last. 'Sexuality
never goes away. It just lies dormant.'

She laughed. 'Well, mine seemed in permanent hibernation.'

'And your feelings for David?' She was conscious of his scrutiny.
'Are they in permanent hibernation?'

'I'm not sure if I still love him,' she admitted. 'I've always thought
it would just go on between us, I've never imagined it ending. I've
never wanted to actually . . .' She seemed unable to form the words.

'Leave him?'

She nodded.

'And now, Claire?' Gary took her hand once more. 'What do you
want to do now?'

'I don't know.' She and Max had shared something special, but
could there be a future to it? She had never thought so, always
assumed that all he'd ever wanted was a diversion – before he took
off to those pastures new he kept talking about. But now, after what
Gary had just told her, she wasn't so sure. Had he cared so very
much?

And as for David . . . He was her husband: how could she hurt
him? How could she ever leave him?

'You'd better make up your mind, Claire.' Gary squeezed her
hand. He could listen, but he wasn't offering any answers.

'I know.'

'Max will be leaving in the next few days. He's not going to
come to you.'

'I know that too.' Claire made her way to the door. He had as
good as told her that himself. 'I'll let myself out,' she told him.

Slowly she walked back to the cottage she shared with David.
She had to untangle her feelings. She had to find those answers.
And she needed time. But that was one commodity that apparently
she just didn't have.

All afternoon, Claire brooded. She and David walked to Rough
Tor, but it only brought back memories of her father. *You go and
see it for me*. His voice came back to her, speaking to Ben . . . And

now Josh Trent would never see it for himself, never enjoy Cornwall any more.

She knew she'd been about as much fun as a wet weekend.

'You don't know what to do with yourself, now you haven't got anyone to organise,' David told her at dinner.

'Maybe I should start organising the Christmas bazaar,' she joked. 'That seems to be what I'm best at.'

'God help us.' David heaped more potatoes on to his plate.

They ate in silence, Claire looking across at her son from time to time. He was very quiet tonight. 'What do you think, Ben?' she asked him at last. 'Got any ideas for me?'

He put down his knife and fork and met her gaze with his solemn blue-grey eyes. 'I shan't be around for Christmas, Mum,' he said.

Claire stopped mid-mouthful.

'You don't normally make plans that much in advance,' David said mildly. He got up to clear his plate, rested a hand briefly on Claire's shoulder.

But she was staring at her son. 'Why not?'

'Because I'll be away.'

'Where are you going?' Her tone changed. She had been half expecting this and she had not meant to sound demanding. It just happened.

'Does it matter?' Ben scowled.

'Yes . . .' Helplessly, Claire looked up at David. It was all very well to take that step back, but not so easy to stay put apparently.

'Of course it matters, son.' David's voice was grave. 'We want the best for you. We always have. We worry. We want to know what you're planning to do with your life.'

'I've been hanging around waiting for long enough . . .' Ben began.

Claire got to her feet. 'If you've been hanging around waiting because of me . . .' She stared at her son. Sometimes he almost seemed a stranger, and she simply couldn't believe in the old maternal intimacy. 'Knowing it would hurt me like hell for you to leave home almost straight after Grandad's death . . .' she was breathing heavily, paying the price for all the emotion that had been floating willy-nilly around her world today, '. . . then you're damn right it hurts.'

'Claire.' David tried to stop her but she wouldn't let him.

'But whatever you think of me,' it was very important that Ben understood this, 'you should know that if you want to go . . . anywhere, then that's what I want for you too.'

'It is?' Ben's scowl collapsed into lopsided confusion.

'I want you to do what you like.' Drained, Claire sat down again. 'No ties. No guilt.'

'Hey, steady on.' David attempted a laugh, as if trying to lighten the atmosphere.

'Anything else is worthless,' Claire whispered. She wanted to let go, she realised. She didn't want Ben to be like Freddie – feeling unable to come home because of what would clutch on to him when he got there. And she didn't want him to be an itinerant like Max, who always had to move on, who never had enough reasons to stay, to settle, to put down roots. She didn't want Ben to be emotionally scarred by an over-possessive mother. She wanted Ben to feel free. And maybe it was about time.

'Mum . . .' There was more that he wasn't telling them, she knew it. His eyes shifted away from hers, elusive, hiding something.

'We can manage without you, you know.' As if to demonstrate this, Claire forced a smile on to her face and began to clear the table.

But inside she was still wondering. What if Ben wanted to cut all ties? Could she accept that? She was still trying to adjust to living without the arts project, for goodness sake, and pretty soon she would have to adjust to living without the presence of Max. Unless . . .

'Course you can. I know that.' Ben's voice was casual but Claire wasn't fooled. She'd never been fooled by Ben.

She grabbed his plate. 'So what – exactly – will you be doing?'

'Hitting Europe.'

'Pardon?'

'Just travelling around. Like I said before.'

Claire took a deep breath. Why did the young have to be so *vague*? 'And where will you go first?'

'I dunno.' He looked apologetic, as if he would answer all her questions if he were capable of doing so. 'France, maybe.'

And there were so many questions the mother in her longed to ask. Like, where will you sleep? What will you eat? How will you manage for money? What will you do if you get mugged? And – if I gave you an unlimited phone card, would you use it? 'And then?' she asked instead. 'Where then?'

'Mum . . .' He took her hands. 'I don't have an itinerary.'

'No, no, of course not.'

'I'll just be bumming around.'

'Bumming around?' Claire tried to feel calm instead of about ninety. She looked at David, but he was silent, leaving this to her as he had always left Ben to her. She had wanted him to, she reminded herself sharply. But she had heard of teenagers who left home to bum around. Some of them – like Freddie – never came back.

'I'll be back, Mum. Don't worry about that.' Would he always know what she was thinking? Her son's eyes pleaded with her, and Claire knew that he wanted her to become brisk and businesslike again. That was easier to cope with than a little mother with crumpled-up emotions who expected something.

'I hope so.' He couldn't know how much.

'But I want a bit of freedom – it's the idea of the open road, you know?'

Claire knew. She thought of the Bonnie. Oh, yes, she understood the feeling. She, too, had wanted to be free.

But still she sensed there was more Ben wanted to tell them. 'And?' She eyed him cautiously.

'And the reason I was hanging around here . . .'

Claire and David waited.

'The reason I didn't leave before . . .'

'Yes?'

'Well,' he said, 'Tiffany wants to come with me, you see.'

Over the next few days, Claire couldn't stop thinking. It had been hard enough explaining the saga of Ben and Tiffany – the saga she'd assumed to be over – to David, who hadn't had the foggiest notion of what had been going on.

'Tiffany *Stickler*?' His tone left Claire in no doubt of his feelings on the subject.

'The very same.' She thought about Ben, and what little might be left in her life without him. She couldn't begin to contemplate how it would be in the cottage. There would be David, working, and there would be Claire, working. And what else? Horrifically polite conversations? And she thought about Max Stockwell and how – unintentionally – he had transformed her world.

Max had been one hell of a catalyst. Through Max she could pause and take stock. She could see possibilities that had never existed before . . .

Claire avoided Gary's cottage for two days, and on the third day she went round there.

Her legs were so weak that she had to hang on to the garden fence, but once again it was Gary who opened the door.

'Hello, Gary.' She waited.

'He's gone.' Gary didn't invite her inside. 'He left yesterday morning.'

Claire nodded. She had half expected it. 'Any message for me?'

'He said to tell you to keep this.' Gary handed her a sheet of paper. On it was written Max's name and a c/o address in Cornwall, scrawled in his distinctive hand. 'They send on his mail.'

Claire folded it in half and shoved it in her pocket. 'Anything else?'

Gary folded his arms, looked reluctant. 'He said he wanted to make it easy for you to find him.'

'Find him?'

'If you ever decide to stop running.'

In Hawthorn House Claire was faintly surprised to find her mother in the residents' lounge, spruced up with a new perm and immaculate make-up chatting to a few of the other residents. Doing her queenly bit, David would have said, but Claire thought it was just a front. David didn't understand how others dealt with grief, and David had declined to come with her today.

'I've got all those blasted pots to fire,' he had growled, the good humour of the weekend apparently evaporated. 'How do you think I can spare the time?'

Patricia took her to the flat and made tea. She seemed to be coping very well, so well that Claire almost felt angry with her. But her father, she knew, would have approved.

She told her mother about Ben and Tiffany. Patricia smiled her distant smile and Claire knew she was thinking about her own son – about Freddie.

'You have to let them go, Claire,' she said.

'I know that. But does Richard?' Richard, she knew, would go barmy, and Ben and Tiffany were planning to tell them tonight. Claire was dreading the outcome – for Ben's sake – although she couldn't deny a small pleasure that Ben had apparently beaten the headmaster, despite all the material weapons Richard had at his disposal.

'Lovely for Ben to see a bit of the world.' Patricia, holding the delicate porcelain tea-cup, might have been talking about the Orient Express from London to Venice, not doing Europe on a shoe-string with a motor-bike. She shot a sharp glance at Claire. 'And plenty of time to get on with the rest of his life when he gets back.'

'Mmm.' If he *did* come back.

'Are you and David going away anywhere this summer?' Carefully, Patricia placed four Bourbon biscuits on a doily and a patterned tea-plate.

'Maybe later, towards the end of the holidays.' But what about her mother? Patricia wouldn't be going anywhere, would she? Not on her own.

'I miss your father, Claire.' Her mother brushed a crumb from her skirt. She sounded remarkably matter-of-fact. 'I miss him more than you would believe possible. As he used to be.'

'I know.' Of course she did. She might not show it, but that had never been Patricia's way. And Claire . . . she missed him too.

Claire held her mother's hand. Strangely it seemed to be coming easily these days, touching her, kissing her goodbye, wanting to care for her. 'I thought you and I might take a little trip,' she whispered.

'You and I?' Patricia's eyes lit up.

'I thought we could go to see Freddie.' After all, hadn't her mother said that she'd always longed to visit him? And as for Claire, she needed a break from Trevarne and all it stood for. Soon Ben would be gone.

'Oh, Claire . . .'

It wasn't really running away . . . 'So I thought perhaps we could go to Amsterdam.'

Chapter 18

———◆———

Richard's face was red, a vein in his neck throbbing. In contrast, Iris, who had accompanied him to the cottage, looked perfectly calm.

'What do you say to all this?' he demanded of David and Claire. 'What the hell do *you* say?'

David's dislike of Richard Stickler showed on his face. 'Ben's eighteen. We can't stop him from doing some travelling. It's his life.'

Claire thought Richard would explode. 'But Tiffany – Tiffany isn't even seventeen yet. She's still at school. She's supposed to be doing her A levels.'

'I know.' David looked suitably grave, although Claire was aware that he himself had managed just fine without A levels and privately doubted their usefulness. 'Perhaps you should be talking to Tiffany,' he said mildly. 'She's your daughter.'

'Yes.' Richard stood up straighter. 'She is my daughter, and I won't let her go.' He turned towards Tiffany and Ben, who were standing folded against each other in the doorway, having followed Richard and Iris back to the cottage. 'You can't go,' he repeated.

'You can't stop me, Dad.' Tiffany was very cool, very determined, and Claire was glad she wasn't *her* daughter. In fact, she was glad she didn't have a daughter. Boys were worry enough . . .

She looked back to Richard. He had got his way last time. And, after the Jeremy Sanderson episode, she couldn't help being curious as to how Ben had won back Tiffany Stickler's affections. Richard was steaming, but his daughter seemed to have been doing a bit of growing up. So who would win this particular battle?

'I refuse to allow it.' He glanced at his wife for confirmation. 'Don't we, Iris?'

'I don't see how we can stop her.' Iris's voice betrayed an understanding that Claire had not been expecting. 'We can't chain her to her bedroom. She's already shown us what she does when we try to dictate the pattern of her life.'

Claire glanced at her in admiration. She had guessed right. There was more to Iris Stickler than met the eye. But still . . . sixteen was so very young. 'Have you really thought this through?' Claire asked the two teenagers. 'Both of you. It's all very well for Ben to put off university –'

'I never said I'd go at all,' he broke in.

'But at least you have the option,' she reminded him. 'If Tiffany leaves school now, without A levels, what choices will *she* have?'

'We want to go now.' Tiffany spoke, but Claire sensed a hesitation in Ben and perhaps a chink in the collective armour.

'What's the big hurry?'

'We've decided.' Tiffany stuck her arm in Ben's. 'That's all.'

A glance at her son persuaded Claire that he was definitely wavering, looking for an out clause in the small print. And Claire thought she understood. He had won the girl and was eager to carry her off into the sunset, but he wouldn't want to deprive her of anything – especially her choices for the future. After all, six months on he might be blamed for it.

'It isn't as easy as all that, my girl.' Richard wagged his finger. But that wasn't the way – Claire could almost see Tiffany digging her heels in.

'You can't stop us,' she said again.

'How about,' they all looked up at David as he spoke, 'a compromise?'

'Like what?' Ben growled.

'Like going for four or five weeks,' he suggested. 'Until September.'

'Four or five weeks?' Tiffany scoffed. 'How far would we get in that time?'

'And we don't want to have to say *exactly* when we're coming back,' Ben chipped in. 'That's the whole idea.'

'Four weeks can be a hell of a long time without a decent bed,' David pointed out. 'You might be quite keen to come back by then.'

'And if we're not?' Ben was looking interested, and Claire noted that David's line of thought had, once again, been very close to her own.

'Come back anyway.' David looked across at Claire, held her gaze for a moment. 'You can always make new plans . . . later on.'

Claire looked down at her lap, fiddled with the buttons of her sweater, feeling uncomfortable. What exactly had David meant by that?

Meanwhile, as Ben apparently tried to gauge Tiffany's response to this suggestion, David pressed home his advantage. 'Keep your parents happy,' he told Tiffany. 'Go off together for the summer. Have a good time. Come back to do your A levels.' He looked at her sharply. 'It may be important to you later, love.'

A lot more was said to elaborate on this plan, but on the whole it seemed to be an acceptable compromise to everyone, with the possible exception of Tiffany, who could – Claire guessed – be safely left to Ben.

And knowing that Ben would be back after a month or two – even if it wouldn't be long before he disappeared again – well, it made it that much easier for Claire to let go. She was getting better at it, she felt. At last . . .

'Amsterdam?' David stared at her as if she were quite mad. 'With your mother?'

Claire bristled. 'Well, why not?' Her mother might be a touch uptight, but she wasn't as bad as David liked to make out. 'My mother can cope with anything. She could cope with Amsterdam with her eyes closed.'

'And when you get to the red-light district, she'll probably have to.'

Claire ignored this. She didn't think even Freddie would take his mother to the more dubious parts of the city. 'Freddie thinks she'll love it.'

'Freddie is off his head.'

'David.' Claire sighed. 'I don't see why I shouldn't take her to

Amsterdam. It's the school holidays. You've got a lot of work on. You don't need me hanging around here just getting in your way.'

He stared at her. 'It's not that I'm scared to let you out of my sight, Claire.'

'I didn't say that.' Now they were almost having a row. And for what? She decided to appeal to his sense of logic. 'Give me one good reason why I shouldn't take her.'

'Because she'll probably want to carry out a citizen's arrest on everyone she sees smoking dope, that's why. And in Amsterdam that's a hell of a lot of people.'

'Oh, David . . .' Claire had to smile. But she knew why David was raising objections. He had assumed that the end of the arts committee's frenetic activity in producing Trevarne's Event in July signalled a change of some kind. That she would now be available for him once more, not always dashing off somewhere every night. And here she was announcing she'd like to go to Amsterdam.

'I don't want you to go, Claire.'

But why not? Did he still want to imprison her in Trevarne for the rest of her life? 'I can afford it,' she said stubbornly. She worked for a living, didn't she? She was independent – she'd had to be.

David frowned. 'It's got nothing to do with money,' he muttered, under his breath.

Then what? 'Mum needs this,' she told him more gently. 'I'm doing it for her. After Dad's death she needs something to take her mind off things. And she's desperate to see Freddie. I want to help her, can't you understand that?'

A strange expression passed over David's face. 'And what about me? Maybe I need –' He halted in mid-sentence.

For the first time, she wavered. Ben was leaving too. Why did this suddenly seem like desertion? 'What is it, David?' *What* did he need?

He turned away. 'Nothing that won't keep.'

'It's only for a few days, David.'

'I can see that you've made up your mind.' He grabbed his overalls, headed for the workshop, still grumbling. 'I don't know why you're even bothering to discuss it with me.'

Claire sensed that, like her, he had no idea if they had a future

together. She was doing this for Patricia, but the fact was that Claire
too needed this break. So much had been happening in her life. It
would be good for her to spend a few days with her mother, and
good to have some time away. And, yes, she wanted to see Freddie
again. She wanted that very much.

Freddie looked – incredibly – just the same.

'Don't people get older in Amsterdam?' Claire hugged him.
'Maybe I should come over here to live. Got any room for me in
your flat?'

'I've always got room for you.' He grinned. 'And actually you'd
like living here, Claire.'

Freddie took them to the botel owned by his friends Stefan and
Marika, a small floating hotel moored in the harbour alongside
narrow boats and a floating Chinese restaurant. He showed them to
their tiny but comfortable cabin, waited for them to get settled in
and then borrowed Stefan's boat to take them to Jordaan by canal.

'I like your friends. Marika is very kind,' Patricia observed, in
her and-why-haven't-*you*-found-yourself-a-nice-woman voice.

'Marika is an angel,' Freddie said. 'There isn't another woman
like her in the entire city.'

'Hmm.' Patricia gazed away from him, off into the distance of
the canal, a strip of water stretching as far as the eye could see, the
view bordered by tall narrow buildings, and broken up by bridges
and walkways, cyclists and pedestrians.

There were bikes everywhere, it was the first thing that Claire
had noticed about the city – bikes stacked row upon row outside
Central Station, cyclists whizzing down the cycle lanes on old bikes
with high handlebars and wicker baskets, ringing their bells to move
ignorant tourists out of their way.

'Any girl would have to be an angel to put up with me,' Freddie
admitted.

'Or mad,' Claire agreed.

'You spoilt me, Mum.' Freddie laughed as he said it, but Patricia
was silent. Claire knew that her mother still wanted to slot Freddie
into a little compartment of her own making, where he might be
safe, she supposed. But she couldn't, could she? And Freddie didn't

want to be safe – he was far too bohemian for that.

'Perhaps you've become a confirmed bachelor,' Claire joked. Or perhaps he had been too long alone.

'Perhaps.' Freddie seemed about to elaborate, and then changed his mind. 'On Wednesday afternoons Stefan and I play backgammon in this café I'm taking you to – my favourite brown café in Jordaan.'

'Brown café?'

But when they got there, Claire could see why it was so called. It wasn't exactly gloomy – in fact, the effect was one of warm and friendly welcome, but the wood panelling, dark curtains, stained walls and heavy wooden tables and benches certainly reflected the name.

'Amsterdammers as good as live in these places,' Freddie told them. 'They're all over the city.' He greeted the owner, and ordered coffee, beer, Dutch gin and spicy Dutch apple cake.

'To soak up the alcohol,' he told Claire, with a wink.

Claire looked around at the other tables – one group of people were engaged in a lively discussion in Dutch, another couple were playing chess, a middle-aged man was reading a paper and a young girl with textbooks spread out in front of her appeared to be writing an essay.

'Home from home,' Freddie explained. 'In the winter I practically live here too. See that stove? It belches out heat, like you wouldn't believe.'

They looked over to where he was pointing and saw a huge pot-bellied stove in the corner surrounded by Delft tiles. Claire certainly would believe.

'Hasn't your flat got proper heating, darling?' Patricia worried.

But Claire could imagine that this was the perfect place to come and chat with your friends. In Amsterdam anyway – she couldn't exactly envisage setting up a brown café in Trevarne. The coffee-coloured walls and ceiling looked as if they'd been stained by centuries of tobacco smoke, and the thin rugs covering the tables seemed to have soaked up an awful lot of spilt beer. Aunt Emily would have a fit.

Claire leant towards him. 'Tell us what it's like living in

Amsterdam, Freddie,' she urged. Already, she was beginning to understand its appeal.

'I don't know where to start.' Freddie grew thoughtful, which in itself wasn't much like the Freddie she remembered. 'But I suppose I'd have to start with tolerance.'

'How do you mean, darling?' Gingerly, Patricia sipped her coffee.

Freddie took a deep breath. 'In Amsterdam, the bohemian lives next door to sleaze, and sleaze lives next door to respectability. And it doesn't matter. Do you see?'

Claire smiled. 'I think so.'

'No one judges the other.' He spread his hands. 'They live in harmony. We all do.'

'Harmony, that sounds nice.' Patricia smiled approvingly.

'Yes, it does,' Claire agreed. And she couldn't help thinking of the contrast between that kind of attitude – live and let live – and the attitude of a small-minded village community like Trevarne.

Okay, given a bit of persuasion most of them had clubbed together to create a community happening, and that had meant a great deal to Claire. But would it last? Would the people of Trevarne work together, let each other be? Or would Iris Stickler go back to picking plums, while Richard kept the village gossip going in her name? Would Richard still be a narrow-minded headmaster at the beginning of the autumn term? Would the parents of Trevarne still try to get rid of a teacher who strayed from their own boundaries of accepted sexual behaviour?

'But apart from that, the life here isn't frantic,' Freddie went on. And it was true that Freddie seemed remarkably relaxed. 'We don't get stressed. We're more laid back, you know. We like to chill out.'

But that could be the drugs, Claire thought to herself with a grin.

'And there's so much to see.' He took a huge bite of apple cake and chewed happily. 'Perhaps I'll take my two favourite ladies on a candlelight canal cruise.'

'Lovely.' Patricia clapped her hands.

Freddie grabbed hold of her to give her a smacking kiss on the cheek, and for a moment she looked like a young girl again. It occurred to Claire that Freddie was very like their father – she had never seen it before, but now that he was older it seemed obvious.

And Patricia clearly saw the same charm in her son as she had seen in Josh, all those years ago.

'It's taken so long to get you here,' Freddie told them, neglecting to mention the fact that he had been more than a little elusive in the past. 'I'm going to make sure you drown in Dutch delights, you'll see.'

'But not in Dutch gin, one hopes.' Claire was sipping her second small glass of jeneva. It was similar to English gin, but besides juniper, it was flavoured with caraway and coriander, which apparently gave it the distinctive taste Freddie had talked of when he persuaded her to try some. She was beginning to feel pleasantly light-headed. No stress, eh? That sounded just perfect.

Freddie grinned. 'Pretty hot stuff, hmm?' He nudged her. 'You can have a beer chaser if you like . . .'

'Don't be disgusting, Freddie.' Claire pulled a face.

'It's traditional,' he teased. 'We call the combination of the two, a *kopstoot*.'

'Which means?'

'A headbanger.'

'I think I'm too old to start indulging in headbangers,' Claire muttered.

'Oh, I'm all for tradition.' Patricia laughed. 'What else is there that's traditional?'

'You name it.' Freddie finished the apple cake and washed it down with a swig of beer. He was clearly enjoying himself hugely. 'The tulip fields might have been and gone – you're a bit late for those – but I can give you flower markets, windmills, clog-making, Edam . . .'

'You should have been a tour operator,' Claire told him drily. Was this how Ben would be one day? Would she visit him in some far-flung place he had made his own?

'And,' he leant closer towards them, 'I can show you backstreet Amsterdam – the part the tourists don't always get to see.'

Claire thought this sounded more promising, but Patricia's eyes had gone suspiciously misty.

'To tell you the truth, darling,' she said, 'all I really want to see is you.'

'You've got me.' Freddie squeezed her hand. He looked up at Claire. 'And I'm a reformed character.'

'Oh, yes?' They laughed. It didn't seem exactly likely.

He grew solemn. 'No drugs . . .'

Claire's eyebrows rose.

'Well . . . nothing serious.'

Patricia was about to speak, but he stopped her, put his finger on her lips. 'No. Ssh. You're not allowed to be cross.'

And Patricia did as he asked.

Claire grinned. Amsterdam clearly had *something*.

'And no drink.'

At this point Claire couldn't restrain herself. 'Honestly, Freddie!'

'Well, not much.' He tapped his chest. 'And I've almost given up smoking.'

'Almost? Sounds about as likely as almost being pregnant.' Claire poked him in the ribs. 'Don't tell me you're trying to give up all the pleasures – and so young in life too.' Freddie was so much younger than her: sometimes he seemed more like her son.

'Now, now, Claire,' Patricia warned her. 'We're here to enjoy Freddie, not make fun of him.'

Claire laughed. That was her mother all over – *she* could criticise but just let anyone else try . . .

'Well, Mum might want you and only you,' she said, 'but I happen to want those delights of Amsterdam.' She finished her gin. She was here for her mother and she was here to do a lot of thinking. But she may as well enjoy herself at the same time. 'So, tell me, where do we start?'

It proved very difficult, however, to leave the brown café that afternoon, what with its warm ambience, the kind of closeted family conversation Claire hadn't experienced for ages and, of course, the gin. In fact, by the time they left that night, Claire was feeling rather inebriated and wondering whether she had been indiscreet. She remembered Freddie asking her about David. But what exactly had she told him?

So they started touring Amsterdam the following morning, at Dam Square, where the busking street performers included a mix

of juggling, fire-eating, music and mime. A band of Dutch youths
with dreadlocks, in baggy black trousers, big boots and threadbare
jumpers, were singing English folk songs and slugging beer. And
as she looked around her, Claire couldn't help noticing what a multi-
ethnic city Amsterdam was. Live and let live indeed. The very
opposite of Trevarne.

To their surprise, several people greeted Freddie with a wave or
a shout.

'I play here sometimes,' he told them, in response to their
questioning looks.

'Still?' Claire remembered the guitar. Freddie loved to play; his
guitar had been about the only possession he hadn't left behind
when he first went off travelling. In Ben's case, it would be his
motor-bike, she supposed.

'You mean people throw money into a hat for you?' Patricia was
aghast.

'My guitar case, actually, Mum.' Freddie laughed.

She gripped his arm. 'And that's how you live?'

'Hey, remember, Mum,' Claire sensed another bout of maternal
concern looming, 'Freddie's been doing it for years. He knows his
way around.' She caught her brother's eye. 'Chill out . . .'

From the square, Freddie took them past the impressive flanks of
the Royal Palace, and the floating flower market, where bucketfuls
of tulips, lilies and irises created a sea of colour, to Vondelpark by
way of one of the trams that roved the city – originally yellow, but
now painted in psychedelic colours that made Claire stare with
delight. They settled down for a picnic lunch under a weeping
willow by the lake, and Patricia announced her intention to spend a
couple of hours relaxing – she already looked tired from Freddie's
sightseeing tour, Claire noted.

Freddie elected to stay with her, and Claire grabbed the
opportunity to take in the Rijksmuseum. Not for anyone would she
miss seeing Rembrandt's *Night Watch*.

Claire had rather surprised herself when she'd first suggested
this trip. She had known it to be her mother's dearest wish to see
Freddie and she had also known that one would never make the
journey alone. Her mother missed Josh Trent – they all missed him.

And Claire had felt the need to try to bring the remainder of the family back together – just for a while.

Freddie had been keen for them to come; Claire could almost hear the guilt in her brother's voice when he phoned her, having finally got the message telling him of his father's death. *I didn't know . . . I didn't know, Claire . . .* He kept repeating the words, and Claire found herself reassuring him as she had reassured him when he was a child. He had been away from the city, he wasn't to blame. Freddie, the baby of the family . . . Claire, the responsible one. Would it never change?

Freddie had wanted to come over to England, and that was a surprise in itself. But by then Claire had already had her brainwave. 'No,' she told Freddie, 'we'll come to you.'

And now, here they were.

But as she made her way to the museum, she couldn't help wondering what it would have been like to come here with Max. To sit around in one of the many old-style brown cafés drinking Dutch gin or the excellent fresh coffee, eating hussar salad or the traditional thick pea soup. Sitting around and putting the world to rights . . .

Claire quickened her step. And, of course, she could imagine coming here with David – although it was odd that they had never visited Freddie in Amsterdam. Surely they had intended to. But she and David had travelled very little – they had remained locked in Trevarne, she supposed.

She and David would probably focus on art and culture, Claire thought, as she was doing now. They would absorb the Dutch masters at the Rijks, imbibe Vincent Van Gogh's wild cornfields, potent irises and vibrant sunflowers . . . not to mention a quick visit to Rembrandt's house to look at his etchings. She grinned. Amsterdam was a painter's paradise.

Fern would love it.

Chilled, she rubbed at the goose-bumps that had sprung up on her bare arms. Perhaps one day David might bring Fern . . .

Claire shook her head in mock rebuke as she entered the museum. Why had she allowed herself to spoil things? At least she was here, even though it was with neither Max nor David. Even though she had never expected to come to Amsterdam with her mother.

When she returned to Vondelpark, she could see that Freddie and Patricia had used the time alone to get to know one another again. Rather incongruously, or so it seemed to Claire, they were lounging on a bench near the bandstand, in front of a huge plaque of what might be called street graffiti – or even modern art. But there was a warm, relaxed look on her mother's face, and Freddie, too, seemed peaceful.

Freddie had come here with just a rucksack on his back and a guitar slung over his shoulder, but now he belonged, Claire realised. He had made his own life – away from his family. And now Ben was doing the same, at least for a while.

That night they had dinner in what Freddie referred to as the wackiest restaurant in Amsterdam where, to Claire's surprise, her mother seemed remarkably unfazed by the odd whiff of hash smoke, and the interesting line in psychedelic knitwear preferred by many of the diners. Although they hadn't actually gone into one, Claire was fascinated by the dope cafés, or wacky cafés as Freddie called them, identifiable by names like Smokey, Out of Your Mind and Beyond Heaven, where you could actually buy drugs quite openly. What would the Friends of Trevarne say to that? she wondered.

The following morning, he took them to the market on Albert Cuypstraat, whose stalls piled high with exotic fish and vegetables, colourful cheeses and bolts of fabric made Patricia exclaim with delight.

'These narrow streets are called the *pijp*. The pipe,' Freddie told them, demonstrating how the long narrow curves resembled an old clay pipe.

'And now,' he drew them to one side, 'it is time to show you my favourite part of the city . . .'

This proved to be the old working-class district of Jordaan where Freddie now lived, a sprawling area of gabled houses, old shuttered warehouses, tiny boutiques, specialist shops, brown cafés and *hofjes*. 'Little courtyards attached to alms-houses,' Freddie explained, opening a heavy oak door under a gablestone to reveal a narrow passageway that led to a rambling garden and a square, in the centre of which was an old water pump. 'Built in the seventeenth century by rich merchants for the poor and destitute.'

'That was very charitable of them,' Claire remarked, taking in the details of the wild garden, sniffing the scents of the herbs, admiring the buddleia and lace-cap hydrangea. It was like taking a step into perfect peace, out of the bustle of the Spui that now seemed miles away.

'They thought it would get them to heaven,' Freddie whispered.

Claire surveyed her surroundings. 'Do people still live here?'

He nodded as he ushered them out. 'But it's okay to look around – it's not private property.'

They bought a sandwich lunch from one of the cheese shops, drawn inside the narrow doorway by the pungent smells to marvel at the rich variation of the cheeses and brightly coloured rinds.

As they left the shop, a young woman with long brown hair and a pleasant smile waved to them and jumped off her bike. 'Hi, Freddie!' she called.

'Alise . . .'

They spoke for a few minutes in Dutch, but from their body language it didn't take a genius to work out their relationship, Claire thought.

'Mum . . . Claire . . .' Freddie smiled. 'Meet Alise.'

They shook hands.

'Do you speak English?' Patricia asked.

'Oh, yes.' Alise seemed enthusiastic. And 'Freddie – he has told me much about you.'

'He has?' Patricia's eyebrows rose.

Freddie has told us absolutely zilch about *you*, Claire thought.

Alise turned to Freddie. 'Will you be home for dinner tonight?'

'I think so.' He kissed her on both cheeks. 'See you later.'

'Those didn't look,' Claire remarked as they made their way to the tram stop, 'like the actions of a confirmed bachelor.'

Freddie laughed as he jumped on to the tram and took Patricia's hand. You had to be quick, or they left without you. Claire saw him look into his mother's face. 'Maybe you're right,' he said softly.

But Patricia said very little about the episode. Perhaps she was wondering how well she knew her son after all, perhaps she was beginning to understand why Freddie kept so much to himself . . .

The journey ended in what was plainly the red-light district.

'Freddie . . .' Claire was reproachful.

'It's perfectly harmless.' He winked.

'Maybe. But I don't think Mum will appreciate –'

'Oh, don't worry darling. I asked Freddie to bring us here.' Patricia took Claire's arm. 'What's the point of only seeing the respectable side of the city? I want to see it all.'

Claire stared at her in amazement. Here in Amsterdam, Patricia seemed a different woman indeed.

But Freddie took her other arm and led her on. 'My sentiments entirely.'

And although the shop-front boudoirs – as Freddie called them – massage parlours and strip shows were undeniably sleazy, Claire had to agree that it was an interesting experience, and that Patricia looked remarkably untainted by it, even when someone of uncertain gender dressed in gold lamé and leather boots stopped them to ask Freddie the whereabouts of a place that sounded suspiciously like Fay's leather disco.

Perhaps I heard wrong, Claire thought, noting that Freddie was able to provide directions.

But she also knew that although Freddie was showing them the red-light district, they were only seeing the superficial and tawdry gloss. It was disturbing to see girls no older than Tiffany parading their bodies for sale – and in broad daylight. It worried her – the very number of sex shops displaying pornography and sex aids graphically, and to every man, woman and child. Tolerance, perhaps, but didn't the openness only make it more acceptable, less shocking? And was that a good thing? She saw a crackhead inhaling in a public tram, she saw the van that provided junkies with clean needles . . . Freddie whisked them past all this – but it bothered her, the underground world of drugs, sex for sale, corruption and danger that existed behind the façade.

By the time Freddie put them on their glass-topped canal cruiser to return to Stefan and Marika's botel for the night – their last night – Patricia and Claire were both exhausted.

Freddie kissed them goodbye. 'So what do you think of Amsterdam, Claire?' he asked her.

'I like it.' And she did. She liked the waterways of the city, bordered by elegant gabled and fretted houses, by trees, by bright and colourful boats. She liked the peace, the bohemian atmosphere, the lack of traffic, exhaust fumes and department stores. She found parts of the city disturbing – but she could see why Freddie had chosen to live here.

'Ah, yes.' Freddie seemed pleased. 'I thought you would. Because here,' he hugged Patricia, 'there's *voor elck wat wils* . . . something for everyone.'

Chapter 19

———◆———

'You know, Claire,' Patricia said, when they were back in their cabin getting ready for bed, 'I'm so glad that we came to Amsterdam, you and I.'

'It's been lovely to see Freddie,' Claire agreed.

'Oh, yes, that, of course.' Patricia seemed distracted. 'It *was* wonderful to see him again after all this time.'

'We won't leave it so long in future.' Claire's instinct was that now he might come to England more often. Freddie had changed. Whether it was the influence of his friend Alise, the effect of their father's death, or simply experience, she didn't know, but she sensed that Freddie wouldn't separate himself so distinctly in the future. And she was pleased – they were still a family, after all. There was something still binding them together.

'Mmm . . .' Patricia's voice grew sad. 'But he lives in a very different world from us now, Claire.'

'He always did.' It was just that her mother hadn't accepted it till now. Claire pulled on her nightdress. 'But I don't know that it's so *very* different.' She grinned at her mother as her head emerged. 'I'd say you've adapted to life in Amsterdam rather well over the past few days.'

'Oh, I pretended to.' Patricia was smoothing moisture cream into her face and neck. Her eyes met Claire's in the mirror. 'It's easy to keep it up for a short while. But it does get wearing – pretending to be relaxed when there's this obstinate little ball of worry rattling away inside you.'

'You shouldn't be worrying about Freddie.' Claire climbed into bed. 'He'll be fine. He's always been fine.'

'I can't help it.' Patricia sighed. 'I think it's because he's never had a steady job, never owned his own house, never had . . .'

'A steady girlfriend?'

Their eyes met once more. 'I hope she was.'

Claire laughed. She didn't want Ben to have to keep parts of his life secret.

'I *do*.'

Her mother looked, Claire observed, as if she were ready to go home. 'You have to start thinking about yourself,' she told her. But she was beginning to wonder if it was a mother's fate. Unconditional love, never-ending worry . . .

'I don't want to think about myself.' Patricia compressed her lips into a thin line. 'I want to give in to this terrible urge.'

'Urge?' Claire smiled. 'What urge?'

'To snatch him away.' Patricia's mouth twitched. 'Take him home, protect him from it all.' She replaced the pot of cream on the small ledge that served as a dressing-table and was still for a moment.

Claire watched her. 'Protect him from what exactly?' Freddie was a grown man, when all was said and done.

'From everything.' Patricia spun round to face her. Claire gazed back at her in a moment of mutual understanding.

'Anything and everything.' They laughed.

'I know.' It was like that for her with Ben, it always had been.

Patricia screwed up her fists. 'That's how it is. But I hate it.'

'Then change it,' Claire said gently.

'How?' Her mother stared back at her. 'He's my child. He always will be, no matter how many years go by.' Patricia seemed exhausted by this speech. Wearily she turned back towards the mirror and began brushing her hair, grey now but still brushed fifty times before bed without fail.

'You're already standing back.' Claire thought of Ben. 'You and me both.' There would always be an impulse to protect, but you could resist it, you could fight it. She had fought it, from Ben's first day at school, from the first time he had gone out alone at night, to his decision to buy a motor-bike. To now. Travelling around Europe wasn't exactly a mother's dream for her child. She would probably worry a little bit every day, but she had stepped back and she was damn well going to stay there.

Her mother was watching her carefully. 'I'm trying to, Claire. But it's been a long time.'

And perhaps it had taken her father's death to change the patterns. 'It's not too late,' Claire told her. 'You haven't lost him.' These past few days had taught her that much.

'I hope you're right.'

She and her mother must be more alike than she had thought. Both of them prone to overdose in the maternal department. Still, there was something niggling at Claire. 'But Freddie's not your only child,' she said softly.

'It's not the same with girls.' Abruptly, Patricia put down the hairbrush and glanced sharply at her daughter, as if ensuring she was not offended by this remark.

'Isn't it?' Claire drew the covers closer to her chin.

'Girls stay with you.'

'For always?' She didn't buy that for starters. She had, after all, left London to go to Cornwall with David.

'No, no.' Patricia waved this away. 'There are times you lose them – of course there are. But you always know they'll come back to you. Whether they're living miles away or next door is immaterial. There's a bond.'

Claire wasn't sure she understood this distinction. Did she have a bond like that with her mother? She'd like to think so . . . But she still wasn't convinced. 'Even when they get married?' she asked her.

'Especially when they get married.' Patricia sounded very certain. 'And even more so when they have children of their own.' She nodded sagely. 'That's when they really come to understand.'

'And why should it be so different with sons?' Claire whispered, thinking once more of Ben.

'I was busy when I had you,' Patricia said. 'I was always busy in those days. We thought you might be the only one. I was happy with that. So was your father. We were quite a compact little unit.' She smiled. 'Freddie, coming as late as he did, he was rather a surprise.'

'But a nice surprise?'

'Oh, yes.' Patricia's eyes grew dreamy.

'Freddie was special,' Claire said. She'd always felt that. 'Like an entirely unexpected gift.'

'Yes.' Her mother paused. 'Did you mind?'

'Not really.' There had been times when perhaps she had. But she'd never doubted her father's affection for her, even though she might have occasionally longed for her mother to look at her the way she looked at Freddie.

'I'd hate for you to have minded.' Patricia approached the bed. 'Josh got cross sometimes. He said I was wrong.'

'Wrong?'

'To treat you two differently.' She came closer. 'And I know I did. But you *were* different, Claire. You were both individuals, you had different needs.' Her voice was earnest. 'You were the self-sufficient one, you were older, you were a girl.' Vaguely, she smiled. 'You were your father's . . .'

'I never minded.' There had been times, yes, when the responsibilities had lain heavy on her shoulders. Times when she had wanted to escape the family ties . . . but underneath it all, 'I adored Freddie,' she said. 'I still do.' Perhaps it was strange that she hadn't been jealous. Children were, she knew, and often without reason. But she wasn't sure her mother was right. Children were different, yes. But they all needed to be loved.

However, Patricia seemed satisfied. Visibly, she relaxed as she sank slowly on to the edge of Claire's bed. 'You see, in some ways Freddie wasn't as lucky as you. I had to look out for him in a different way.'

'How do you mean?'

'I knew there was something.' She was looking around her, as if searching for the words. 'Right from the start, Freddie was what you might call rootless, unsure. He didn't care very much for himself.'

Claire nodded, understanding. 'So someone else had to do it for him?'

Patricia smiled. 'But I clung too hard.'

Claire knew what she was saying. She had clung too hard and Freddie had broken free. She had lost him – at least for a while.

Patricia was still speaking. 'But I know you won't make the same mistake, darling Claire. You're so sensible. You've always been so sensible.'

'I have?' Claire wanted to laugh. She thought of her childhood, her teenage dreams when the Bonnie had represented everything that was not sensible. She thought of all that wild riding, that search for a certain freedom, a new thrill . . . Sensible, eh?

And then she thought of David, her impulsive decision to marry him, her horror at having to live in a small village in Cornwall for the rest of her life. She thought of Max and his kiss. Those had not been the actions of a sensible woman.

And then there was Ben. Had she too clung too hard? Was Patricia wrong? Had she already made exactly the same mistake as her own mother? Was that why he wanted to go away?

Patricia took her hand. 'And when I say that I'm glad that you and I came here to Amsterdam, I'm not saying thank you for bringing me to see Freddie.'

'You're not?' Claire was confused.

'Well, I am.' Patricia smiled. 'But I'm also saying thank you for these few days alone with you. Thank you for being there for your father and me at the end. For caring.'

Claire was more than a little taken aback by this. Taken aback and unutterably moved. 'Oh, I care,' she whispered. 'I care very much.'

'And thank you for giving us this chance to get close to one another again.' Patricia nodded with satisfaction.

And it was true. It had happened almost without Claire noticing. Beginning with a certain ease of touch, a spontaneous affection between them, back in Cornwall. And then coming here . . .

Here in Amsterdam she had talked with her mother more than she had probably ever talked to her before. She had enjoyed her company. No, she wasn't the travelling companion Claire would have chosen. But now she was very glad that she had come to Amsterdam with Patricia.

'You were always so close to your father,' Patricia went on. 'I used to tease him – I told him he never gave me a look in.'

Claire was puzzled. She had never seen it from that aspect before.

'But there was a time, when you were little more than a baby . . .'

'We've still got that bond, Mum.' Claire moved closer to hug her.

'I know.' Patricia smiled back at her. Gently, she stroked her hair. 'And I also know that your father used to talk to you all the time, give you advice.'

'Yes . . .' That was true enough. And how she missed him . . .

Patricia's hands were on her shoulders, she was looking into her eyes. 'And I think that now, perhaps, you need him more than ever.'

Claire gazed back at her, surprised at her mother's perception. And at some distant memory that she could hardly place.

'And so I wanted to let you know, darling Claire . . .' She paused. 'I'm not your father. He was much wiser than I'll ever be, and I've made an awful lot more mistakes than he ever could.' Patricia's voice wavered and then became strong again. 'But I want you to know, whenever you need me, I'm here.'

The next morning Claire was surprised to get a call from Marika in reception, saying that Freddie was in the breakfast room and wanted a private word.

She looked across at her mother. Patricia was still in bed asleep, a small smile on her face, so Claire sat down and scribbled a quick note so she wouldn't be worried when she woke.

Freddie was lounging in the breakfast room, reading a newspaper. He got to his feet when she came in and they kissed on both cheeks.

'What on earth's brought you out here at this hour?' she asked him. It was only half past eight: he wasn't due to collect them to take them to the airport until eleven.

'I wanted a little talk.'

'Fire away.' They sat down at a table and Claire poured coffee for them both.

'Number one,' he said, 'thanks for bringing Mum over. It was great to see both of you. Really great.'

'You could always visit *us*,' Claire reminded him sharply. 'Or is England out of bounds?'

'Yes. No.' He laughed. 'I always meant to. I will do.'

'Good.' Claire sipped her coffee. It was nice and strong, the way she liked it.

'And what's number two?' Because he could certainly have thanked her for bringing their mother to Amsterdam when Patricia was around. But, there again, Freddie enjoyed a bit of cloak and dagger.

'Number two . . .' He was slightly shame-faced, and Claire had to remind herself that this expression had always been one of Freddie's ploys to gain sympathy.

'Yes?'

'Number two . . . Well, I may as well get to the point.'

'Please.'

'It's just that I was wondering . . .' Freddie put down his cup and grasped her hand. His brown birdlike eyes were brilliant and over-excited, she observed. As if he'd been up all night. 'Do you think she would consider moving?'

'Moving?'

'Moving over here, I mean.'

Claire gazed at him in astonishment. Whatever she had been expecting – and Freddie asking for money had been top of her list, for he had always been broke and from the look of him nothing much had changed – it hadn't been this. 'Mum? Come here? What, to live in Amsterdam, you mean?'

'Well, why not?' He let go of her hand and poured more coffee.

Claire began to giggle.

'What's so funny?'

'Can you really see Mum . . .?' Claire had a vision of her respectable and rather conservative mother living in an apartment in the Jordaan district, drinking her morning coffee in the brown cafés, watching her son busking in Dam Square.

'See her doing what?' Freddie's eyes were just a little bit cross now. 'I thought she liked it here. She's had a good time, hasn't she?'

'Yes, Freddie, she has.' As she patted his hand, Claire recalled her mother's voice . . . *It does get wearing . . . pretending.*

'Well, then?'

'She's had a wonderful time,' Claire told him, 'but Mum couldn't live like that on a daily basis. She's . . . well, she's Mum.'

He watched her over the thick white rim of the coffee cup, his eyes sad now. 'But I could ask her, couldn't I?'

'You could . . .' Freddie was here, of course. But what else was there in Amsterdam for a woman like Patricia?

'You wouldn't mind?'

She smiled. 'I wouldn't mind.' Although it was ironic that Freddie wanted to remove their mother – always primarily *his* mother, she acknowledged – at the very time that Claire had rediscovered her.

'You see . . . now, I'm more settled.'

'With Alise?' She smiled. She had guessed as much.

Freddie nodded. 'I didn't tell Mum before, because you know what she's like. There would have been non-stop verbals. She would have tried to get us married off in minutes.' He spoke in a rush, the words pouring out.

'I understand.' She patted his hand once more. 'Mum understands. But . . .'

'What?' He looked at her with that childlike expression of his. Everything was so black and white for Freddie, Claire thought.

'You don't have to try to make up to her for anything in the past, you know.' She understood the way his mind was working, she always had. But wasn't it a bit late in the day for Freddie to feel guilt for his previous neglect?

'Don't I?' He fiddled with his teaspoon. 'But it isn't just Mum. What about you?'

'What about me?'

'Would you fancy living here?'

'Me?' Claire almost choked on her coffee. 'What on earth would you want me to live here for?'

'I was thinking of you, Claire,' he told her reproachfully. 'I thought you might need a bit of a change.'

Her eyes narrowed. 'What makes you say that?'

He shrugged. 'You and Mum, you're the only family I've got left now.'

'You couldn't get away from us all quickly enough in London,' she reminded him. Well, honestly . . . 'And you've practically never come to see us since.'

He spread his hands. 'I never have the spare cash.'

'You know quite well Mum would have sent you the fare.' She'd probably sent quite a few fares over the years.

He remained silent.

'You've broken all the ties, Freddie. How come you want to change everything now?'

'I miss you all.'

She must have looked surprised by this admission.

'It hit me hard – when Dad died. You don't realise what you have – you know, family and all that – until you lose a part of it.' His eyes, which had been solemn, changed expression and the Freddie she knew rather better, the brother who was rarely serious, returned. 'Jesus, I must be getting old, I guess.'

'I think you must.' Claire smiled, but she had the odd feeling that, despite their childhood closeness, despite these last few days, there was a side to Freddie that she'd never understood, never allowed for. Her mother had seen it, of course, she had as good as told her so. But, then, mothers usually did.

'And, anyway,' Freddie sat back in his chair, 'it's not such a daft idea, you coming to live in Amsterdam.'

'You don't give up, do you?'

'Nope. There's plenty of work here, Claire. Lots of nice people.'

'Work? Don't you think I'm getting a bit old for the shop-front boudoir routine?' she joked.

He put his head to one side, surveying her critically, looking remarkably like the little boy she remembered. 'You look pretty good to me,' he said, 'but there's no need for that. Stefan would give you a job.'

-'As a waitress?' He seemed to have all their futures well worked out. 'Freddie, I run a school in Cornwall, single-handed practically.' Well, maybe that was a slight exaggeration, but it felt like that sometimes.

'But you said you hated it.'

'Did I?' Claire couldn't remember saying anything of the kind. 'It must have been all that gin you made me drink.'

'Ah . . .' He wagged his finger. 'The truth will out.'

'Everyone hates their job sometimes.' She remained non-committal. It was a feature of the long summer holidays, to dread going back. Once she'd slotted into the routine, she'd be okay.

'So you don't think the school is an out-dated institution run by a narrow-minded hypocrite whose brain is closely connected with the contents of his trousers?' Freddie watched her.

God, she *had* been indiscreet. Claire felt shell-shocked. 'Well . . .'

'And you don't think Trevarne is a small-minded village full of pathetic little people with nothing better to do than gossip all day?'

'I said that?'

'You sure did.'

'That gin must have been even stronger than I thought.' It was true that she'd never liked Trevarne, never wanted to live there, begged David to consider moving. And never forgiven him for his refusal. David . . .

'So, Claire . . .'

'I'm married,' she said bleakly. Freddie seemed to have forgotten that.

'Oh, yeah . . . David.'

Claire looked sharply across at him. 'Okay, Freddie. What else did I say? What did I tell you about David?'

'Not a lot.' He grinned. God, he was infuriating at times, she thought.

'But what – exactly?'

'Something about not having slept together for ages, and how you might as well give up on your marriage, and why the hell hadn't you gone to bed with Max when you had the chance?'

Claire wanted to go and hide her face in a deep hole somewhere. 'Oh.' She obviously hadn't left out a thing.

Freddie leant over the table. 'So who's Max?'

'Oh, he's . . .' She glared at him for he was still grinning. 'Never mind who he is.' A thought occurred to her. 'Mum didn't hear all this, did she?'

Freddie shook his head. 'She was in the loo.'

'Thank God for that.' But she had managed to tell Freddie a hell of a lot in the time it took one person to go to the bathroom.

'If you want to talk about it, Claire . . .' Freddie let his offer hang in the air between them. 'Any time.'

Funny, Claire thought. Just lately, everyone seemed to want her to talk about it. It was kind of him, but . . . 'Thanks, Freddie. But no thanks.' It was something she had to work out for herself.

He was clearly not offended in the least. 'And about Amsterdam.'

'Yes?'

'Think about it, Claire. Please. For me?' He smiled. 'And maybe for yourself as well.'

When had she ever been able to refuse Freddie anything, when he smiled like that?

It would mean a whole new life.

'Yes, I'll think about it,' she promised.

Chapter 20

———◆———

Not only did everyone seem to want her to talk to them about her problems, Claire thought, but everyone also seemed to want her to move house.

It was the first thing David said when she got back, before even hello, before a kiss. And she was so nervous of seeing him, her mind had been looping between terror and anticipation all day. Because she still didn't *know*.

She put her key in the familiar lock, heaved her case inside, listened for him. Ben was gone. There would be only David in the cottage now.

The house was quiet, but not unwelcoming. She walked into the sitting room, and there he was, standing by the window, waiting for her.

'I've been thinking,' he said. 'I reckon we should move out of here.'

Claire stared at him in astonishment. 'What?'

'I said . . .' David took a step towards her, seemed to hesitate, and then grabbed a glass of whisky from the coffee table. It didn't look as if it was his first.

'I heard you.' No hello. No kiss. 'But what are you talking about, David?' She eyed him cautiously, not sure that she knew him quite as well as she'd always thought.

'What I say. About moving out of here.' His voice had grown belligerent, and this irritated her. Some welcome.

'No, "Hello, Claire, how was Amsterdam?" Just, "I reckon we should move out of here?" ' She pulled off her jacket and flung it on the back of a chair.

His eyes, when he looked up at her, showed pain, and not a lot more. 'What do you want, Claire? Small-talk?'

She stared back at him, wondering. Slowly, she shook her head. 'No, I don't want that.'

'Good.' He picked up his glass.

She pointed to it. 'Can I have one?' It looked as though she was going to need it.

'You don't drink whisky,' he growled.

'Until I went to Amsterdam I didn't drink gin.'

David's smile failed to reach his eyes. He got to his feet, went over to the drinks cupboard and poured her a hefty measure.

'Cheers.' As he handed her the glass, their fingers touched and she had to stop herself from pulling away. David was scaring her. There was a kind of hollow look about him that she didn't recognise, didn't trust.

For a moment they both sat in silence until Claire couldn't bear it any longer. Perhaps she and David needed more than small-talk, but silence wouldn't get them very far. 'Are you saying that this cottage is too big for the two of us, now that Ben's gone?' Because, if so, that's absolutely ridiculous, she felt like adding. Ben hadn't gone for good – she hoped – and the cottage had only two bedrooms. Besides, it would be pleasant to have a guest room after all these years. Maybe they could even have friends to stay.

'No, I'm not saying that.'

Well, that was something. She thought again. 'Is there another house in the village that you like the look of? One that's come up for sale? With a bigger workshop or something?' It was all she could think of, and she knew she was gabbling. But this was crazy. They both loved the cottage, didn't they?

David drained his glass. 'I'm talking about leaving Trevarne, Claire.'

She gaped at him. 'But Trevarne is your home.'

'Ah.' His brow creased. 'But is it yours?'

Claire thought of Amsterdam. She thought of London. And then she thought of Max. 'Of course it is,' she said softly. 'You love Trevarne, David. You always have.' And for some reason this thought, which had always caused resentment before, left her feeling perfectly calm.

'I used to.' He got up for a refill. 'But I'm not sure that I do love the place any more. What good is it, if . . . if . . .' He didn't complete the sentence.

Was that how he felt about her too? Claire looked away, to a safe place, to the other side of the room where David wasn't standing. But his big figure seemed to fill the entire sitting room somehow. 'What are you trying to tell me, David?' As he returned to his chair, she dropped down to her knees beside him.

He glanced at her briefly, indifferently. 'I thought you'd be pleased.'

'Pleased?' She blinked back at him. Why the hell should she be pleased?

'You never wanted to live here, did you?'

'Well, no . . . I . . .'

'You've always nagged me to leave.'

Had she? Had she nagged? Claire had always hoped nagging was for other wives, not her. 'But . . .'

'You always said we'd never be happy here.'

'Not exactly . . .' She registered the bitterness in his voice, and recalled the early days of their marriage, when they had first come to Cornwall, the manner in which excitement had been replaced by boredom. Yes, she had been desperate to leave. There had been times when – if it had not been for the love she felt for David, and the existence of their son – she would have left herself. No doubt she *had* said that. She must have said lots of things.

'Oh, yes, I remember. And you turned out to be right, didn't you? We're both miserable. This entire marriage is a farce.'

She was silent. What did he expect her to say?

'Neither of us is happy.' He glared at her. 'We've been into that before, haven't we? But – Are you happy, Claire?'

She stared at the rug where they had once made passionate love. 'No, I'm not happy.'

She had only said it to try to make him move, the great stubborn lump. But it wasn't true. They had been happy here in the beginning . . . until those bleak days of isolation.

Young motherhood. It was supposed to be so fulfilling. No one told you what to do if you were bored out of your skull, if you were depressed all the time. She recalled bleak times, when David had worked all day and every day. All for them, he said, but it was hard to see it that way. She watched him getting more and more tired every evening, every night, becoming more and more distant, oblivious to her needs.

All she had for company was a screaming baby. And so she clung to that baby, didn't she? She had to – he became all there was in her world. The highlight of her day was walking down to the village store. No friends. No fun. No lights in her life.

'No, David,' she repeated. 'I'm not happy.'

He slammed down his glass. 'So what do you say?' He glared at her. 'Shall we move?'

Claire hugged her knees. 'I don't believe you want to leave Trevarne. Your family's here. Your work is here. You belong.' And what about Fern?

'But you don't.'

There it was again. Claire hugged her knees so tight that her wrists were hurting. Even David was saying it now. But she had tried so hard to belong, hadn't she? She had worked in the village school, she had become a Friend of Trevarne, she had even organised the summer fête. What more could she have done?

'And that's why we have to go,' he said.

Claire realised what he was saying. 'So you think we should leave Trevarne because of me? Because I've always wanted to?' After all this time. It seemed incredible.

'Of course I bloody do.' He tore his fingers through his shaggy dark hair. Bits of grey, bits of ginger, she thought. 'What the bloody hell did you think I was talking about?'

She grinned.

'What's so funny?'

'It's funny because . . .' Claire struggled to put it into words. 'I can't imagine leaving Trevarne.'

'What the hell do you mean?'

'Just that.' It seemed so obvious now. 'I can't imagine living anywhere else.'

After Freddie's suggestion, of course she had thought about it. Putting the matter of her marriage aside for a moment, she had considered what moving to Amsterdam would mean. And that was when she realised that – horror of horrors – for all Trevarne's petty small-mindedness, for all it drove her crazy with frustration at times, she had grown to love the damn place. It had become home.

It had given her such a thrill when everyone worked together for the Event. Like Max had said, it was a challenge, it had been something from nothing. And that was how she felt about Trevarne. But, unlike Max, she didn't want to leave now that she had achieved what she had set out to achieve. She wanted to build on it – to make it strong.

Amsterdam had been fun, and it would have been a new life, sure enough – one to which her mother had said a very decisive no, to. Freddie, apparently, no longer got exactly what he wanted. But, without realising it, she appeared to have grown ridiculously fond of the old life.

David was staring at her. 'But you'd like to live somewhere else,' he said.

'No, I bloody well would not.'

His eyes narrowed. 'Claire, I don't get you.'

She stretched her legs out in front of her. Couldn't he see? 'I would never have bothered to help organise the Event if I didn't want to do something for Trevarne. If I wasn't fond of the place.'

David leant closer. 'When you did that – for Trevarne – I was so proud. I hoped for a minute, that things had changed. But . . .'

'But?'

'But then I realised you only did all that to get away from me.'

'What on earth do you mean, David?' Was he mad?

'Oh, you know, a chance for you to get out of the house. And because . . .'

He didn't elaborate, but she knew he was thinking about Max. She knew about village gossip better than most. And she knew what David believed.

'I didn't have an affair with Max Stockwell, David.'

He looked away. 'I don't want to know.'

'But *I* want you to know.' It seemed very important. 'Although I was tempted,' she admitted.

He looked back at her.

'But I didn't.' And she knew she'd inadvertently answered her own drunken question to Freddie in Amsterdam. She hadn't slept with Max because whatever she and David had shared . . . it was unfinished. It might not be strong, in fact it had done more than its fair share of precarious wobbling, but it was still there. It could be built on. They were still together, they hadn't parted.

David's expression was inscrutable. He moved over to where he'd left his whisky glass, took a gulp, before slamming it back down on the coffee table. The amber liquid shook, shot out and spilt on the antique pine.

'Then if you don't want to move, what do you want?' They both stared at the stain on the coffee table as it spread and sank slowly into the wood.

'I don't know.'

Suddenly he was on his knees, next to her on the floor. 'How can I make it better?' he demanded.

'Oh, David.' Tentatively she put a hand on his shoulder.

He grabbed it, crushed it in his big palm. 'I can't stand this any more, Claire. It's driving me crazy . . .'

'David . . .' He was hurting her hand but she didn't really care.

'Is it over between us? I need to know. If I can't make you happy . . .' His voice faltered. 'If you don't want me, then I need to know now.'

She tried to speak, but he wasn't finished.

'That night you pushed me away, the things you said . . . You made me feel like a monster.'

She stared at him in amazement. How could he be so wrong?

'And if that's how you see me – then for God's sake tell me, and we'll put an end to this sham of a marriage right now.' He was out of breath, watching her, waiting.

'You're no monster,' she whispered. 'How could you be? But I've been lonely. You've got your work, your fishing. We've grown so far apart.'

'No.'

'But we have, and that's why . . .'

'I want you, Claire.' He freed her hand, and grabbed hold of her by the shoulders.

His face was very close. She was scared. She found she was staring into his eyes, and she could feel it again – that strange half-forgotten current of longing that she had felt the night he helped her mould her clay pot at the wheel.

His lips moved towards hers and suddenly she wasn't scared any longer. She felt like she was coming home.

'Claire, Claire . . .'

The kiss went on and on, and she gave herself up to it, wallowing in a past passion, marvelling at how easily it had been lost, how completely it could return.

They drew apart, their breathing heavy, their eyes searching each other's faces. For some clue . . .'

And then all she was conscious of was her need for him.

She pulled him closer, arched away from him and felt them – his warm, soft kisses, raining on her face, her throat, her neck.

His hands were on her shoulders, her breasts.

Caught in whatever was pulling them forward, they grew more urgent, loosening one another's clothing, ripping at it, desperate for the touch of bare skin, needing the comfort.

She trembled, closed her eyes, smelling that scent of him, so familiar, that fragrance of damp river, of grass, bark and dry clay. The scent of the earth that was David. She heard the sound of his fast, shallow breathing, his murmured 'Claire, Claire . . .'

She tasted his lips, again and again. And then, as she leant over him, her hands on his bare chest, she tasted with her tongue the dry saltiness of his skin that she loved.

'David . . .' How could she have let this go from her life? It didn't seem possible.

They made love, hungrily, aching and intense, on the rug in front of the fireplace, just like they had when they were first married, the first time he had brought her here to this cottage, the first time he'd brought her home.

'Why did we ever stop?' she asked him when it was over.

Propping herself up on her elbow, she tangled strands of his hair between her fingers.

'Work. The baby. Habit.' He grinned, and she realised the pain had gone from his eyes. So easy . . . 'I don't know, Claire.'

David was her ballast. It might have seemed to be just Claire and Ben for years. But a family was the sum of its individual members, and David had always balanced theirs. Claire found it hard to believe that she had let herself diminish his role, undervalue his contribution. 'But we won't stop again,' she said.

'We certainly won't.' He grabbed her hand. 'We won't live in separate worlds. We'll find things we want to do together – like we used to. Like walking and talking and going out for dinner and . . .' He brought her hand to his lips.

She took a deep breath as the passion streaked through her once again. 'David, about that night . . .' The nightmare still haunted her.

He put a finger to her lips. 'Ssh.'

'No.' She nibbled his fingertip, then moved it gently away. 'I have to tell you.' No love without pain . . .

And she told him, lying there on the rug, what she should have told him years ago. About why she'd stopped riding the Bonneville. About Dorking, Jerry, and the time she was raped in the car park of the bikers' café. Her voice remained unemotional and flat, she didn't want sympathy, she simply wanted him to be the only one who knew.

He listened, growing angry from time to time, holding her close. 'Why did you never tell anyone?'

'The police, you mean?'

'Or your father. Someone. Anyone.'

'I was ashamed.' Claire stroked a fingertip along his left eyebrow. 'I was ashamed of what had happened, that I could have been so stupid, *letting* it happen like that. I was ashamed of the whole sordid thing.'

'It wasn't your fault.'

She put her finger on his lips just as he had done to her. 'I know that now. But at the time . . .' Her voice wavered. It had felt as if freedom was being snatched from her. She wanted to forget. All she'd wanted was to be safe.

'I'll look after you, Claire,' he whispered. 'It's all I ever wanted to do.'

'All I wanted you to do,' she told him.

'Did you marry me because you were running away?'

It was very close to the truth, and all Claire wanted now was honesty between them. Because she should have been honest before. 'I was in love with you,' she told him.

'But?'

'But, yes, I think perhaps I did.' A different life, a gentle man who would care for her, always look after her, never force her to do anything she didn't want to do. Safety. My God . . . Claire put a hand to her mouth. What sort of a fantasy world had she been living in? She thought of Max – but not with the usual pang of regret. Silently she thanked him, because it had been Max who recognised that she was still running. Perhaps because he was busy doing it too. Max had seen what her father already knew. Yes, she had been running. But not from Max. 'I was running away from life,' she said.

He smiled. 'And you ended up getting more life than you bargained for in Trevarne.'

She thought about it. 'I felt cheated. When you told me there was no chance of us leaving Trevarne, I thought I was taking second place for you. That your family and your work would always come before me.' She stroked his arm. 'I thought that you simply didn't love me enough.'

'I should have listened properly.' David caught hold of her fingers. 'I didn't understand how important it was to you. And you were so used to life in London . . . It was way outside my experience. I couldn't believe my luck in getting you in the first place. I thought I'd lose you if we left Trevarne.'

She clung to him. Why hadn't they ever talked like this back then?

'You made Trevarne seem like such a dull sort of place.' He stroked her hair. 'And I suppose it was.'

Angrily, she shook her head. 'I was unbearable. I never forgave you for wanting to stay in your own home. I was ridiculous.'

He kissed her ear. 'Never. Never ridiculous. But I almost got to hating this place myself when I thought it had driven you away. This place, the people, me . . .'

'I want to stay. I want to be with you.' She didn't know when she had forgiven him for keeping her here in Trevarne. The odd thing was that it had happened without her noticing.

He grinned. 'Then we'll stay.'

Claire smiled back at him. 'But . . .' She had to ask, it was torturing her. 'But what about Fern?'

She wondered if she could blame him. She had as good as ejected him from her bed, from her life . . . What man wouldn't feel the need to look elsewhere? What woman, come to that? *She* had looked elsewhere – she alone knew how close she had come with Max Stockwell.

'Fern?' He looked puzzled.

'I thought . . .' With them lying here like this, she was almost embarrassed to say it. But she wanted everything out in the open now. 'You and she . . .'

David grew serious. 'Claire, Fern is my cousin.'

'What?'

'I always thought you would guess. She's Veronica's child.'

'Veronica's?' Claire remembered the bond she had sensed between the two of them, the bond between Veronica and Fern that she had recognised at the market.

'I should have told you before, I suppose,' David said. 'So many times I almost did. But the aunts swore me to secrecy before I even met you, and Fern was terrified that it would get out, be round the village in five minutes flat and hurt her mother even more than she'd been hurt already. I didn't think it mattered that much,' he added ruefully. 'And as for Emily – she can't bear the thought of anyone knowing. She can't bear –'

'Fern,' Claire supplied, beginning to understand.

He stared at her. 'But you didn't think . . .?'

Claire tried to smile, conscious only of an overwhelming relief. 'There was that time you said you had a business meeting, and the business was Fern. There were the craft fairs . . . You always seemed so much more than just good friends.' Of course even cousins could fall in love – but she knew now that the link between Fern and

David that she had suspected to be love . . . was actually something quite different.

'I suppose we are more than friends.' David's fingers trailed down her spine and she shivered with a slow delight. 'But it never crossed my mind you'd take it that way, you daft thing. Fern is like a sister. I feel sorry for her. A bit responsible too, I suppose. The craft fairs were because I genuinely want to help her succeed. And the business meeting . . .' She could see he was trying to remember. 'I think we were wooing a potential sponsor.'

'And maybe you wanted to get out of the house?' With her parents in residence all the time, who could blame him for needing a break?

David grinned. 'Families, eh?'

'That's why she stays.' Claire remembered her conversation with Fern.

'That's why we both stay.' David clenched his fist. 'She may be my aunt but Emily is a bully. She never lets poor Veronica forget her fall from grace – probably because she always fancied the same chap herself, or so Veronica says. Who knows?' Slowly he unclenched his palm. 'If not for Emily, Veronica might even have married him.'

'She scared him off?' Claire could understand that. Emily would scare all but the bravest.

He nodded. 'Veronica won't leave her. And Fern won't leave her mother.'

'I see.' She became thoughtful.

'Claire.' He was watching her. 'Don't you know? I only ever wanted you. Why else would I have waited for you so long, stopped you from speaking out when I thought you were about to end our marriage for good? Why else would I have prayed like crazy for you to come back to me?' He smiled. 'The day of the fête – when you were crying – that gave me a bit of hope. But then you went away again. I couldn't think what else to do. But for my own sanity, I had to know.'

David, she realised, was no ordinary man. And she had almost lost him.

Abruptly, he jumped to his feet. 'Oh, I nearly forgot.'

'What?' She smiled at him, because he was standing there stark naked and utterly unselfconscious.

Taking her point, he went across to draw the curtains. 'We don't want Iris coming to the right conclusions.'

'Or Richard.' They both laughed.

'And what did you nearly forget?' she asked him.

He went over to the mantelpiece, retrieving a postcard that was propped up against some weird-looking object she didn't recognize. 'From Ben.'

He passed it to her.

Claire read the scrawled lines.

Having a good time. See you soon. Ben.

'Doesn't exactly tell you a lot.' David laughed.

But for Claire it was all she could hope for, and more. Two weeks ago she had managed to say goodbye to her son without a tear. And when he returned she would say hello with a smile. She missed him, but she was getting there. 'See you soon,' she echoed. 'Not too soon, I hope.' Because this was something they could never have done with Ben living in the cottage. Made love on the rug in the sitting room . . . And to think that she had worried that there would be nothing left.

David sat on the floor beside her. 'There's lots of things we can do while he's away . . .' His fingers moved from her shoulder down to her wrist.

She kissed the warm skin of his upper arm. 'Like what?'

'Like this.' He stroked her shoulder blade, she felt the pressure of his thumbs.

'Mmm.' She snuggled back into his arms.

'We could even make a few more pots together.' He pointed to the unrecognisable object on the mantelpiece. 'We could set up a display cabinet.'

'Looks like another constipated penguin,' she said, realising what it was. David had been using the kiln while she had been in Amsterdam.

'I love it.' He squeezed her waist. 'After all, we made it together.'

Claire shivered. They'd certainly done that. 'And what else?' she asked him.

'We could go down to the bike shop so I can buy you your heart's desire.'

She pulled away and stared at him. 'Oh, I don't know, David . . .' But her heart was thudding as if she were a young girl again. Standing outside Jerry's, dreaming of her first Bonneville. Of freedom.

'You've put it behind you, haven't you?' he asked. 'The fear.'

'Yes, but . . .'

'Remember the pleasures,' he said.

Claire sank against the warmth that was David and let herself remember. It was remarkably easy and, boy, did it feel good.

She smiled. She had let Ben go, and she would let her fears go too. But she would hang on to what she had with David. A family wasn't just about responsibility, it was about love, it was about commitment. Her father would be proud. It had taken a while. But now her running days were over.